J 741.594 Gra
Graley, Sarah,
Donut the Destroyer /
$14.99   on1156806070

WITHDRAWN

W9-BGS-070

THE DESTROYER

SARAH GRALEY AND STEF PURENINS

An Imprint of
SCHOLASTIC

This book is for all the heroes out there,
who always try to do the right thing
and help make the world a better
place for everyone.

Copyright © 2020 by Sarah Graley and Stef Purenins

All rights reserved. Published by Graphix, an imprint of Scholastic Inc.,
Publishers since 1920. SCHOLASTIC, GRAPHIX, and associated logos are
trademarks and/or registered trademarks of Scholastic Inc.

The publisher does not have any control over and does not assume
any responsibility for author or third-party websites or their content.

No part of this publication may be reproduced, stored in a retrieval
system, or transmitted in any form or by any means, electronic, mechanical,
photocopying, recording, or otherwise, without written permission of the
publisher. For information regarding permission, write to Scholastic Inc.,
Attention: Permissions Department, 557 Broadway, New York, NY 10012.

This book is a work of fiction. Names, characters, places, and incidents
are either the product of the author's imagination or are used fictitiously,
and any resemblance to actual persons, living or dead, business
establishments, events, or locales is entirely coincidental.

Library of Congress Control Number: 2019945255

ISBN 978-1-338-54193-9 (hardcover)
ISBN 978-1-338-54192-2 (paperback)

10 9 8 7 6 5 4 3 2 1   20 21 22 23 24

Printed in China   62
First edition, June 2020
Edited by Cassandra Pelham Fulton
Book design by Shivana Sookdeo
Creative Director: Phil Falco
Publisher: David Saylor

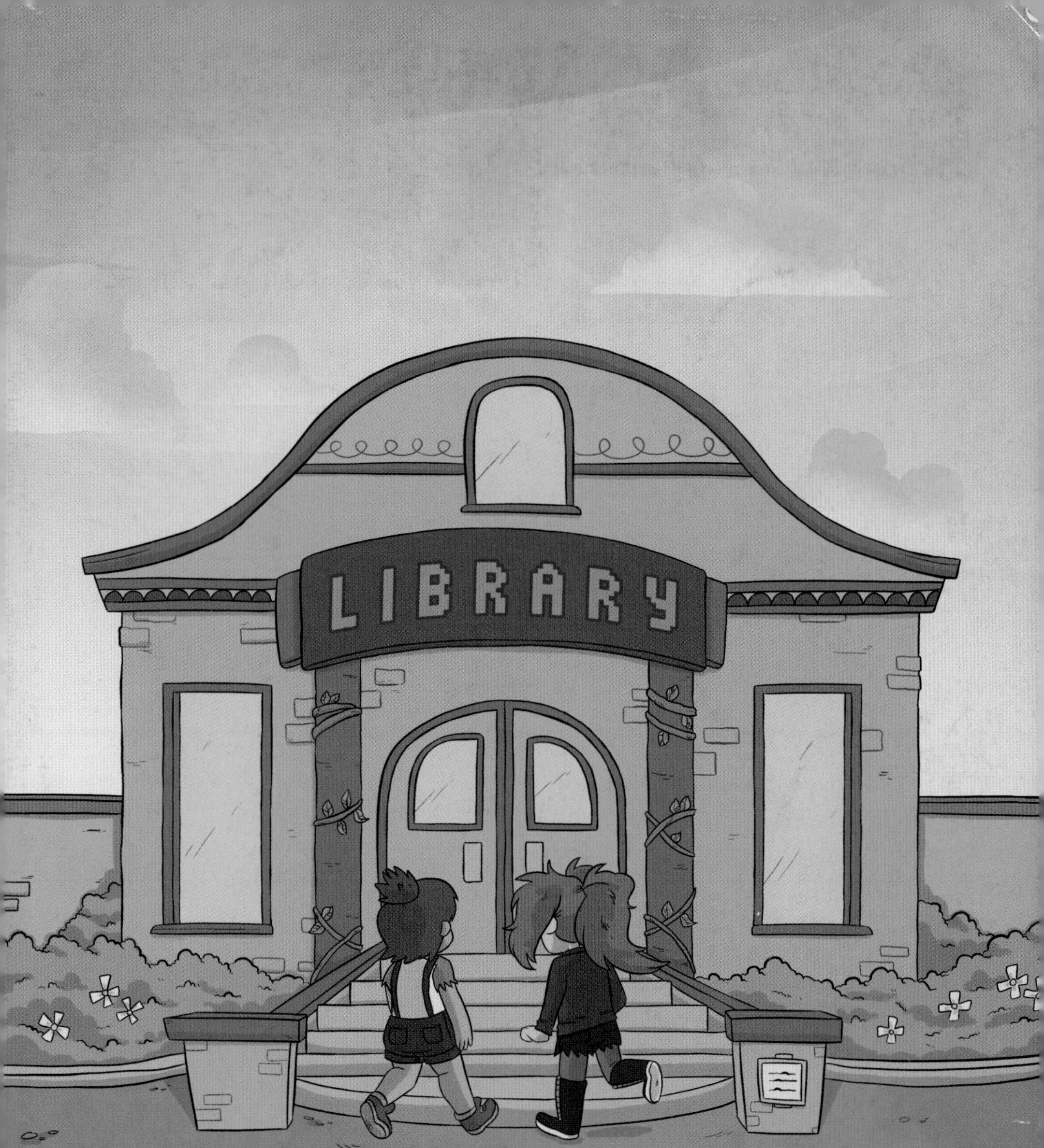
LIBRARY

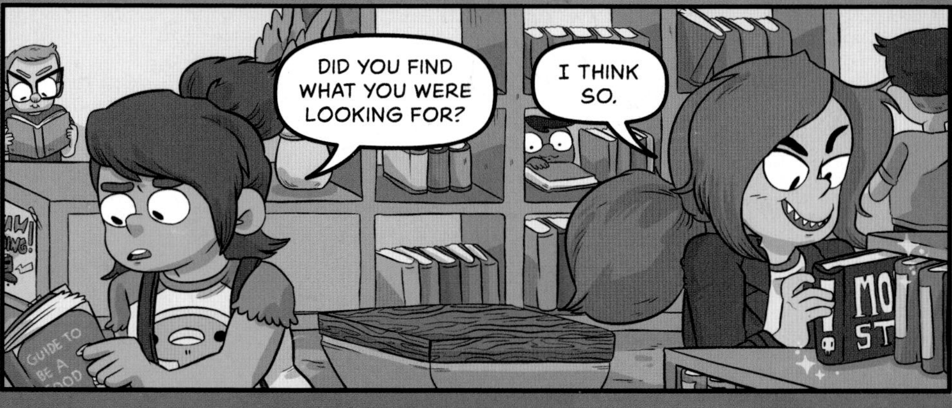
DID YOU FIND WHAT YOU WERE LOOKING FOR?
I THINK SO.

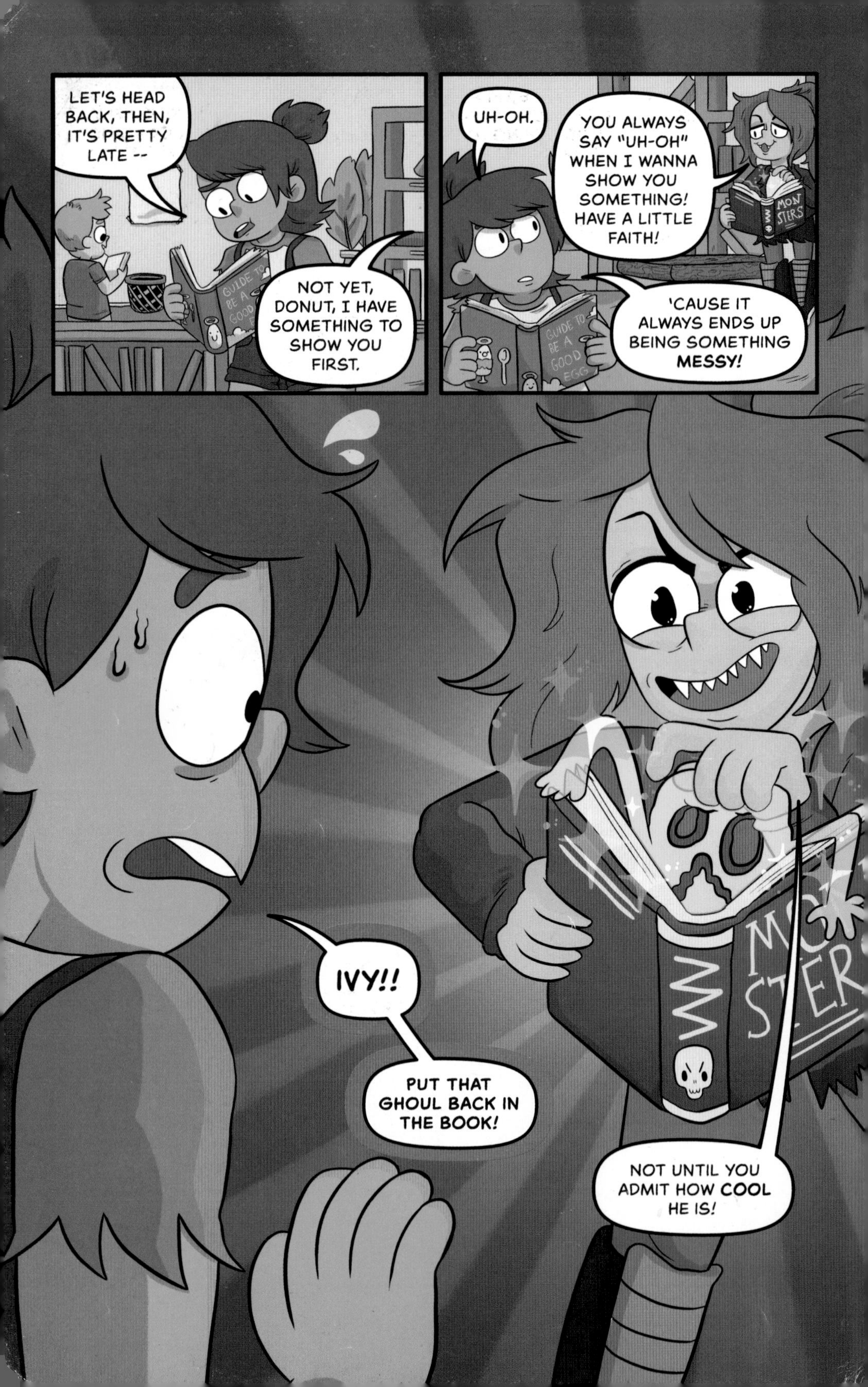
LET'S HEAD BACK, THEN, IT'S PRETTY LATE --
NOT YET, DONUT, I HAVE SOMETHING TO SHOW YOU FIRST.
GUIDE TO BE A GOOD
UH-OH.
YOU ALWAYS SAY "UH-OH" WHEN I WANNA SHOW YOU SOMETHING! HAVE A LITTLE FAITH!
MON STERS
'CAUSE IT ALWAYS ENDS UP BEING SOMETHING **MESSY!**
GUIDE TO BE A GOOD EGG
IVY!!
PUT THAT GHOUL BACK IN THE BOOK!
NOT UNTIL YOU ADMIT HOW **COOL** HE IS!

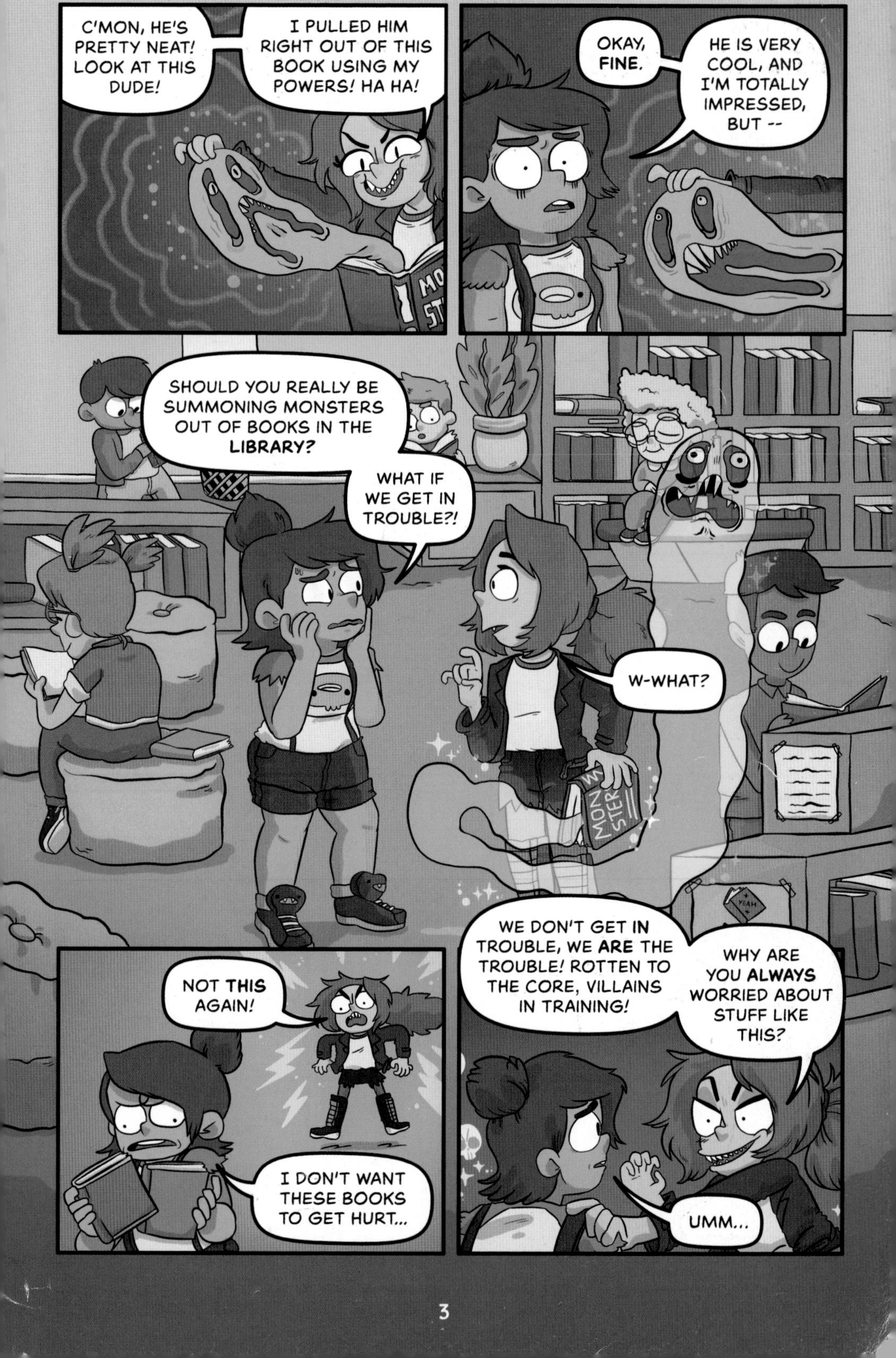
C'MON, HE'S PRETTY NEAT! LOOK AT THIS DUDE!
I PULLED HIM RIGHT OUT OF THIS BOOK USING MY POWERS! HA HA!
MON STER
OKAY, FINE.
HE IS VERY COOL, AND I'M TOTALLY IMPRESSED, BUT --
SHOULD YOU REALLY BE SUMMONING MONSTERS OUT OF BOOKS IN THE LIBRARY?
WHAT IF WE GET IN TROUBLE?!
W-WHAT?
MON STER
WE DON'T GET IN TROUBLE, WE ARE THE TROUBLE! ROTTEN TO THE CORE, VILLAINS IN TRAINING!
WHY ARE YOU ALWAYS WORRIED ABOUT STUFF LIKE THIS?
NOT THIS AGAIN!
I DON'T WANT THESE BOOKS TO GET HURT...
UMM...

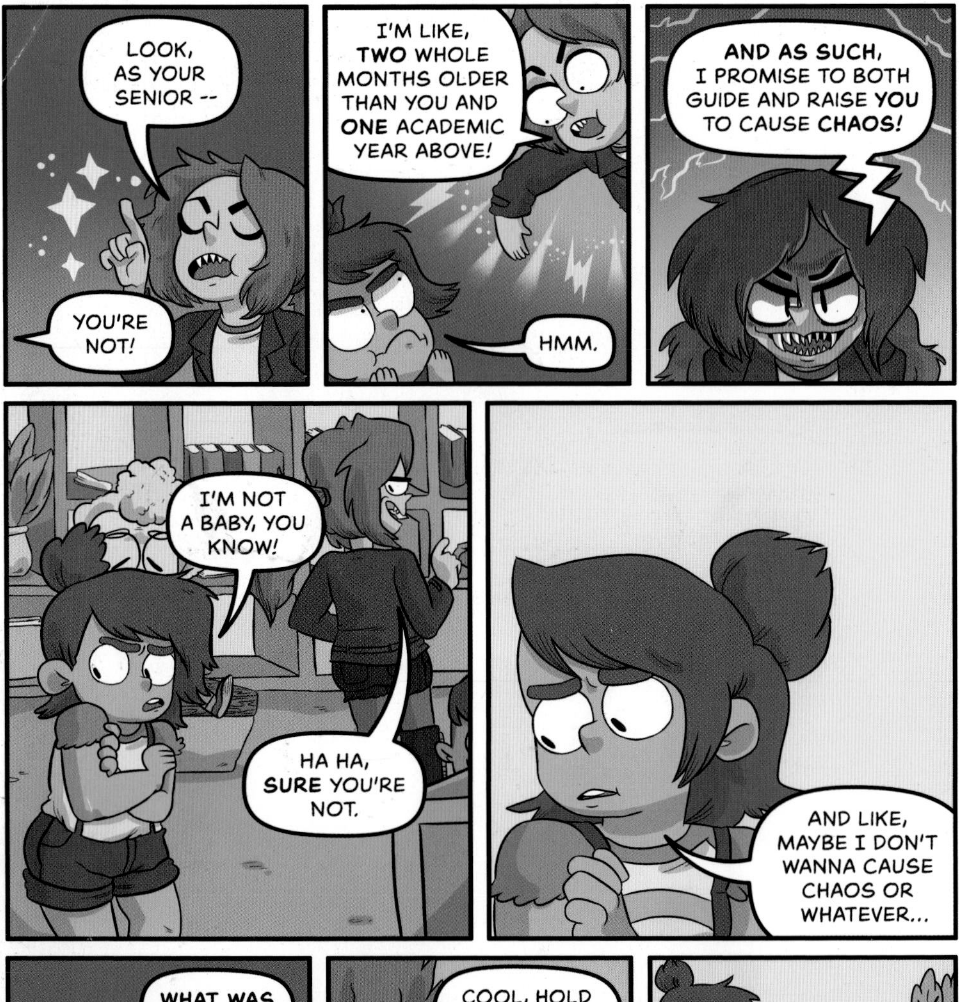
LOOK, AS YOUR SENIOR --
YOU'RE NOT!
I'M LIKE, **TWO** WHOLE MONTHS OLDER THAN YOU AND **ONE** ACADEMIC YEAR ABOVE!
HMM.
AND AS SUCH, I PROMISE TO BOTH GUIDE AND RAISE **YOU** TO CAUSE **CHAOS!**
I'M NOT A BABY, YOU KNOW!
HA HA, **SURE** YOU'RE NOT.
AND LIKE, MAYBE I DON'T WANNA CAUSE CHAOS OR WHATEVER...
WHAT WAS THAT?
NOTHING!!
COOL, HOLD THESE BOOKS FOR ME.
GHOULS FOR DAYS
UH...
YOU'RE NOT GOING TO GET US BANNED FROM THE LIBRARY, ARE YOU?
IT'S A START! GOTTA BUILD OUR EVIL REPUTATION SOMEHOW!

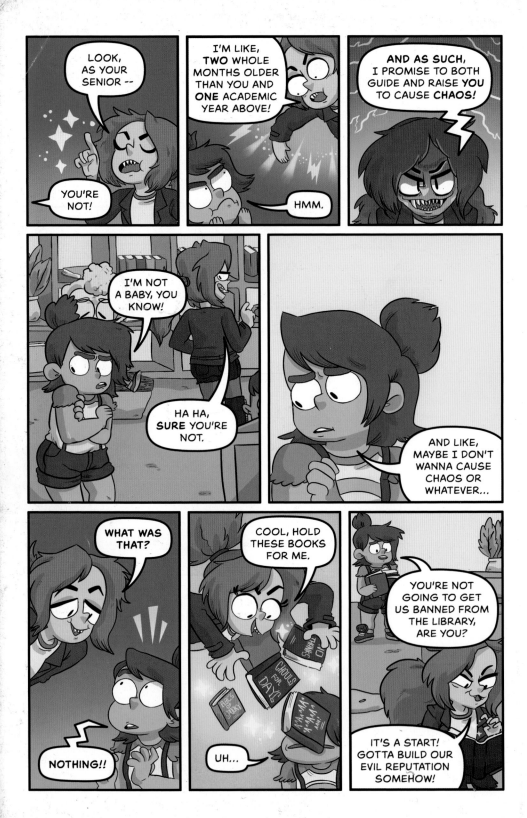

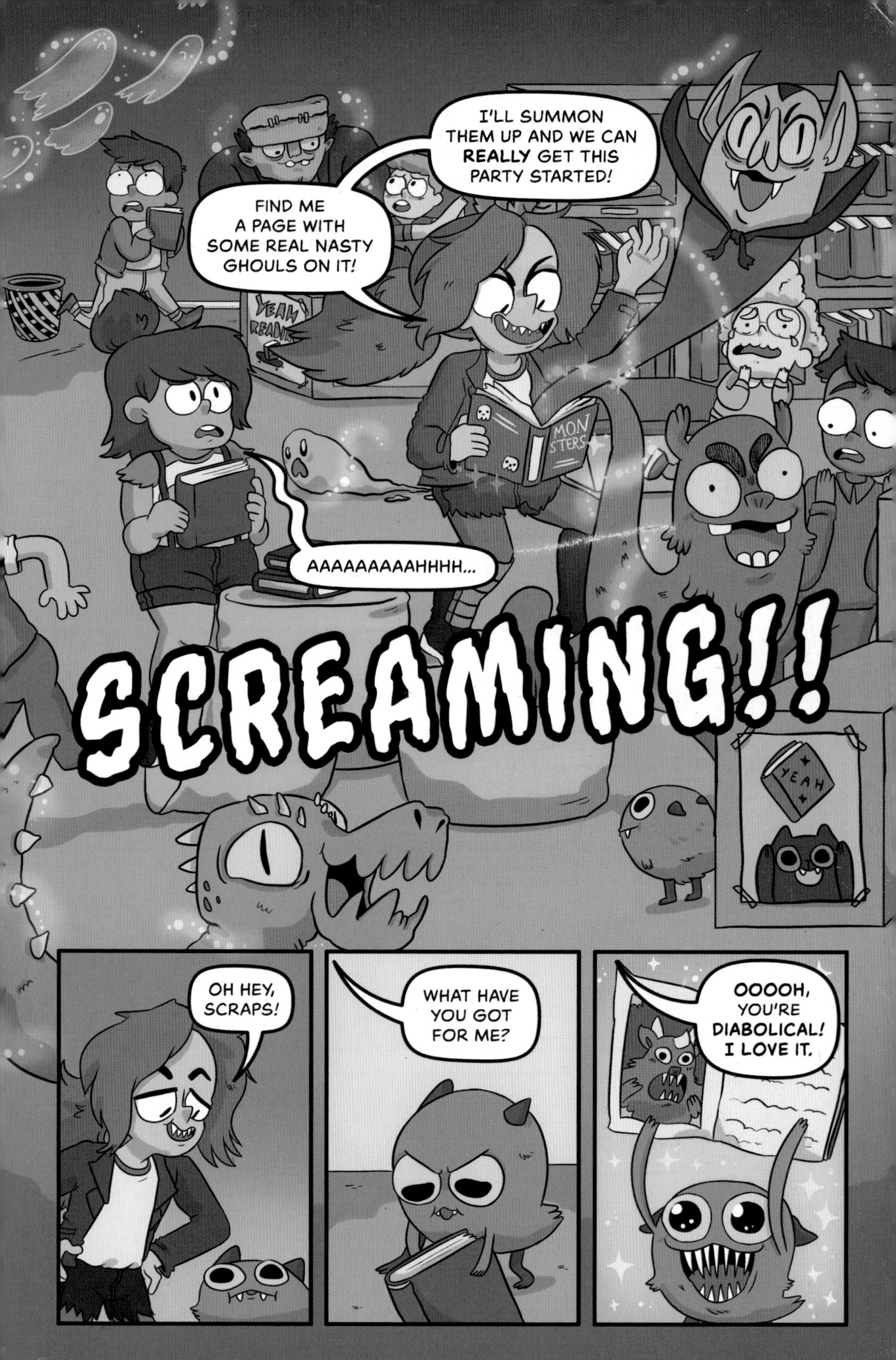
FIND ME A PAGE WITH SOME REAL NASTY GHOULS ON IT!
I'LL SUMMON THEM UP AND WE CAN REALLY GET THIS PARTY STARTED!
YEAH READING
MONSTERS
AAAAAAAAAHHHH...
SCREAMING!!
YEAH
OH HEY, SCRAPS!
WHAT HAVE YOU GOT FOR ME?
OOOOH, YOU'RE DIABOLICAL! I LOVE IT.

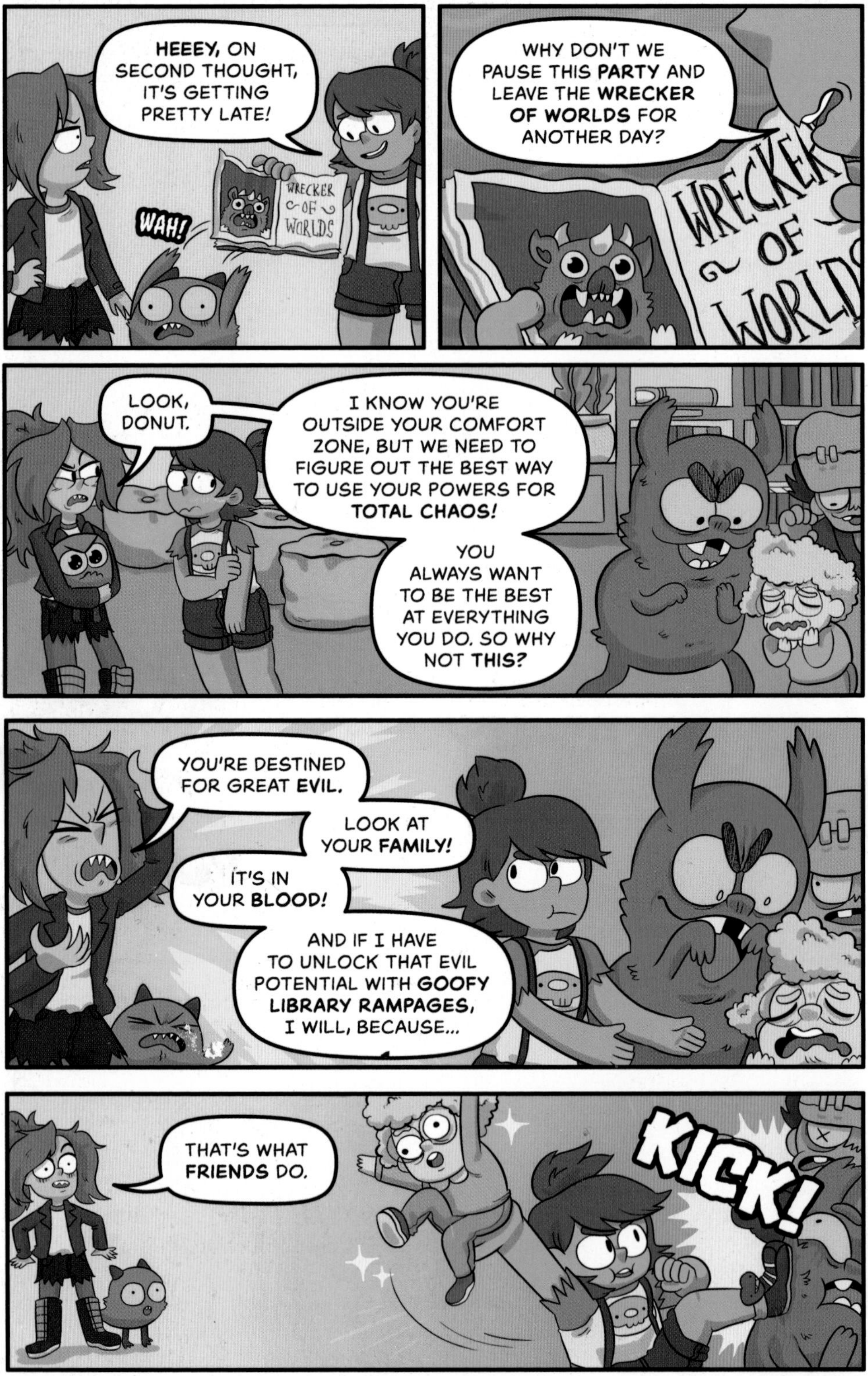
HEEEY, ON SECOND THOUGHT, IT'S GETTING PRETTY LATE!
WAH!
WRECKER OF WORLDS
WHY DON'T WE PAUSE THIS PARTY AND LEAVE THE WRECKER OF WORLDS FOR ANOTHER DAY?
WRECKER OF WORLDS
LOOK, DONUT.
I KNOW YOU'RE OUTSIDE YOUR COMFORT ZONE, BUT WE NEED TO FIGURE OUT THE BEST WAY TO USE YOUR POWERS FOR TOTAL CHAOS!
YOU ALWAYS WANT TO BE THE BEST AT EVERYTHING YOU DO. SO WHY NOT THIS?
YOU'RE DESTINED FOR GREAT EVIL.
LOOK AT YOUR FAMILY!
IT'S IN YOUR BLOOD!
AND IF I HAVE TO UNLOCK THAT EVIL POTENTIAL WITH GOOFY LIBRARY RAMPAGES, I WILL, BECAUSE...
THAT'S WHAT FRIENDS DO.
KICK!

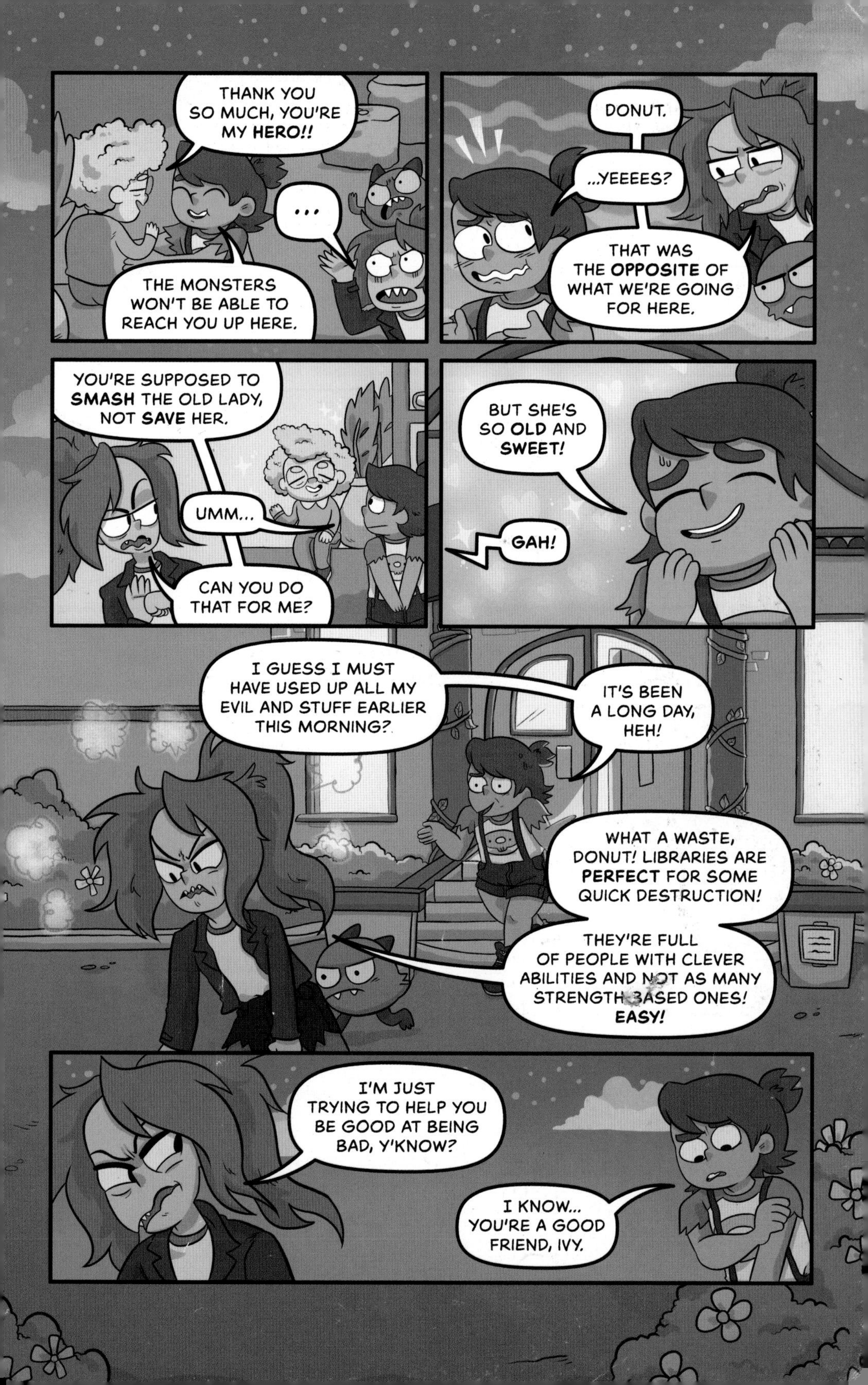
THANK YOU SO MUCH, YOU'RE MY HERO!!
THE MONSTERS WON'T BE ABLE TO REACH YOU UP HERE.
...
DONUT.
...YEEEES?
THAT WAS THE OPPOSITE OF WHAT WE'RE GOING FOR HERE.
YOU'RE SUPPOSED TO SMASH THE OLD LADY, NOT SAVE HER.
UMM...
CAN YOU DO THAT FOR ME?
BUT SHE'S SO OLD AND SWEET!
GAH!
I GUESS I MUST HAVE USED UP ALL MY EVIL AND STUFF EARLIER THIS MORNING?
IT'S BEEN A LONG DAY, HEH!
WHAT A WASTE, DONUT! LIBRARIES ARE PERFECT FOR SOME QUICK DESTRUCTION!
THEY'RE FULL OF PEOPLE WITH CLEVER ABILITIES AND NOT AS MANY STRENGTH-BASED ONES! EASY!
I'M JUST TRYING TO HELP YOU BE GOOD AT BEING BAD, Y'KNOW?
I KNOW... YOU'RE A GOOD FRIEND, IVY.

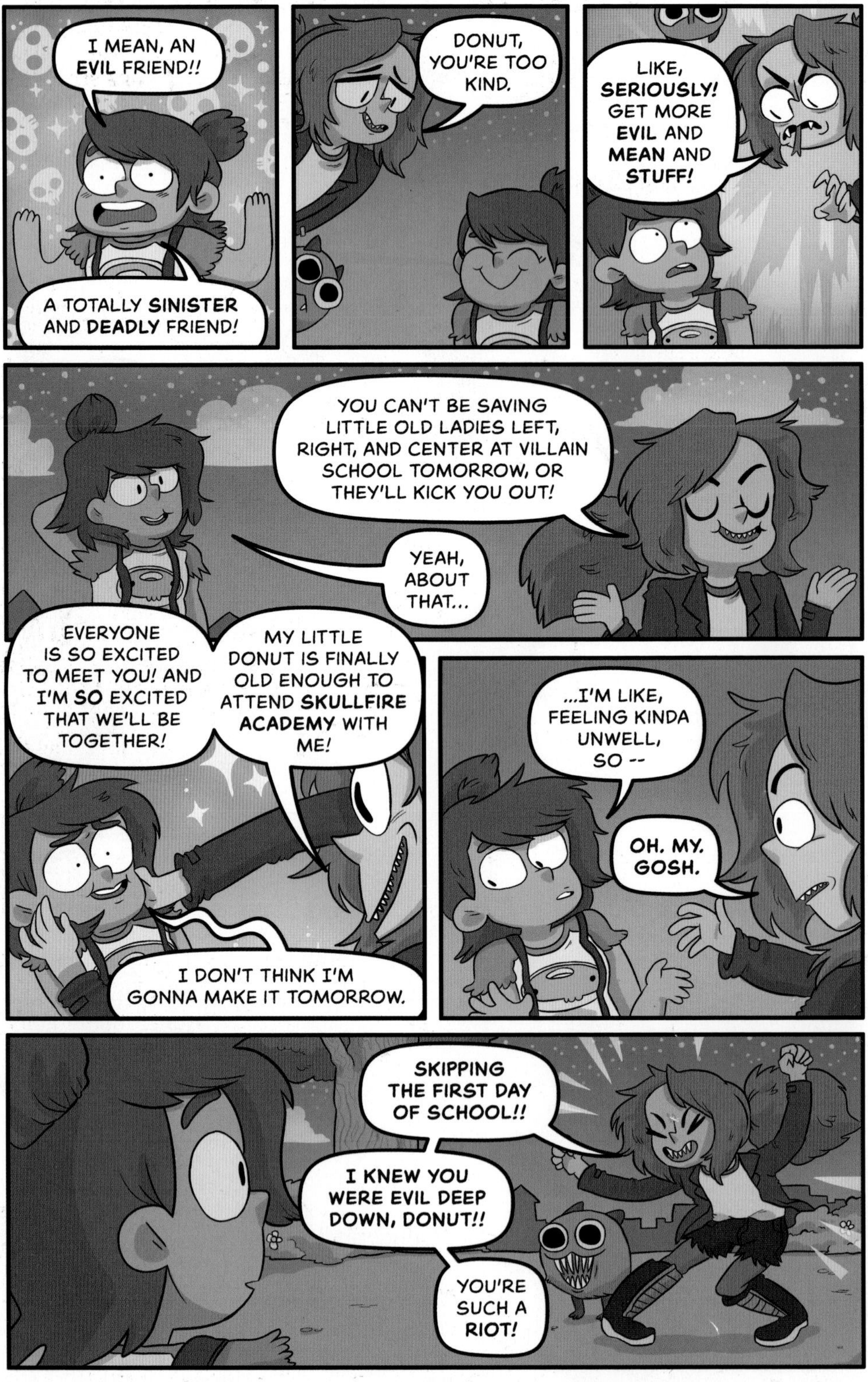
I MEAN, AN **EVIL** FRIEND!!
A TOTALLY **SINISTER** AND **DEADLY** FRIEND!
DONUT, YOU'RE TOO KIND.
LIKE, **SERIOUSLY!** GET MORE **EVIL** AND **MEAN** AND **STUFF!**
YOU CAN'T BE SAVING LITTLE OLD LADIES LEFT, RIGHT, AND CENTER AT VILLAIN SCHOOL TOMORROW, OR THEY'LL KICK YOU OUT!
YEAH, ABOUT THAT...
EVERYONE IS SO EXCITED TO MEET YOU! AND I'M **SO** EXCITED THAT WE'LL BE TOGETHER!
MY LITTLE DONUT IS FINALLY OLD ENOUGH TO ATTEND **SKULLFIRE ACADEMY** WITH ME!
I DON'T THINK I'M GONNA MAKE IT TOMORROW.
...I'M LIKE, FEELING KINDA UNWELL, SO --
OH. MY. GOSH.
SKIPPING THE FIRST DAY OF SCHOOL!!
I KNEW YOU WERE EVIL DEEP DOWN, DONUT!!
YOU'RE SUCH A **RIOT!**

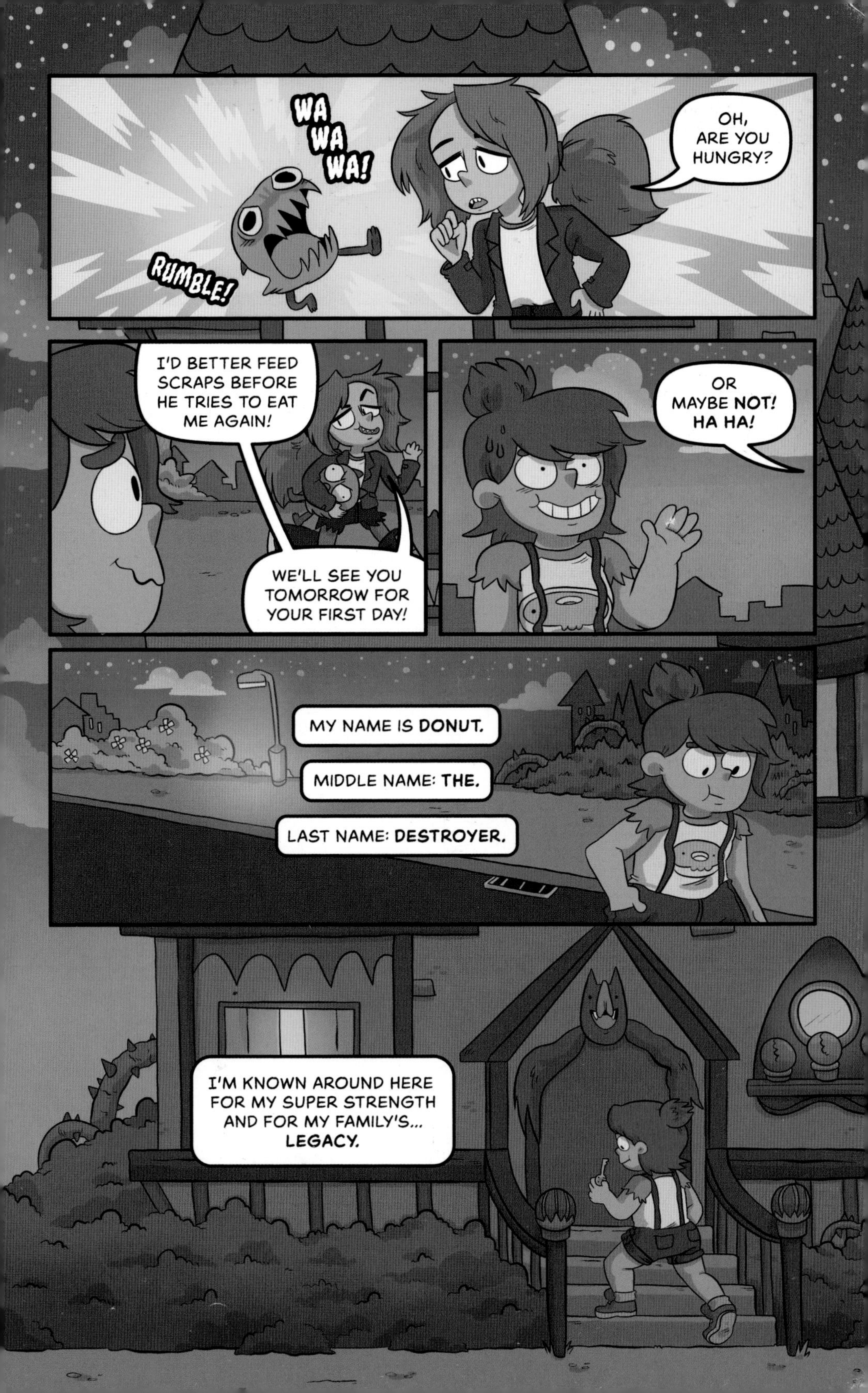
WA WA WA!
RUMBLE!
OH, ARE YOU HUNGRY?
I'D BETTER FEED SCRAPS BEFORE HE TRIES TO EAT ME AGAIN!
WE'LL SEE YOU TOMORROW FOR YOUR FIRST DAY!
OR MAYBE NOT! HA HA!
MY NAME IS DONUT.
MIDDLE NAME: THE.
LAST NAME: DESTROYER.
I'M KNOWN AROUND HERE FOR MY SUPER STRENGTH AND FOR MY FAMILY'S... LEGACY.

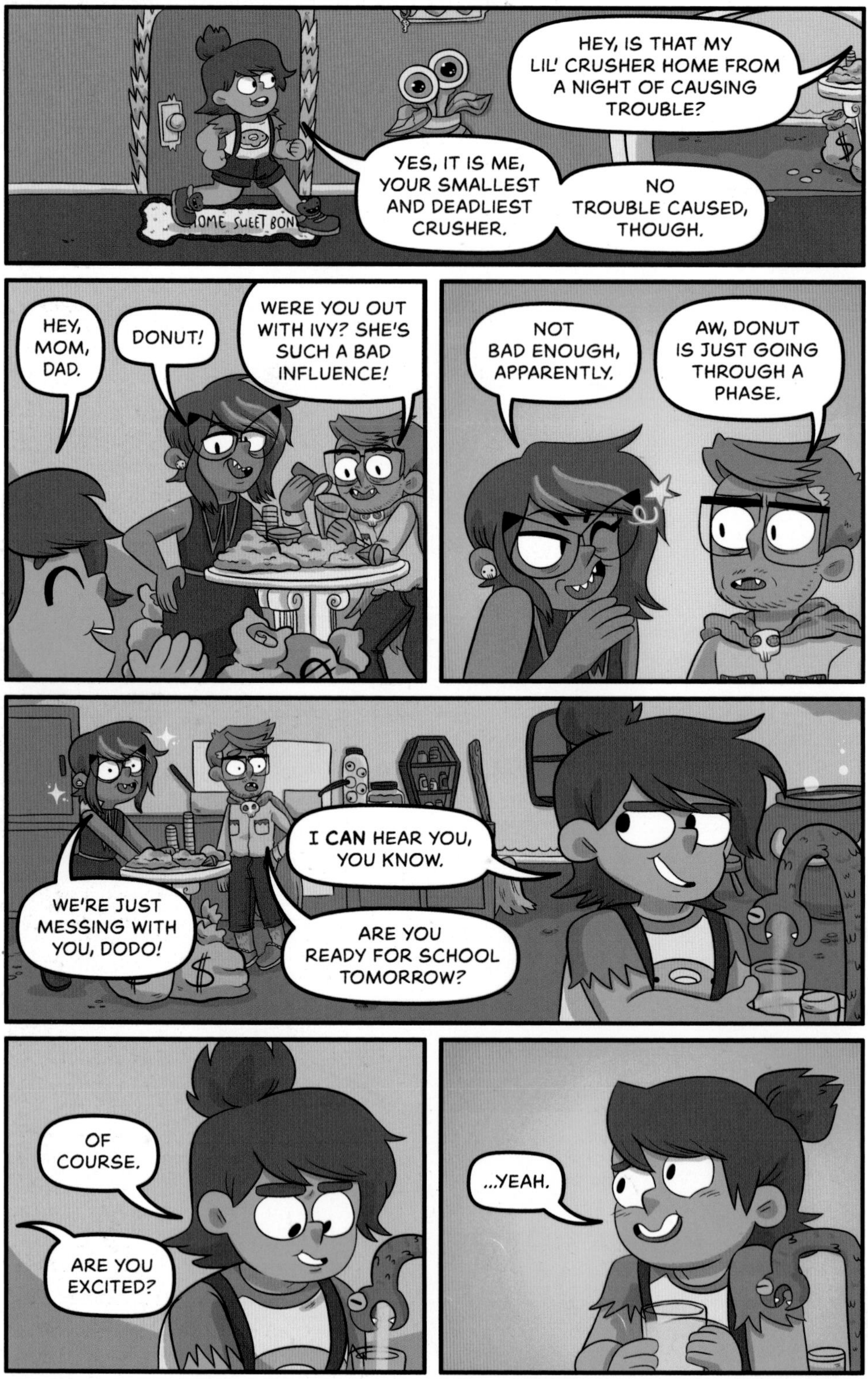
HOME SWEET BON
HEY, IS THAT MY LIL' CRUSHER HOME FROM A NIGHT OF CAUSING TROUBLE?
YES, IT IS ME, YOUR SMALLEST AND DEADLIEST CRUSHER.
NO TROUBLE CAUSED, THOUGH.
HEY, MOM, DAD.
DONUT!
WERE YOU OUT WITH IVY? SHE'S SUCH A BAD INFLUENCE!
NOT BAD ENOUGH, APPARENTLY.
AW, DONUT IS JUST GOING THROUGH A PHASE.
I CAN HEAR YOU, YOU KNOW.
WE'RE JUST MESSING WITH YOU, DODO!
ARE YOU READY FOR SCHOOL TOMORROW?
OF COURSE.
ARE YOU EXCITED?
...YEAH.

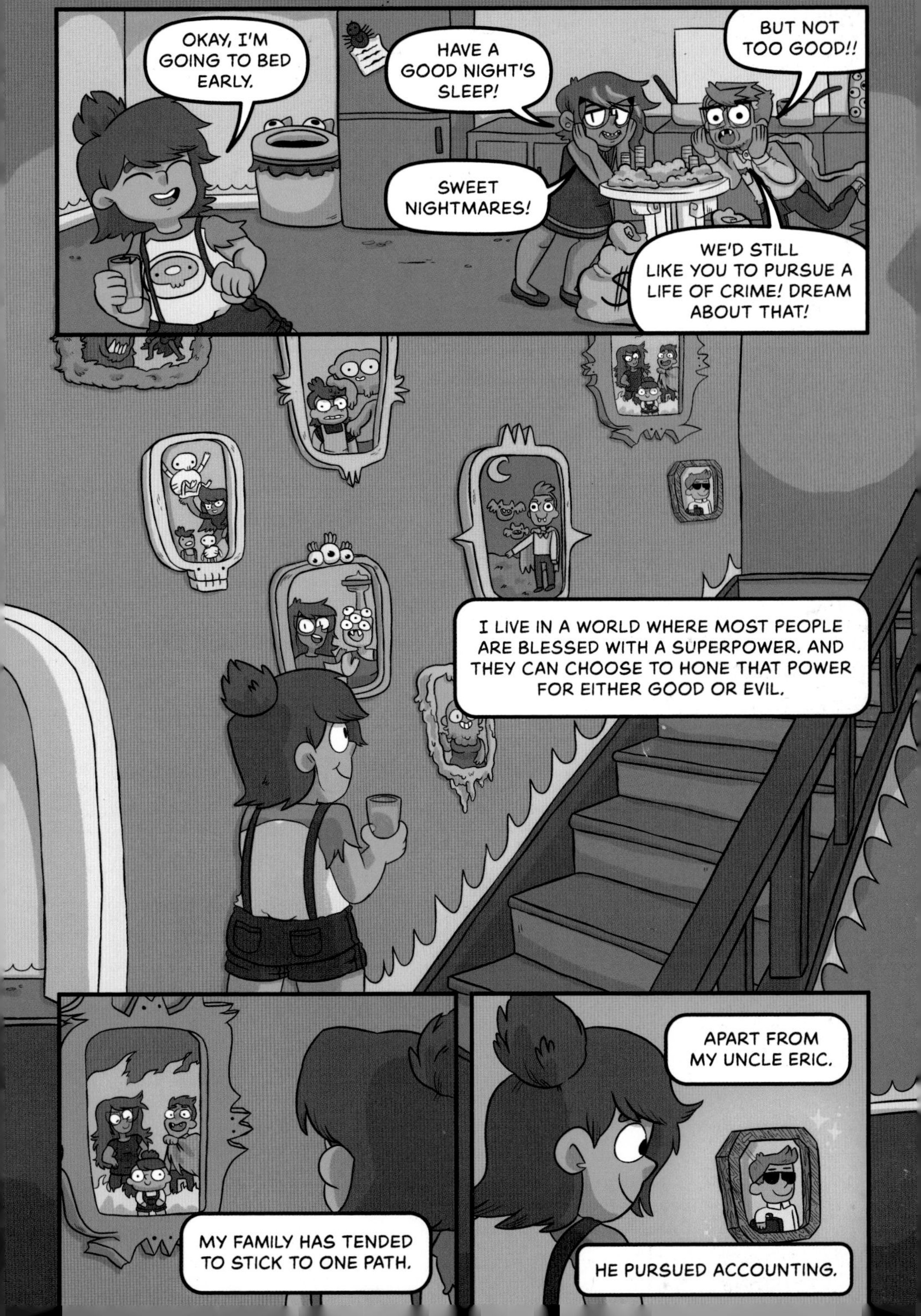
OKAY, I'M GOING TO BED EARLY.
HAVE A GOOD NIGHT'S SLEEP!
BUT NOT TOO GOOD!!
SWEET NIGHTMARES!
WE'D STILL LIKE YOU TO PURSUE A LIFE OF CRIME! DREAM ABOUT THAT!
I LIVE IN A WORLD WHERE MOST PEOPLE ARE BLESSED WITH A SUPERPOWER. AND THEY CAN CHOOSE TO HONE THAT POWER FOR EITHER GOOD OR EVIL.
MY FAMILY HAS TENDED TO STICK TO ONE PATH.
APART FROM MY UNCLE ERIC.
HE PURSUED ACCOUNTING.

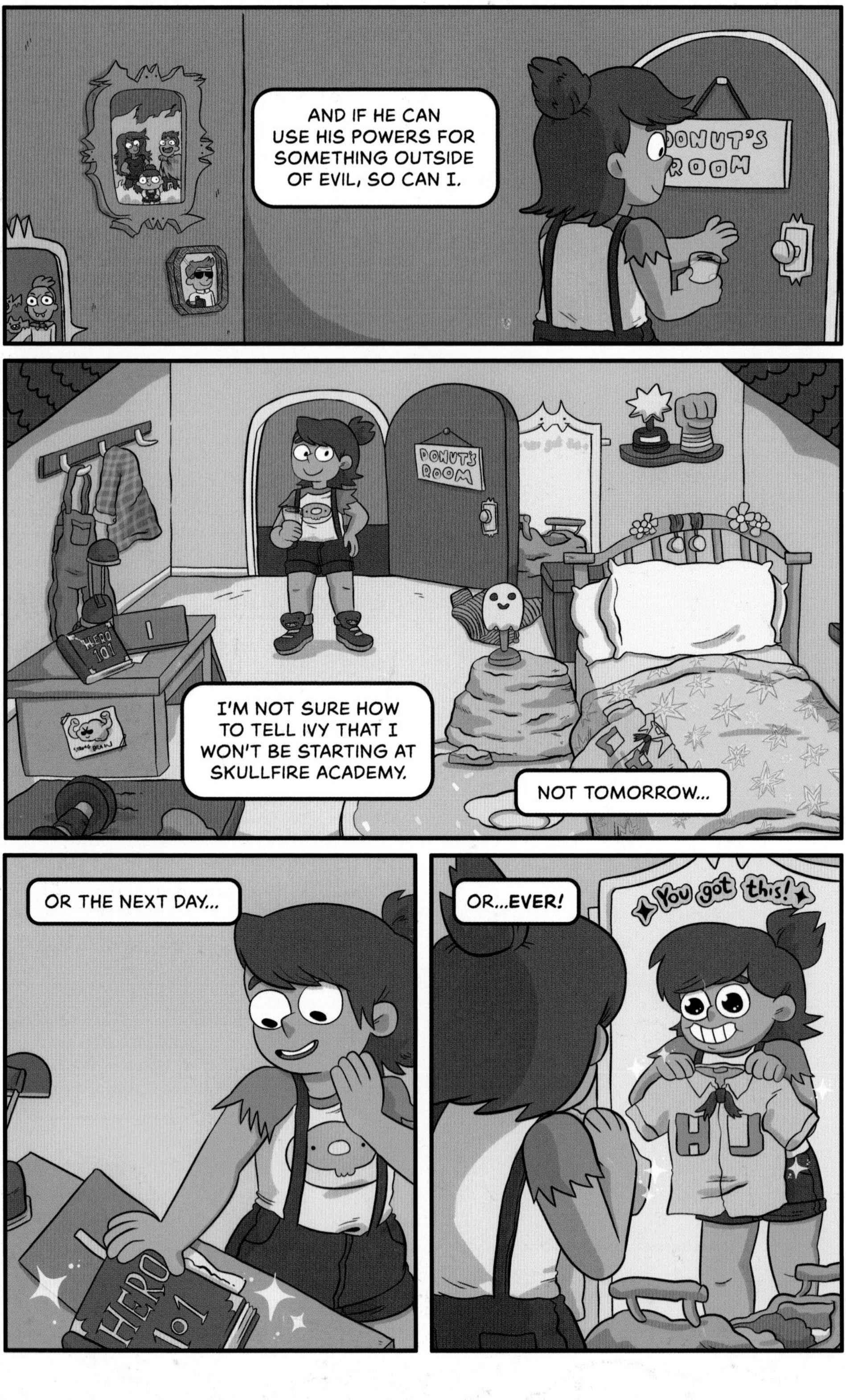
AND IF HE CAN USE HIS POWERS FOR SOMETHING OUTSIDE OF EVIL, SO CAN I.
DONUT'S ROOM
DONUT'S ROOM
HERO 101
I'M NOT SURE HOW TO TELL IVY THAT I WON'T BE STARTING AT SKULLFIRE ACADEMY.
NOT TOMORROW...
OR THE NEXT DAY...
HERO 101
OR...EVER!
You got this!
HU

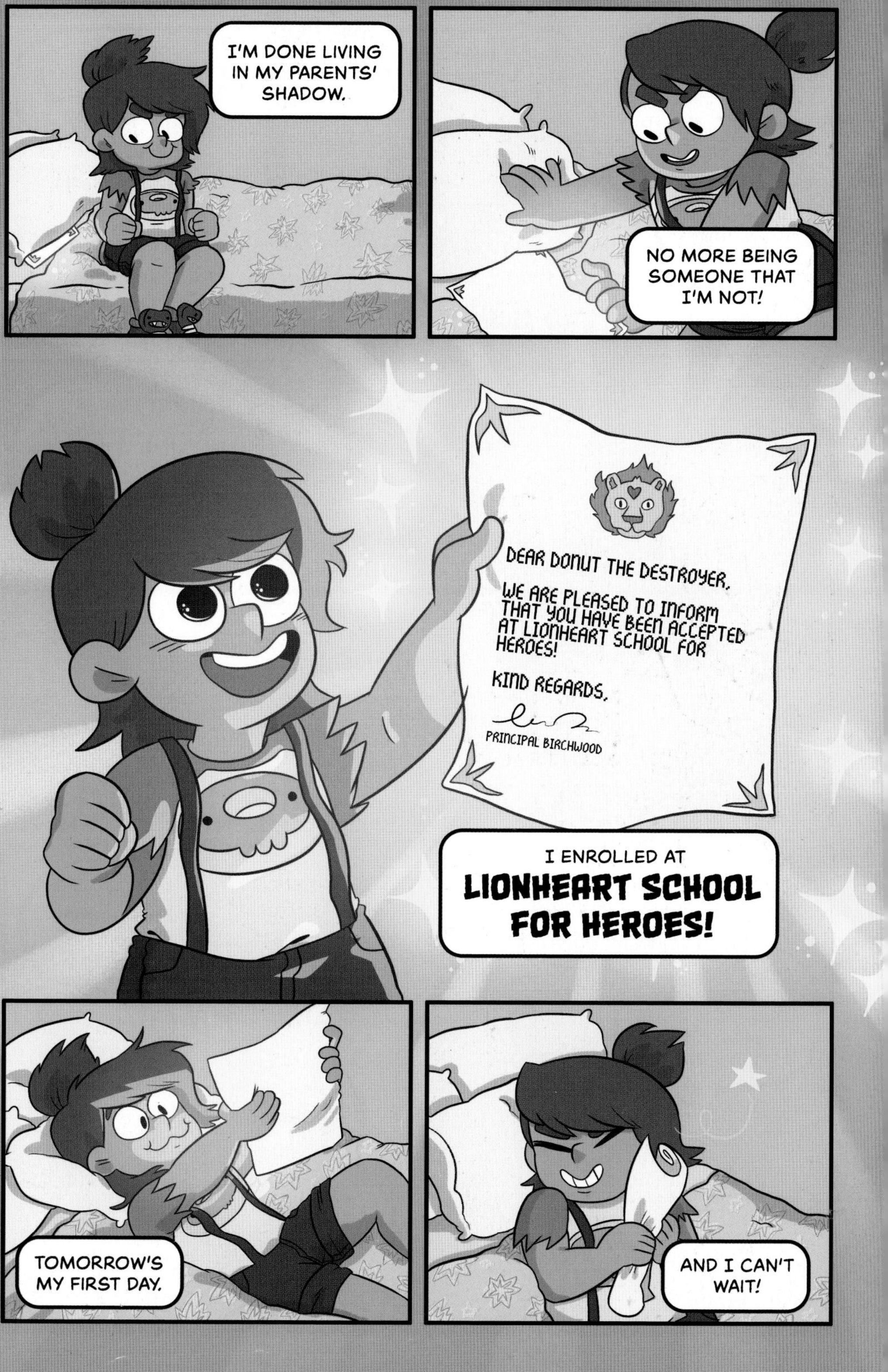
I'M DONE LIVING IN MY PARENTS' SHADOW.
NO MORE BEING SOMEONE THAT I'M NOT!
DEAR DONUT THE DESTROYER,
WE ARE PLEASED TO INFORM THAT YOU HAVE BEEN ACCEPTED AT LIONHEART SCHOOL FOR HEROES!
KIND REGARDS,
PRINCIPAL BIRCHWOOD
I ENROLLED AT LIONHEART SCHOOL FOR HEROES!
TOMORROW'S MY FIRST DAY.
AND I CAN'T WAIT!

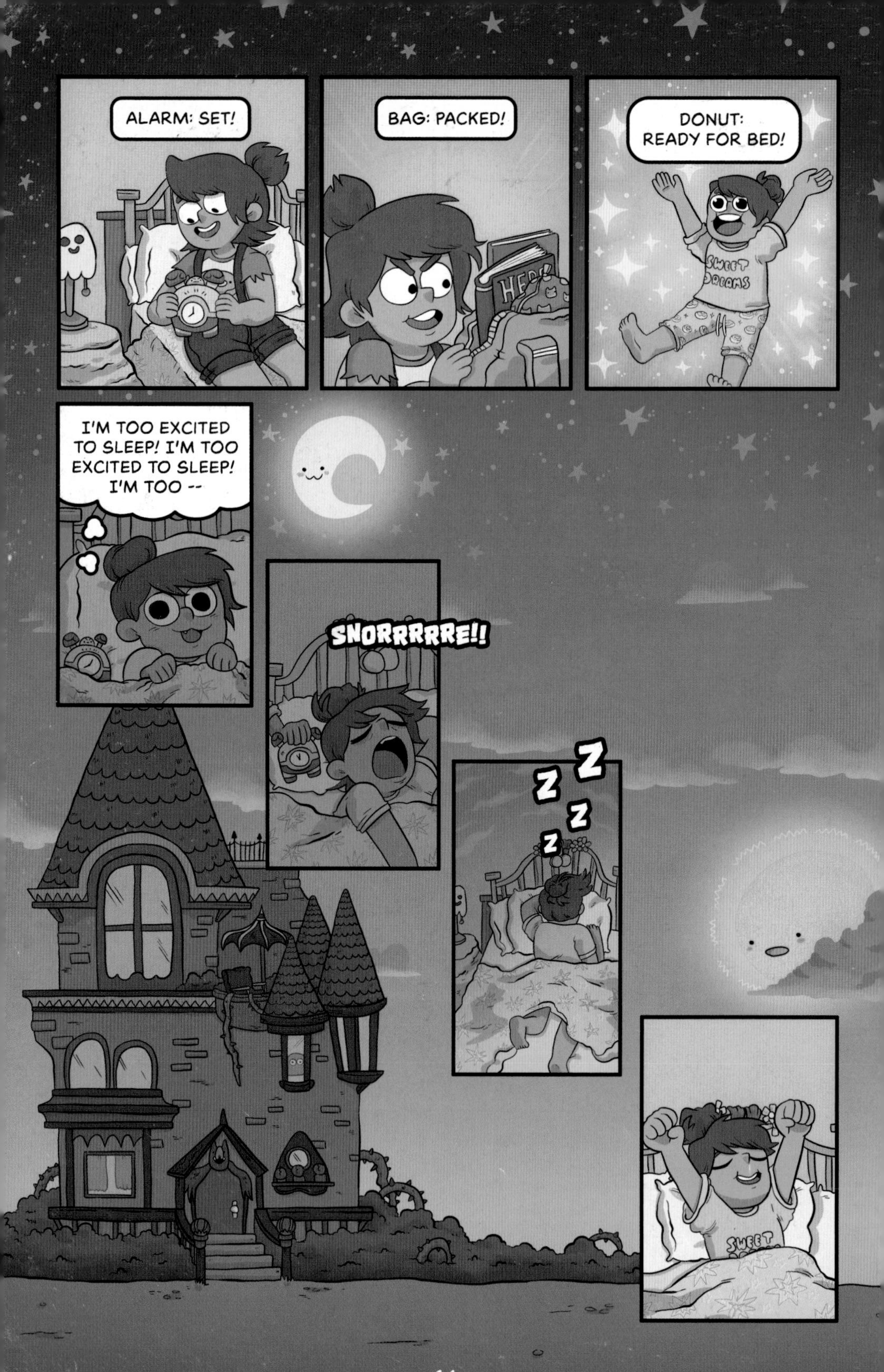
ALARM: SET!
BAG: PACKED!
DONUT: READY FOR BED!
SWEET DREAMS
I'M TOO EXCITED TO SLEEP! I'M TOO EXCITED TO SLEEP! I'M TOO --
SNORRRRRE!!
Z Z Z Z
SWEET

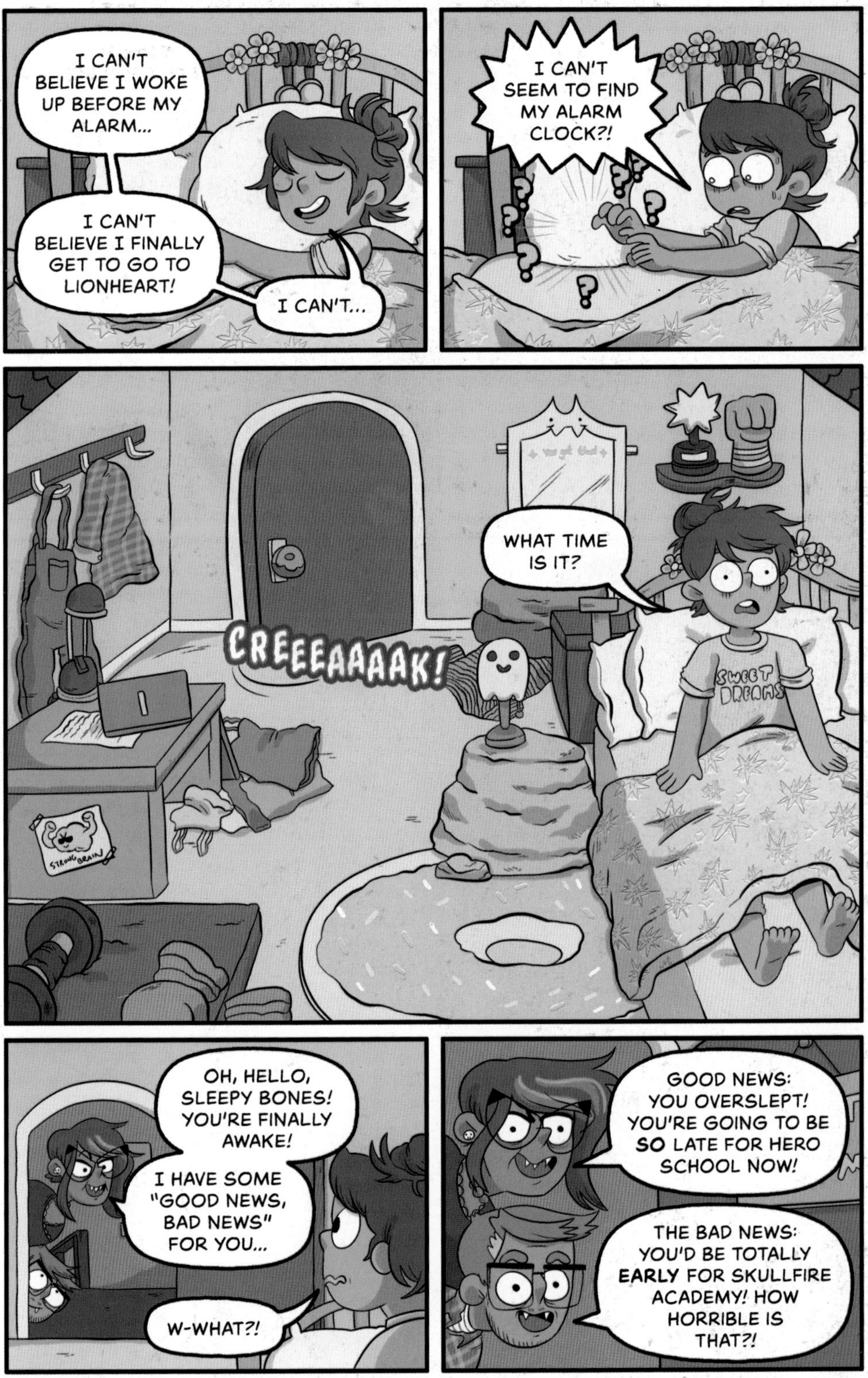
I CAN'T BELIEVE I WOKE UP BEFORE MY ALARM...
I CAN'T BELIEVE I FINALLY GET TO GO TO LIONHEART!
I CAN'T...
I CAN'T SEEM TO FIND MY ALARM CLOCK?!
WHAT TIME IS IT?
CREEEAAAAK!
STRONG BRAIN
SWEET DREAMS
OH, HELLO, SLEEPY BONES! YOU'RE FINALLY AWAKE!
I HAVE SOME "GOOD NEWS, BAD NEWS" FOR YOU...
W-WHAT?!
GOOD NEWS: YOU OVERSLEPT! YOU'RE GOING TO BE SO LATE FOR HERO SCHOOL NOW!
THE BAD NEWS: YOU'D BE TOTALLY EARLY FOR SKULLFIRE ACADEMY! HOW HORRIBLE IS THAT?!

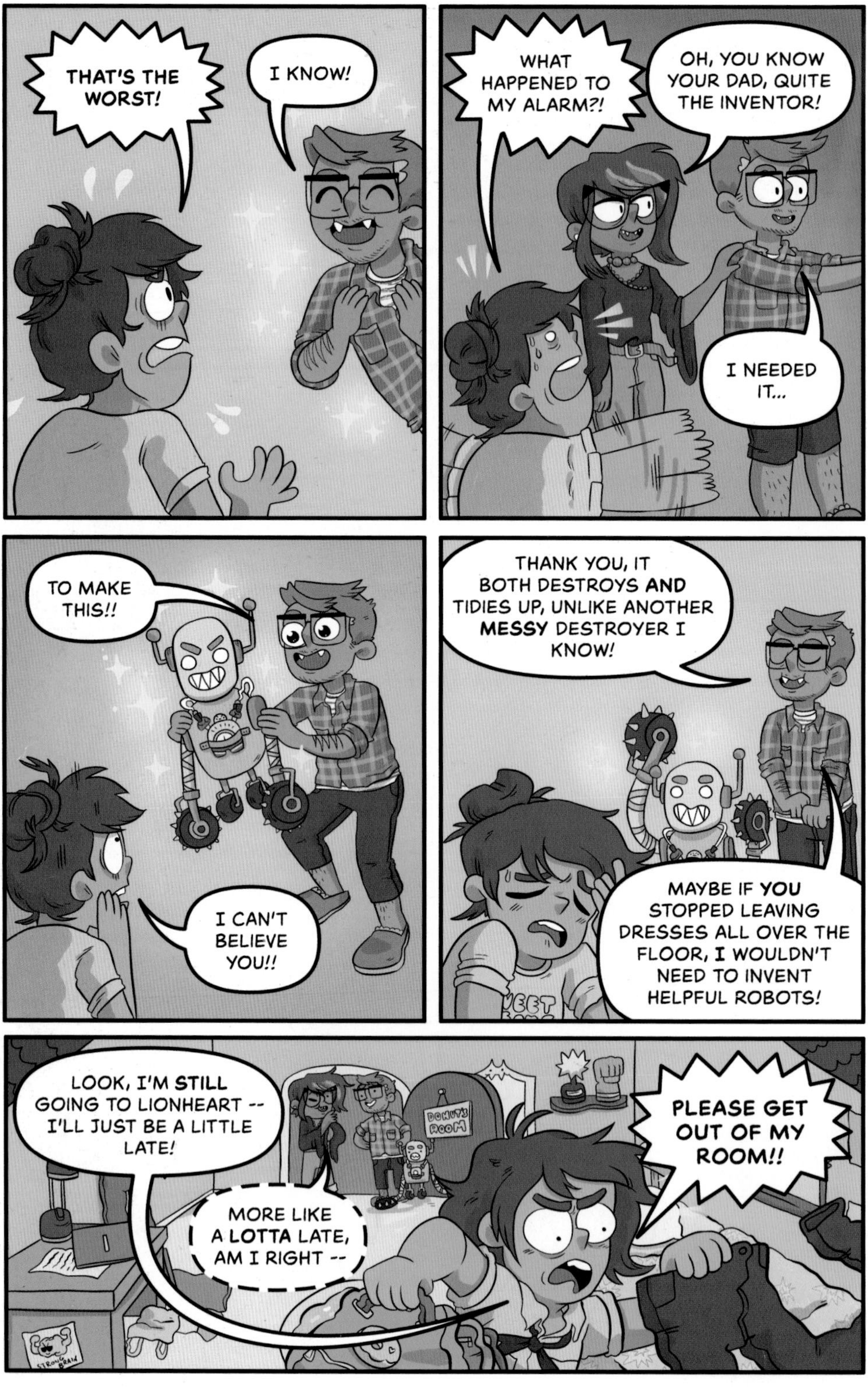
THAT'S THE WORST!
I KNOW!
WHAT HAPPENED TO MY ALARM?!
OH, YOU KNOW YOUR DAD, QUITE THE INVENTOR!
I NEEDED IT...
TO MAKE THIS!!
I CAN'T BELIEVE YOU!!
THANK YOU, IT BOTH DESTROYS AND TIDIES UP, UNLIKE ANOTHER MESSY DESTROYER I KNOW!
MAYBE IF YOU STOPPED LEAVING DRESSES ALL OVER THE FLOOR, I WOULDN'T NEED TO INVENT HELPFUL ROBOTS!
LOOK, I'M STILL GOING TO LIONHEART -- I'LL JUST BE A LITTLE LATE!
DONUT'S ROOM
MORE LIKE A LOTTA LATE, AM I RIGHT --
PLEASE GET OUT OF MY ROOM!!

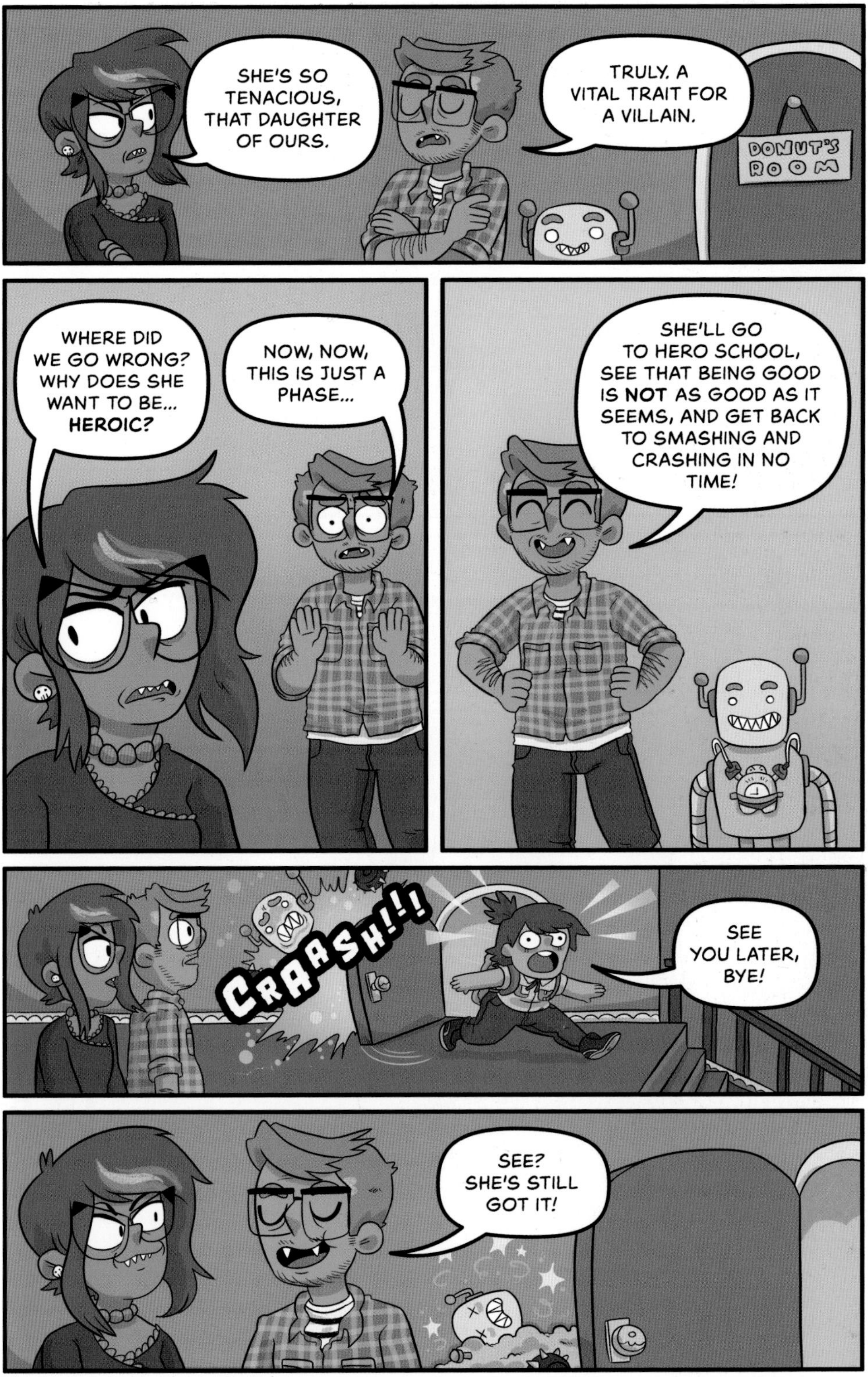
SHE'S SO TENACIOUS, THAT DAUGHTER OF OURS.
TRULY, A VITAL TRAIT FOR A VILLAIN.
DONUT'S ROOM
WHERE DID WE GO WRONG? WHY DOES SHE WANT TO BE... **HEROIC?**
NOW, NOW, THIS IS JUST A PHASE...
SHE'LL GO TO HERO SCHOOL, SEE THAT BEING GOOD IS **NOT** AS GOOD AS IT SEEMS, AND GET BACK TO SMASHING AND CRASHING IN NO TIME!
CRAASH!!!
SEE YOU LATER, BYE!
SEE? SHE'S STILL GOT IT!

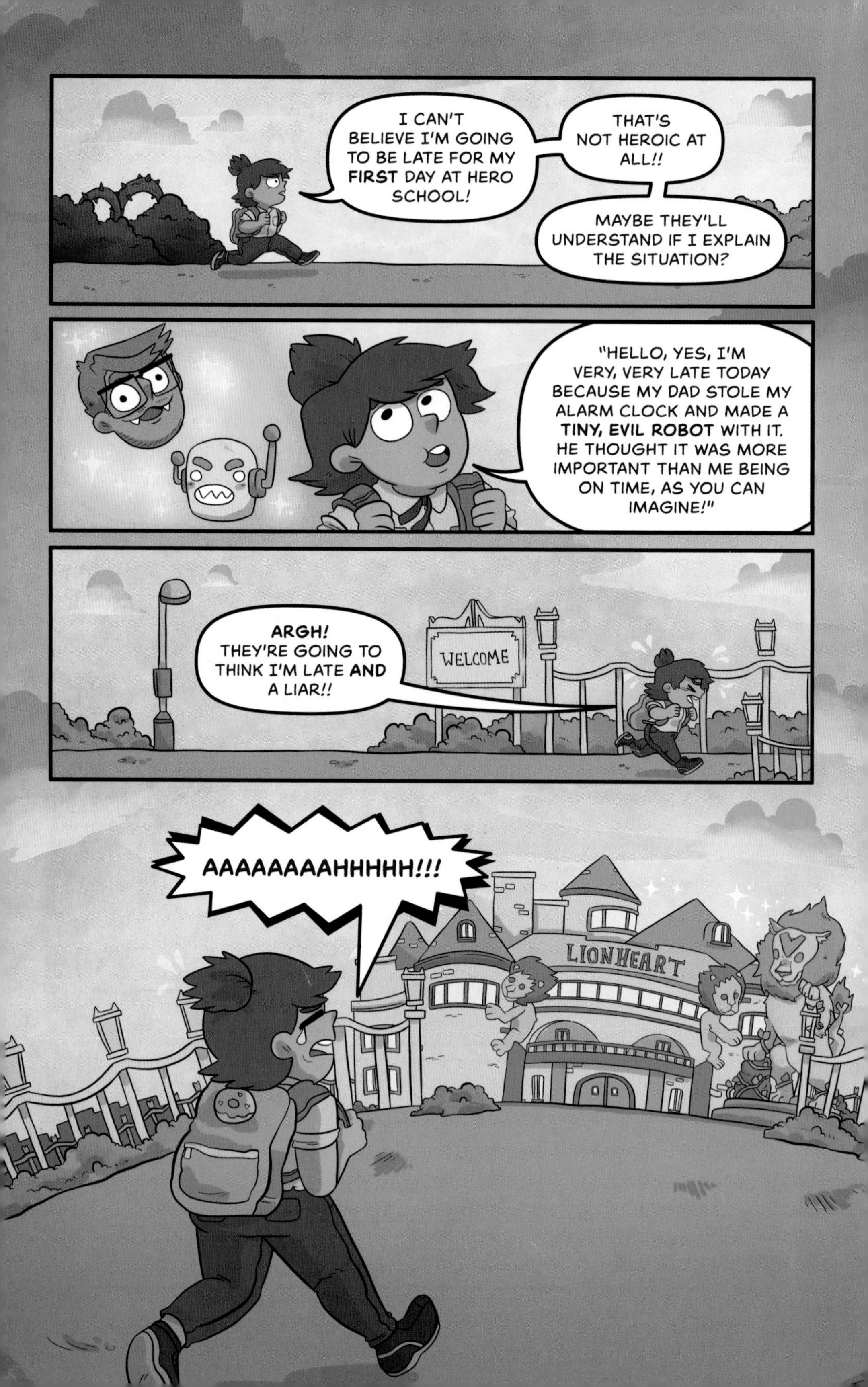
I CAN'T BELIEVE I'M GOING TO BE LATE FOR MY FIRST DAY AT HERO SCHOOL!
THAT'S NOT HEROIC AT ALL!!
MAYBE THEY'LL UNDERSTAND IF I EXPLAIN THE SITUATION?
"HELLO, YES, I'M VERY, VERY LATE TODAY BECAUSE MY DAD STOLE MY ALARM CLOCK AND MADE A TINY, EVIL ROBOT WITH IT. HE THOUGHT IT WAS MORE IMPORTANT THAN ME BEING ON TIME, AS YOU CAN IMAGINE!"
WELCOME
ARGH! THEY'RE GOING TO THINK I'M LATE AND A LIAR!!
AAAAAAAAHHHHH!!!
LIONHEART

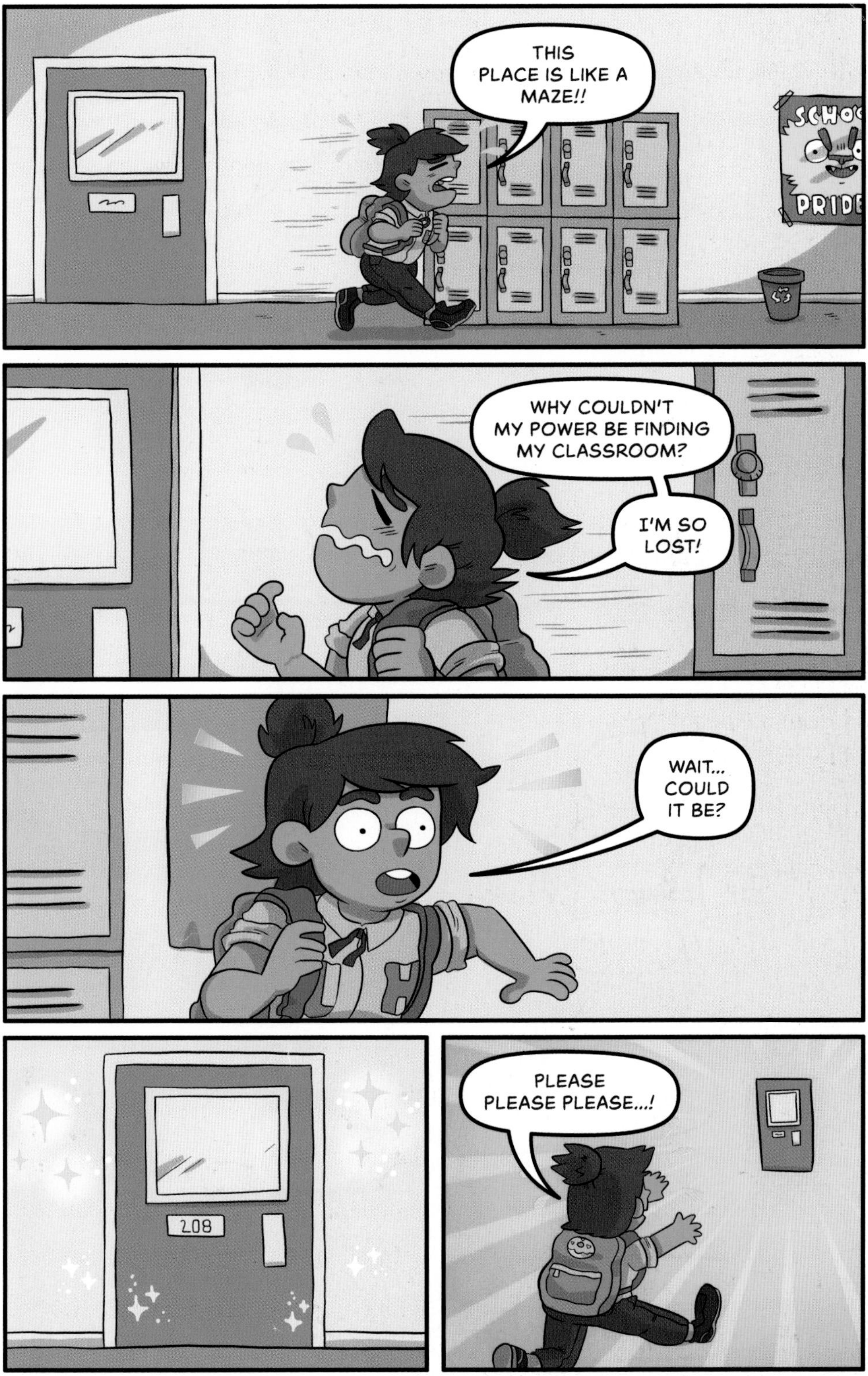

THIS PLACE IS LIKE A MAZE!!
PRIDE
WHY COULDN'T MY POWER BE FINDING MY CLASSROOM?
I'M SO LOST!
WAIT... COULD IT BE?
208
PLEASE PLEASE PLEASE...!

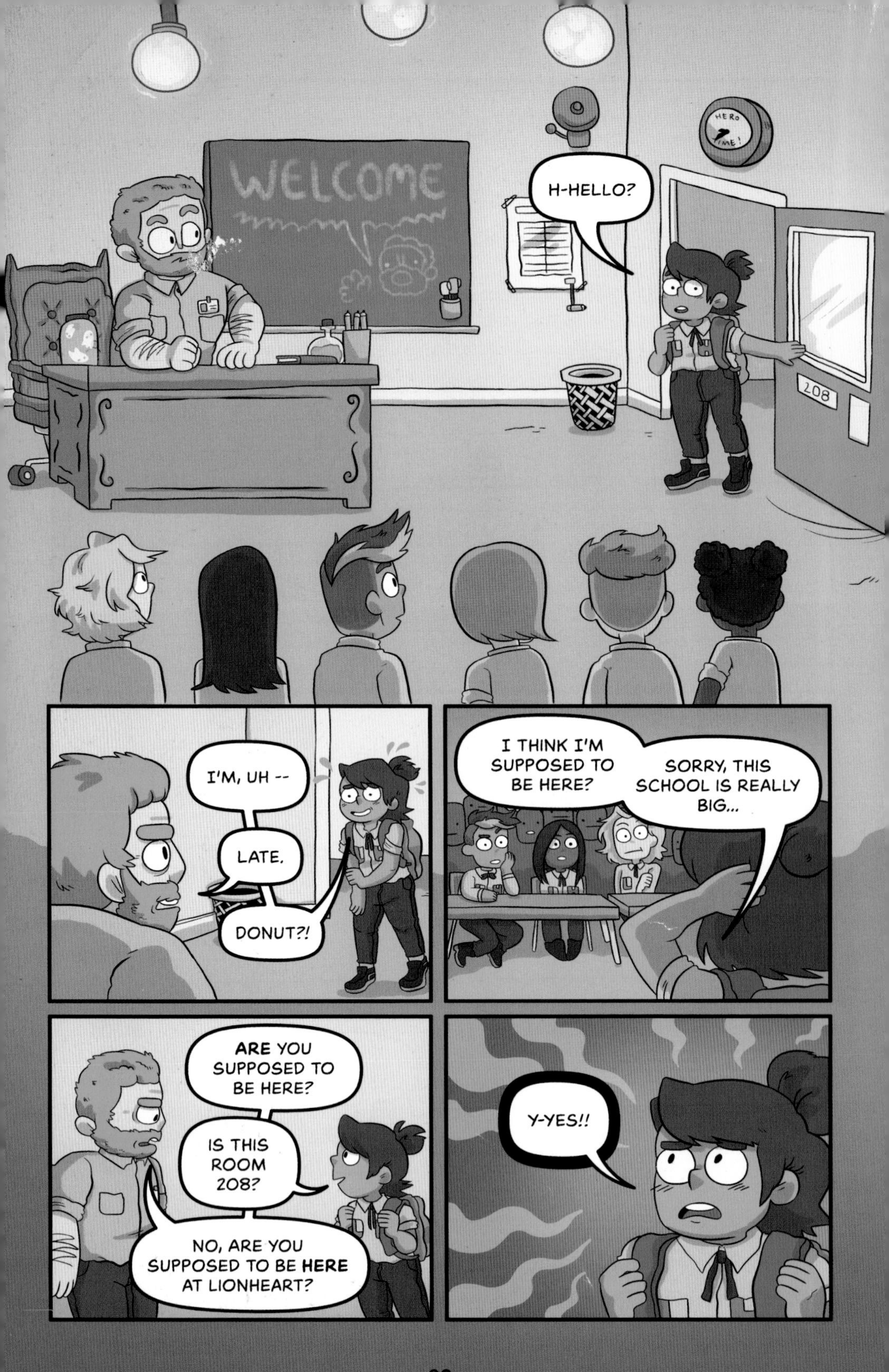
WELCOME
HERO TIME!
H-HELLO?
208
I'M, UH --
LATE.
DONUT?!
I THINK I'M SUPPOSED TO BE HERE?
SORRY, THIS SCHOOL IS REALLY BIG...
ARE YOU SUPPOSED TO BE HERE?
IS THIS ROOM 208?
NO, ARE YOU SUPPOSED TO BE **HERE** AT LIONHEART?
Y-YES!!

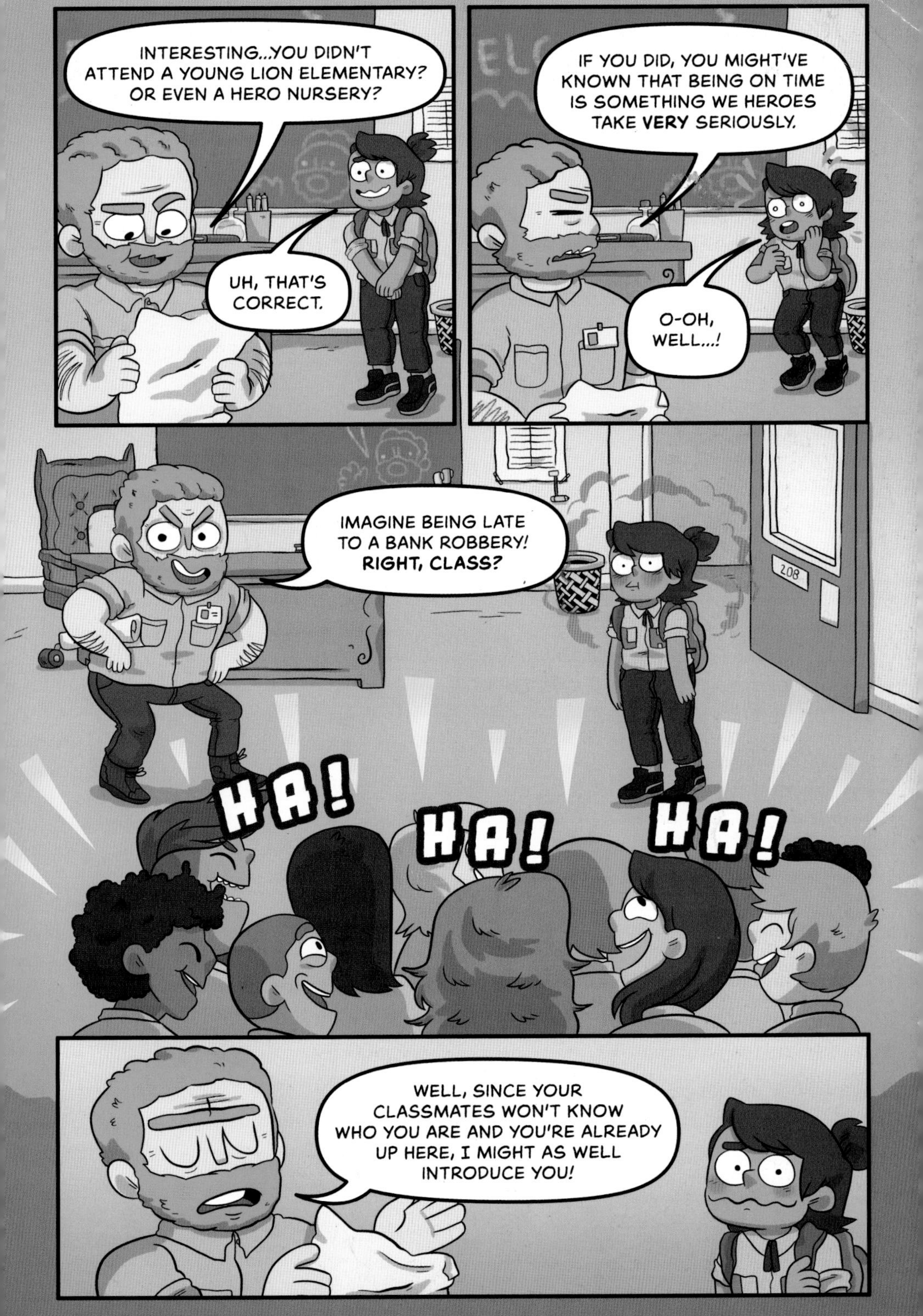
INTERESTING...YOU DIDN'T ATTEND A YOUNG LION ELEMENTARY? OR EVEN A HERO NURSERY?
UH, THAT'S CORRECT.
IF YOU DID, YOU MIGHT'VE KNOWN THAT BEING ON TIME IS SOMETHING WE HEROES TAKE **VERY** SERIOUSLY.
O-OH, WELL...!
IMAGINE BEING LATE TO A BANK ROBBERY! **RIGHT, CLASS?**
208
HA! HA! HA!
WELL, SINCE YOUR CLASSMATES WON'T KNOW WHO YOU ARE AND YOU'RE ALREADY UP HERE, I MIGHT AS WELL INTRODUCE YOU!

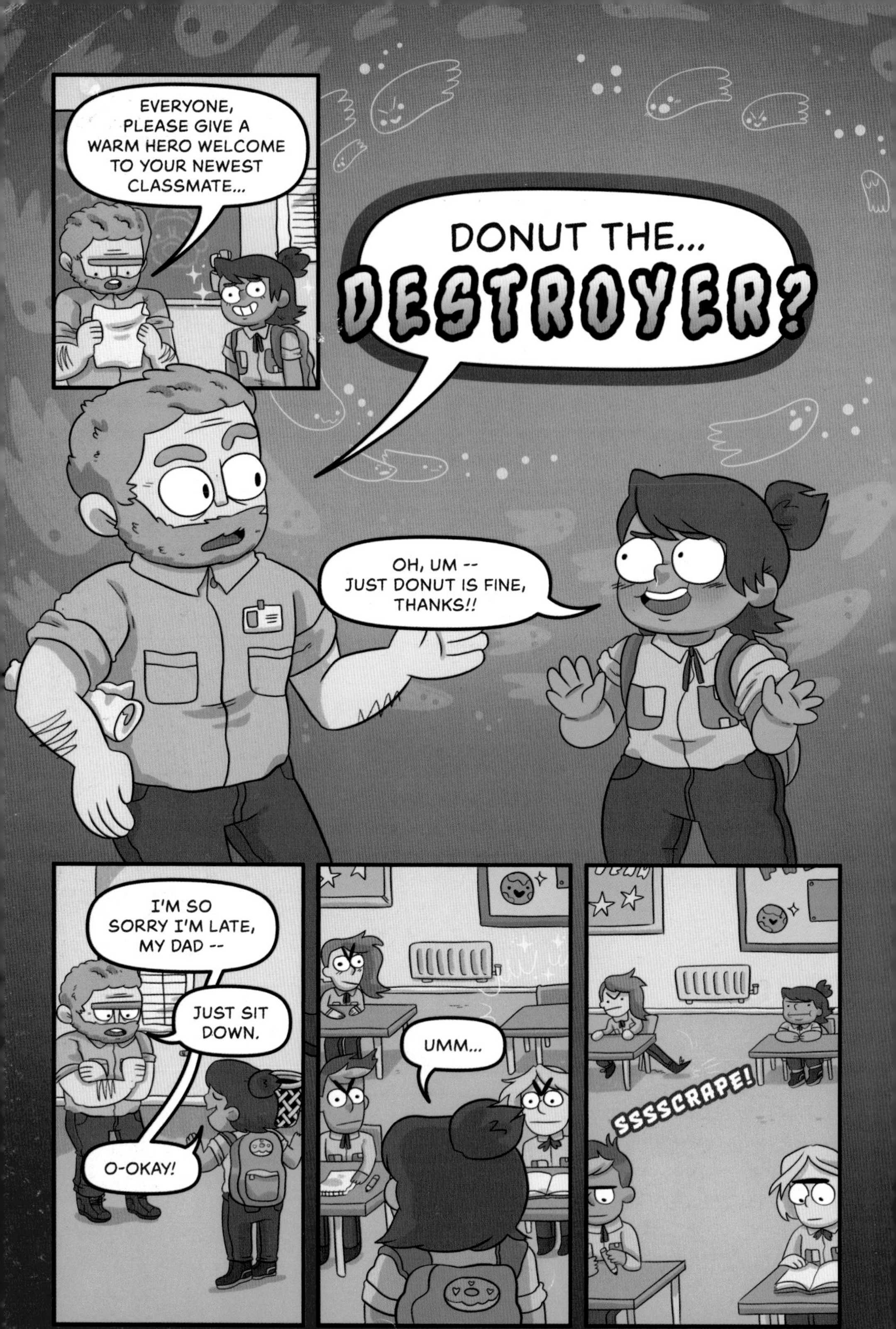
EVERYONE, PLEASE GIVE A WARM HERO WELCOME TO YOUR NEWEST CLASSMATE...
DONUT THE... DESTROYER?
OH, UM -- JUST DONUT IS FINE, THANKS!!
I'M SO SORRY I'M LATE, MY DAD --
JUST SIT DOWN.
O-OKAY!
UMM...
SSSSCRAPE!

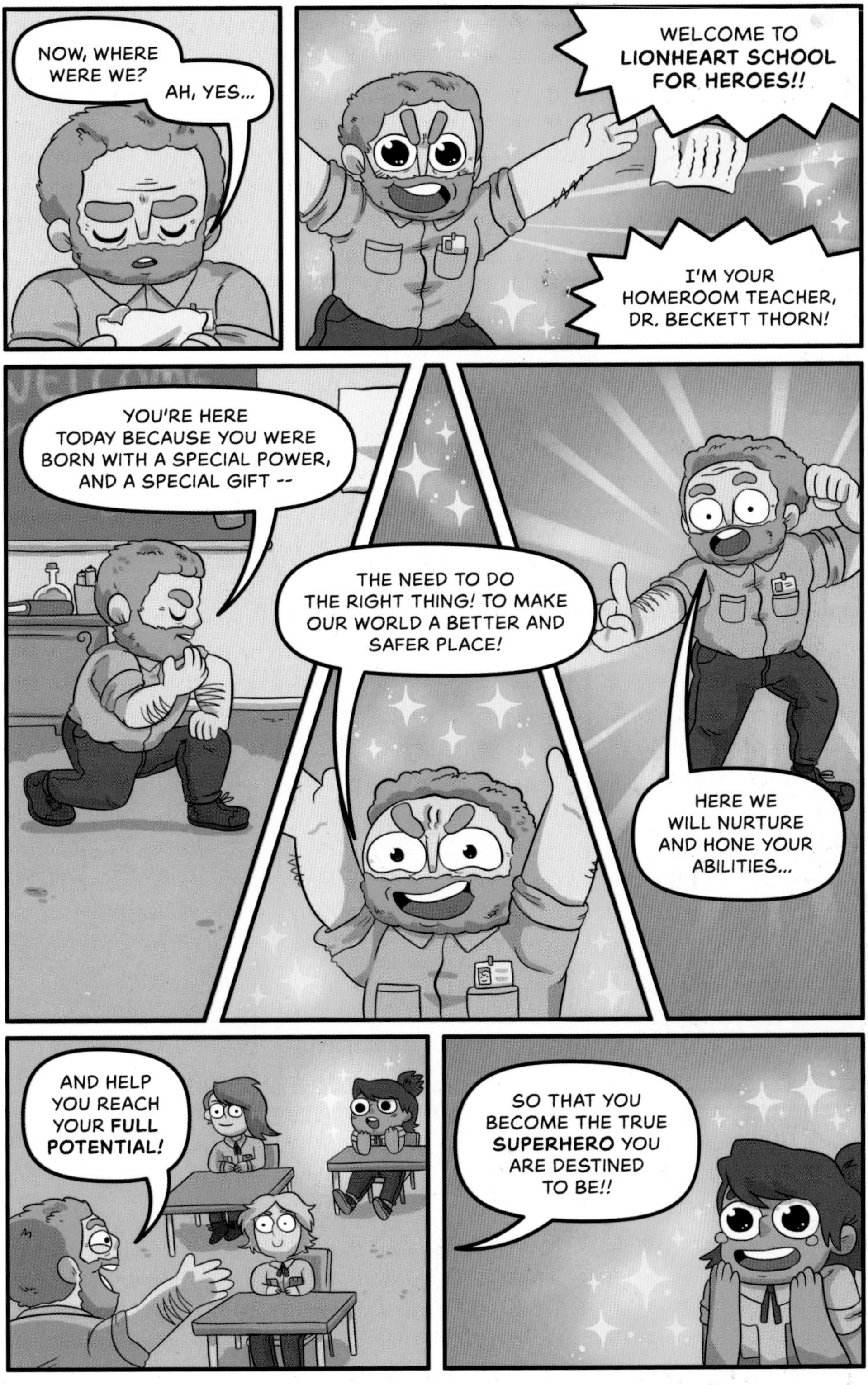
NOW, WHERE WERE WE?
AH, YES...
WELCOME TO LIONHEART SCHOOL FOR HEROES!!
I'M YOUR HOMEROOM TEACHER, DR. BECKETT THORN!
YOU'RE HERE TODAY BECAUSE YOU WERE BORN WITH A SPECIAL POWER, AND A SPECIAL GIFT --
THE NEED TO DO THE RIGHT THING! TO MAKE OUR WORLD A BETTER AND SAFER PLACE!
HERE WE WILL NURTURE AND HONE YOUR ABILITIES...
AND HELP YOU REACH YOUR **FULL POTENTIAL!**
SO THAT YOU BECOME THE TRUE **SUPERHERO** YOU ARE DESTINED TO BE!!

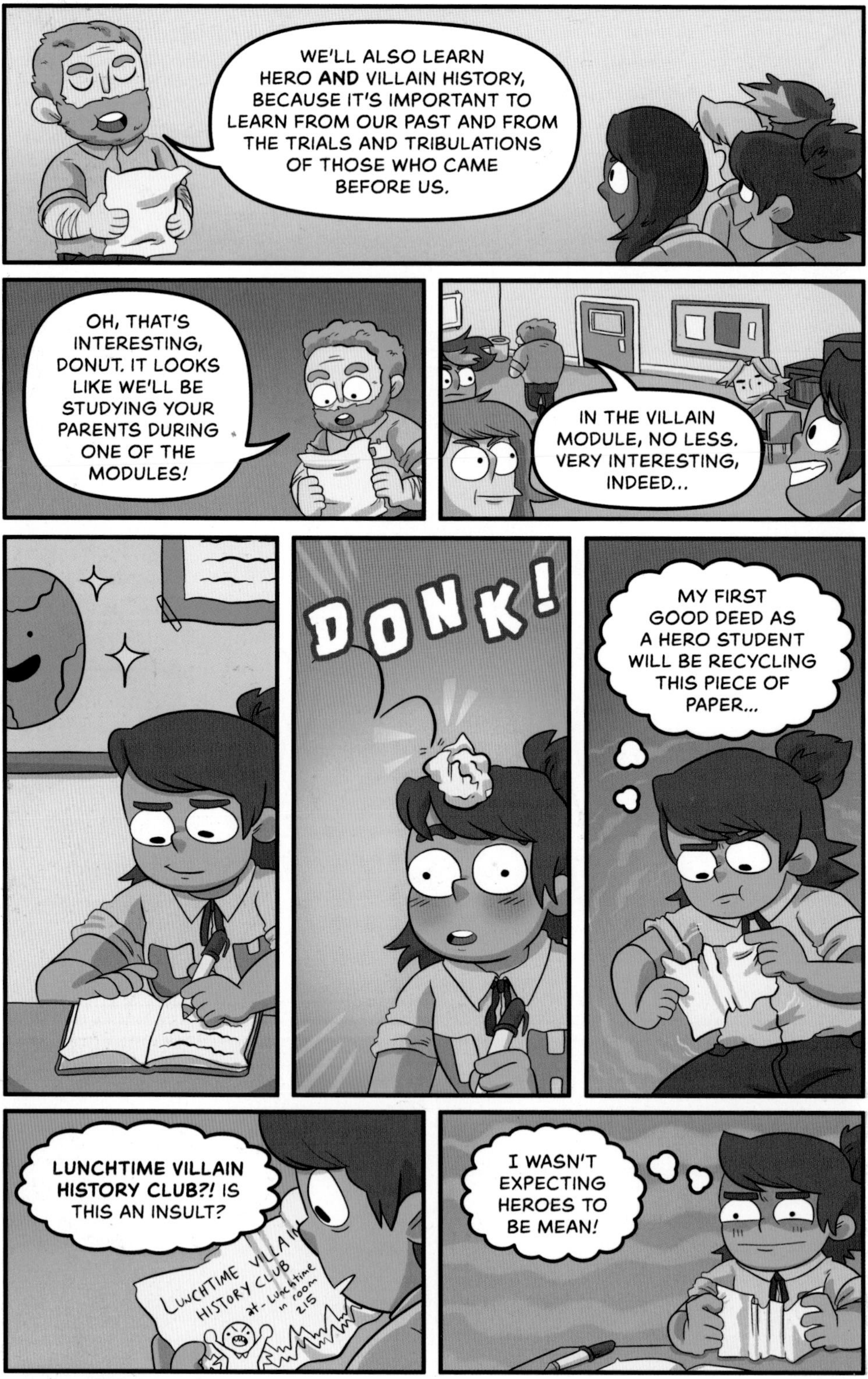

WE'LL ALSO LEARN HERO **AND** VILLAIN HISTORY, BECAUSE IT'S IMPORTANT TO LEARN FROM OUR PAST AND FROM THE TRIALS AND TRIBULATIONS OF THOSE WHO CAME BEFORE US.
OH, THAT'S INTERESTING, DONUT. IT LOOKS LIKE WE'LL BE STUDYING YOUR PARENTS DURING ONE OF THE MODULES!
IN THE VILLAIN MODULE, NO LESS. VERY INTERESTING, INDEED...
DONK!
MY FIRST GOOD DEED AS A HERO STUDENT WILL BE RECYCLING THIS PIECE OF PAPER...
LUNCHTIME VILLAIN HISTORY CLUB?! IS THIS AN INSULT?
LUNCHTIME VILLAIN HISTORY CLUB
at - Lunchtime in room 215
I WASN'T EXPECTING HEROES TO BE MEAN!

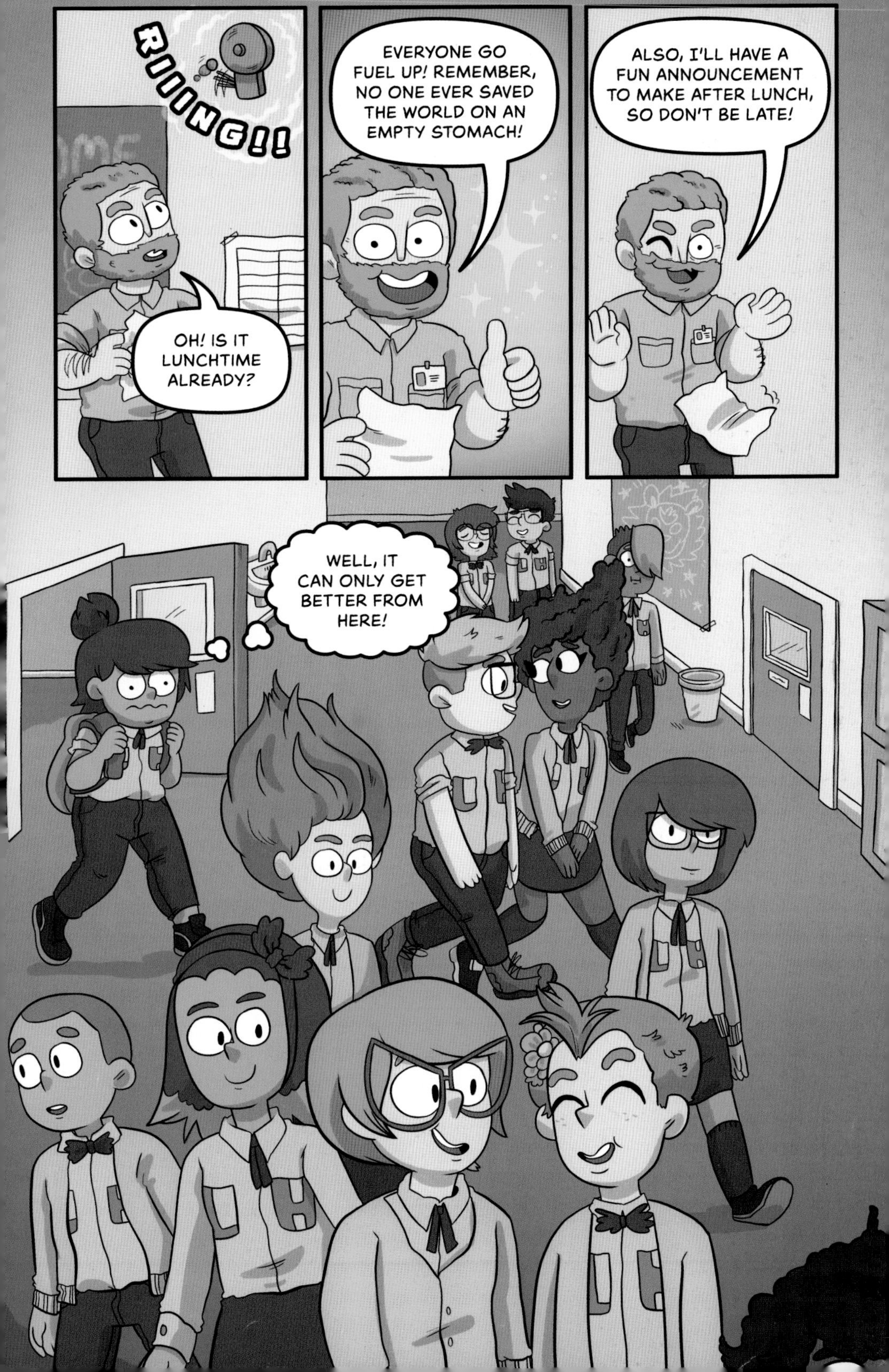
RIIING!!
OH! IS IT LUNCHTIME ALREADY?
EVERYONE GO FUEL UP! REMEMBER, NO ONE EVER SAVED THE WORLD ON AN EMPTY STOMACH!
ALSO, I'LL HAVE A FUN ANNOUNCEMENT TO MAKE AFTER LUNCH, SO DON'T BE LATE!
WELL, IT CAN ONLY GET BETTER FROM HERE!

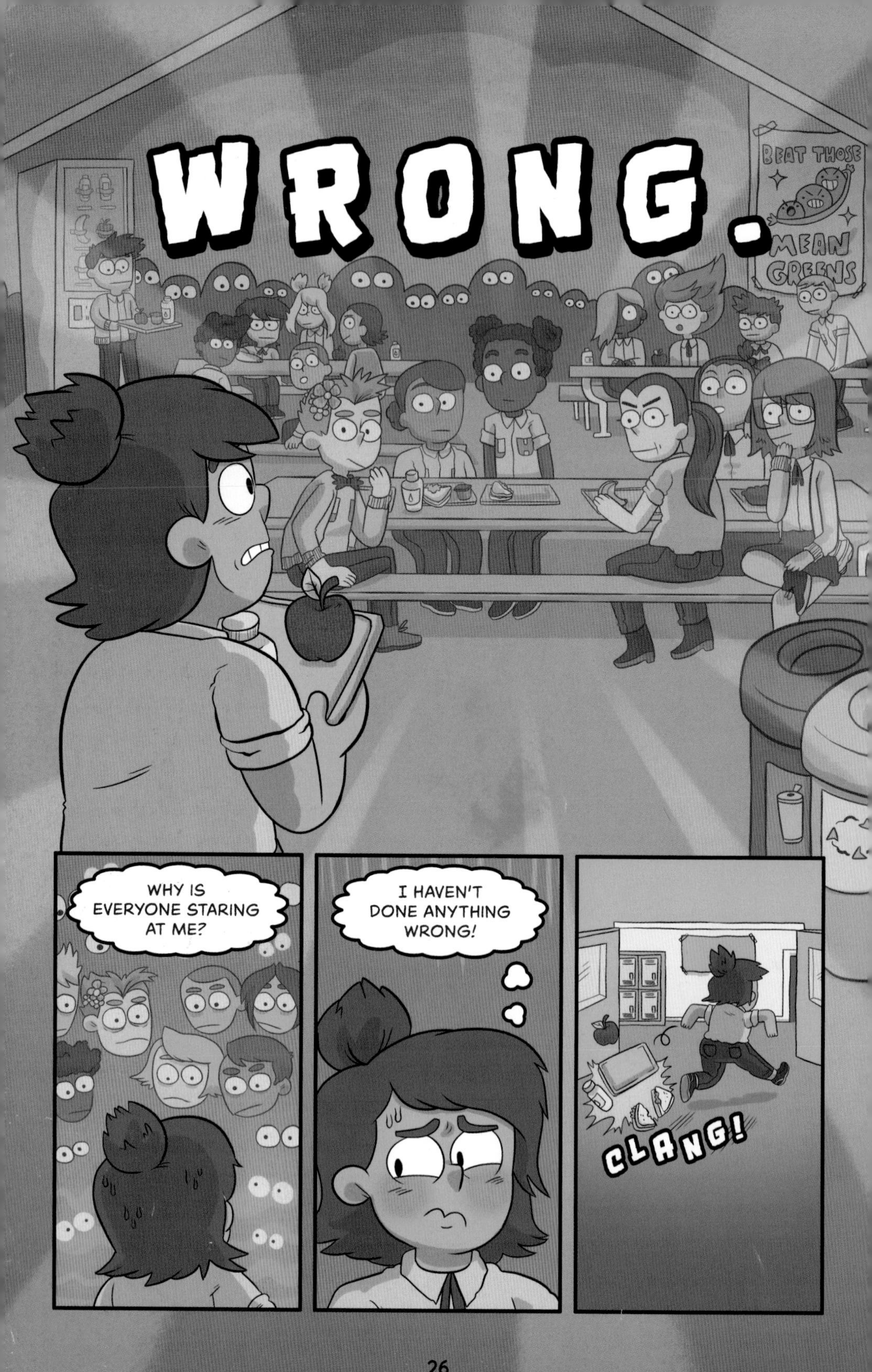
WRONG.
BEAT THOSE MEAN GREENS
WHY IS EVERYONE STARING AT ME?
I HAVEN'T DONE ANYTHING WRONG!
CLANG!

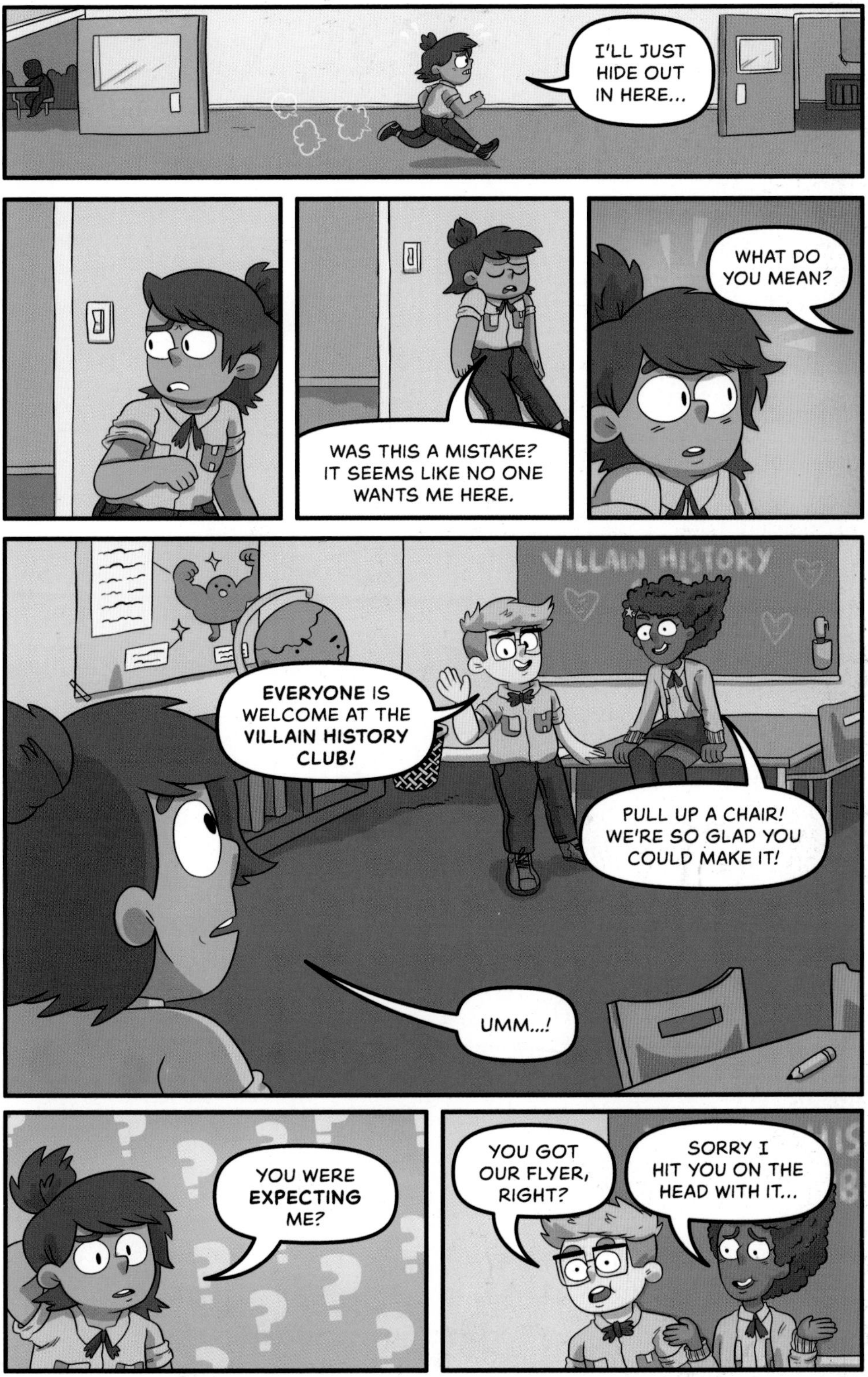
I'LL JUST HIDE OUT IN HERE...
WAS THIS A MISTAKE? IT SEEMS LIKE NO ONE WANTS ME HERE.
WHAT DO YOU MEAN?
VILLAIN HISTORY
EVERYONE IS WELCOME AT THE VILLAIN HISTORY CLUB!
PULL UP A CHAIR! WE'RE SO GLAD YOU COULD MAKE IT!
UMM...!
YOU WERE EXPECTING ME?
YOU GOT OUR FLYER, RIGHT?
SORRY I HIT YOU ON THE HEAD WITH IT...

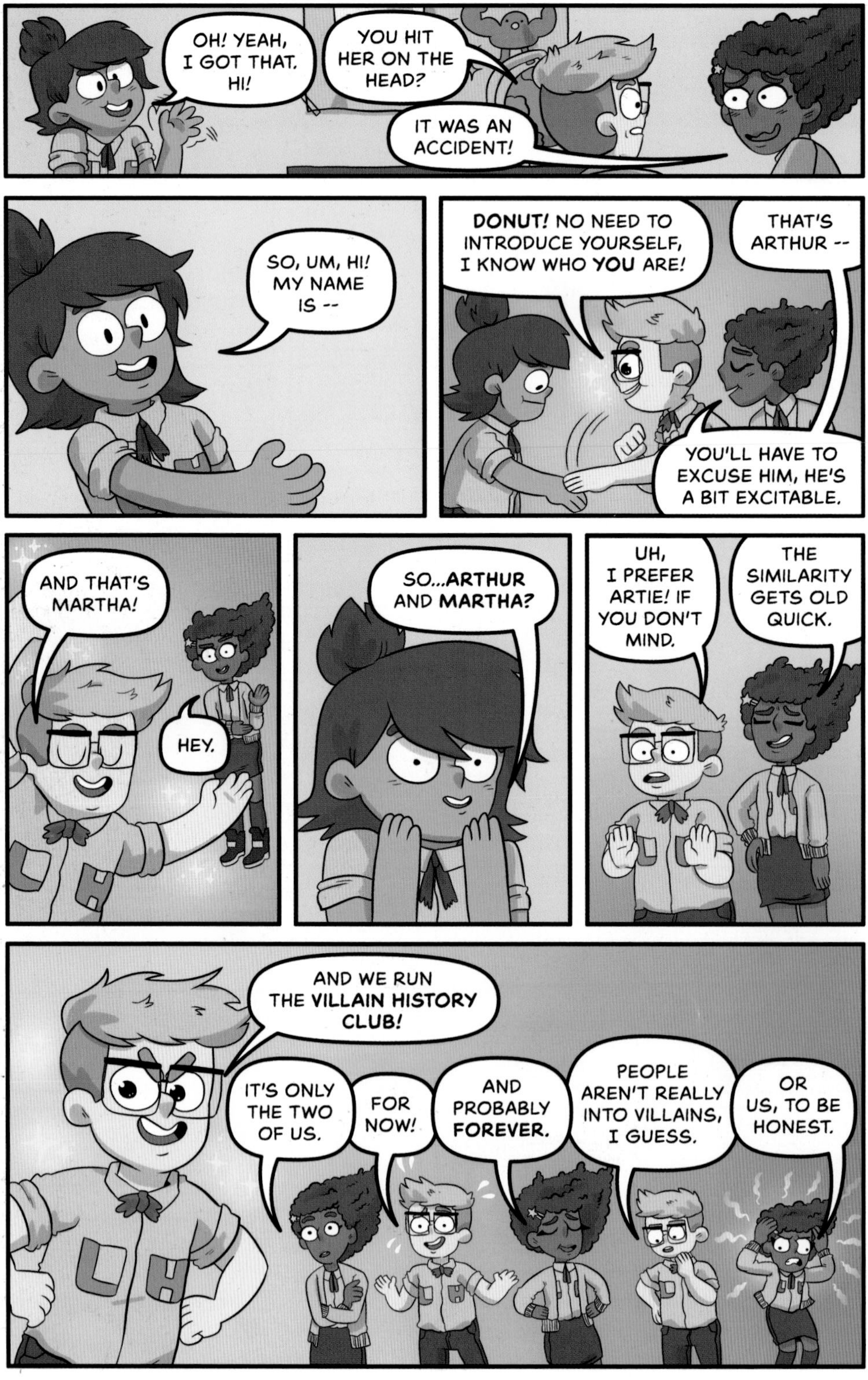
OH! YEAH, I GOT THAT. HI!
YOU HIT HER ON THE HEAD?
IT WAS AN ACCIDENT!
SO, UM, HI! MY NAME IS --
DONUT! NO NEED TO INTRODUCE YOURSELF, I KNOW WHO **YOU** ARE!
THAT'S ARTHUR --
YOU'LL HAVE TO EXCUSE HIM, HE'S A BIT EXCITABLE.
AND THAT'S MARTHA!
HEY.
SO...**ARTHUR** AND **MARTHA?**
UH, I PREFER ARTIE! IF YOU DON'T MIND.
THE SIMILARITY GETS OLD QUICK.
AND WE RUN THE **VILLAIN HISTORY CLUB!**
IT'S ONLY THE TWO OF US.
FOR NOW!
AND PROBABLY **FOREVER.**
PEOPLE AREN'T REALLY INTO VILLAINS, I GUESS.
OR US, TO BE HONEST.

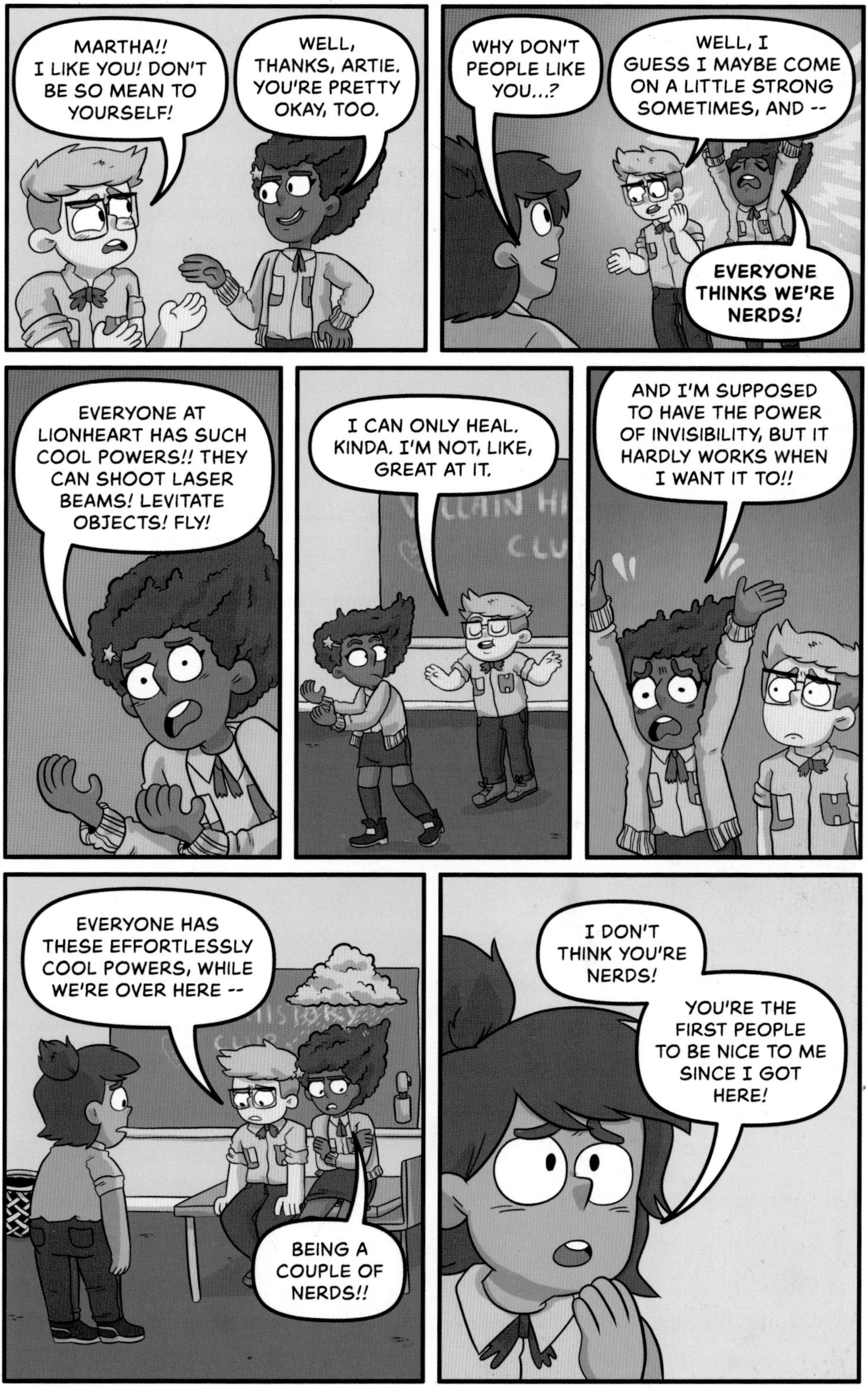

MARTHA!! I LIKE YOU! DON'T BE SO MEAN TO YOURSELF!
WELL, THANKS, ARTIE. YOU'RE PRETTY OKAY, TOO.
WHY DON'T PEOPLE LIKE YOU...?
WELL, I GUESS I MAYBE COME ON A LITTLE STRONG SOMETIMES, AND --
EVERYONE THINKS WE'RE NERDS!
EVERYONE AT LIONHEART HAS SUCH COOL POWERS!! THEY CAN SHOOT LASER BEAMS! LEVITATE OBJECTS! FLY!
I CAN ONLY HEAL, KINDA. I'M NOT, LIKE, GREAT AT IT.
AND I'M SUPPOSED TO HAVE THE POWER OF INVISIBILITY, BUT IT HARDLY WORKS WHEN I WANT IT TO!!
EVERYONE HAS THESE EFFORTLESSLY COOL POWERS, WHILE WE'RE OVER HERE --
BEING A COUPLE OF NERDS!!
I DON'T THINK YOU'RE NERDS!
YOU'RE THE FIRST PEOPLE TO BE NICE TO ME SINCE I GOT HERE!

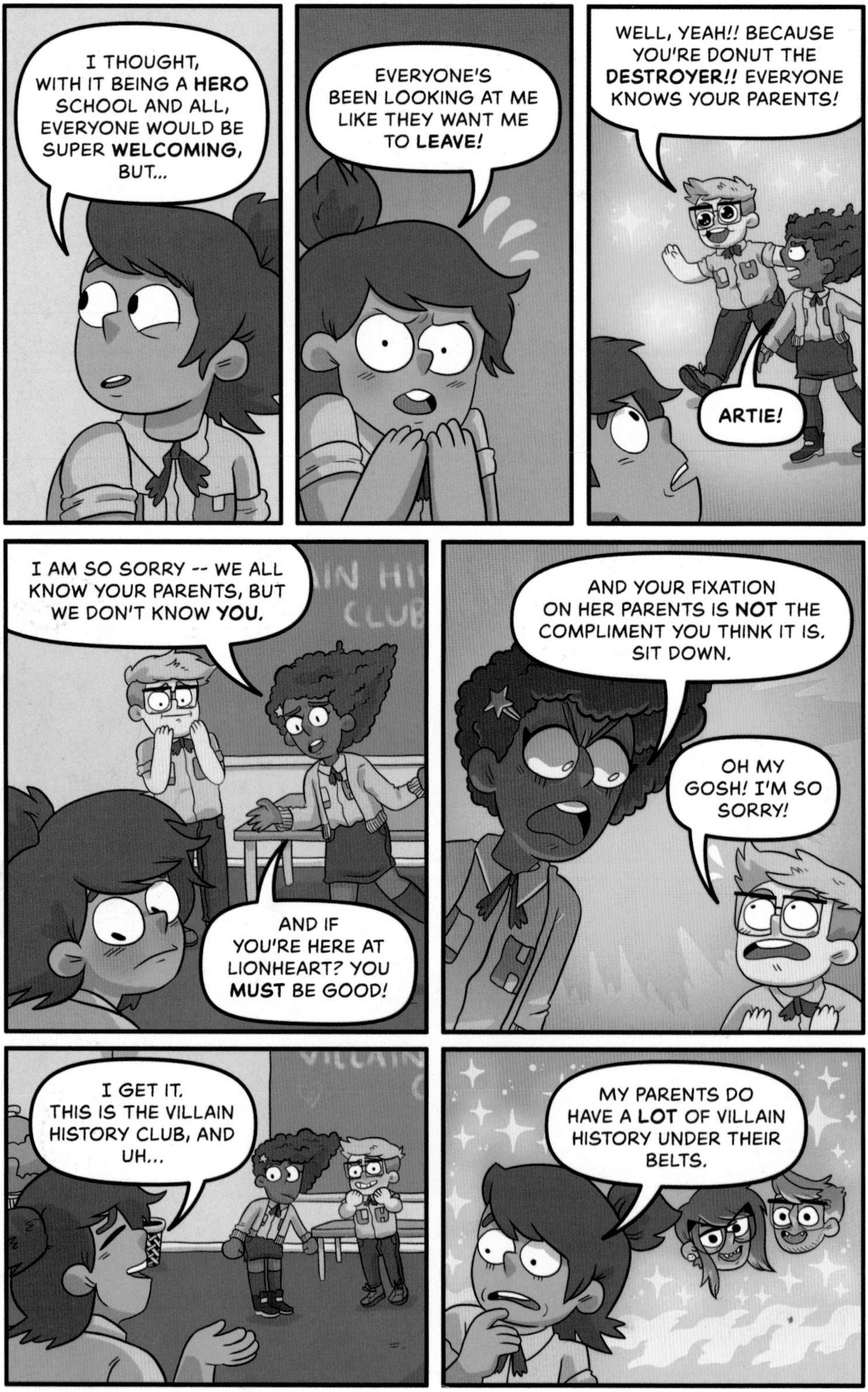
I THOUGHT, WITH IT BEING A HERO SCHOOL AND ALL, EVERYONE WOULD BE SUPER WELCOMING, BUT...
EVERYONE'S BEEN LOOKING AT ME LIKE THEY WANT ME TO LEAVE!
WELL, YEAH!! BECAUSE YOU'RE DONUT THE DESTROYER!! EVERYONE KNOWS YOUR PARENTS!
ARTIE!
I AM SO SORRY -- WE ALL KNOW YOUR PARENTS, BUT WE DON'T KNOW YOU.
AND IF YOU'RE HERE AT LIONHEART? YOU MUST BE GOOD!
AND YOUR FIXATION ON HER PARENTS IS NOT THE COMPLIMENT YOU THINK IT IS. SIT DOWN.
OH MY GOSH! I'M SO SORRY!
I GET IT. THIS IS THE VILLAIN HISTORY CLUB, AND UH...
MY PARENTS DO HAVE A LOT OF VILLAIN HISTORY UNDER THEIR BELTS.

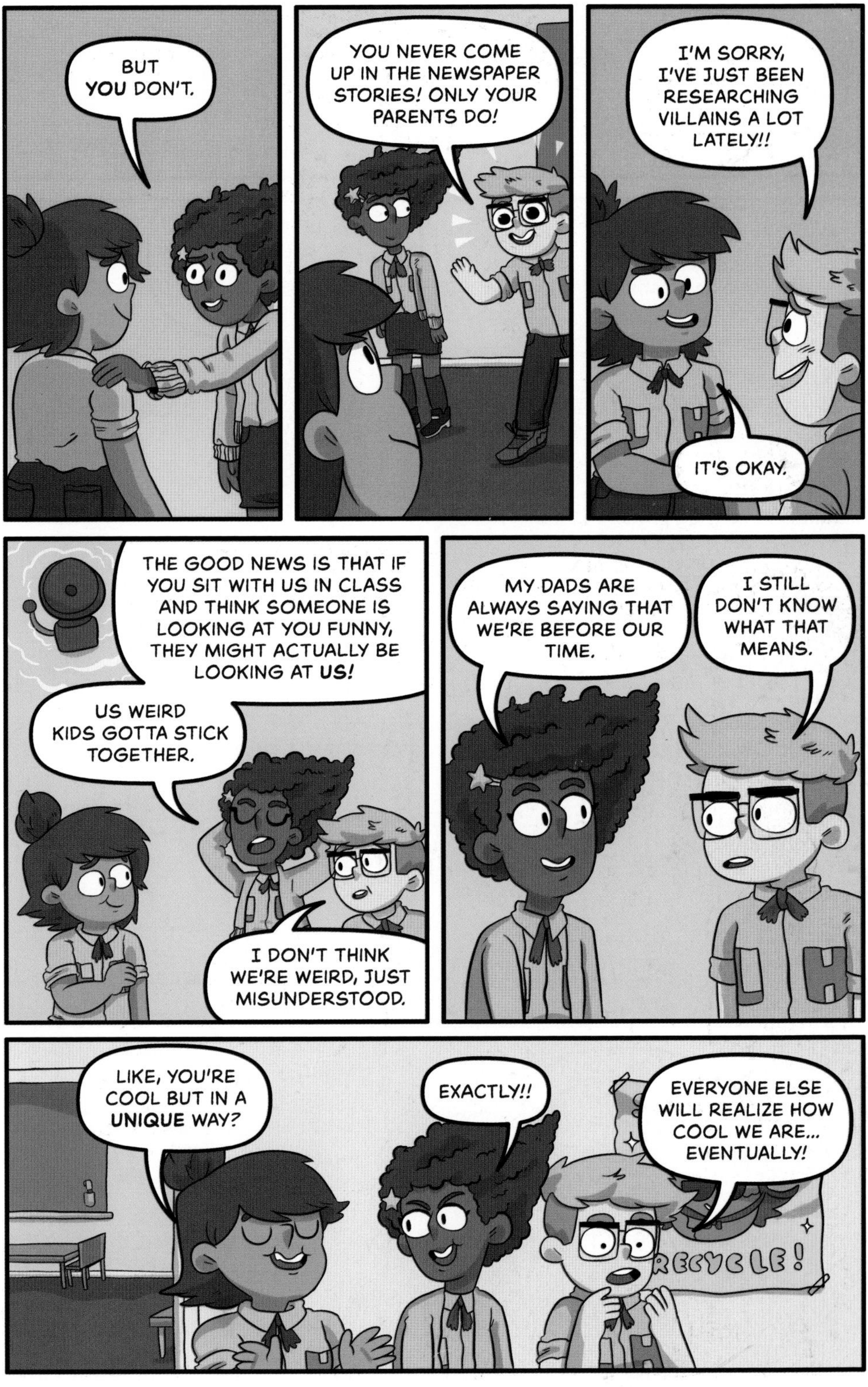
BUT YOU DON'T.
YOU NEVER COME UP IN THE NEWSPAPER STORIES! ONLY YOUR PARENTS DO!
I'M SORRY, I'VE JUST BEEN RESEARCHING VILLAINS A LOT LATELY!!
IT'S OKAY.
THE GOOD NEWS IS THAT IF YOU SIT WITH US IN CLASS AND THINK SOMEONE IS LOOKING AT YOU FUNNY, THEY MIGHT ACTUALLY BE LOOKING AT US!
US WEIRD KIDS GOTTA STICK TOGETHER.
I DON'T THINK WE'RE WEIRD, JUST MISUNDERSTOOD.
MY DADS ARE ALWAYS SAYING THAT WE'RE BEFORE OUR TIME.
I STILL DON'T KNOW WHAT THAT MEANS.
LIKE, YOU'RE COOL BUT IN A UNIQUE WAY?
EXACTLY!!
EVERYONE ELSE WILL REALIZE HOW COOL WE ARE... EVENTUALLY!
RECYCLE!

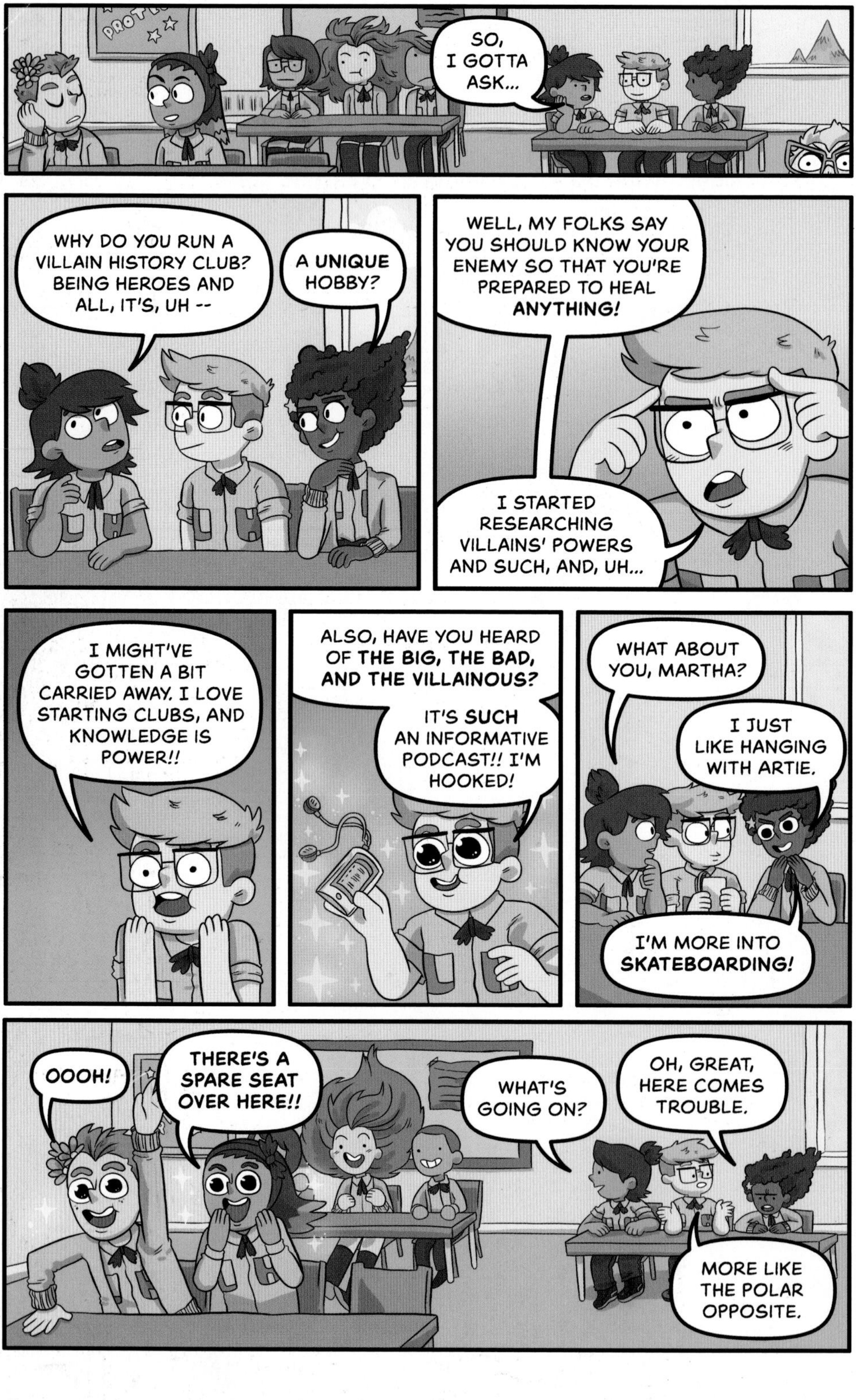
SO, I GOTTA ASK...
WHY DO YOU RUN A VILLAIN HISTORY CLUB? BEING HEROES AND ALL, IT'S, UH --
A **UNIQUE** HOBBY?
WELL, MY FOLKS SAY YOU SHOULD KNOW YOUR ENEMY SO THAT YOU'RE PREPARED TO HEAL **ANYTHING!**
I STARTED RESEARCHING VILLAINS' POWERS AND SUCH, AND, UH...
I MIGHT'VE GOTTEN A BIT CARRIED AWAY. I LOVE STARTING CLUBS, AND KNOWLEDGE IS POWER!!
ALSO, HAVE YOU HEARD OF **THE BIG, THE BAD, AND THE VILLAINOUS?**
IT'S **SUCH** AN INFORMATIVE PODCAST!! I'M HOOKED!
WHAT ABOUT YOU, MARTHA?
I JUST LIKE HANGING WITH ARTIE.
I'M MORE INTO **SKATEBOARDING!**
OOOH!
THERE'S A SPARE SEAT OVER HERE!!
WHAT'S GOING ON?
OH, GREAT, HERE COMES TROUBLE.
MORE LIKE THE POLAR OPPOSITE.

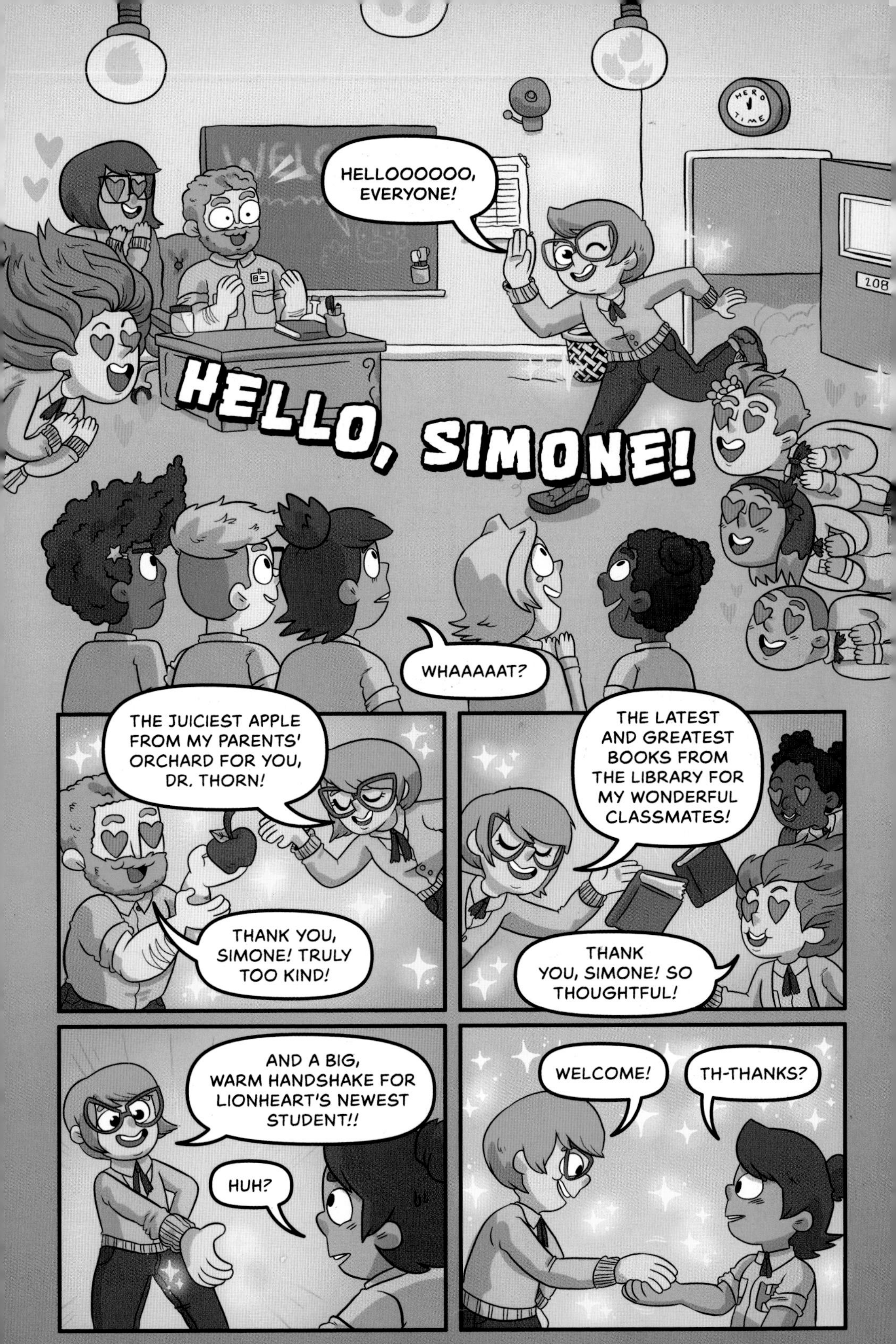
HELLOOOOOO, EVERYONE!
HELLO, SIMONE!
WHAAAAAT?
THE JUICIEST APPLE FROM MY PARENTS' ORCHARD FOR YOU, DR. THORN!
THANK YOU, SIMONE! TRULY TOO KIND!
THE LATEST AND GREATEST BOOKS FROM THE LIBRARY FOR MY WONDERFUL CLASSMATES!
THANK YOU, SIMONE! SO THOUGHTFUL!
AND A BIG, WARM HANDSHAKE FOR LIONHEART'S NEWEST STUDENT!!
HUH?
WELCOME!
TH-THANKS?

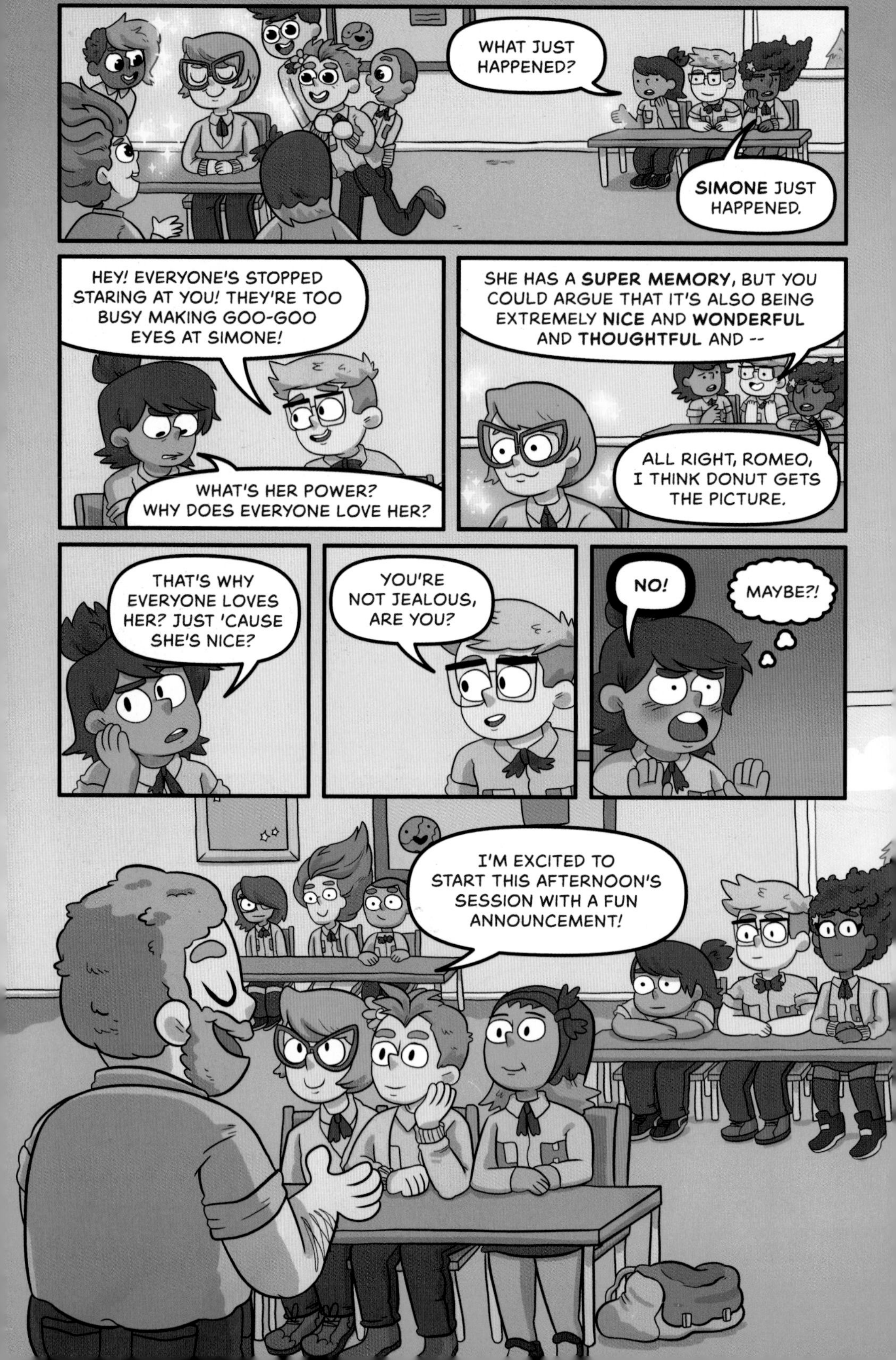

WHAT JUST HAPPENED?
SIMONE JUST HAPPENED.
HEY! EVERYONE'S STOPPED STARING AT YOU! THEY'RE TOO BUSY MAKING GOO-GOO EYES AT SIMONE!
WHAT'S HER POWER? WHY DOES EVERYONE LOVE HER?
SHE HAS A SUPER MEMORY, BUT YOU COULD ARGUE THAT IT'S ALSO BEING EXTREMELY NICE AND WONDERFUL AND THOUGHTFUL AND --
ALL RIGHT, ROMEO, I THINK DONUT GETS THE PICTURE.
THAT'S WHY EVERYONE LOVES HER? JUST 'CAUSE SHE'S NICE?
YOU'RE NOT JEALOUS, ARE YOU?
NO!
MAYBE?!
I'M EXCITED TO START THIS AFTERNOON'S SESSION WITH A FUN ANNOUNCEMENT!

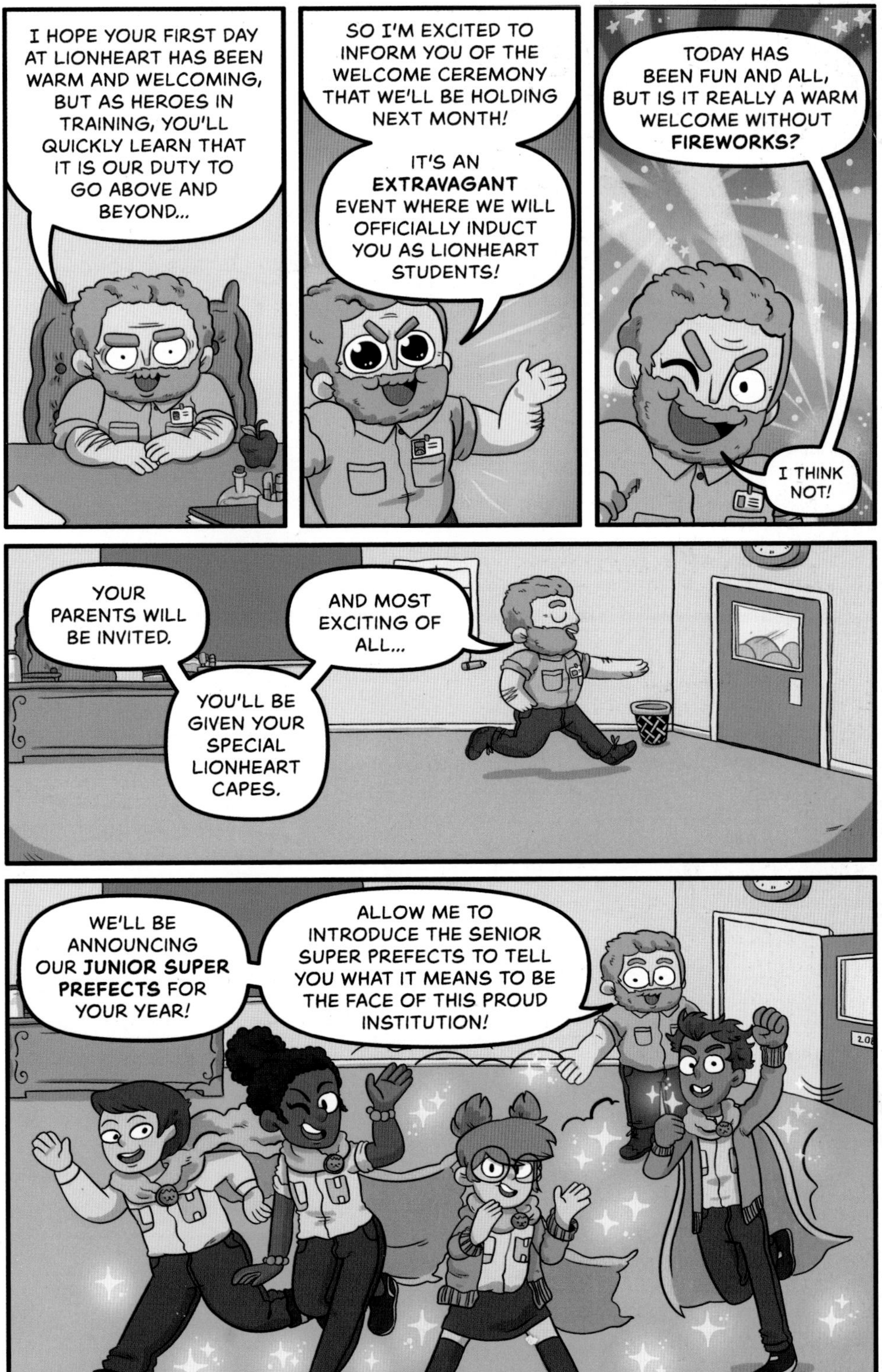
I HOPE YOUR FIRST DAY AT LIONHEART HAS BEEN WARM AND WELCOMING, BUT AS HEROES IN TRAINING, YOU'LL QUICKLY LEARN THAT IT IS OUR DUTY TO GO ABOVE AND BEYOND...
SO I'M EXCITED TO INFORM YOU OF THE WELCOME CEREMONY THAT WE'LL BE HOLDING NEXT MONTH!
IT'S AN **EXTRAVAGANT** EVENT WHERE WE WILL OFFICIALLY INDUCT YOU AS LIONHEART STUDENTS!
TODAY HAS BEEN FUN AND ALL, BUT IS IT REALLY A WARM WELCOME WITHOUT **FIREWORKS?**
I THINK NOT!
YOUR PARENTS WILL BE INVITED.
YOU'LL BE GIVEN YOUR SPECIAL LIONHEART CAPES.
AND MOST EXCITING OF ALL...
WE'LL BE ANNOUNCING OUR **JUNIOR SUPER PREFECTS** FOR YOUR YEAR!
ALLOW ME TO INTRODUCE THE SENIOR SUPER PREFECTS TO TELL YOU WHAT IT MEANS TO BE THE FACE OF THIS PROUD INSTITUTION!

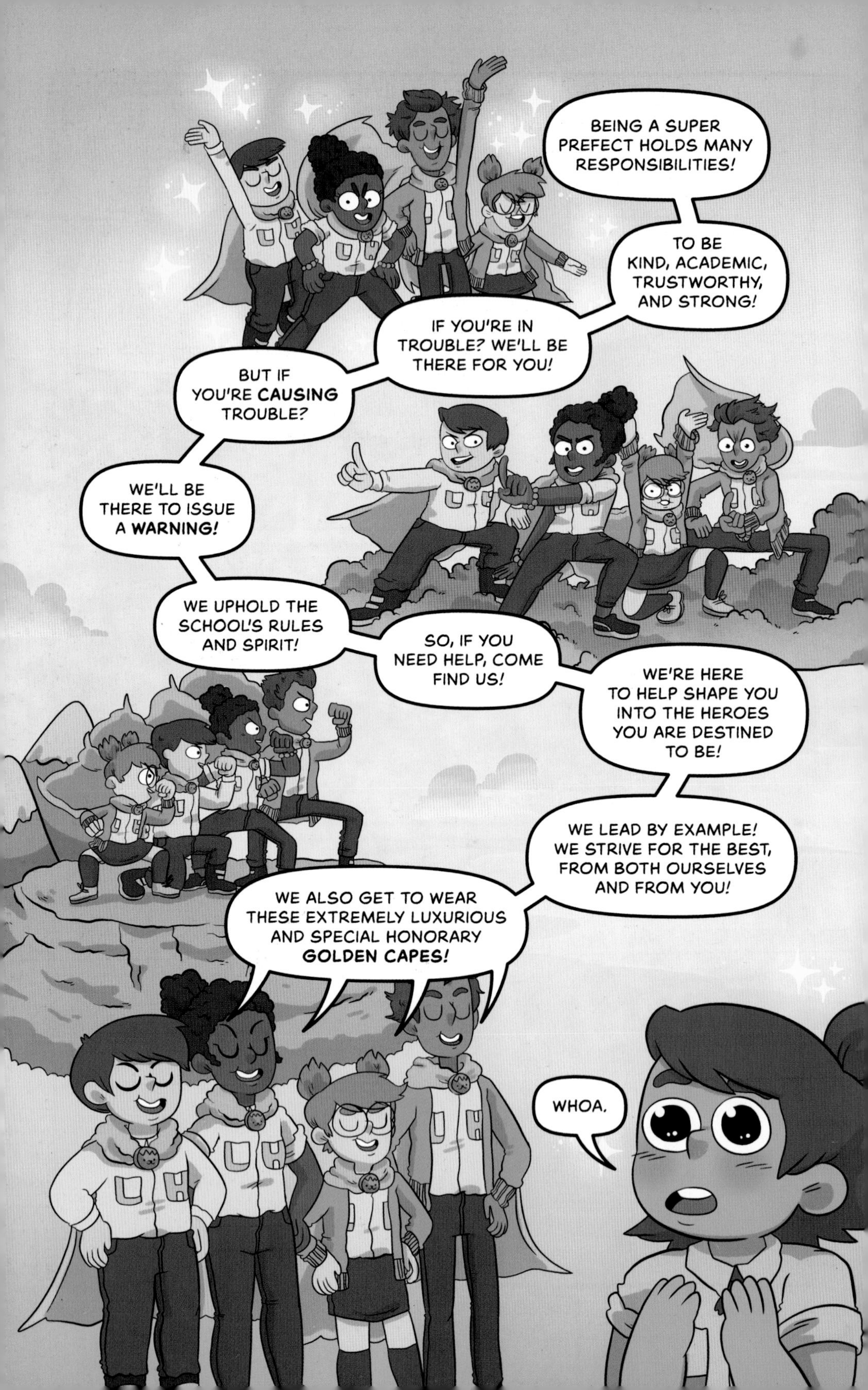
BEING A SUPER PREFECT HOLDS MANY RESPONSIBILITIES!
TO BE KIND, ACADEMIC, TRUSTWORTHY, AND STRONG!
IF YOU'RE IN TROUBLE? WE'LL BE THERE FOR YOU!
BUT IF YOU'RE **CAUSING** TROUBLE?
WE'LL BE THERE TO ISSUE A **WARNING!**
WE UPHOLD THE SCHOOL'S RULES AND SPIRIT!
SO, IF YOU NEED HELP, COME FIND US!
WE'RE HERE TO HELP SHAPE YOU INTO THE HEROES YOU ARE DESTINED TO BE!
WE LEAD BY EXAMPLE! WE STRIVE FOR THE BEST, FROM BOTH OURSELVES AND FROM YOU!
WE ALSO GET TO WEAR THESE EXTREMELY LUXURIOUS AND SPECIAL HONORARY **GOLDEN CAPES!**
WHOA.

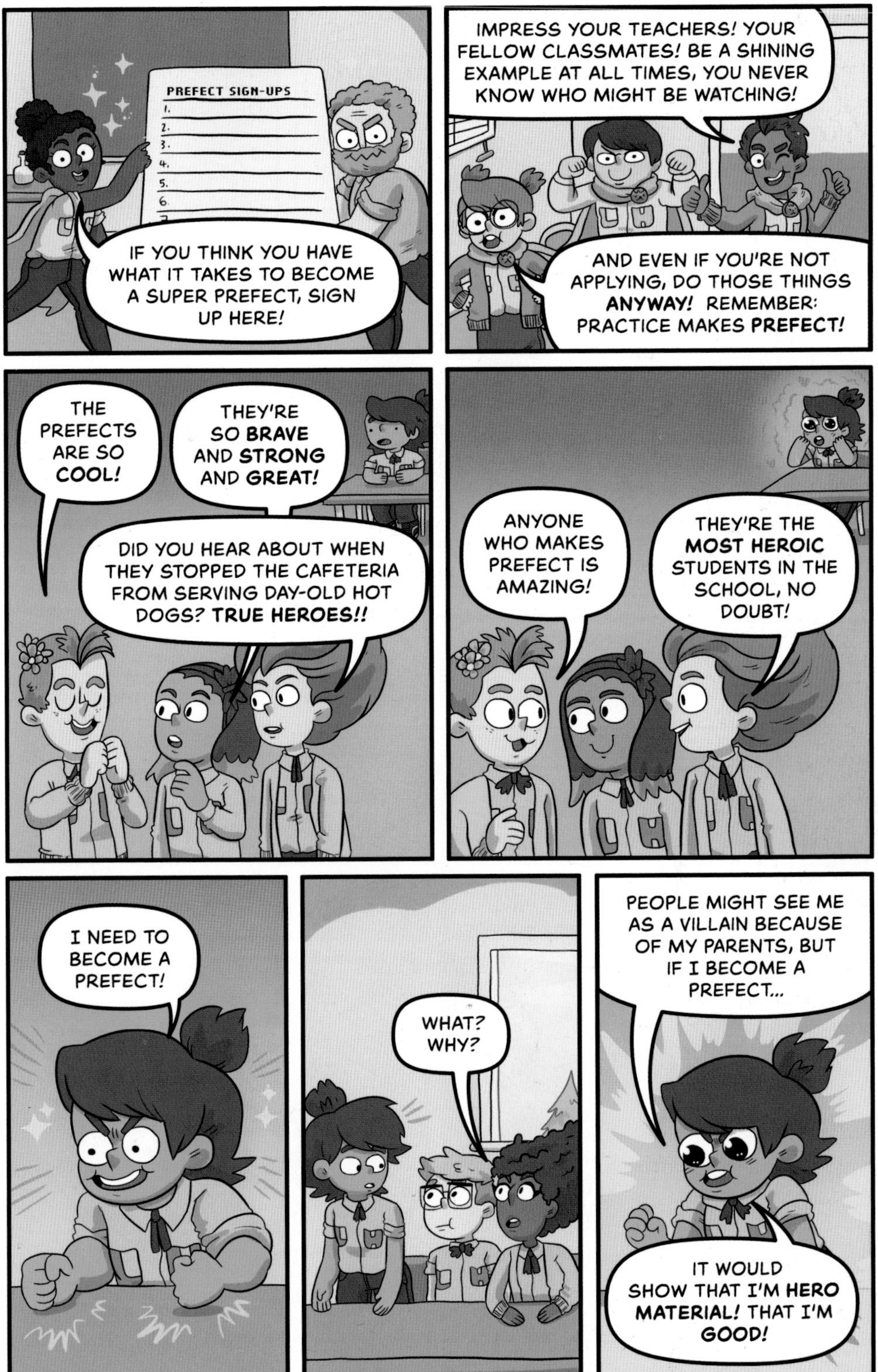
PREFECT SIGN-UPS
1.
2.
3.
4.
5.
6.
IF YOU THINK YOU HAVE WHAT IT TAKES TO BECOME A SUPER PREFECT, SIGN UP HERE!
IMPRESS YOUR TEACHERS! YOUR FELLOW CLASSMATES! BE A SHINING EXAMPLE AT ALL TIMES, YOU NEVER KNOW WHO MIGHT BE WATCHING!
AND EVEN IF YOU'RE NOT APPLYING, DO THOSE THINGS **ANYWAY!** REMEMBER: PRACTICE MAKES **PREFECT!**
THE PREFECTS ARE SO **COOL!**
THEY'RE SO **BRAVE** AND **STRONG** AND **GREAT!**
DID YOU HEAR ABOUT WHEN THEY STOPPED THE CAFETERIA FROM SERVING DAY-OLD HOT DOGS? **TRUE HEROES!!**
ANYONE WHO MAKES PREFECT IS AMAZING!
THEY'RE THE **MOST HEROIC** STUDENTS IN THE SCHOOL, NO DOUBT!
I NEED TO BECOME A PREFECT!
WHAT? WHY?
PEOPLE MIGHT SEE ME AS A VILLAIN BECAUSE OF MY PARENTS, BUT IF I BECOME A PREFECT...
IT WOULD SHOW THAT I'M **HERO MATERIAL!** THAT I'M **GOOD!**

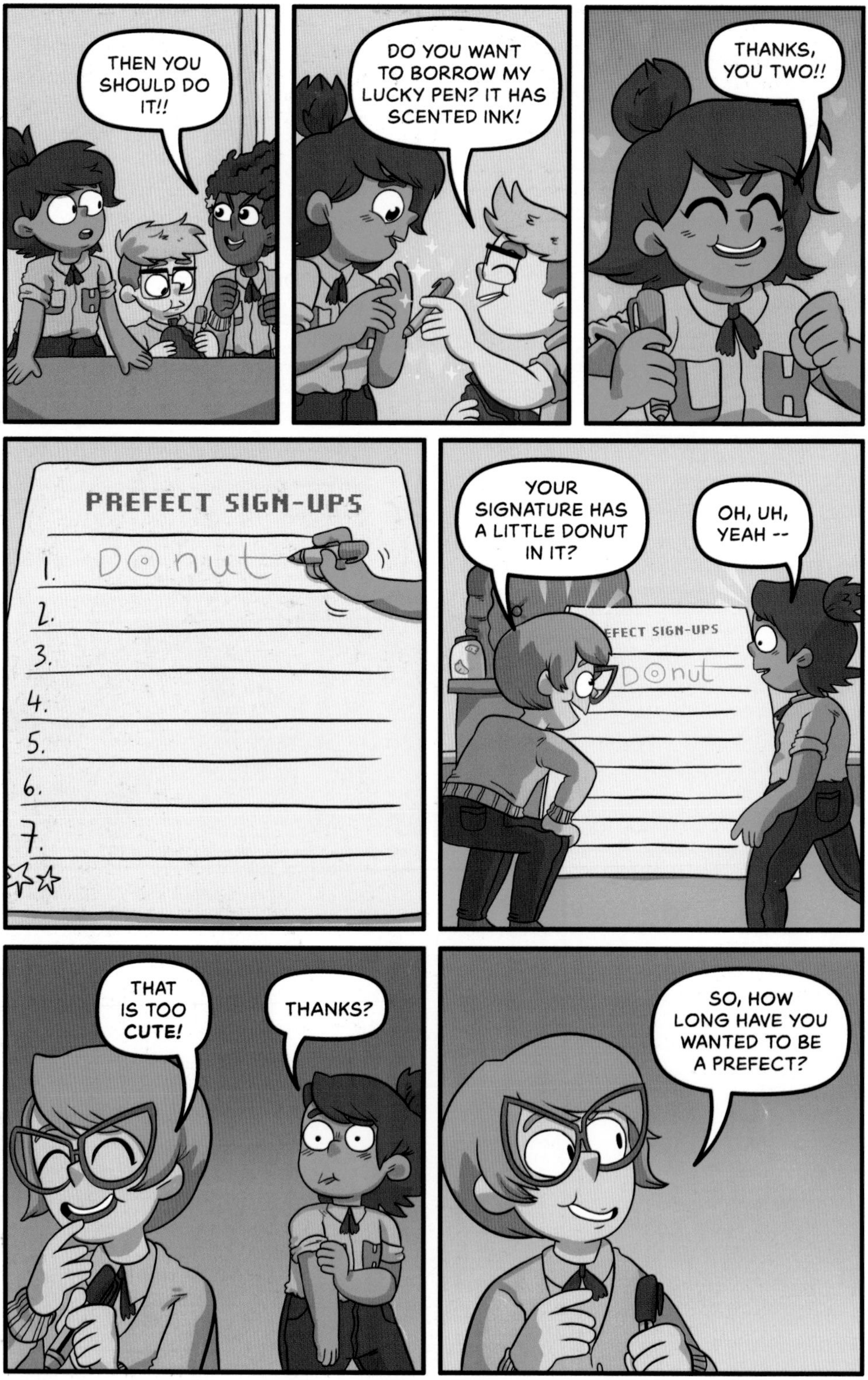
THEN YOU SHOULD DO IT!!
DO YOU WANT TO BORROW MY LUCKY PEN? IT HAS SCENTED INK!
THANKS, YOU TWO!!
PREFECT SIGN-UPS
1. DONUT
2.
3.
4.
5.
6.
7.
YOUR SIGNATURE HAS A LITTLE DONUT IN IT?
OH, UH, YEAH --
THAT IS TOO CUTE!
THANKS?
SO, HOW LONG HAVE YOU WANTED TO BE A PREFECT?

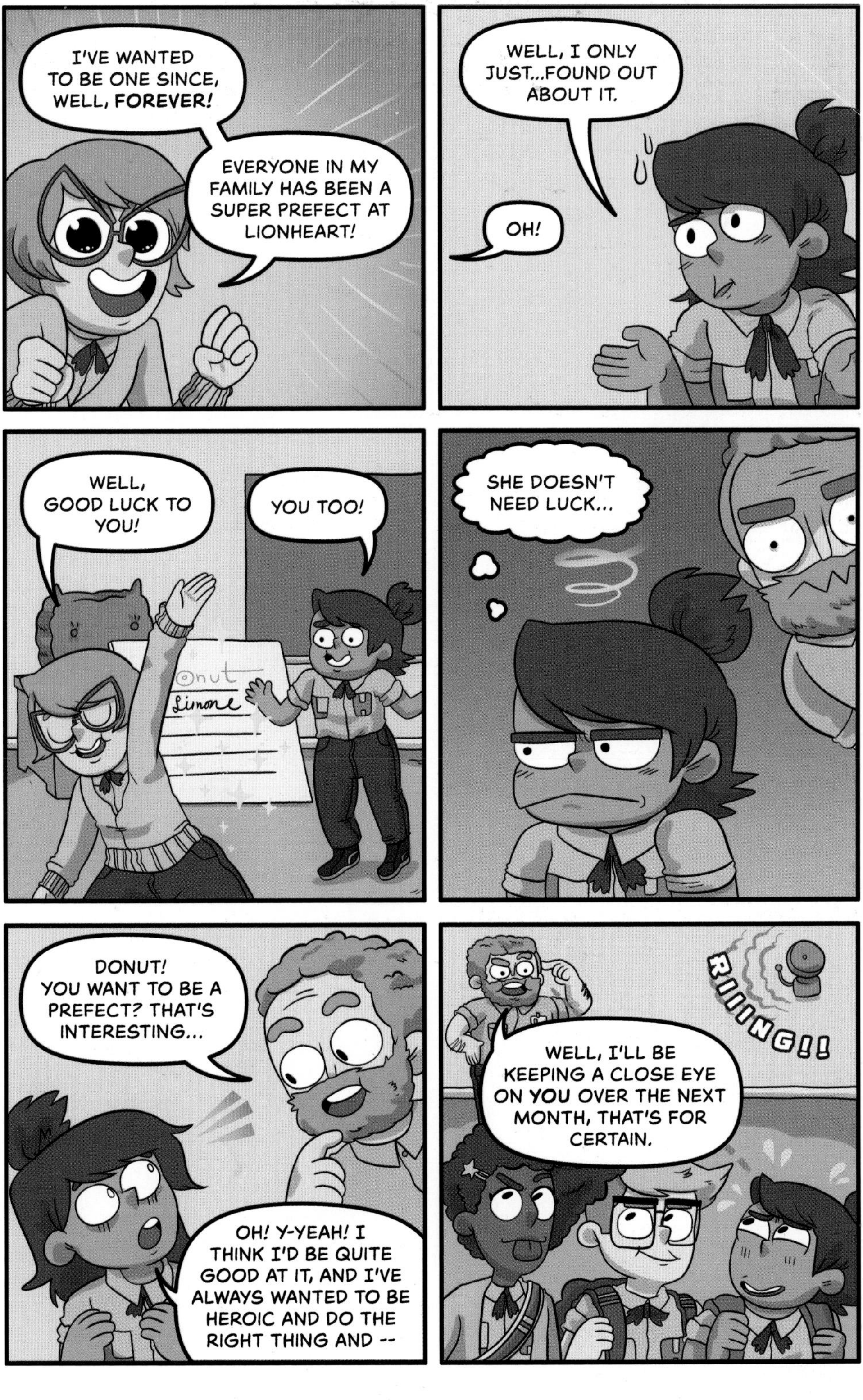
I'VE WANTED TO BE ONE SINCE, WELL, FOREVER!
EVERYONE IN MY FAMILY HAS BEEN A SUPER PREFECT AT LIONHEART!
WELL, I ONLY JUST...FOUND OUT ABOUT IT.
OH!
WELL, GOOD LUCK TO YOU!
YOU TOO!
Donut
Simone
SHE DOESN'T NEED LUCK...
DONUT! YOU WANT TO BE A PREFECT? THAT'S INTERESTING...
OH! Y-YEAH! I THINK I'D BE QUITE GOOD AT IT, AND I'VE ALWAYS WANTED TO BE HEROIC AND DO THE RIGHT THING AND --
RIIIING!!
WELL, I'LL BE KEEPING A CLOSE EYE ON YOU OVER THE NEXT MONTH, THAT'S FOR CERTAIN.

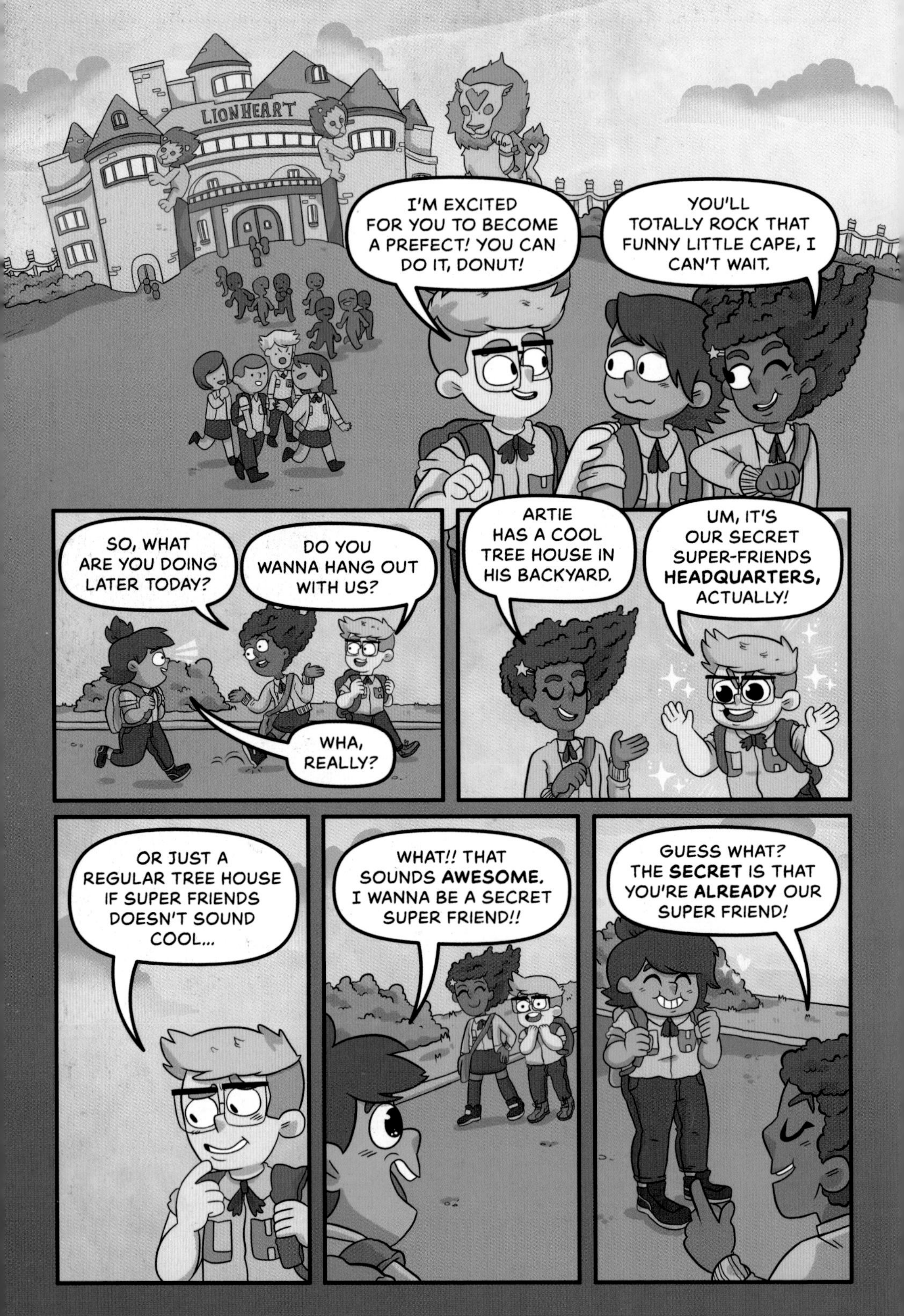
LIONHEART
I'M EXCITED FOR YOU TO BECOME A PREFECT! YOU CAN DO IT, DONUT!
YOU'LL TOTALLY ROCK THAT FUNNY LITTLE CAPE, I CAN'T WAIT.
SO, WHAT ARE YOU DOING LATER TODAY?
DO YOU WANNA HANG OUT WITH US?
WHA, REALLY?
ARTIE HAS A COOL TREE HOUSE IN HIS BACKYARD.
UM, IT'S OUR SECRET SUPER-FRIENDS **HEADQUARTERS,** ACTUALLY!
OR JUST A REGULAR TREE HOUSE IF SUPER FRIENDS DOESN'T SOUND COOL...
WHAT!! THAT SOUNDS **AWESOME.** I WANNA BE A SECRET SUPER FRIEND!!
GUESS WHAT? THE **SECRET** IS THAT YOU'RE **ALREADY** OUR SUPER FRIEND!

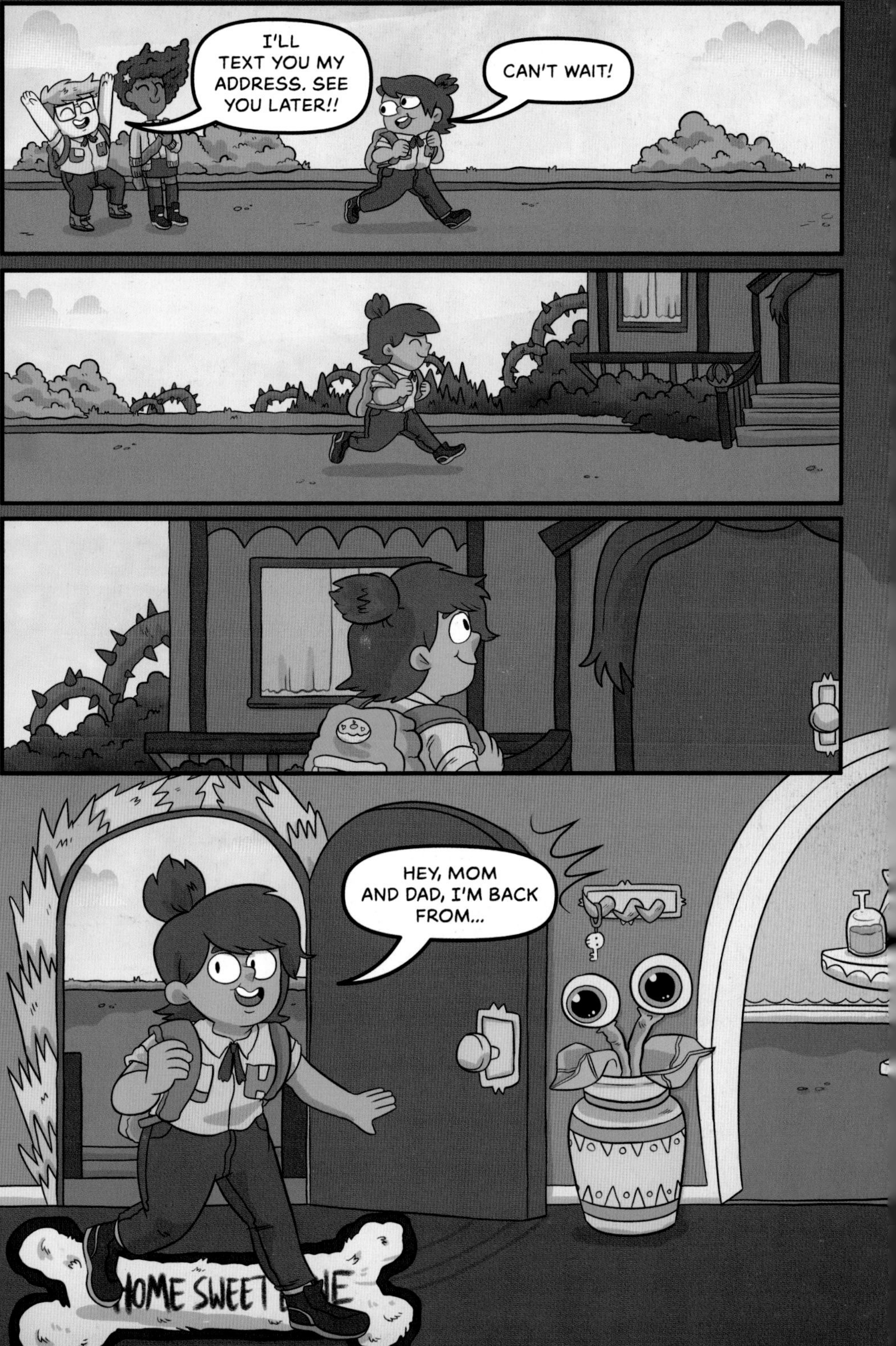
I'LL TEXT YOU MY ADDRESS. SEE YOU LATER!!
CAN'T WAIT!
HEY, MOM AND DAD, I'M BACK FROM...
HOME SWEET

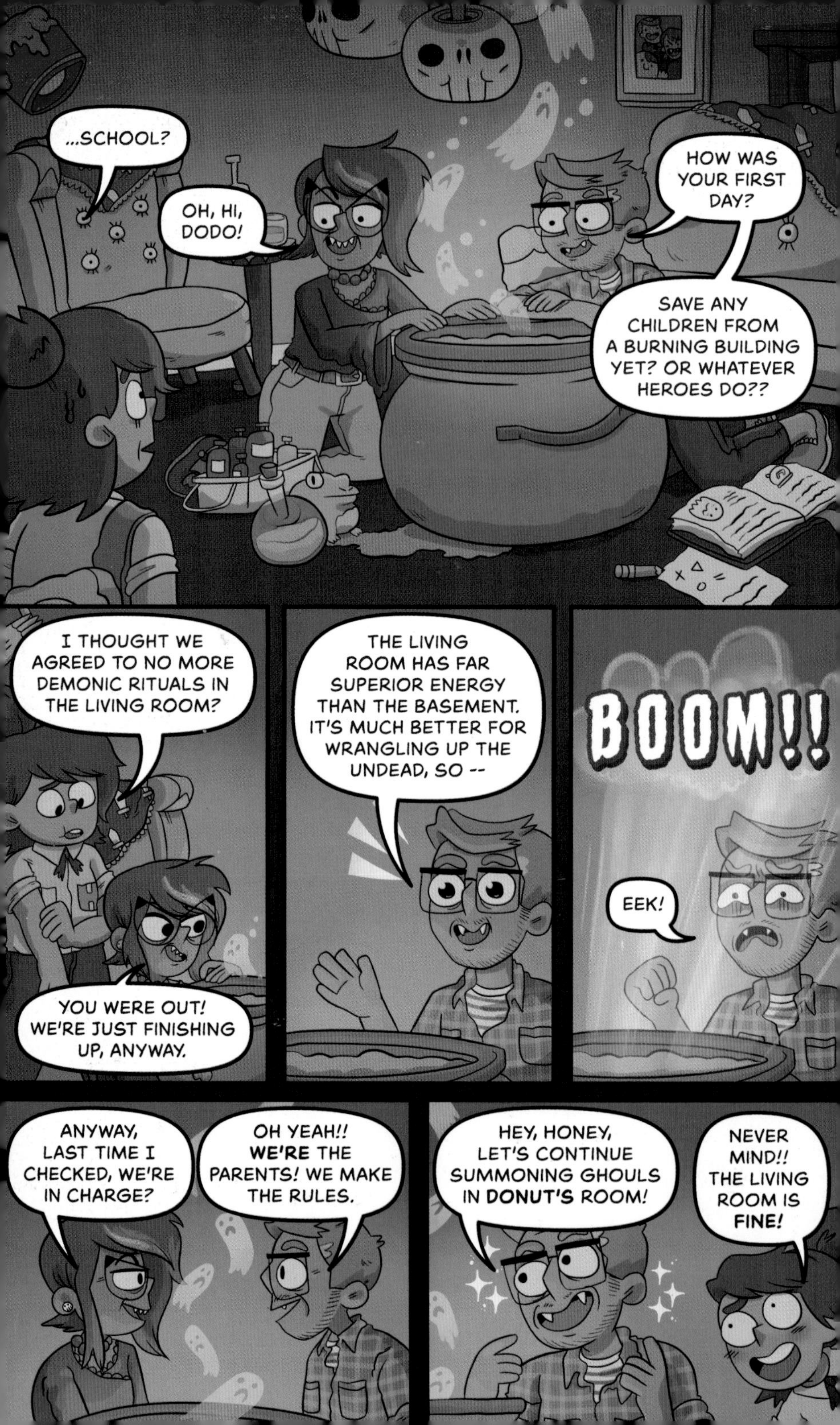
...SCHOOL?
OH, HI, DODO!
HOW WAS YOUR FIRST DAY?
SAVE ANY CHILDREN FROM A BURNING BUILDING YET? OR WHATEVER HEROES DO??
I THOUGHT WE AGREED TO NO MORE DEMONIC RITUALS IN THE LIVING ROOM?
YOU WERE OUT! WE'RE JUST FINISHING UP, ANYWAY.
THE LIVING ROOM HAS FAR SUPERIOR ENERGY THAN THE BASEMENT. IT'S MUCH BETTER FOR WRANGLING UP THE UNDEAD, SO --
BOOM!!
EEK!
ANYWAY, LAST TIME I CHECKED, WE'RE IN CHARGE?
OH YEAH!! **WE'RE** THE PARENTS! WE MAKE THE RULES.
HEY, HONEY, LET'S CONTINUE SUMMONING GHOULS IN **DONUT'S** ROOM!
NEVER MIND!! THE LIVING ROOM IS **FINE!**

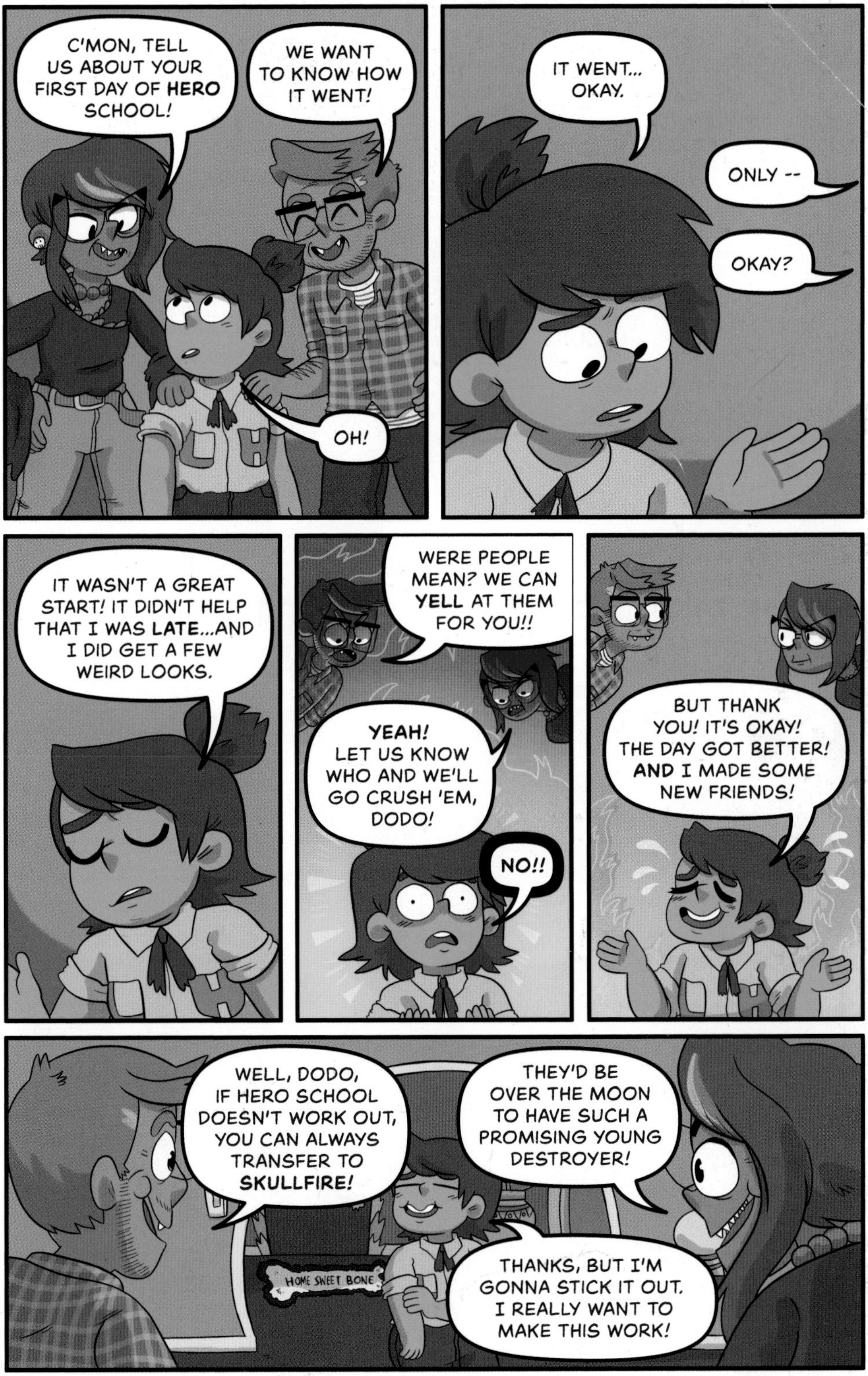
C'MON, TELL US ABOUT YOUR FIRST DAY OF HERO SCHOOL!
WE WANT TO KNOW HOW IT WENT!
OH!
IT WENT... OKAY.
ONLY --
OKAY?
IT WASN'T A GREAT START! IT DIDN'T HELP THAT I WAS LATE...AND I DID GET A FEW WEIRD LOOKS.
WERE PEOPLE MEAN? WE CAN YELL AT THEM FOR YOU!!
YEAH! LET US KNOW WHO AND WE'LL GO CRUSH 'EM, DODO!
NO!!
BUT THANK YOU! IT'S OKAY! THE DAY GOT BETTER! AND I MADE SOME NEW FRIENDS!
WELL, DODO, IF HERO SCHOOL DOESN'T WORK OUT, YOU CAN ALWAYS TRANSFER TO SKULLFIRE!
THEY'D BE OVER THE MOON TO HAVE SUCH A PROMISING YOUNG DESTROYER!
HOME SWEET BONE
THANKS, BUT I'M GONNA STICK IT OUT. I REALLY WANT TO MAKE THIS WORK!

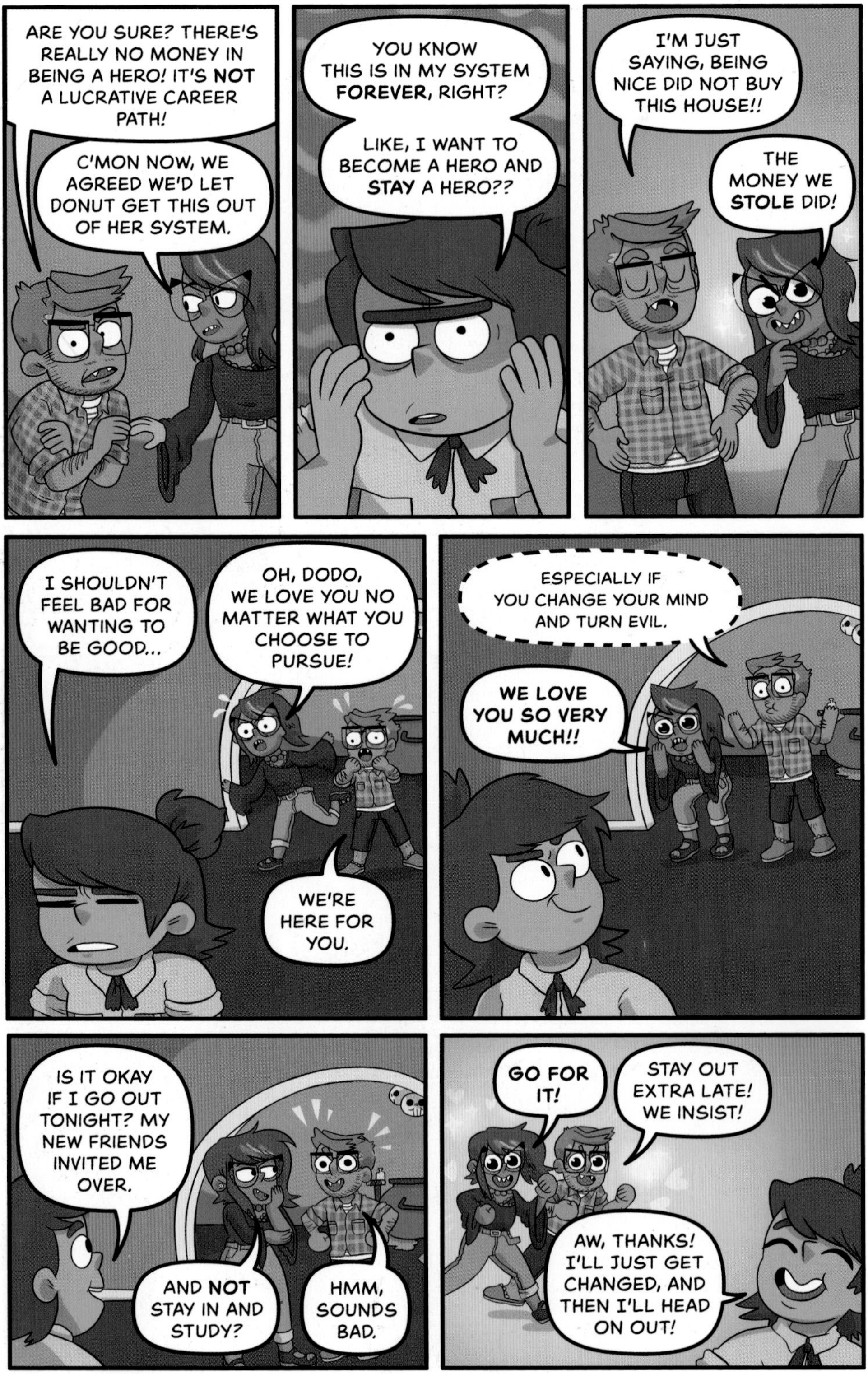

ARE YOU SURE? THERE'S REALLY NO MONEY IN BEING A HERO! IT'S **NOT** A LUCRATIVE CAREER PATH!
C'MON NOW, WE AGREED WE'D LET DONUT GET THIS OUT OF HER SYSTEM.
YOU KNOW THIS IS IN MY SYSTEM **FOREVER**, RIGHT?
LIKE, I WANT TO BECOME A HERO AND **STAY** A HERO??
I'M JUST SAYING, BEING NICE DID NOT BUY THIS HOUSE!!
THE MONEY WE **STOLE** DID!
I SHOULDN'T FEEL BAD FOR WANTING TO BE GOOD...
OH, DODO, WE LOVE YOU NO MATTER WHAT YOU CHOOSE TO PURSUE!
WE'RE HERE FOR YOU.
ESPECIALLY IF YOU CHANGE YOUR MIND AND TURN EVIL.
WE LOVE YOU SO VERY MUCH!!
IS IT OKAY IF I GO OUT TONIGHT? MY NEW FRIENDS INVITED ME OVER.
AND **NOT** STAY IN AND STUDY?
HMM, SOUNDS BAD.
GO FOR IT!
STAY OUT EXTRA LATE! WE INSIST!
AW, THANKS! I'LL JUST GET CHANGED, AND THEN I'LL HEAD ON OUT!

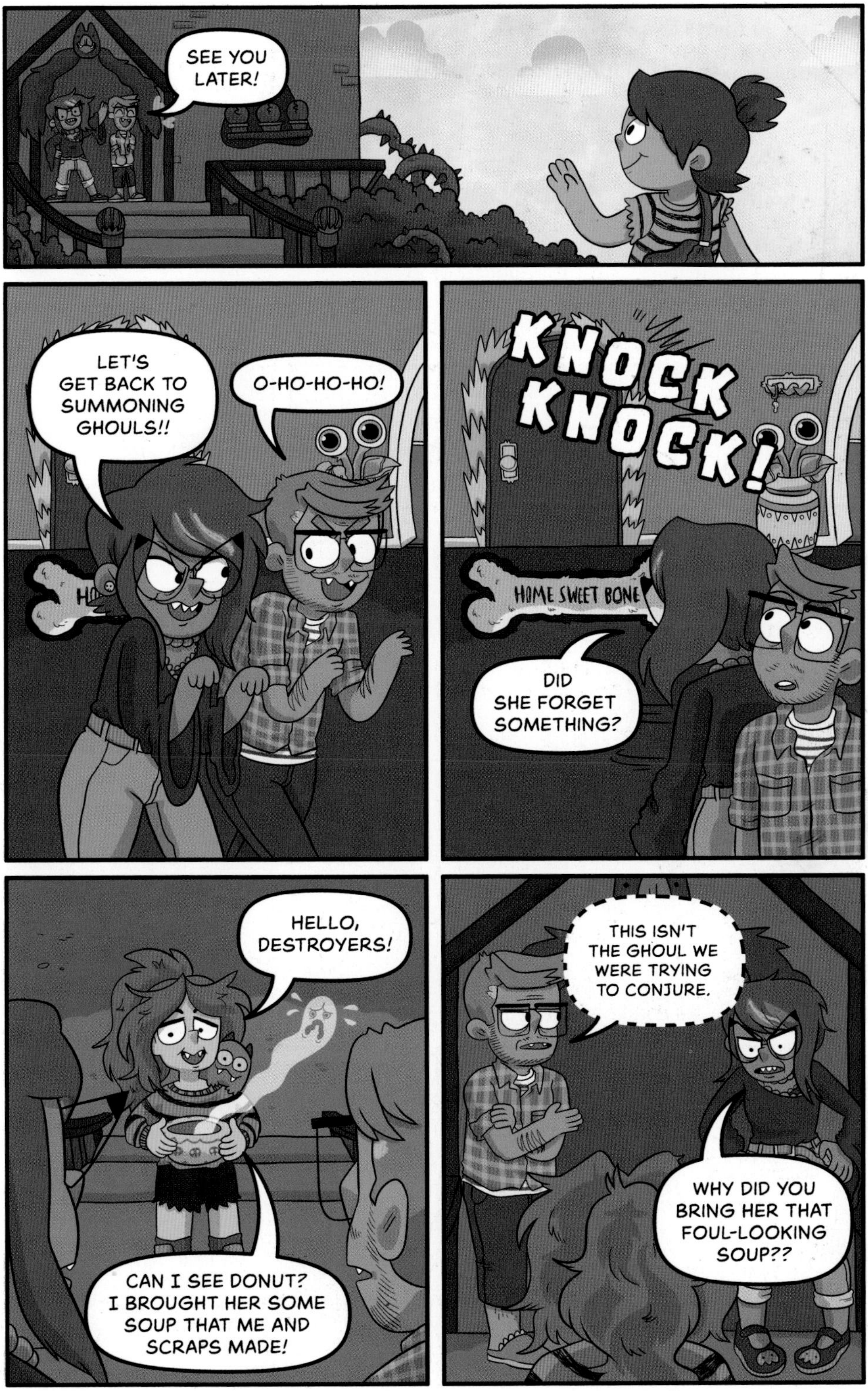
SEE YOU LATER!
LET'S GET BACK TO SUMMONING GHOULS!!
O-HO-HO-HO!
KNOCK KNOCK!
HOME SWEET BONE
DID SHE FORGET SOMETHING?
HELLO, DESTROYERS!
CAN I SEE DONUT? I BROUGHT HER SOME SOUP THAT ME AND SCRAPS MADE!
THIS ISN'T THE GHOUL WE WERE TRYING TO CONJURE.
WHY DID YOU BRING HER THAT FOUL-LOOKING SOUP??

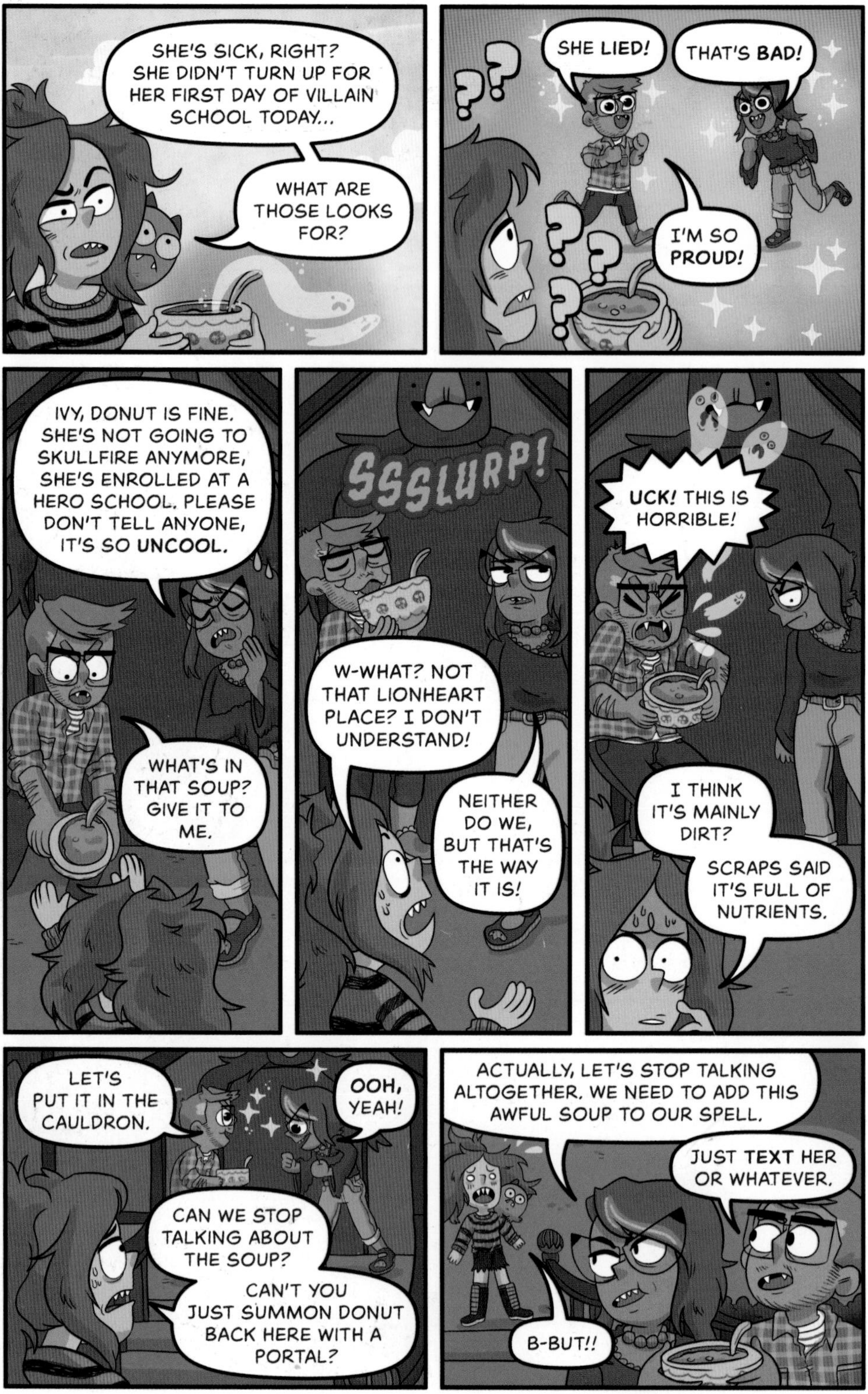
SHE'S SICK, RIGHT? SHE DIDN'T TURN UP FOR HER FIRST DAY OF VILLAIN SCHOOL TODAY...
WHAT ARE THOSE LOOKS FOR?
SHE LIED!
THAT'S BAD!
I'M SO PROUD!
IVY, DONUT IS FINE. SHE'S NOT GOING TO SKULLFIRE ANYMORE, SHE'S ENROLLED AT A HERO SCHOOL. PLEASE DON'T TELL ANYONE, IT'S SO UNCOOL.
WHAT'S IN THAT SOUP? GIVE IT TO ME.
SSSLURP!
W-WHAT? NOT THAT LIONHEART PLACE? I DON'T UNDERSTAND!
NEITHER DO WE, BUT THAT'S THE WAY IT IS!
UCK! THIS IS HORRIBLE!
I THINK IT'S MAINLY DIRT?
SCRAPS SAID IT'S FULL OF NUTRIENTS.
LET'S PUT IT IN THE CAULDRON.
OOH, YEAH!
CAN WE STOP TALKING ABOUT THE SOUP?
CAN'T YOU JUST SUMMON DONUT BACK HERE WITH A PORTAL?
ACTUALLY, LET'S STOP TALKING ALTOGETHER. WE NEED TO ADD THIS AWFUL SOUP TO OUR SPELL.
JUST TEXT HER OR WHATEVER.
B-BUT!!

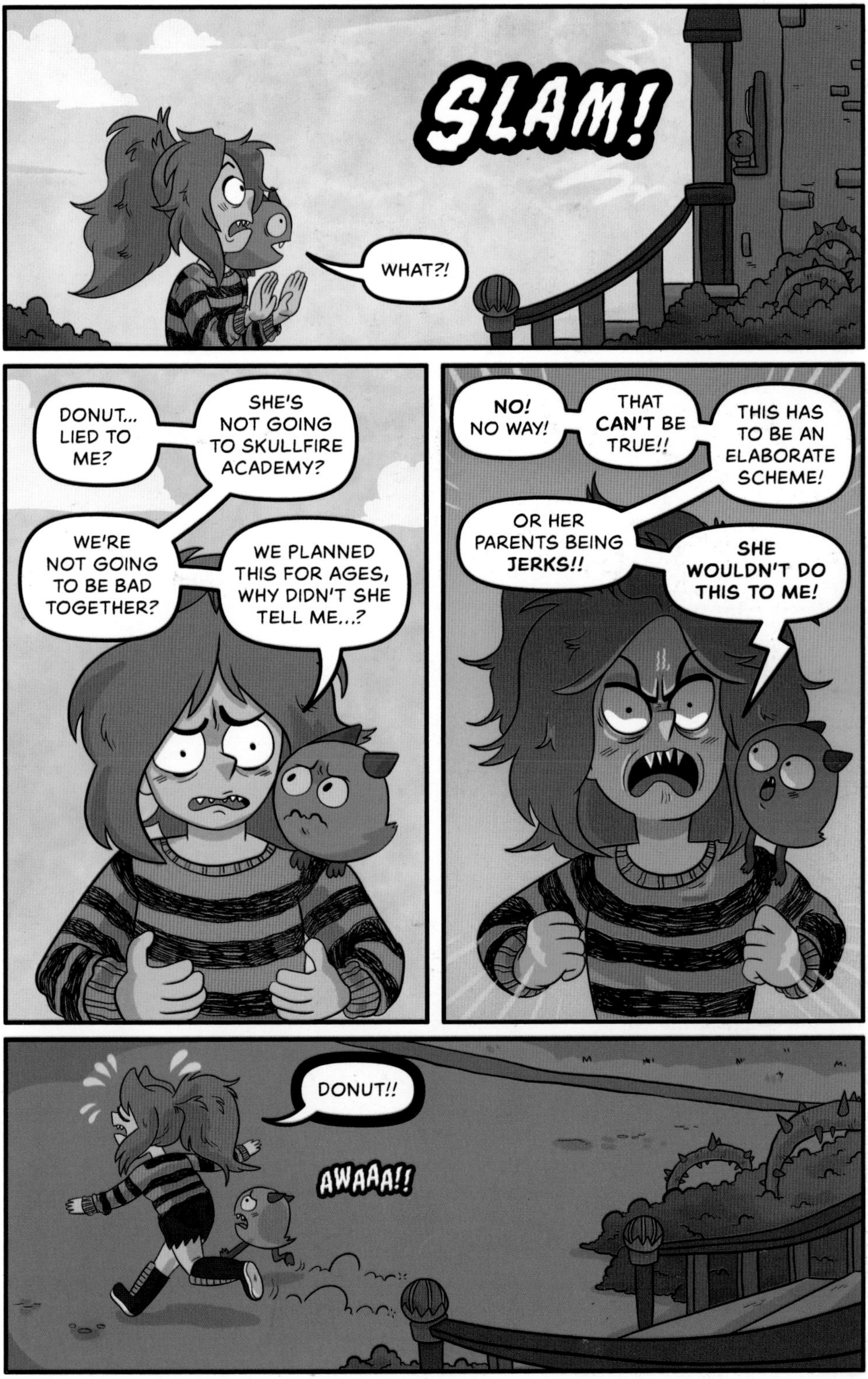
SLAM!
WHAT?!
DONUT... LIED TO ME?
SHE'S NOT GOING TO SKULLFIRE ACADEMY?
WE'RE NOT GOING TO BE BAD TOGETHER?
WE PLANNED THIS FOR AGES, WHY DIDN'T SHE TELL ME...?
NO! NO WAY!
THAT CAN'T BE TRUE!!
THIS HAS TO BE AN ELABORATE SCHEME!
OR HER PARENTS BEING JERKS!!
SHE WOULDN'T DO THIS TO ME!
DONUT!!
AWAAA!!

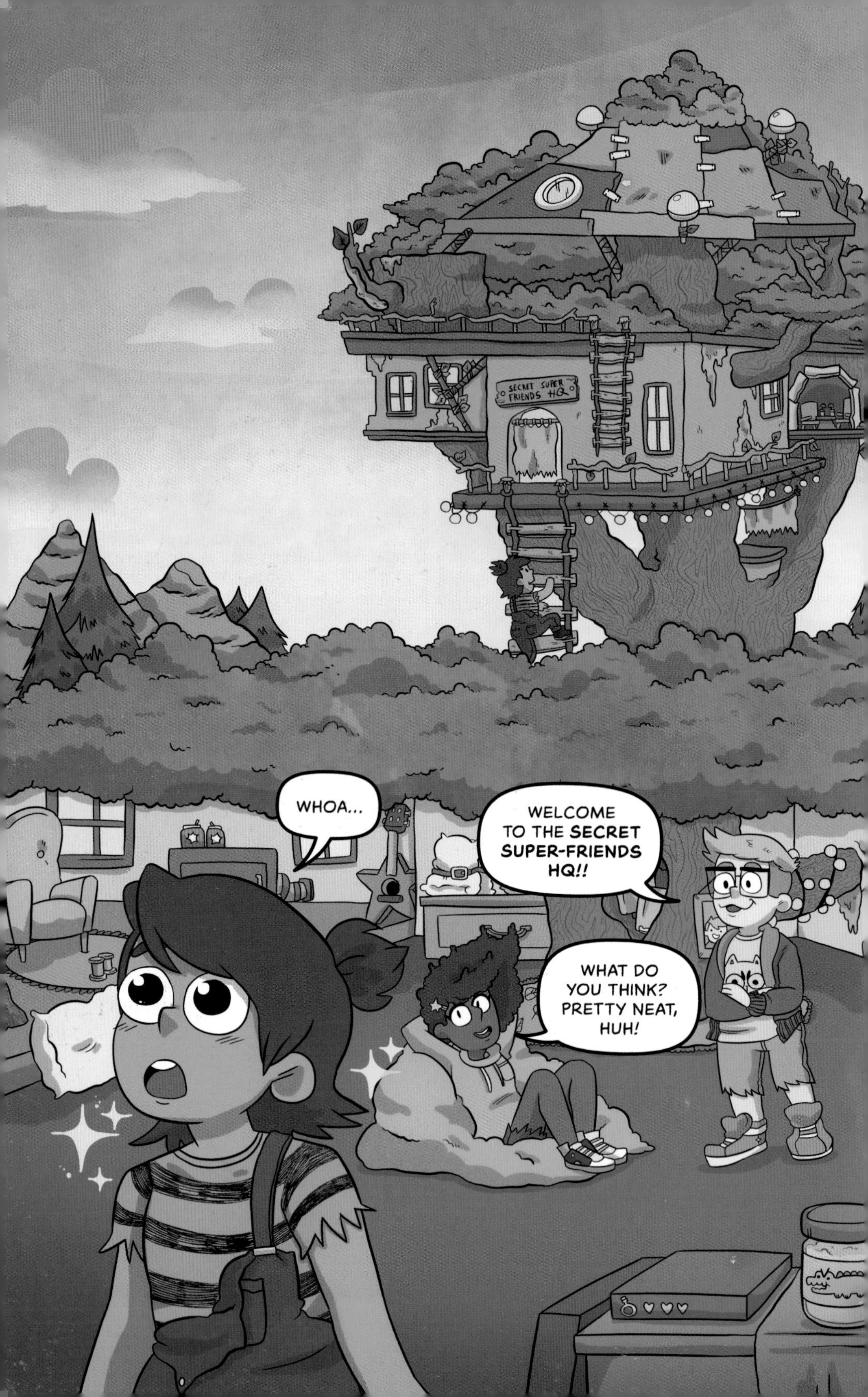
SECRET SUPER FRIENDS HQ
WHOA...
WELCOME TO THE SECRET SUPER-FRIENDS HQ!!
WHAT DO YOU THINK? PRETTY NEAT, HUH!

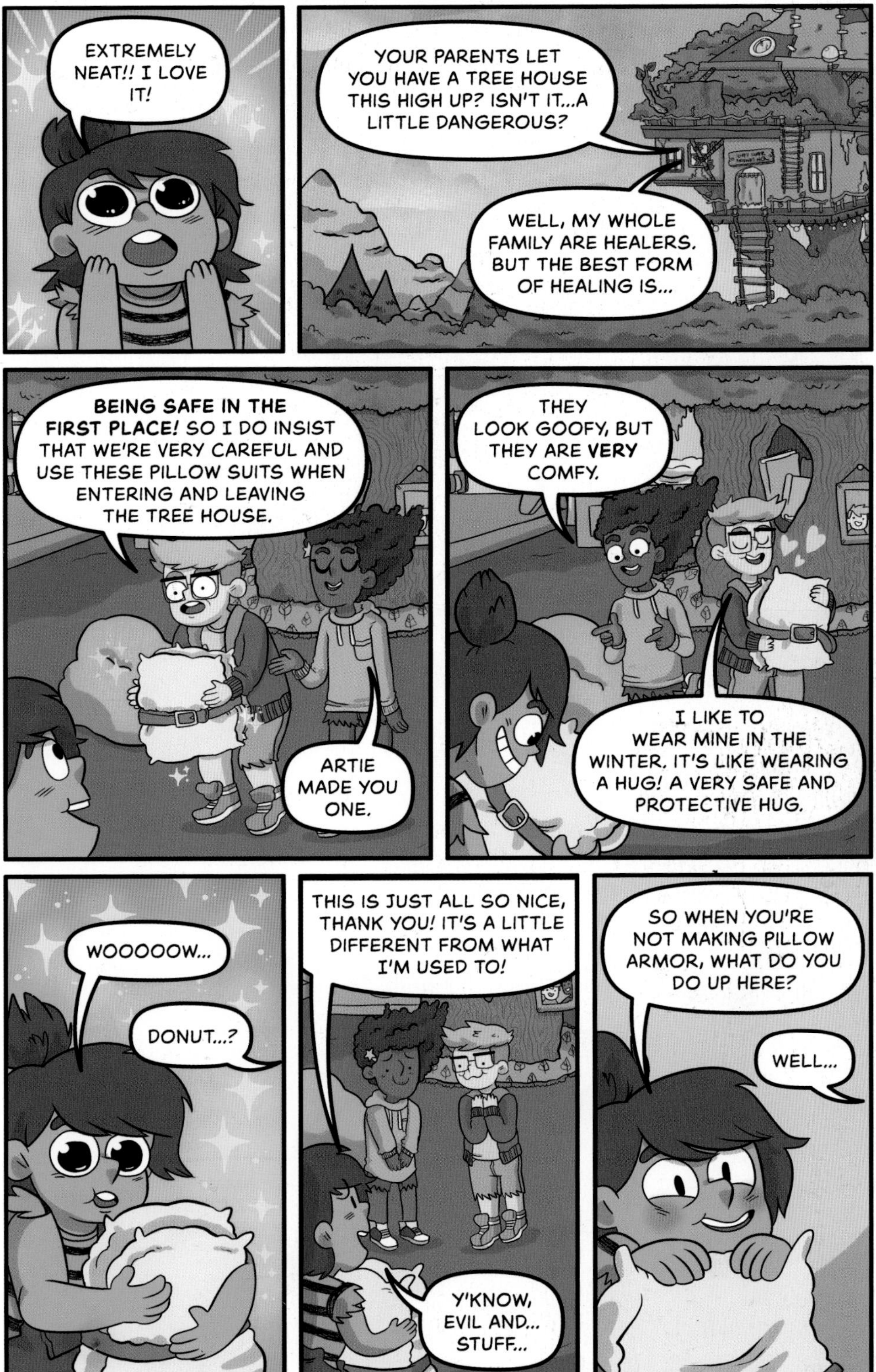
EXTREMELY NEAT!! I LOVE IT!
YOUR PARENTS LET YOU HAVE A TREE HOUSE THIS HIGH UP? ISN'T IT...A LITTLE DANGEROUS?
WELL, MY WHOLE FAMILY ARE HEALERS. BUT THE BEST FORM OF HEALING IS...
BEING SAFE IN THE FIRST PLACE! SO I DO INSIST THAT WE'RE VERY CAREFUL AND USE THESE PILLOW SUITS WHEN ENTERING AND LEAVING THE TREE HOUSE.
ARTIE MADE YOU ONE.
THEY LOOK GOOFY, BUT THEY ARE VERY COMFY.
I LIKE TO WEAR MINE IN THE WINTER. IT'S LIKE WEARING A HUG! A VERY SAFE AND PROTECTIVE HUG.
WOOOOOW...
DONUT...?
THIS IS JUST ALL SO NICE, THANK YOU! IT'S A LITTLE DIFFERENT FROM WHAT I'M USED TO!
Y'KNOW, EVIL AND... STUFF...
SO WHEN YOU'RE NOT MAKING PILLOW ARMOR, WHAT DO YOU DO UP HERE?
WELL...

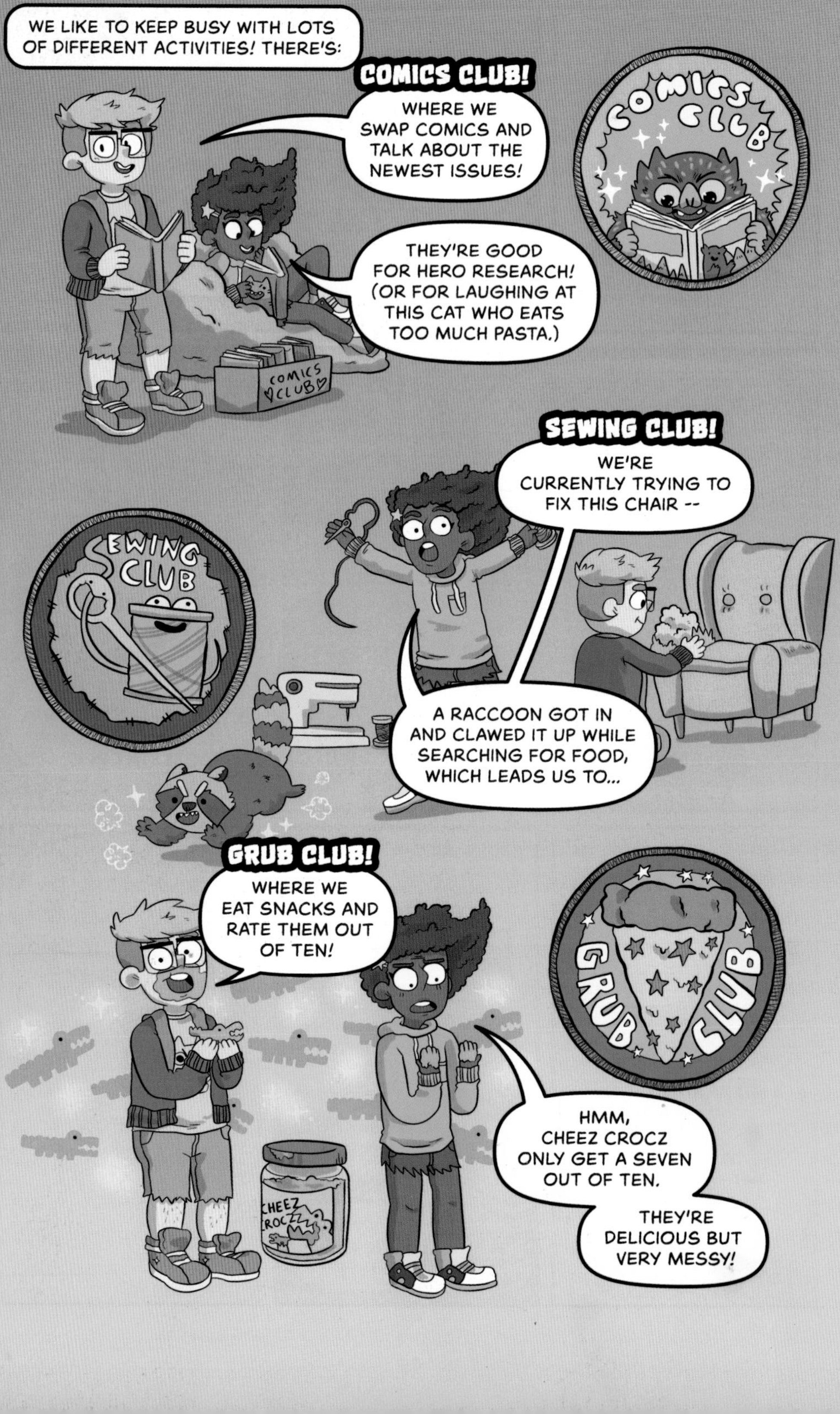
WE LIKE TO KEEP BUSY WITH LOTS OF DIFFERENT ACTIVITIES! THERE'S:
COMICS CLUB!
WHERE WE SWAP COMICS AND TALK ABOUT THE NEWEST ISSUES!
THEY'RE GOOD FOR HERO RESEARCH! (OR FOR LAUGHING AT THIS CAT WHO EATS TOO MUCH PASTA.)
COMICS CLUB
COMICS CLUB
SEWING CLUB!
WE'RE CURRENTLY TRYING TO FIX THIS CHAIR --
SEWING CLUB
A RACCOON GOT IN AND CLAWED IT UP WHILE SEARCHING FOR FOOD, WHICH LEADS US TO...
GRUB CLUB!
WHERE WE EAT SNACKS AND RATE THEM OUT OF TEN!
GRUB CLUB
CHEEZ CROCZZ
HMM, CHEEZ CROCZ ONLY GET A SEVEN OUT OF TEN.
THEY'RE DELICIOUS BUT VERY MESSY!

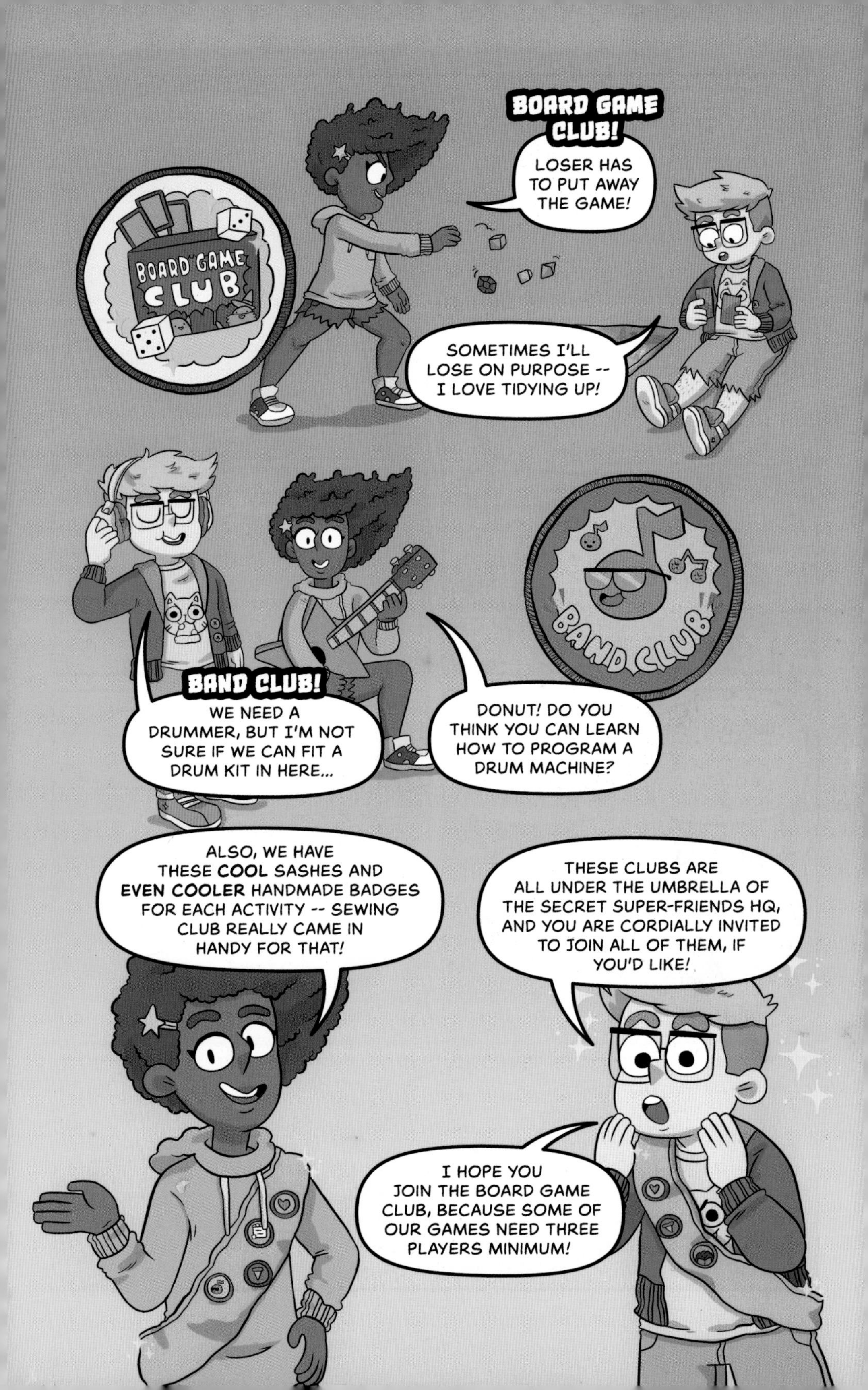
BOARD GAME CLUB
BOARD GAME CLUB!
LOSER HAS TO PUT AWAY THE GAME!
SOMETIMES I'LL LOSE ON PURPOSE -- I LOVE TIDYING UP!
BAND CLUB
BAND CLUB!
WE NEED A DRUMMER, BUT I'M NOT SURE IF WE CAN FIT A DRUM KIT IN HERE...
DONUT! DO YOU THINK YOU CAN LEARN HOW TO PROGRAM A DRUM MACHINE?
ALSO, WE HAVE THESE COOL SASHES AND EVEN COOLER HANDMADE BADGES FOR EACH ACTIVITY -- SEWING CLUB REALLY CAME IN HANDY FOR THAT!
THESE CLUBS ARE ALL UNDER THE UMBRELLA OF THE SECRET SUPER-FRIENDS HQ, AND YOU ARE CORDIALLY INVITED TO JOIN ALL OF THEM, IF YOU'D LIKE!
I HOPE YOU JOIN THE BOARD GAME CLUB, BECAUSE SOME OF OUR GAMES NEED THREE PLAYERS MINIMUM!

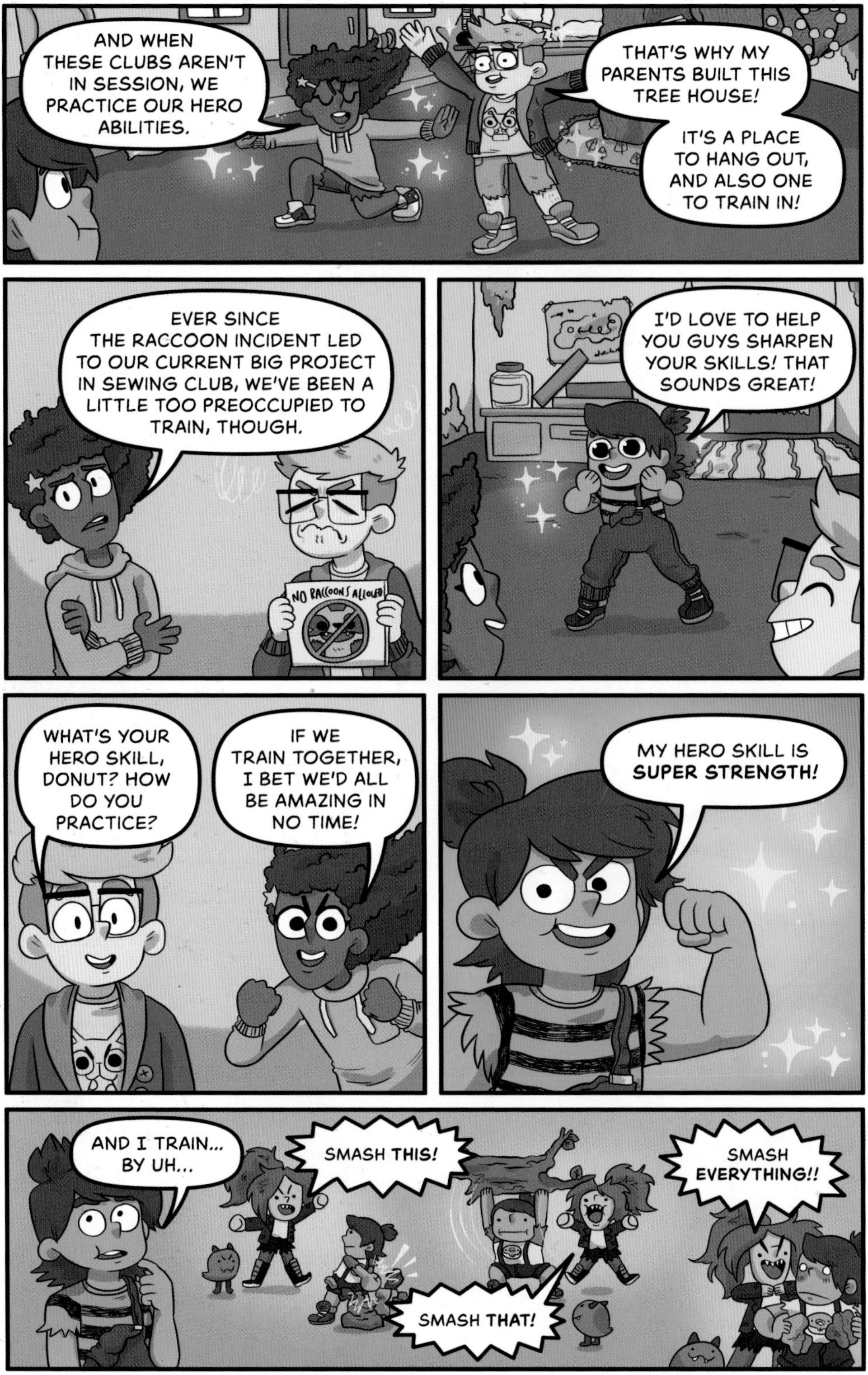
AND WHEN THESE CLUBS AREN'T IN SESSION, WE PRACTICE OUR HERO ABILITIES.
THAT'S WHY MY PARENTS BUILT THIS TREE HOUSE!
IT'S A PLACE TO HANG OUT, AND ALSO ONE TO TRAIN IN!
EVER SINCE THE RACCOON INCIDENT LED TO OUR CURRENT BIG PROJECT IN SEWING CLUB, WE'VE BEEN A LITTLE TOO PREOCCUPIED TO TRAIN, THOUGH.
NO RACCOONS ALLOWED
I'D LOVE TO HELP YOU GUYS SHARPEN YOUR SKILLS! THAT SOUNDS GREAT!
WHAT'S YOUR HERO SKILL, DONUT? HOW DO YOU PRACTICE?
IF WE TRAIN TOGETHER, I BET WE'D ALL BE AMAZING IN NO TIME!
MY HERO SKILL IS **SUPER STRENGTH!**
AND I TRAIN... BY UH...
SMASH **THIS!**
SMASH **EVERYTHING!!**
SMASH **THAT!**

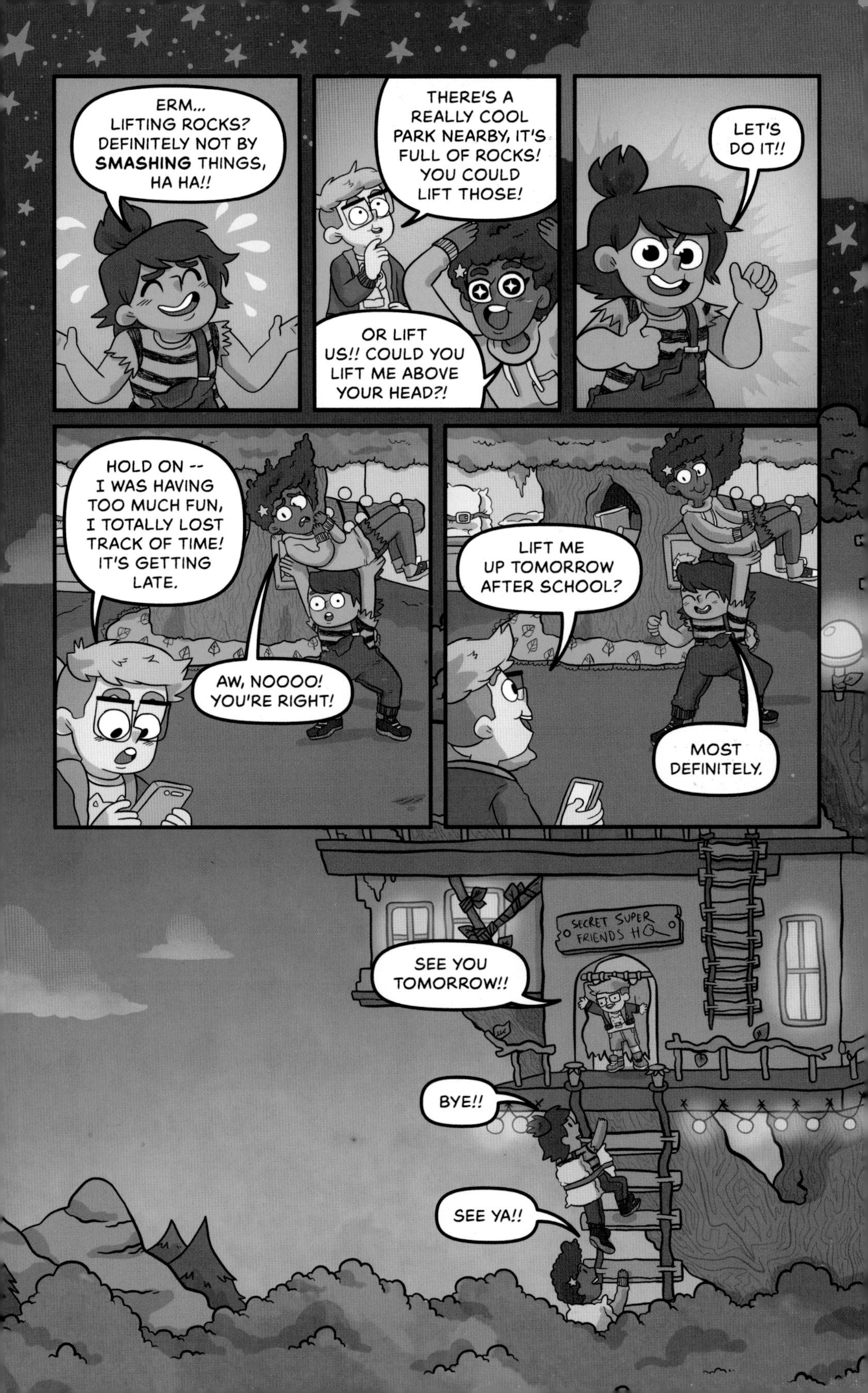
ERM... LIFTING ROCKS? DEFINITELY NOT BY **SMASHING** THINGS, HA HA!!
THERE'S A REALLY COOL PARK NEARBY, IT'S FULL OF ROCKS! YOU COULD LIFT THOSE!
OR LIFT US!! COULD YOU LIFT ME ABOVE YOUR HEAD?!
LET'S DO IT!!
HOLD ON -- I WAS HAVING TOO MUCH FUN, I TOTALLY LOST TRACK OF TIME! IT'S GETTING LATE.
AW, NOOOO! YOU'RE RIGHT!
LIFT ME UP TOMORROW AFTER SCHOOL?
MOST DEFINITELY.
SECRET SUPER FRIENDS HQ
SEE YOU TOMORROW!!
BYE!!
SEE YA!!

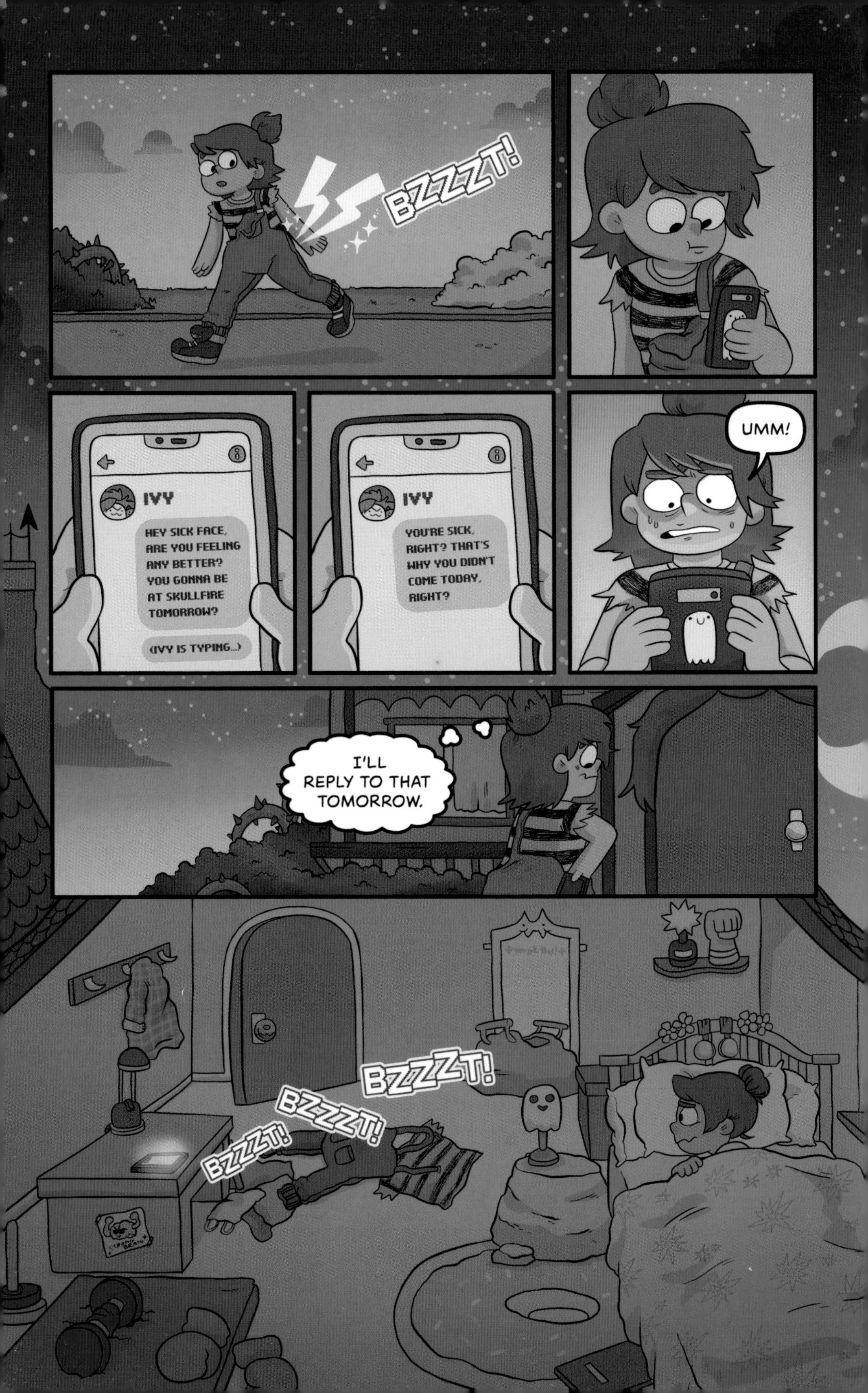
BZZZZT!
IVY
HEY SICK FACE, ARE YOU FEELING ANY BETTER? YOU GONNA BE AT SKULLFIRE TOMORROW?
(IVY IS TYPING...)
IVY
YOU'RE SICK, RIGHT? THAT'S WHY YOU DIDN'T COME TODAY, RIGHT?
UMM!
I'LL REPLY TO THAT TOMORROW.
BZZZZT!
BZZZZT!
BZZZZT!

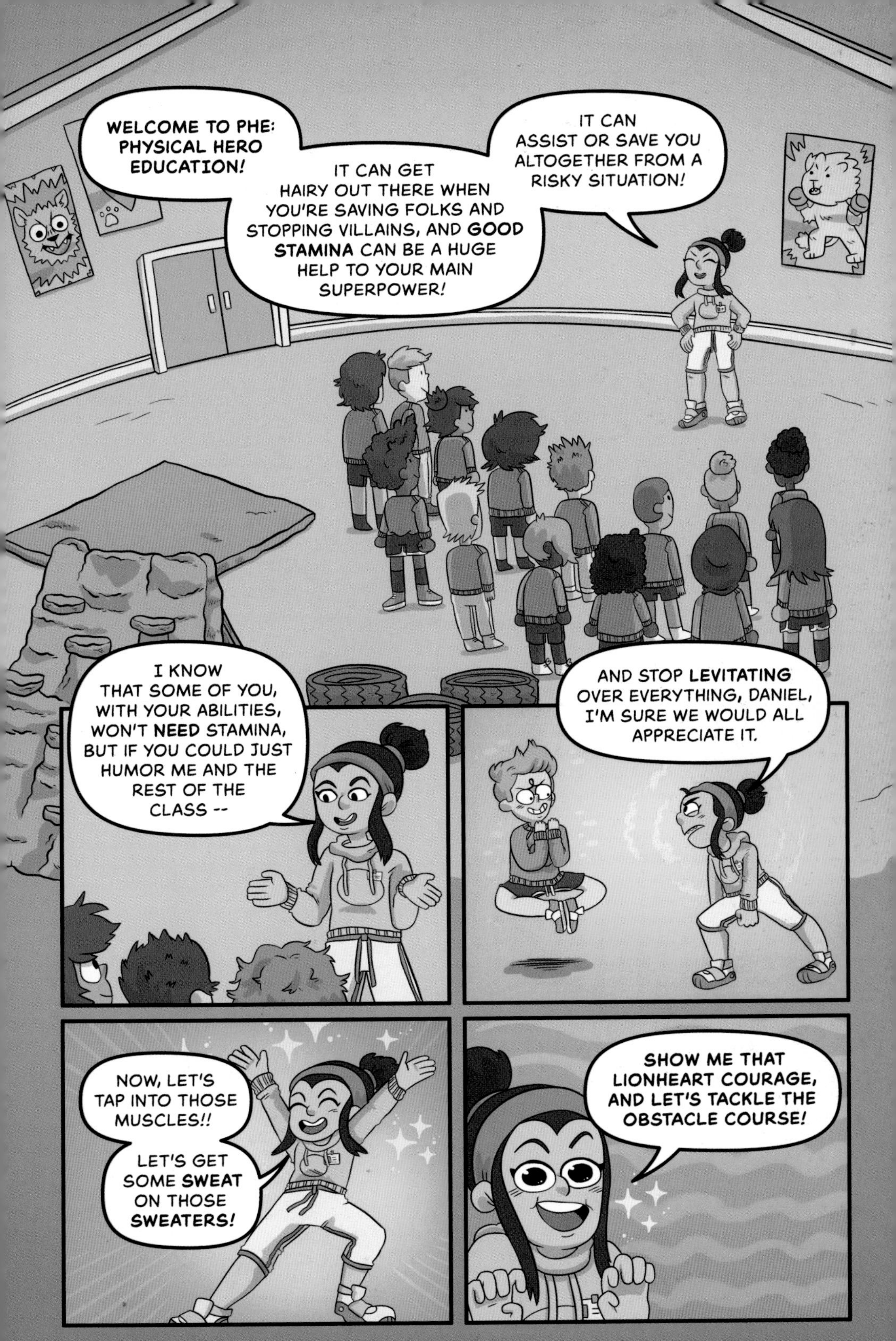
WELCOME TO PHE: PHYSICAL HERO EDUCATION!
IT CAN GET HAIRY OUT THERE WHEN YOU'RE SAVING FOLKS AND STOPPING VILLAINS, AND GOOD STAMINA CAN BE A HUGE HELP TO YOUR MAIN SUPERPOWER!
IT CAN ASSIST OR SAVE YOU ALTOGETHER FROM A RISKY SITUATION!
I KNOW THAT SOME OF YOU, WITH YOUR ABILITIES, WON'T NEED STAMINA, BUT IF YOU COULD JUST HUMOR ME AND THE REST OF THE CLASS --
AND STOP LEVITATING OVER EVERYTHING, DANIEL, I'M SURE WE WOULD ALL APPRECIATE IT.
NOW, LET'S TAP INTO THOSE MUSCLES!!
LET'S GET SOME SWEAT ON THOSE SWEATERS!
SHOW ME THAT LIONHEART COURAGE, AND LET'S TACKLE THE OBSTACLE COURSE!

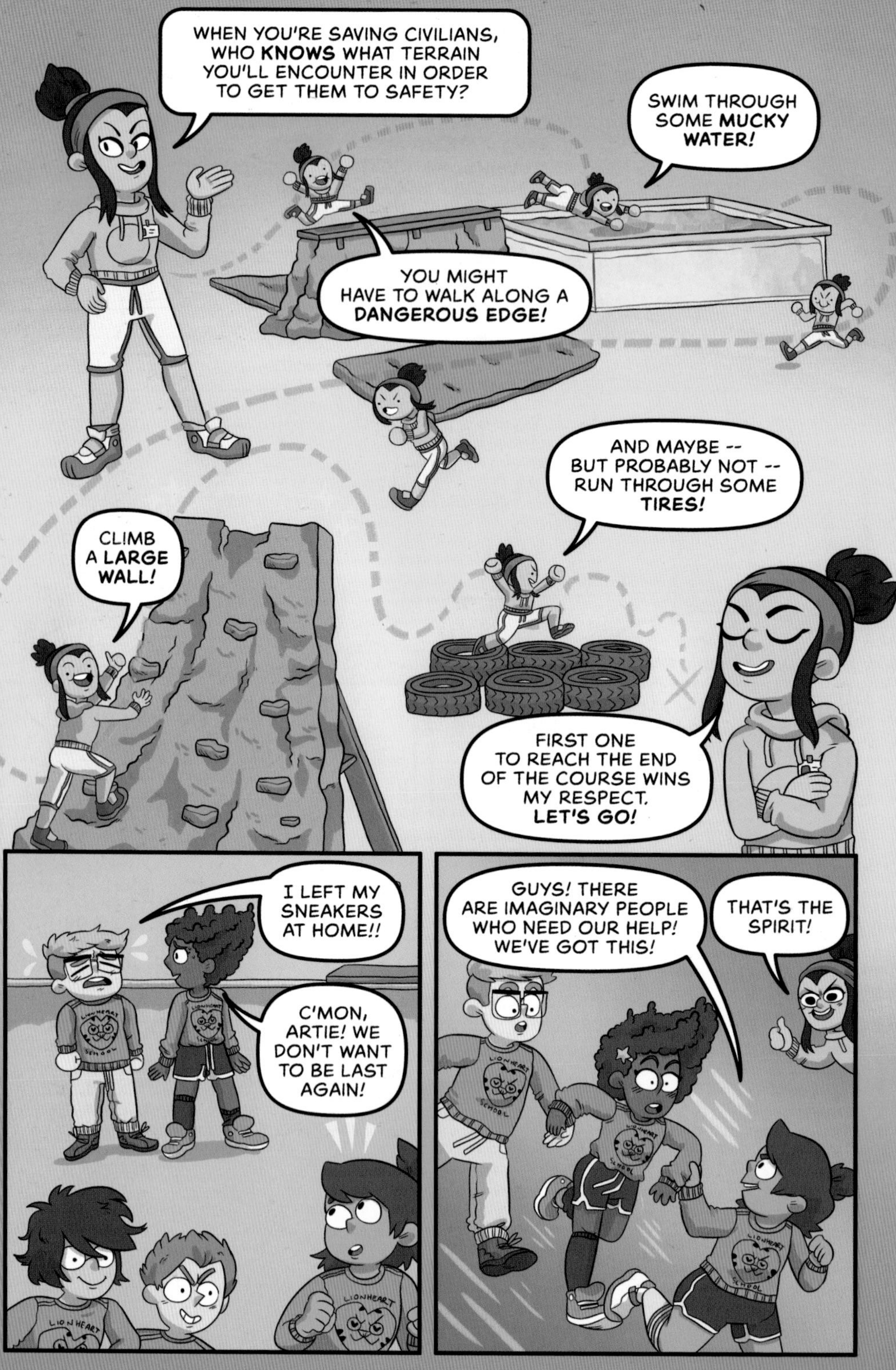
WHEN YOU'RE SAVING CIVILIANS, WHO KNOWS WHAT TERRAIN YOU'LL ENCOUNTER IN ORDER TO GET THEM TO SAFETY?
SWIM THROUGH SOME MUCKY WATER!
YOU MIGHT HAVE TO WALK ALONG A DANGEROUS EDGE!
AND MAYBE -- BUT PROBABLY NOT -- RUN THROUGH SOME TIRES!
CLIMB A LARGE WALL!
FIRST ONE TO REACH THE END OF THE COURSE WINS MY RESPECT. LET'S GO!
I LEFT MY SNEAKERS AT HOME!!
C'MON, ARTIE! WE DON'T WANT TO BE LAST AGAIN!
GUYS! THERE ARE IMAGINARY PEOPLE WHO NEED OUR HELP! WE'VE GOT THIS!
THAT'S THE SPIRIT!

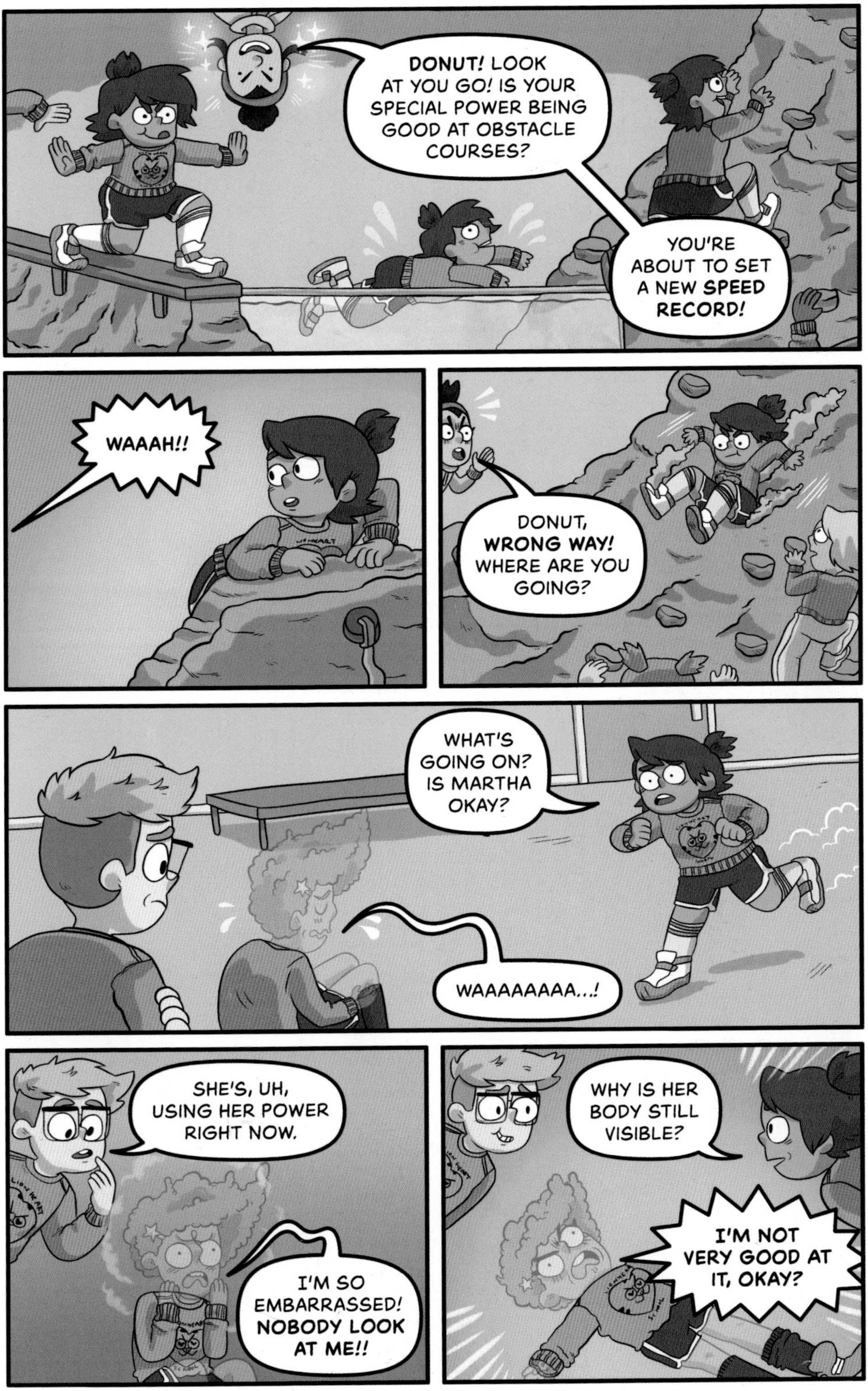
DONUT! LOOK AT YOU GO! IS YOUR SPECIAL POWER BEING GOOD AT OBSTACLE COURSES?
YOU'RE ABOUT TO SET A NEW SPEED RECORD!
WAAAH!!
DONUT, WRONG WAY! WHERE ARE YOU GOING?
WHAT'S GOING ON? IS MARTHA OKAY?
WAAAAAAAA...!
SHE'S, UH, USING HER POWER RIGHT NOW.
I'M SO EMBARRASSED! NOBODY LOOK AT ME!!
WHY IS HER BODY STILL VISIBLE?
I'M NOT VERY GOOD AT IT, OKAY?

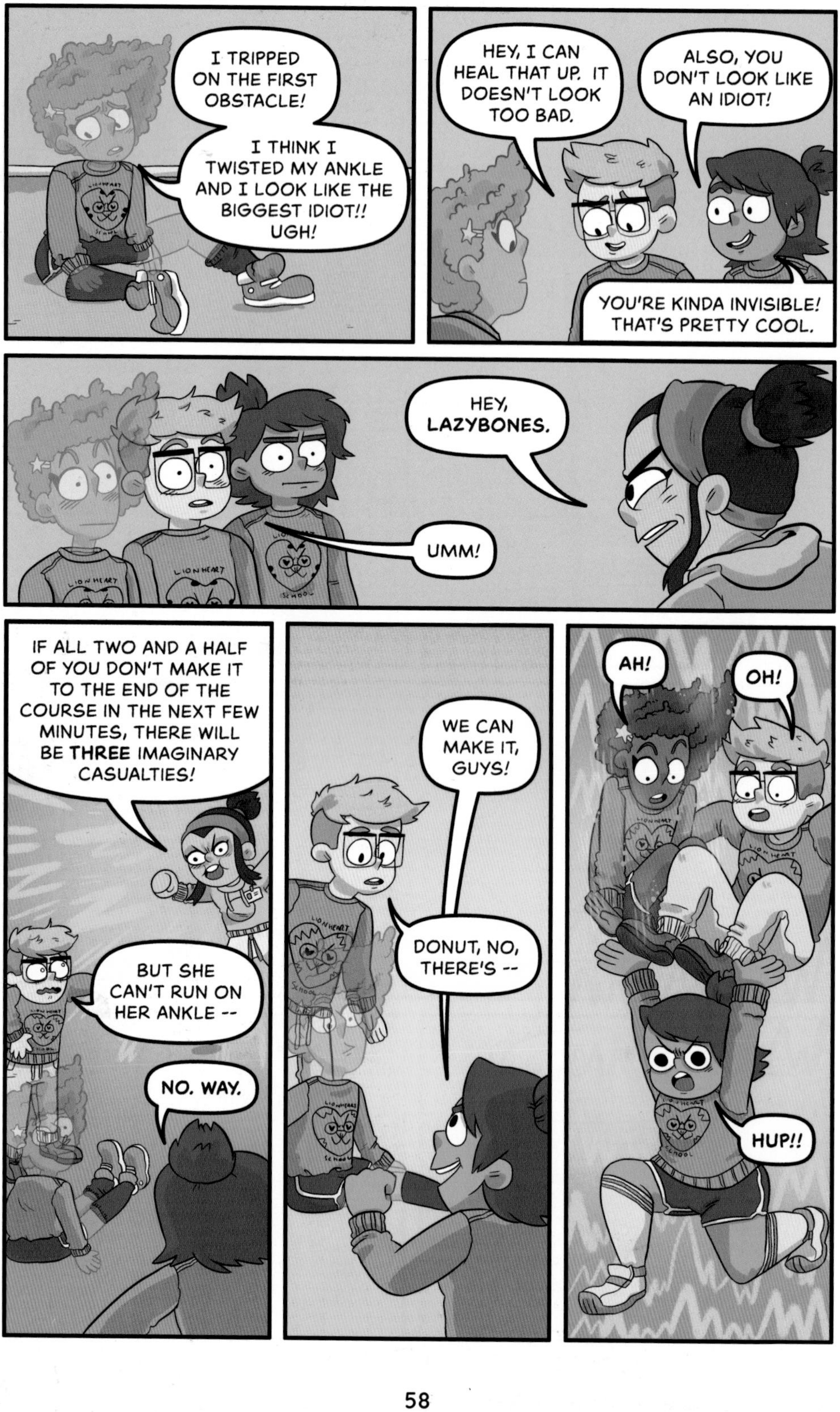
I TRIPPED ON THE FIRST OBSTACLE!
I THINK I TWISTED MY ANKLE AND I LOOK LIKE THE BIGGEST IDIOT!! UGH!
HEY, I CAN HEAL THAT UP. IT DOESN'T LOOK TOO BAD.
ALSO, YOU DON'T LOOK LIKE AN IDIOT!
YOU'RE KINDA INVISIBLE! THAT'S PRETTY COOL.
HEY, LAZYBONES.
UMM!
IF ALL TWO AND A HALF OF YOU DON'T MAKE IT TO THE END OF THE COURSE IN THE NEXT FEW MINUTES, THERE WILL BE THREE IMAGINARY CASUALTIES!
BUT SHE CAN'T RUN ON HER ANKLE --
NO. WAY.
WE CAN MAKE IT, GUYS!
DONUT, NO, THERE'S --
AH!
OH!
HUP!!

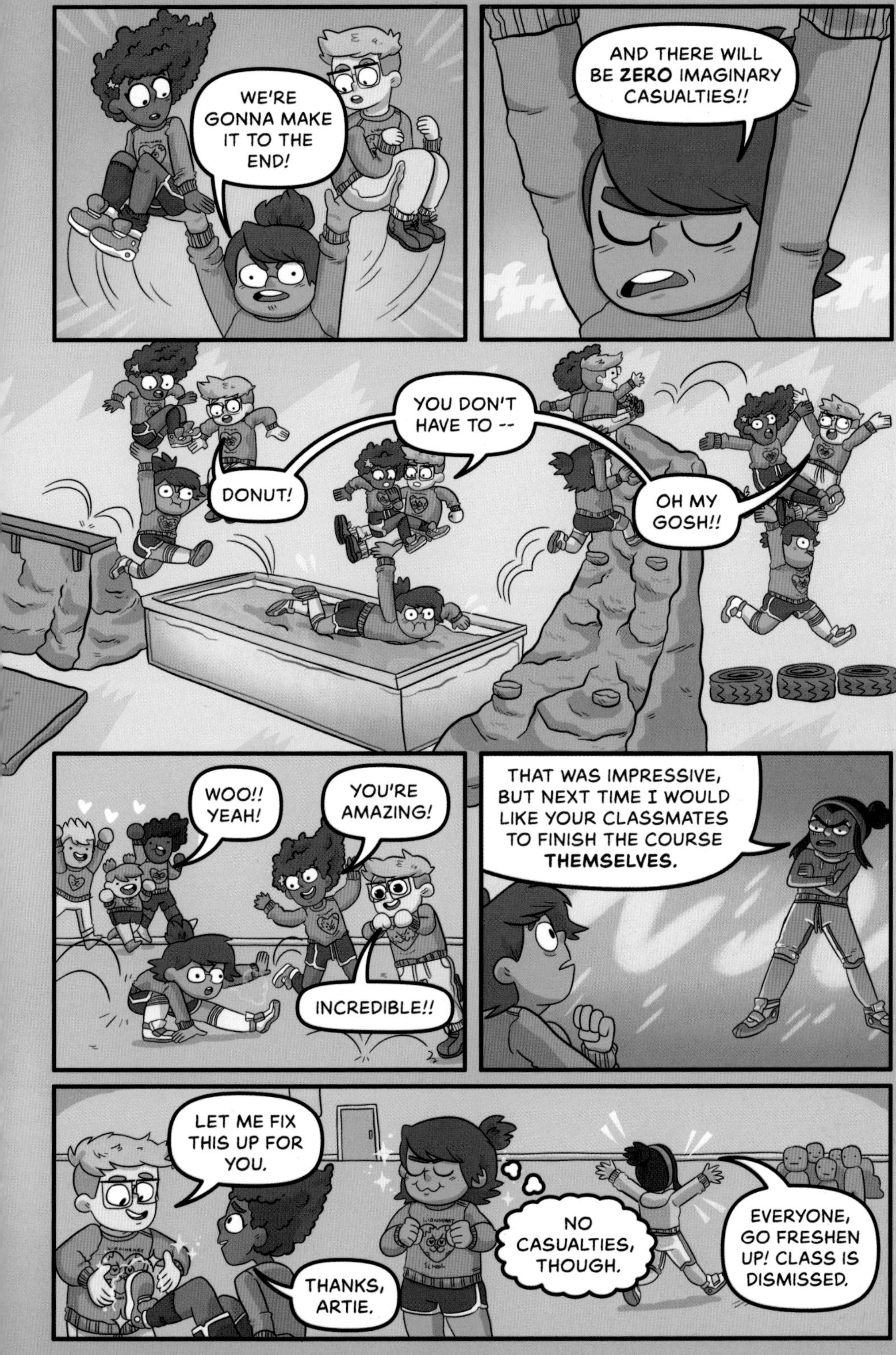
WE'RE GONNA MAKE IT TO THE END!
AND THERE WILL BE ZERO IMAGINARY CASUALTIES!!
DONUT!
YOU DON'T HAVE TO --
OH MY GOSH!!
WOO!! YEAH!
YOU'RE AMAZING!
INCREDIBLE!!
THAT WAS IMPRESSIVE, BUT NEXT TIME I WOULD LIKE YOUR CLASSMATES TO FINISH THE COURSE THEMSELVES.
LET ME FIX THIS UP FOR YOU.
THANKS, ARTIE.
NO CASUALTIES, THOUGH.
EVERYONE, GO FRESHEN UP! CLASS IS DISMISSED.

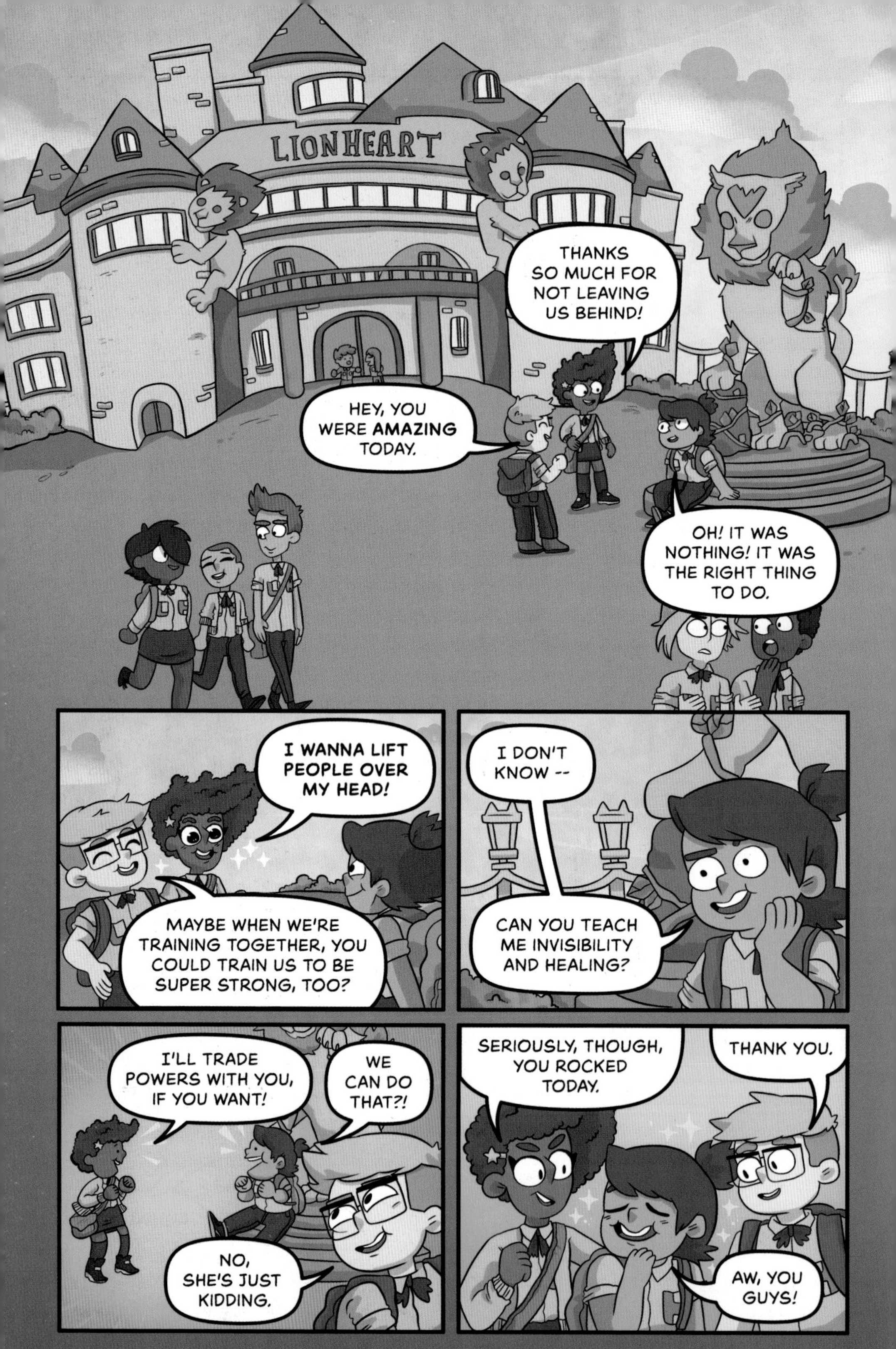
LIONHEART
THANKS SO MUCH FOR NOT LEAVING US BEHIND!
HEY, YOU WERE **AMAZING** TODAY.
OH! IT WAS NOTHING! IT WAS THE RIGHT THING TO DO.
I WANNA LIFT PEOPLE OVER MY HEAD!
MAYBE WHEN WE'RE TRAINING TOGETHER, YOU COULD TRAIN US TO BE SUPER STRONG, TOO?
I DON'T KNOW --
CAN YOU TEACH ME INVISIBILITY AND HEALING?
I'LL TRADE POWERS WITH YOU, IF YOU WANT!
WE CAN DO THAT?!
NO, SHE'S JUST KIDDING.
SERIOUSLY, THOUGH, YOU ROCKED TODAY.
THANK YOU.
AW, YOU GUYS!

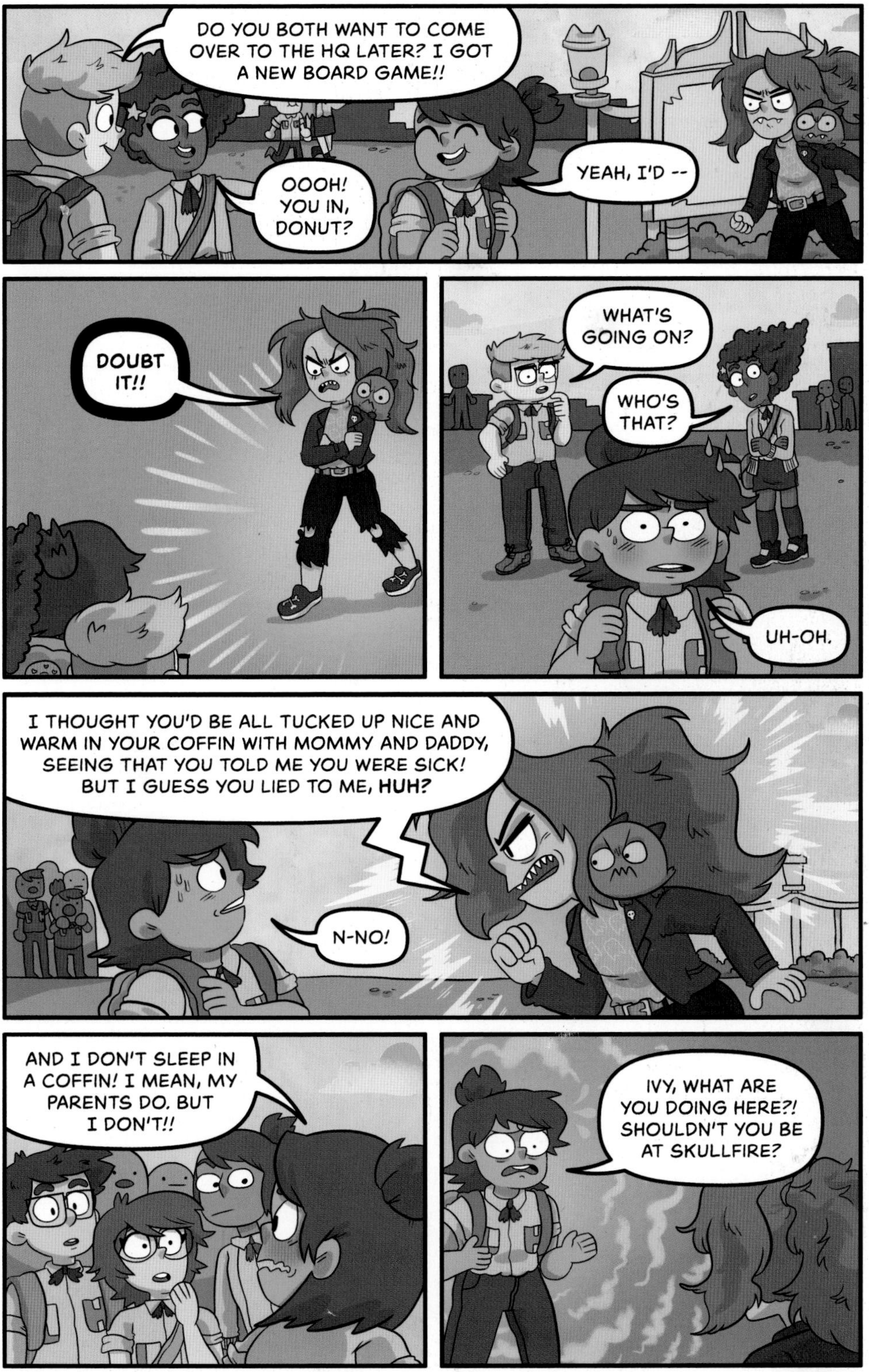

DO YOU BOTH WANT TO COME OVER TO THE HQ LATER? I GOT A NEW BOARD GAME!!
OOOH! YOU IN, DONUT?
YEAH, I'D --
DOUBT IT!!
WHAT'S GOING ON?
WHO'S THAT?
UH-OH.
I THOUGHT YOU'D BE ALL TUCKED UP NICE AND WARM IN YOUR COFFIN WITH MOMMY AND DADDY, SEEING THAT YOU TOLD ME YOU WERE SICK! BUT I GUESS YOU LIED TO ME, HUH?
N-NO!
AND I DON'T SLEEP IN A COFFIN! I MEAN, MY PARENTS DO, BUT I DON'T!!
IVY, WHAT ARE YOU DOING HERE?! SHOULDN'T YOU BE AT SKULLFIRE?

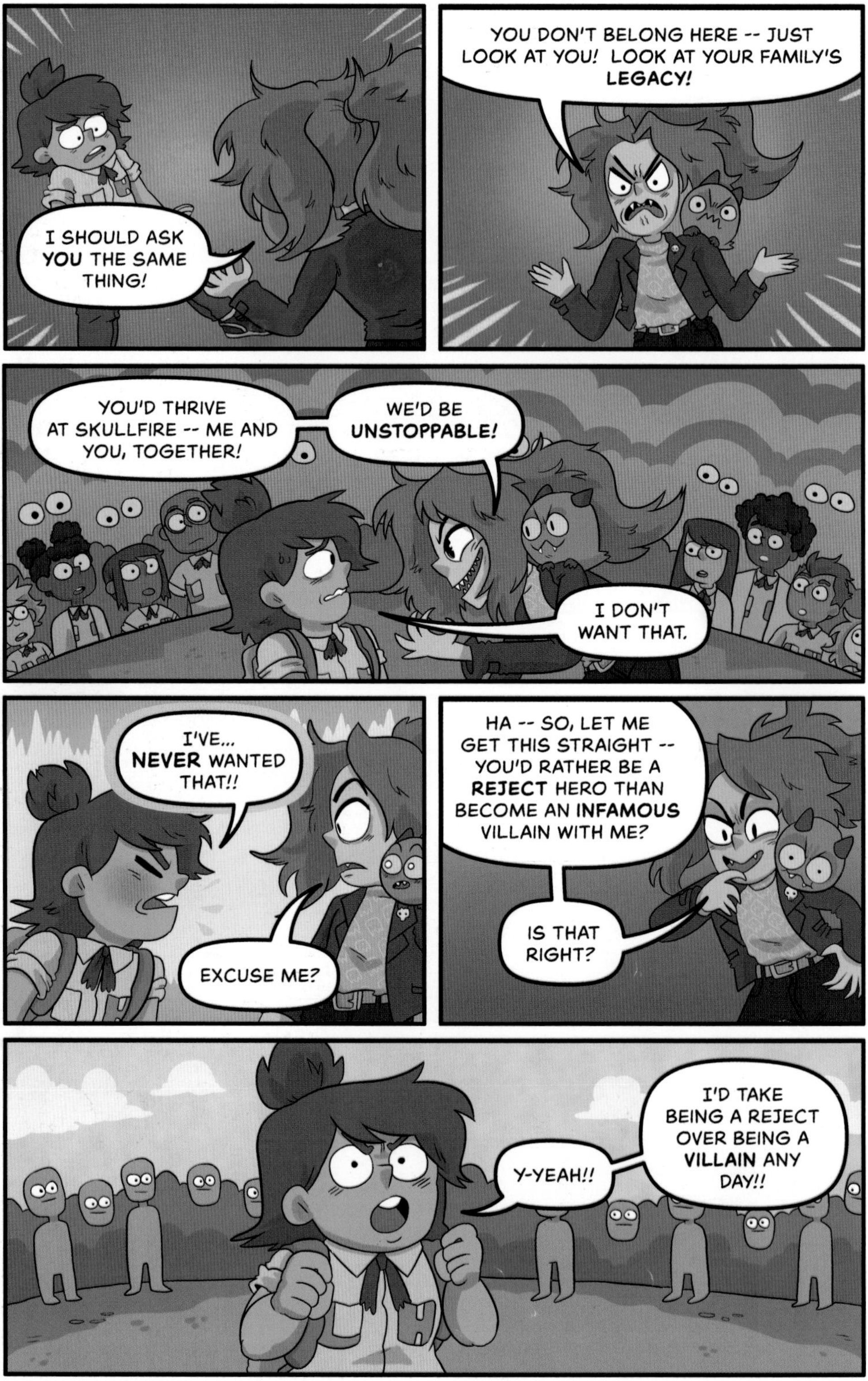
I SHOULD ASK YOU THE SAME THING!
YOU DON'T BELONG HERE -- JUST LOOK AT YOU! LOOK AT YOUR FAMILY'S LEGACY!
YOU'D THRIVE AT SKULLFIRE -- ME AND YOU, TOGETHER!
WE'D BE UNSTOPPABLE!
I DON'T WANT THAT.
I'VE... NEVER WANTED THAT!!
EXCUSE ME?
HA -- SO, LET ME GET THIS STRAIGHT -- YOU'D RATHER BE A REJECT HERO THAN BECOME AN INFAMOUS VILLAIN WITH ME?
IS THAT RIGHT?
Y-YEAH!!
I'D TAKE BEING A REJECT OVER BEING A VILLAIN ANY DAY!!

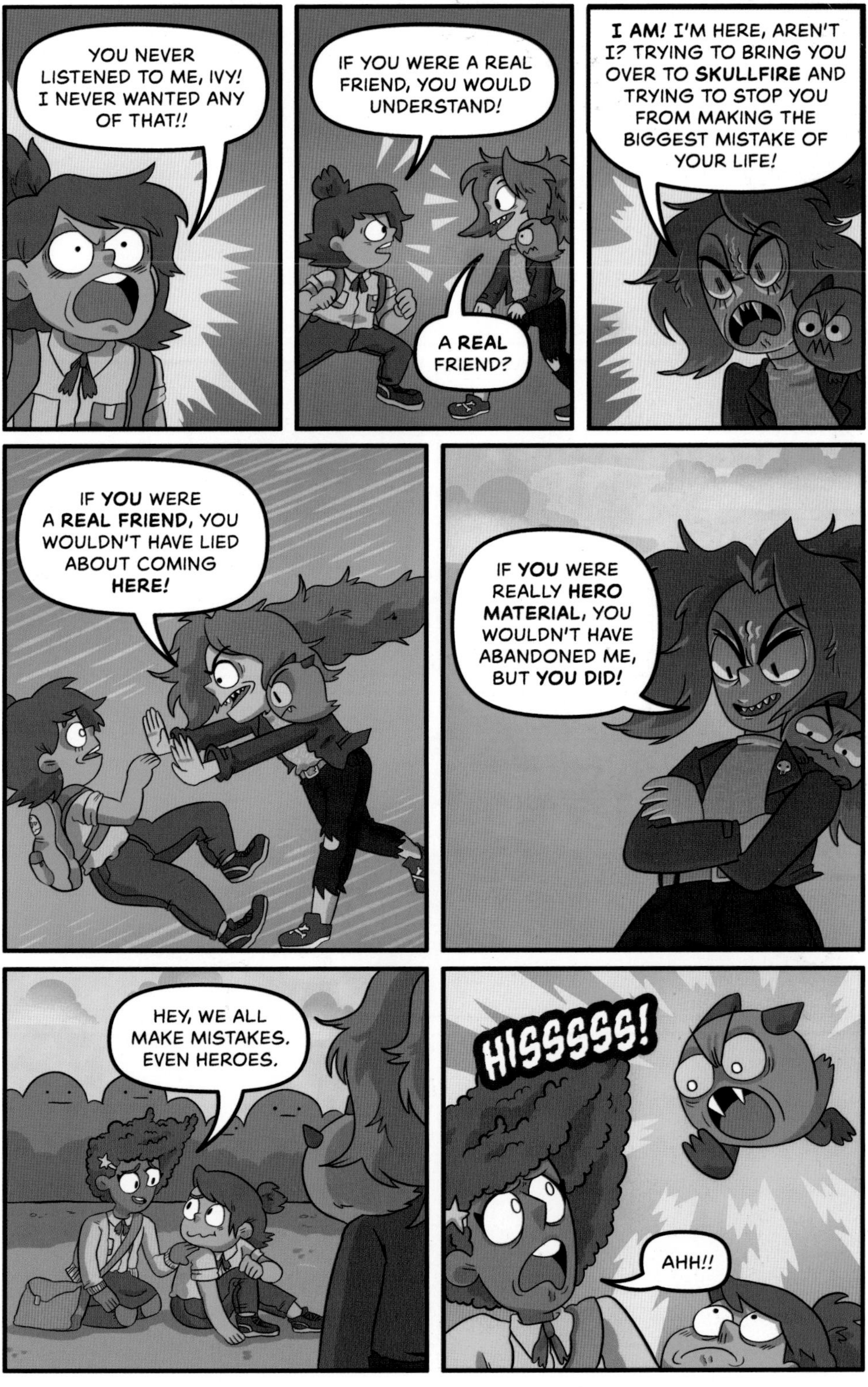
YOU NEVER LISTENED TO ME, IVY! I NEVER WANTED ANY OF THAT!!
IF YOU WERE A REAL FRIEND, YOU WOULD UNDERSTAND!
A REAL FRIEND?
I AM! I'M HERE, AREN'T I? TRYING TO BRING YOU OVER TO SKULLFIRE AND TRYING TO STOP YOU FROM MAKING THE BIGGEST MISTAKE OF YOUR LIFE!
IF YOU WERE A REAL FRIEND, YOU WOULDN'T HAVE LIED ABOUT COMING HERE!
IF YOU WERE REALLY HERO MATERIAL, YOU WOULDN'T HAVE ABANDONED ME, BUT YOU DID!
HEY, WE ALL MAKE MISTAKES. EVEN HEROES.
HISSSSS!
AHH!!

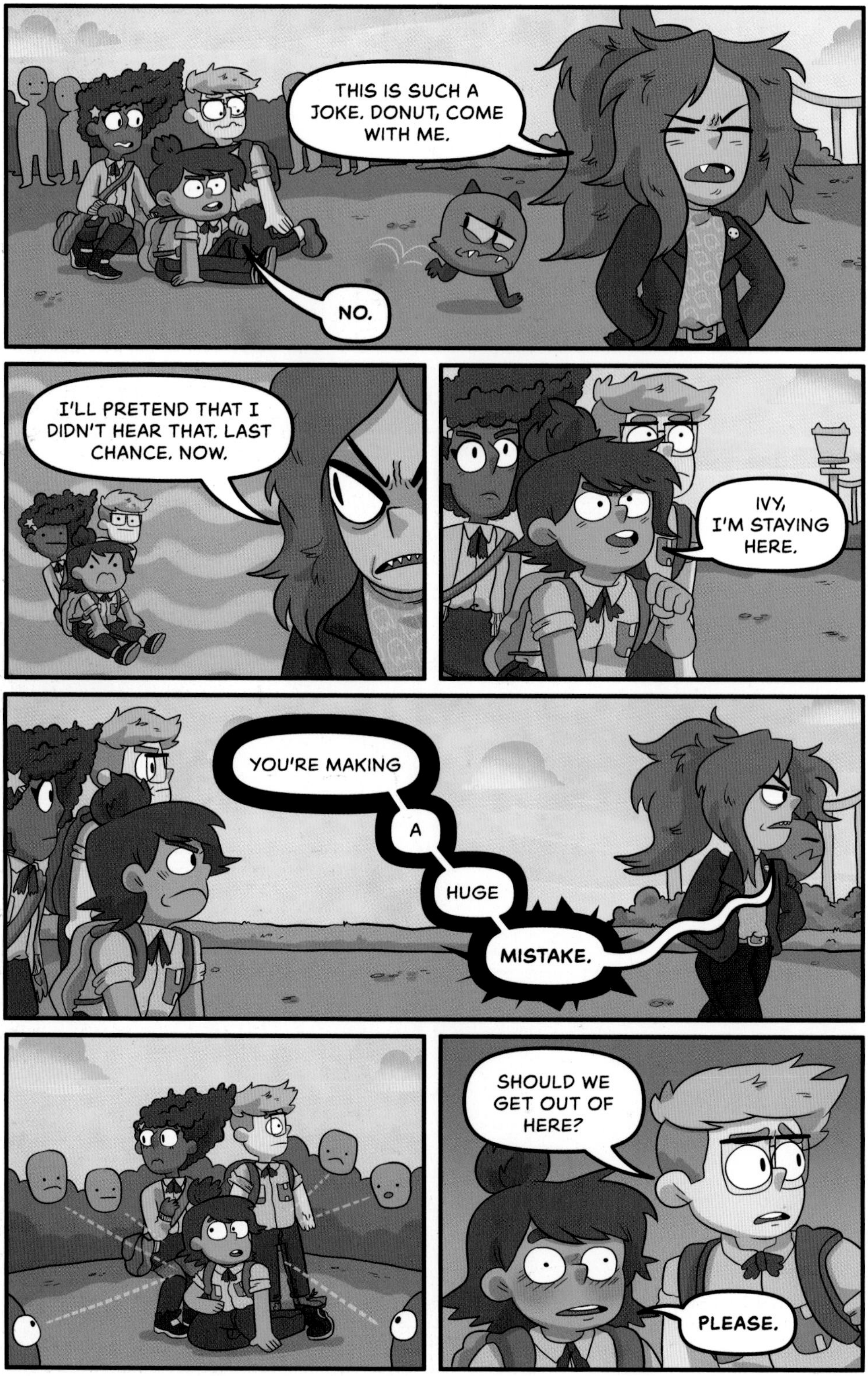
THIS IS SUCH A JOKE. DONUT, COME WITH ME.
NO.
I'LL PRETEND THAT I DIDN'T HEAR THAT. LAST CHANCE. NOW.
IVY, I'M STAYING HERE.
YOU'RE MAKING A HUGE MISTAKE.
SHOULD WE GET OUT OF HERE?
PLEASE.

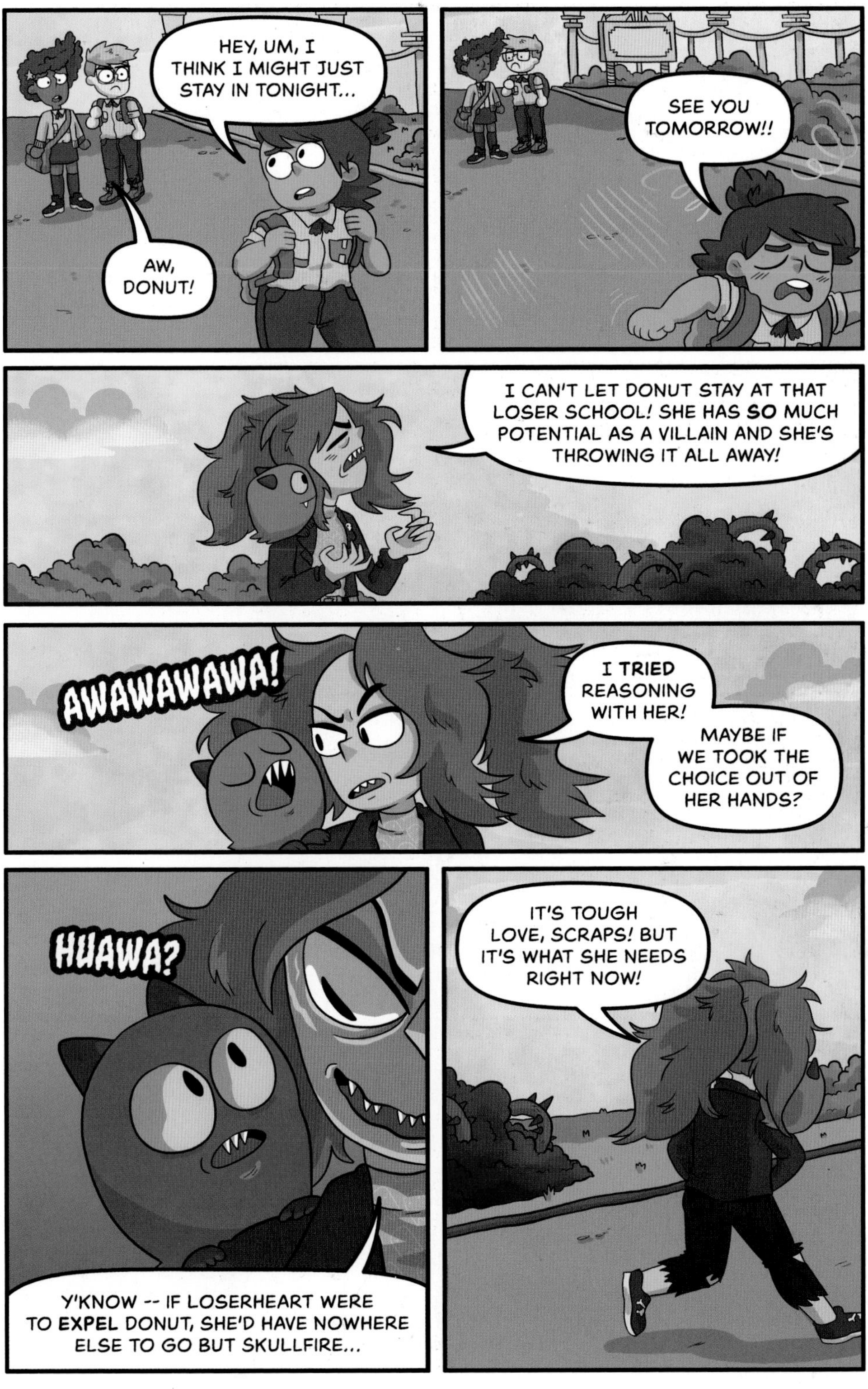
HEY, UM, I THINK I MIGHT JUST STAY IN TONIGHT...
AW, DONUT!
SEE YOU TOMORROW!!
I CAN'T LET DONUT STAY AT THAT LOSER SCHOOL! SHE HAS **SO** MUCH POTENTIAL AS A VILLAIN AND SHE'S THROWING IT ALL AWAY!
AWAWAWAWA!
I **TRIED** REASONING WITH HER!
MAYBE IF WE TOOK THE CHOICE OUT OF HER HANDS?
HUAWA?
Y'KNOW -- IF LOSERHEART WERE TO **EXPEL** DONUT, SHE'D HAVE NOWHERE ELSE TO GO BUT SKULLFIRE...
IT'S TOUGH LOVE, SCRAPS! BUT IT'S WHAT SHE NEEDS RIGHT NOW!

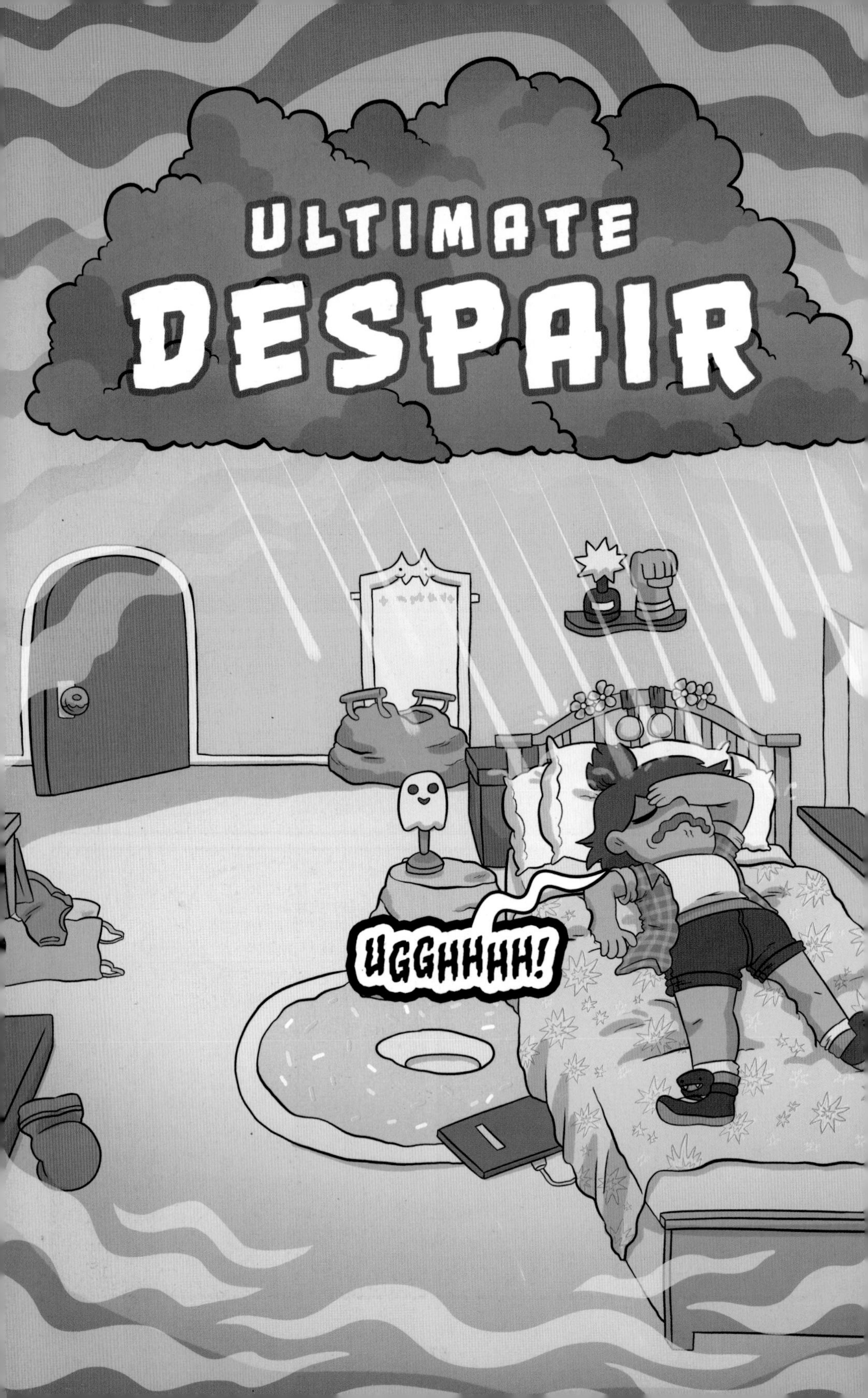
ULTIMATE DESPAIR
UGGHHHH!

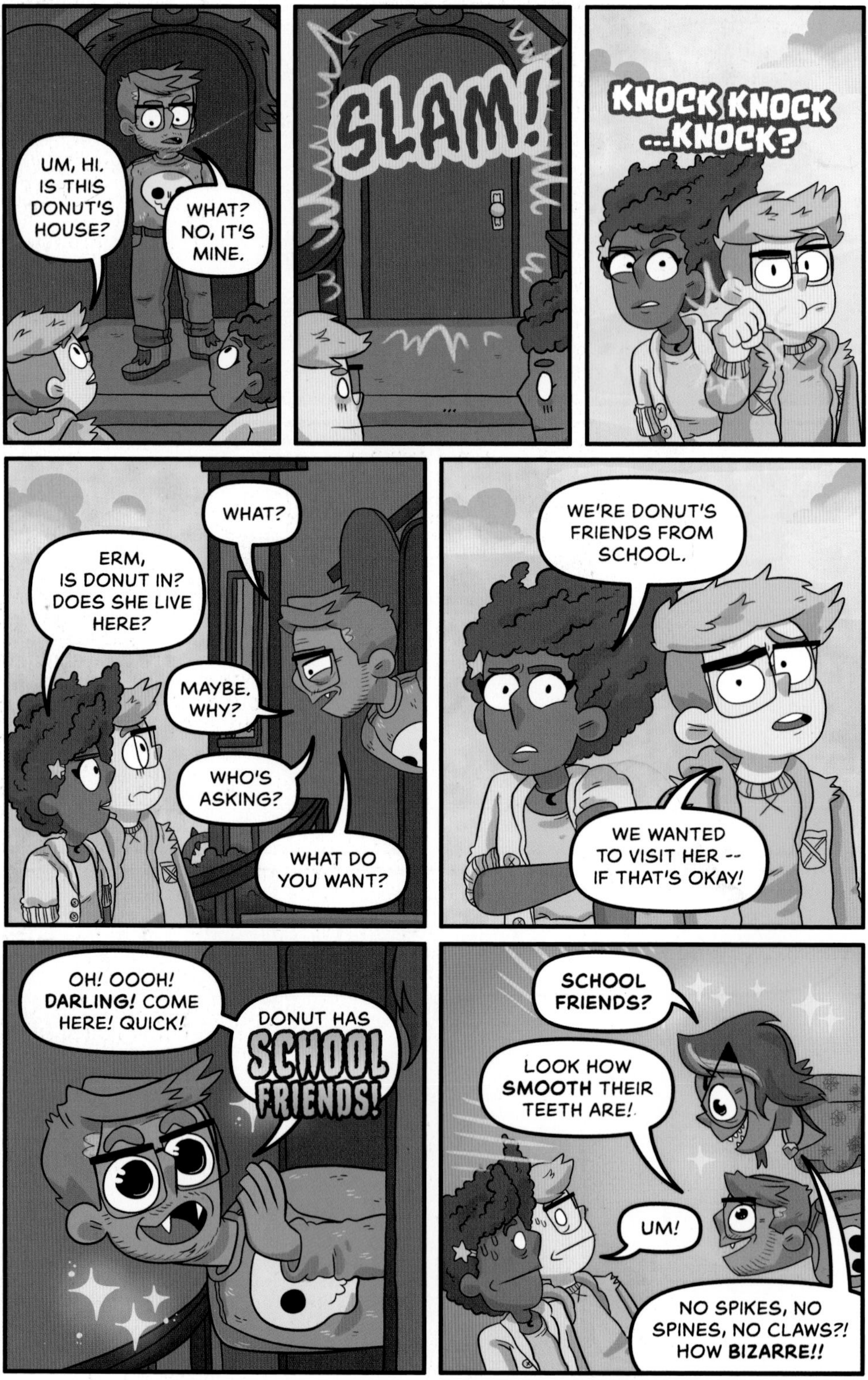
UM, HI. IS THIS DONUT'S HOUSE?
WHAT? NO, IT'S MINE.
SLAM!
KNOCK KNOCK ...KNOCK?
WHAT?
ERM, IS DONUT IN? DOES SHE LIVE HERE?
MAYBE. WHY?
WHO'S ASKING?
WHAT DO YOU WANT?
WE'RE DONUT'S FRIENDS FROM SCHOOL.
WE WANTED TO VISIT HER -- IF THAT'S OKAY!
OH! OOOH! **DARLING!** COME HERE! QUICK!
DONUT HAS SCHOOL FRIENDS!
SCHOOL FRIENDS?
LOOK HOW **SMOOTH** THEIR TEETH ARE!
UM!
NO SPIKES, NO SPINES, NO CLAWS?! HOW **BIZARRE!!**

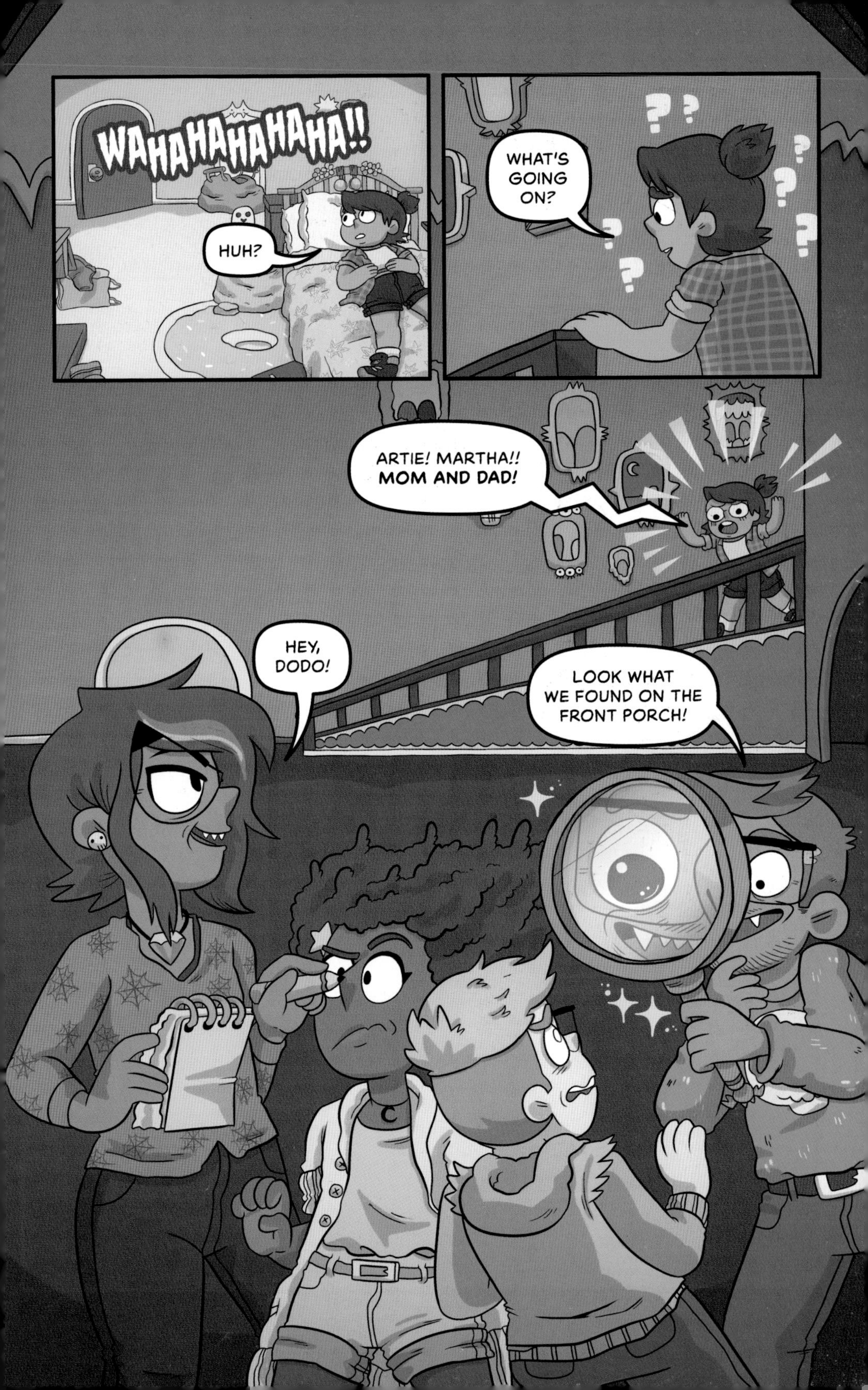
WAHAHAHAHAHAHA!!
HUH?
WHAT'S GOING ON?
ARTIE! MARTHA!! MOM AND DAD!
HEY, DODO!
LOOK WHAT WE FOUND ON THE FRONT PORCH!

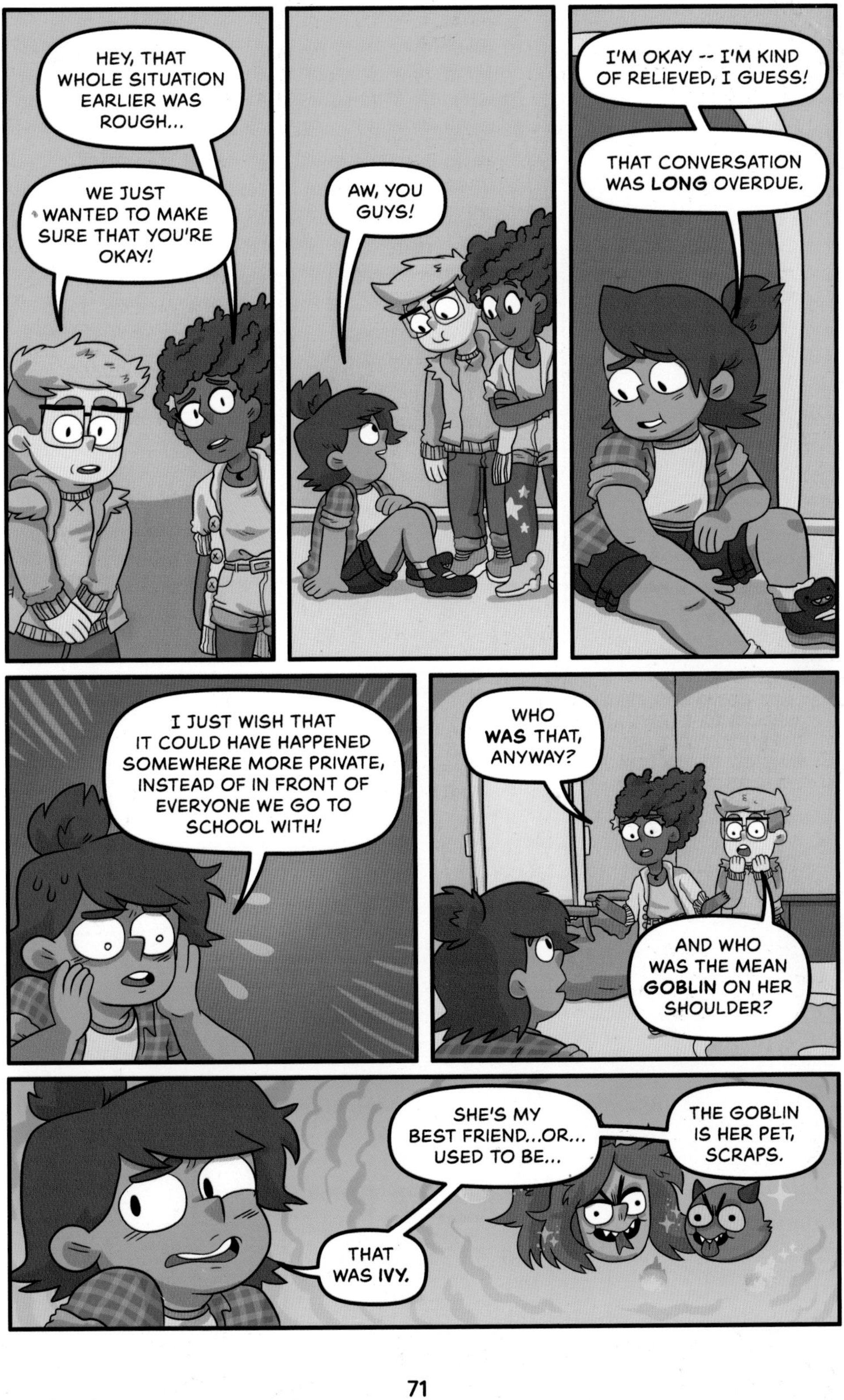
HEY, THAT WHOLE SITUATION EARLIER WAS ROUGH...
WE JUST WANTED TO MAKE SURE THAT YOU'RE OKAY!
AW, YOU GUYS!
I'M OKAY -- I'M KIND OF RELIEVED, I GUESS!
THAT CONVERSATION WAS **LONG** OVERDUE.
I JUST WISH THAT IT COULD HAVE HAPPENED SOMEWHERE MORE PRIVATE, INSTEAD OF IN FRONT OF EVERYONE WE GO TO SCHOOL WITH!
WHO **WAS** THAT, ANYWAY?
AND WHO WAS THE MEAN **GOBLIN** ON HER SHOULDER?
THAT WAS IVY.
SHE'S MY BEST FRIEND...OR... USED TO BE...
THE GOBLIN IS HER PET, SCRAPS.

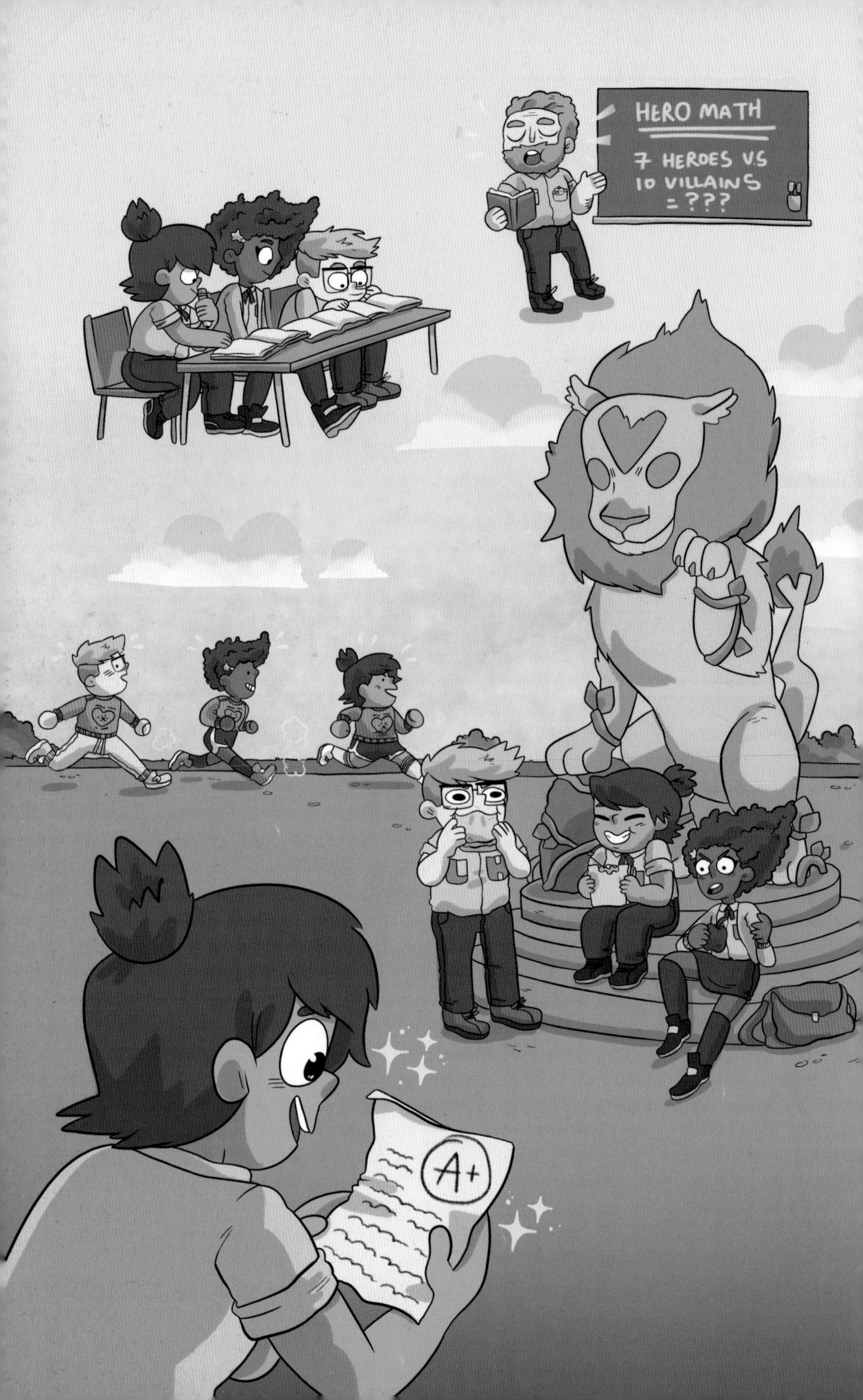
HERO MATH
7 HEROES V.S
10 VILLAINS
= ???
A+

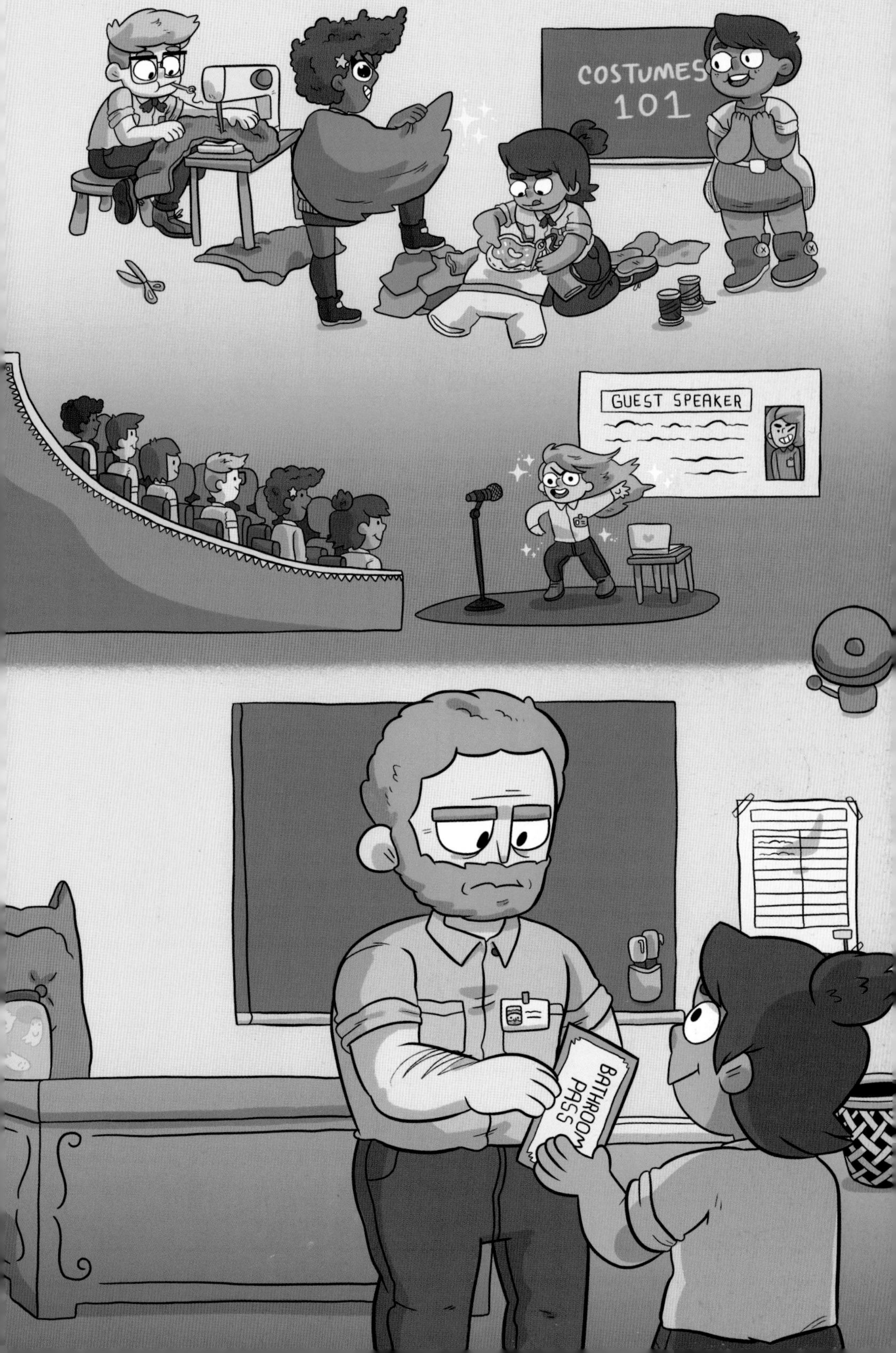
COSTUMES 101
GUEST SPEAKER
BATHROOM PASS

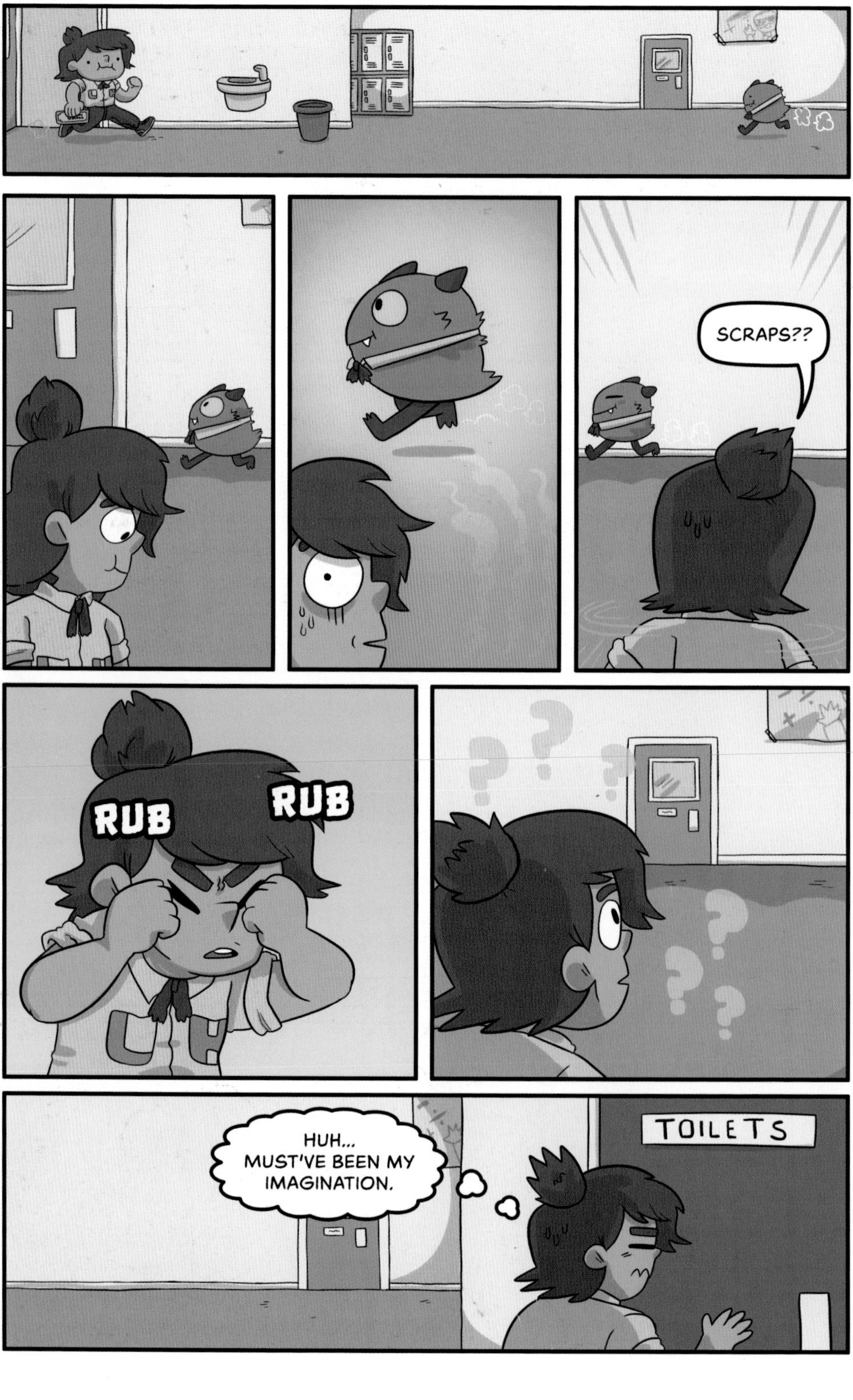
SCRAPS??
RUB
RUB
HUH... MUST'VE BEEN MY IMAGINATION.
TOILETS

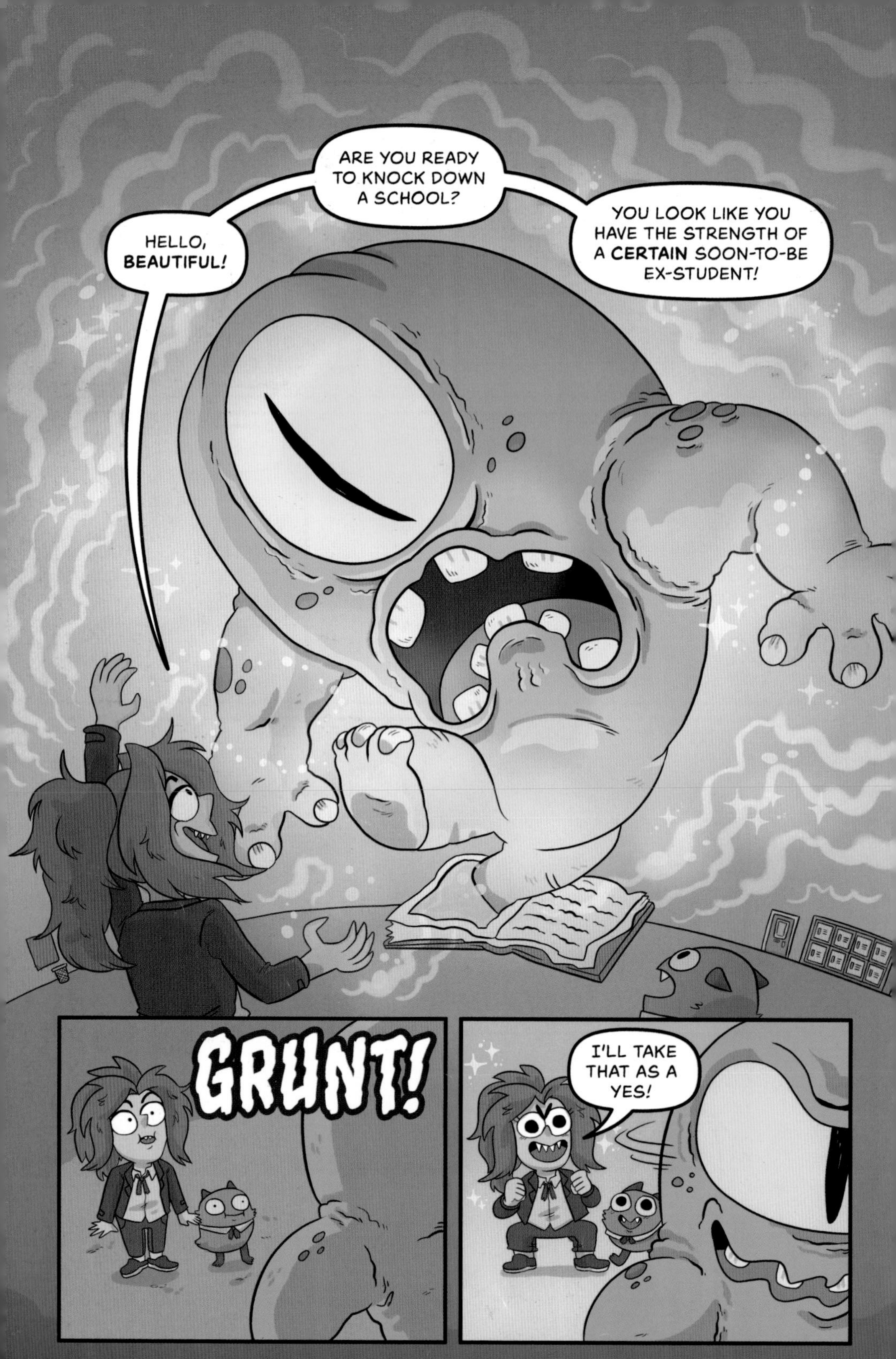
HELLO, BEAUTIFUL!
ARE YOU READY TO KNOCK DOWN A SCHOOL?
YOU LOOK LIKE YOU HAVE THE STRENGTH OF A CERTAIN SOON-TO-BE EX-STUDENT!
GRUNT!
I'LL TAKE THAT AS A YES!

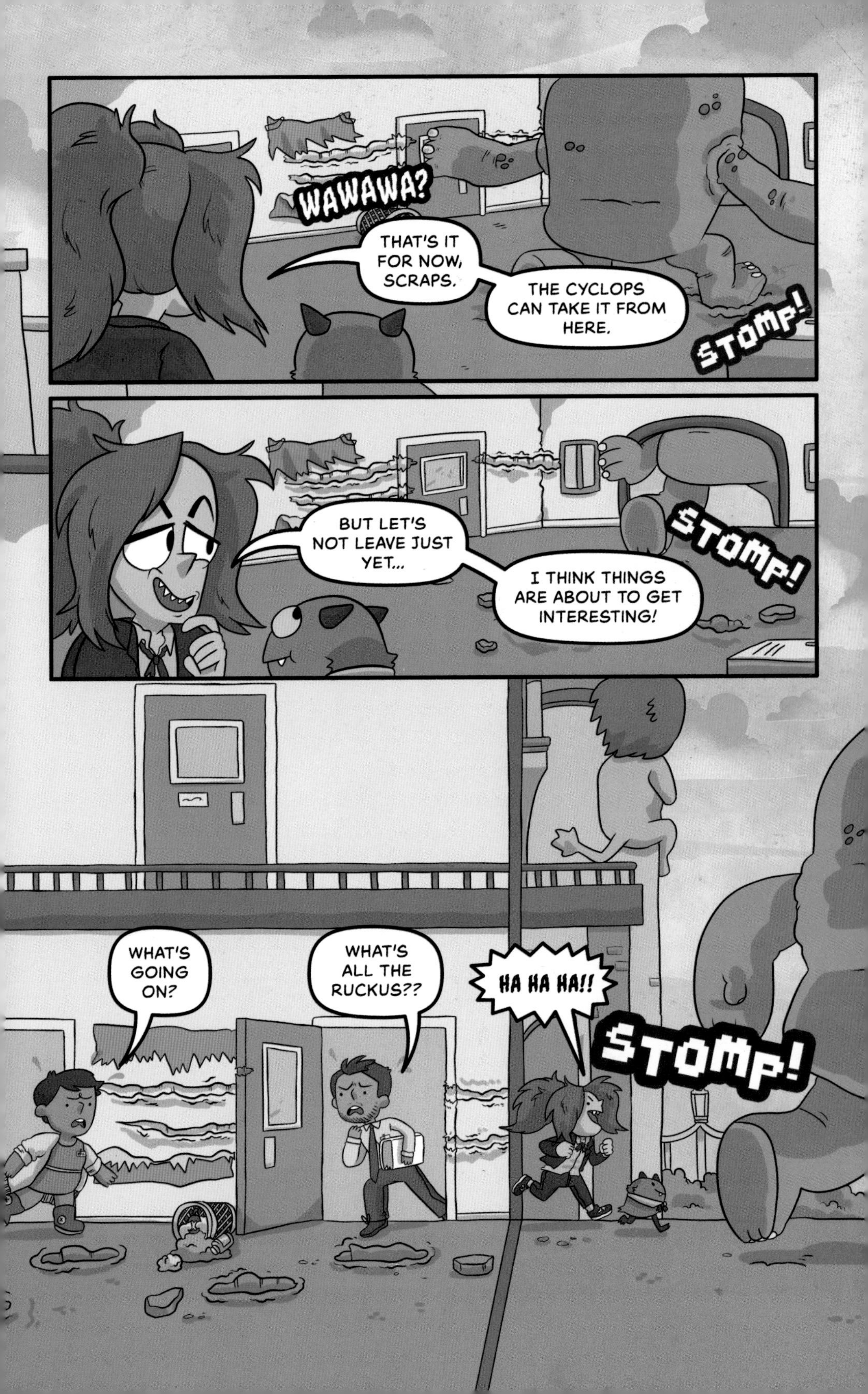
WAWAWA?
THAT'S IT FOR NOW, SCRAPS.
THE CYCLOPS CAN TAKE IT FROM HERE.
STOMP!
BUT LET'S NOT LEAVE JUST YET...
I THINK THINGS ARE ABOUT TO GET INTERESTING!
STOMP!
WHAT'S GOING ON?
WHAT'S ALL THE RUCKUS??
HA HA HA!!
STOMP!

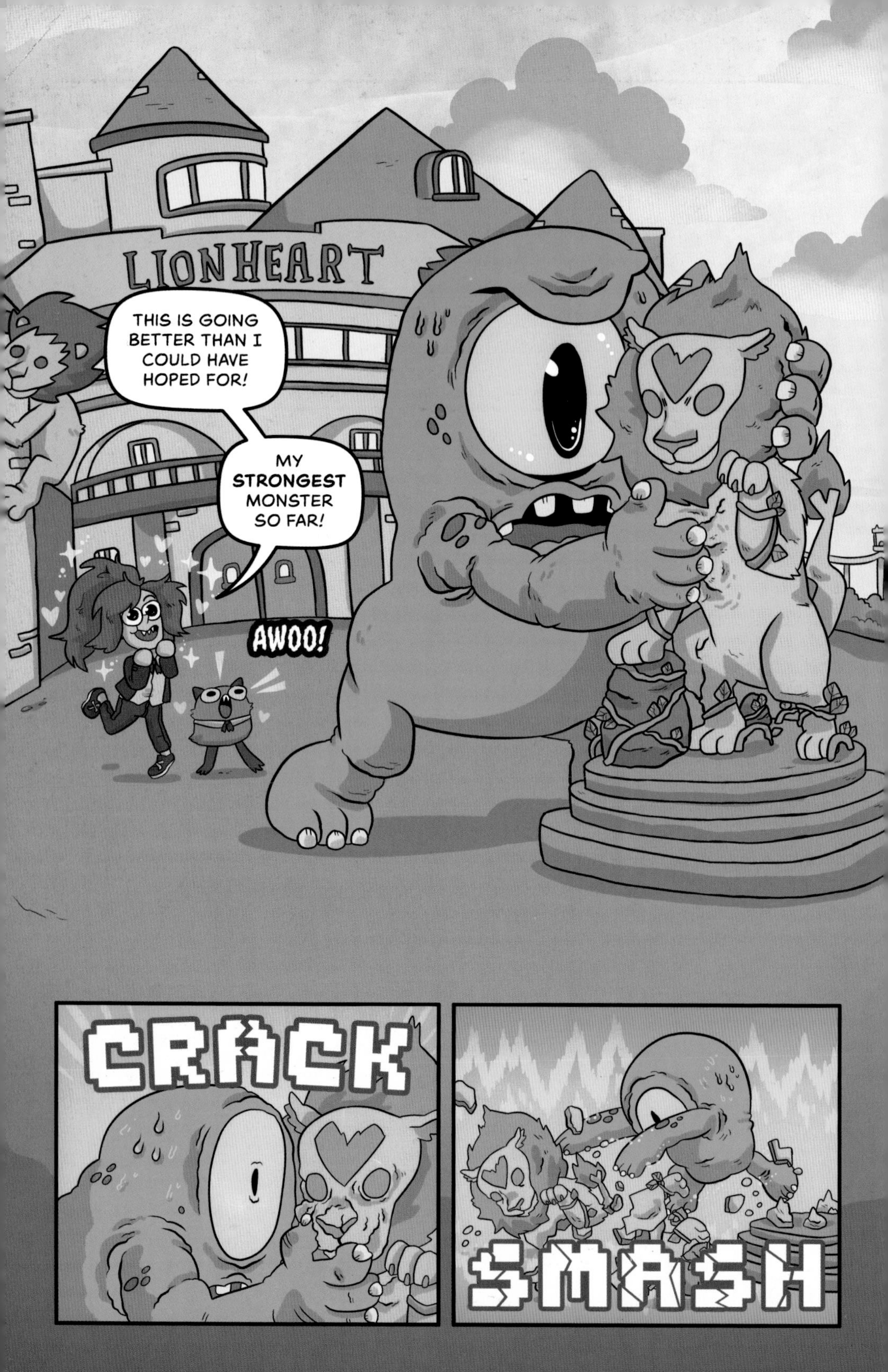
LIONHEART
THIS IS GOING BETTER THAN I COULD HAVE HOPED FOR!
MY STRONGEST MONSTER SO FAR!
AWOO!
CRACK
SMASH

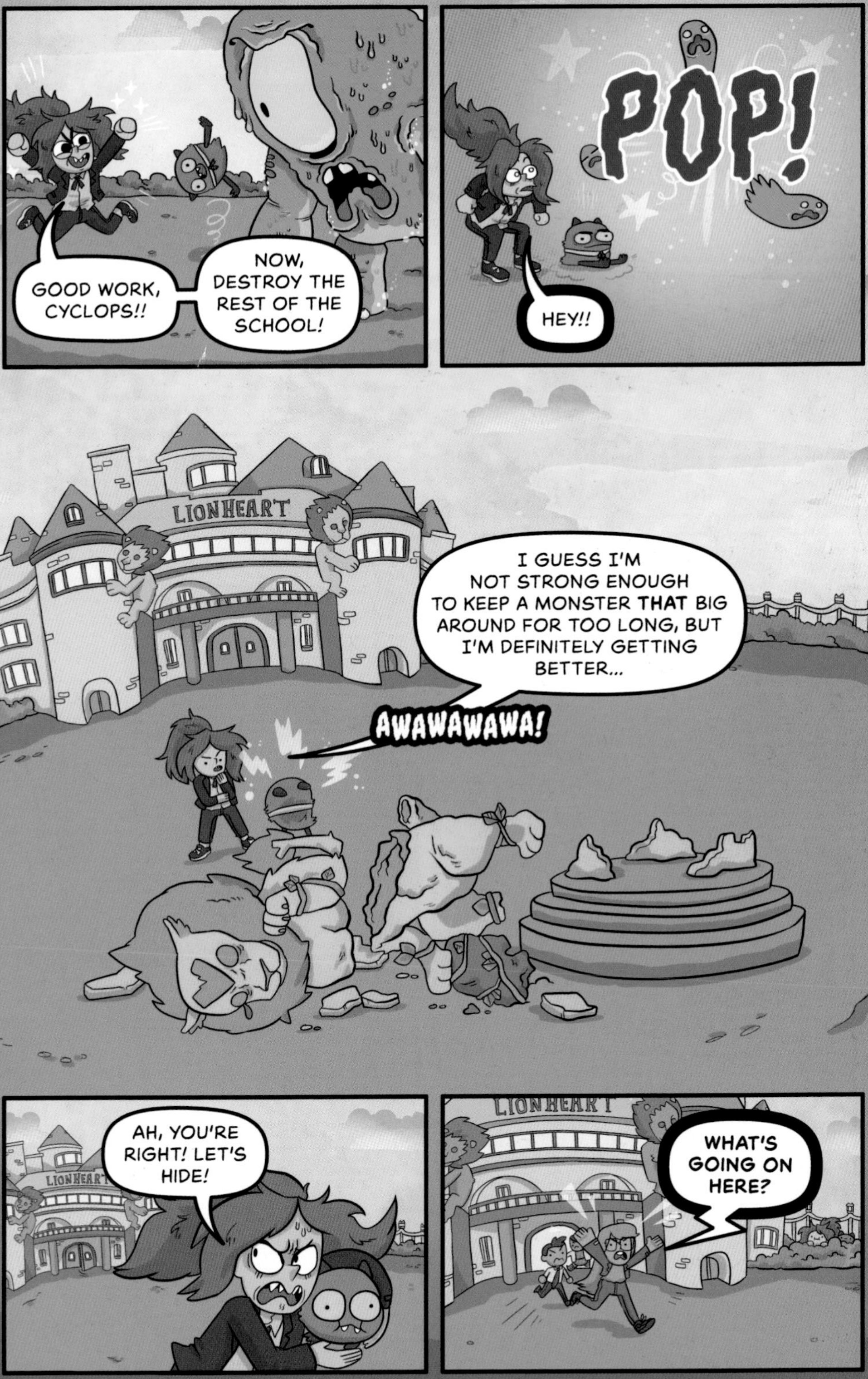
GOOD WORK, CYCLOPS!!
NOW, DESTROY THE REST OF THE SCHOOL!
POP!
HEY!!
LIONHEART
I GUESS I'M NOT STRONG ENOUGH TO KEEP A MONSTER **THAT** BIG AROUND FOR TOO LONG, BUT I'M DEFINITELY GETTING BETTER...
AWAWAWAWA!
AH, YOU'RE RIGHT! LET'S HIDE!
WHAT'S GOING ON HERE?

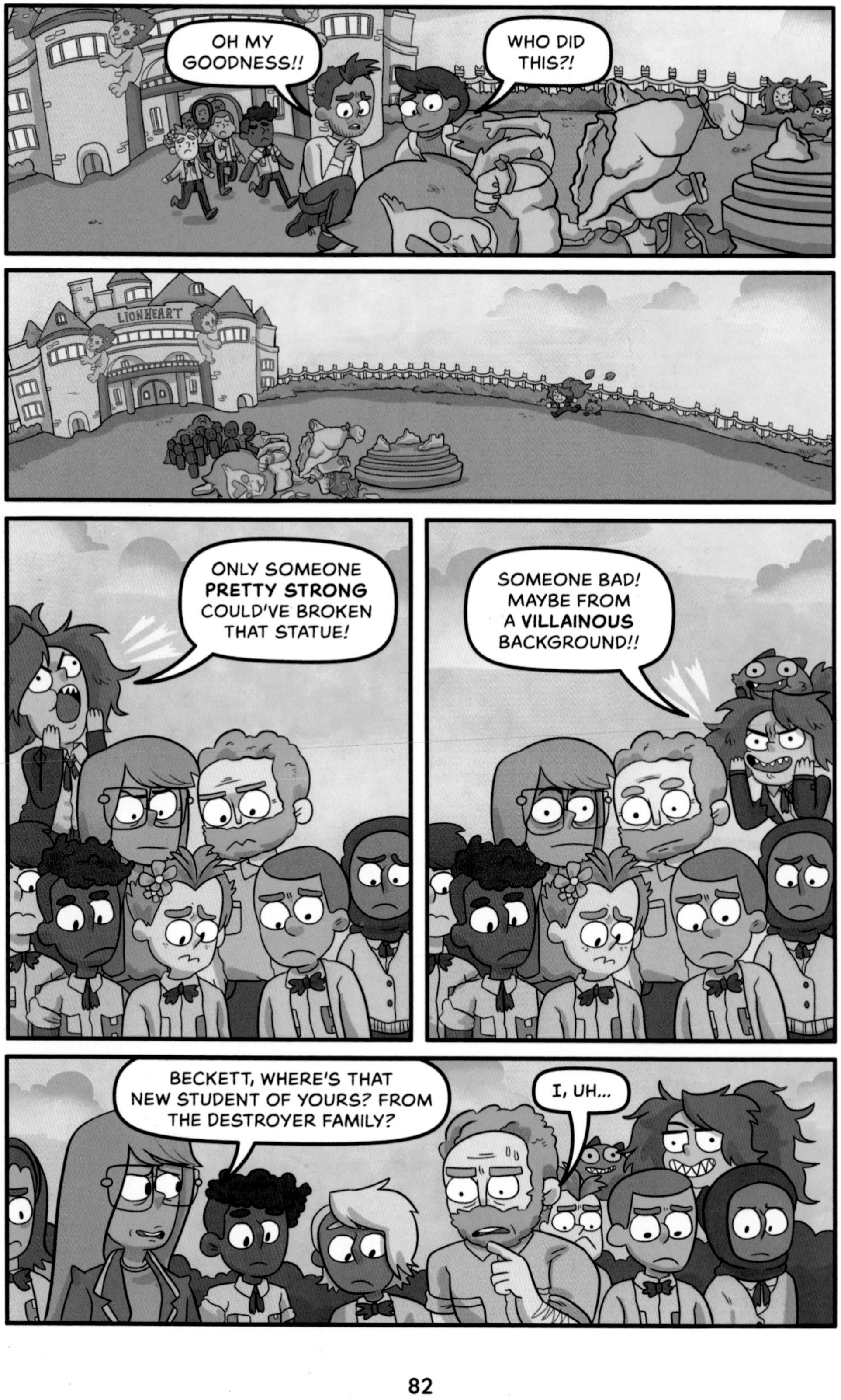
OH MY GOODNESS!!
WHO DID THIS?!
LIONHEART
ONLY SOMEONE PRETTY STRONG COULD'VE BROKEN THAT STATUE!
SOMEONE BAD! MAYBE FROM A VILLAINOUS BACKGROUND!!
BECKETT, WHERE'S THAT NEW STUDENT OF YOURS? FROM THE DESTROYER FAMILY?
I, UH...

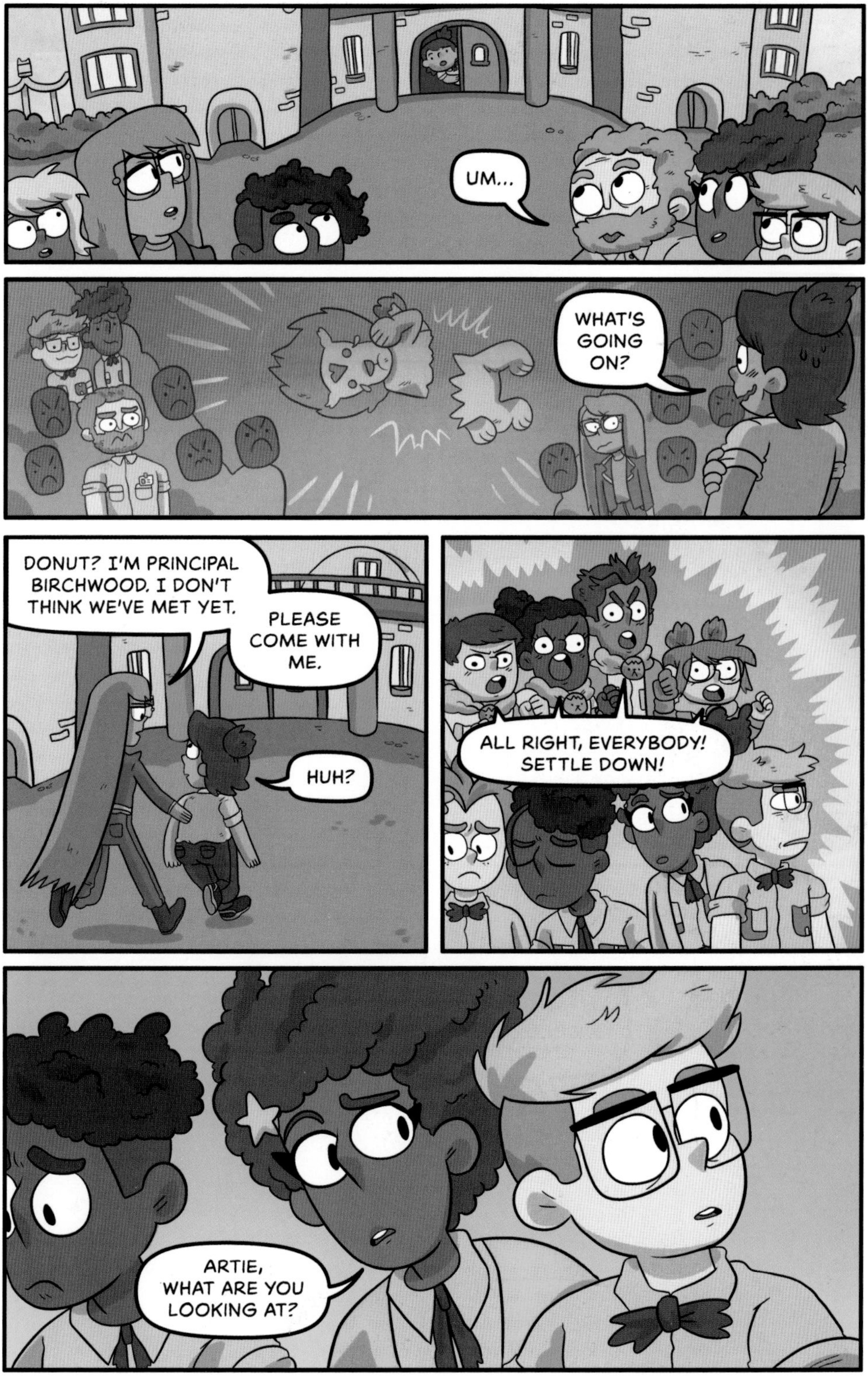
UM...
WHAT'S GOING ON?
DONUT? I'M PRINCIPAL BIRCHWOOD. I DON'T THINK WE'VE MET YET.
PLEASE COME WITH ME.
HUH?
ALL RIGHT, EVERYBODY! SETTLE DOWN!
ARTIE, WHAT ARE YOU LOOKING AT?

84

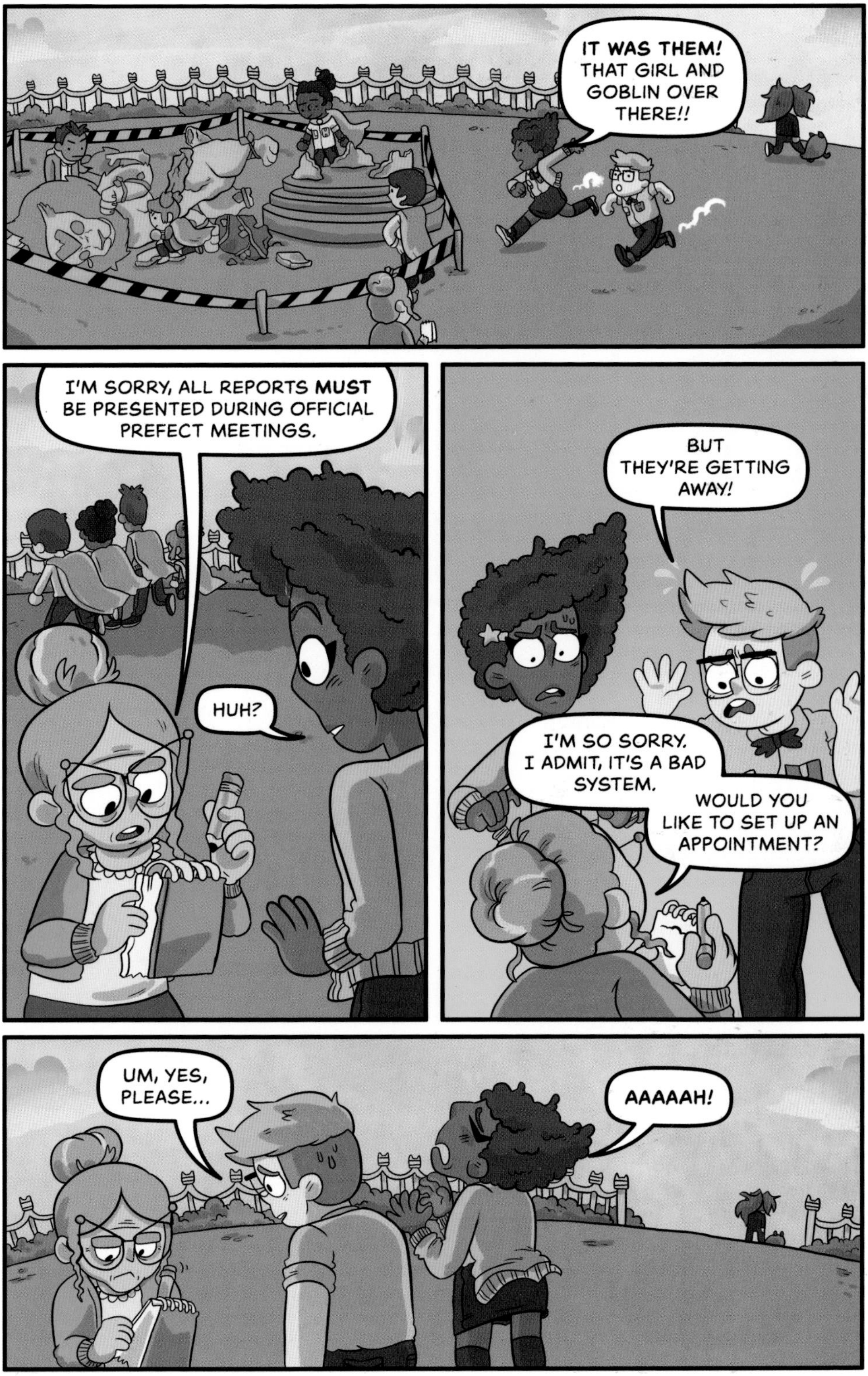
IT WAS THEM! THAT GIRL AND GOBLIN OVER THERE!!
I'M SORRY, ALL REPORTS MUST BE PRESENTED DURING OFFICIAL PREFECT MEETINGS.
HUH?
BUT THEY'RE GETTING AWAY!
I'M SO SORRY. I ADMIT, IT'S A BAD SYSTEM.
WOULD YOU LIKE TO SET UP AN APPOINTMENT?
UM, YES, PLEASE...
AAAAAH!

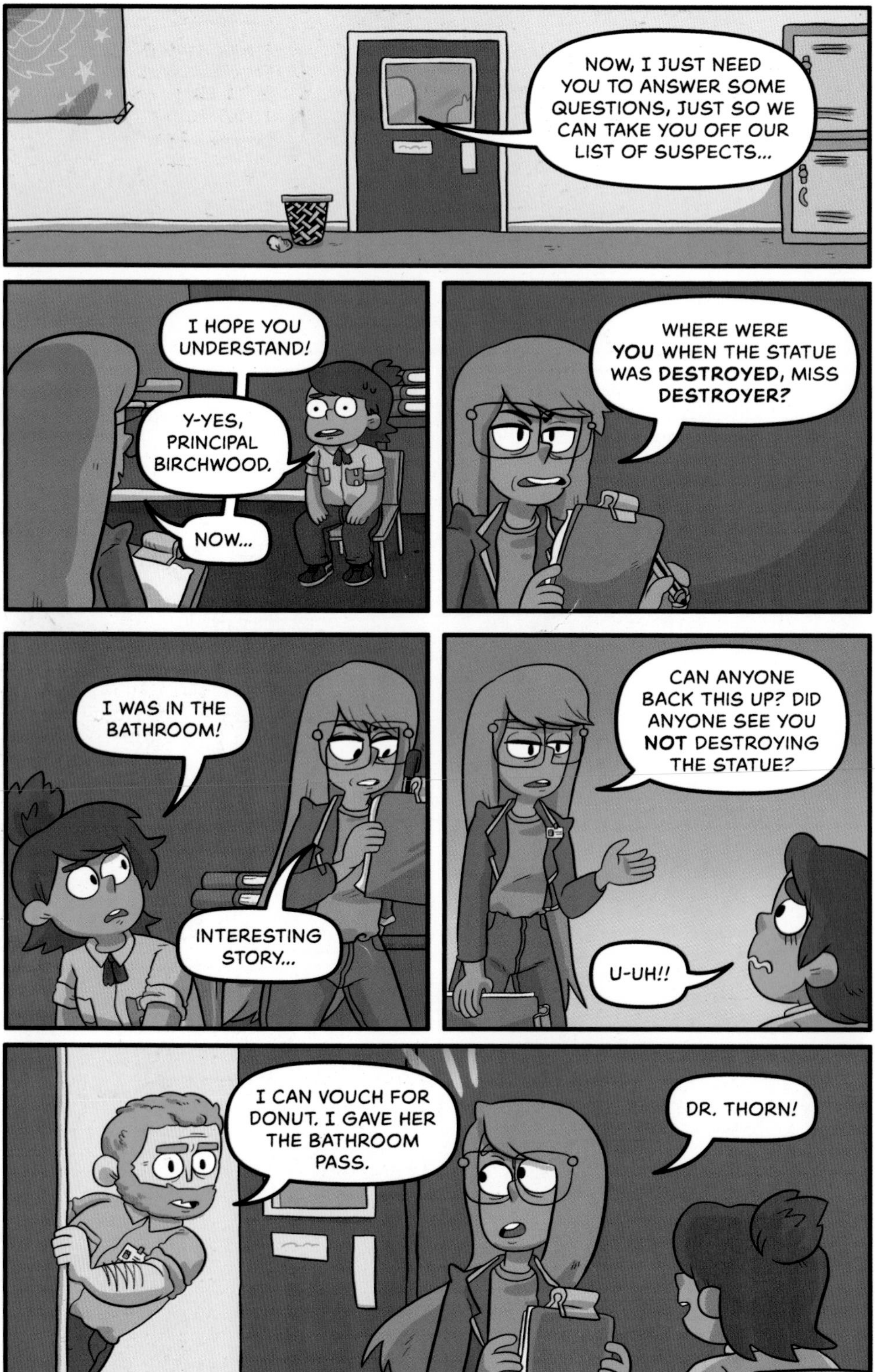
NOW, I JUST NEED YOU TO ANSWER SOME QUESTIONS, JUST SO WE CAN TAKE YOU OFF OUR LIST OF SUSPECTS...
I HOPE YOU UNDERSTAND!
Y-YES, PRINCIPAL BIRCHWOOD.
NOW...
WHERE WERE YOU WHEN THE STATUE WAS DESTROYED, MISS DESTROYER?
I WAS IN THE BATHROOM!
INTERESTING STORY...
CAN ANYONE BACK THIS UP? DID ANYONE SEE YOU NOT DESTROYING THE STATUE?
U-UH!!
I CAN VOUCH FOR DONUT. I GAVE HER THE BATHROOM PASS.
DR. THORN!

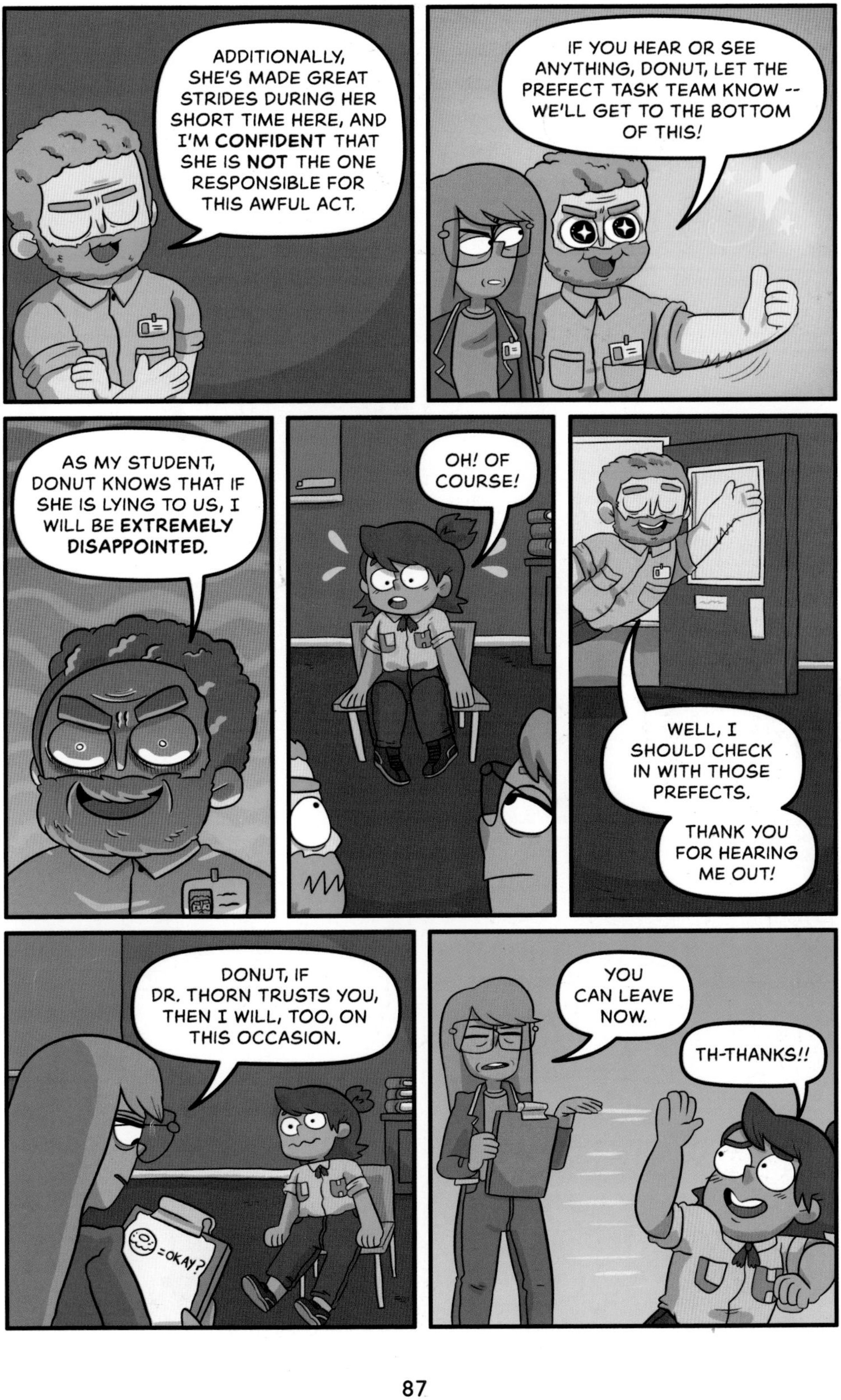

ADDITIONALLY, SHE'S MADE GREAT STRIDES DURING HER SHORT TIME HERE, AND I'M **CONFIDENT** THAT SHE IS **NOT** THE ONE RESPONSIBLE FOR THIS AWFUL ACT.
IF YOU HEAR OR SEE ANYTHING, DONUT, LET THE PREFECT TASK TEAM KNOW -- WE'LL GET TO THE BOTTOM OF THIS!
AS MY STUDENT, DONUT KNOWS THAT IF SHE IS LYING TO US, I WILL BE **EXTREMELY DISAPPOINTED.**
OH! OF COURSE!
WELL, I SHOULD CHECK IN WITH THOSE PREFECTS.
THANK YOU FOR HEARING ME OUT!
DONUT, IF DR. THORN TRUSTS YOU, THEN I WILL, TOO, ON THIS OCCASION.
=OKAY?
YOU CAN LEAVE NOW.
TH-THANKS!!

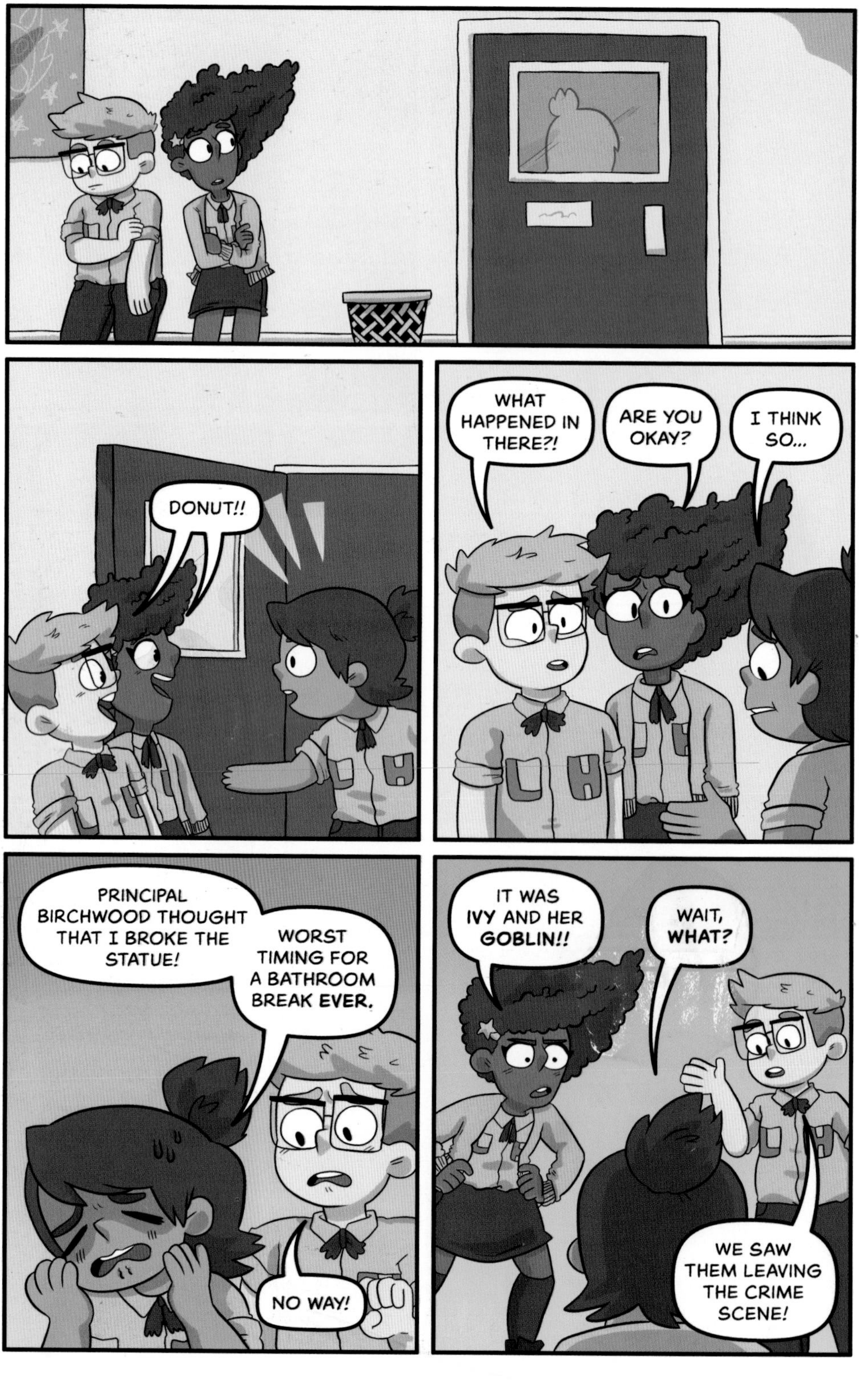
DONUT!!
WHAT HAPPENED IN THERE?!
ARE YOU OKAY?
I THINK SO...
PRINCIPAL BIRCHWOOD THOUGHT THAT I BROKE THE STATUE!
WORST TIMING FOR A BATHROOM BREAK **EVER.**
NO WAY!
IT WAS IVY AND HER **GOBLIN!!**
WAIT, **WHAT?**
WE SAW THEM LEAVING THE CRIME SCENE!

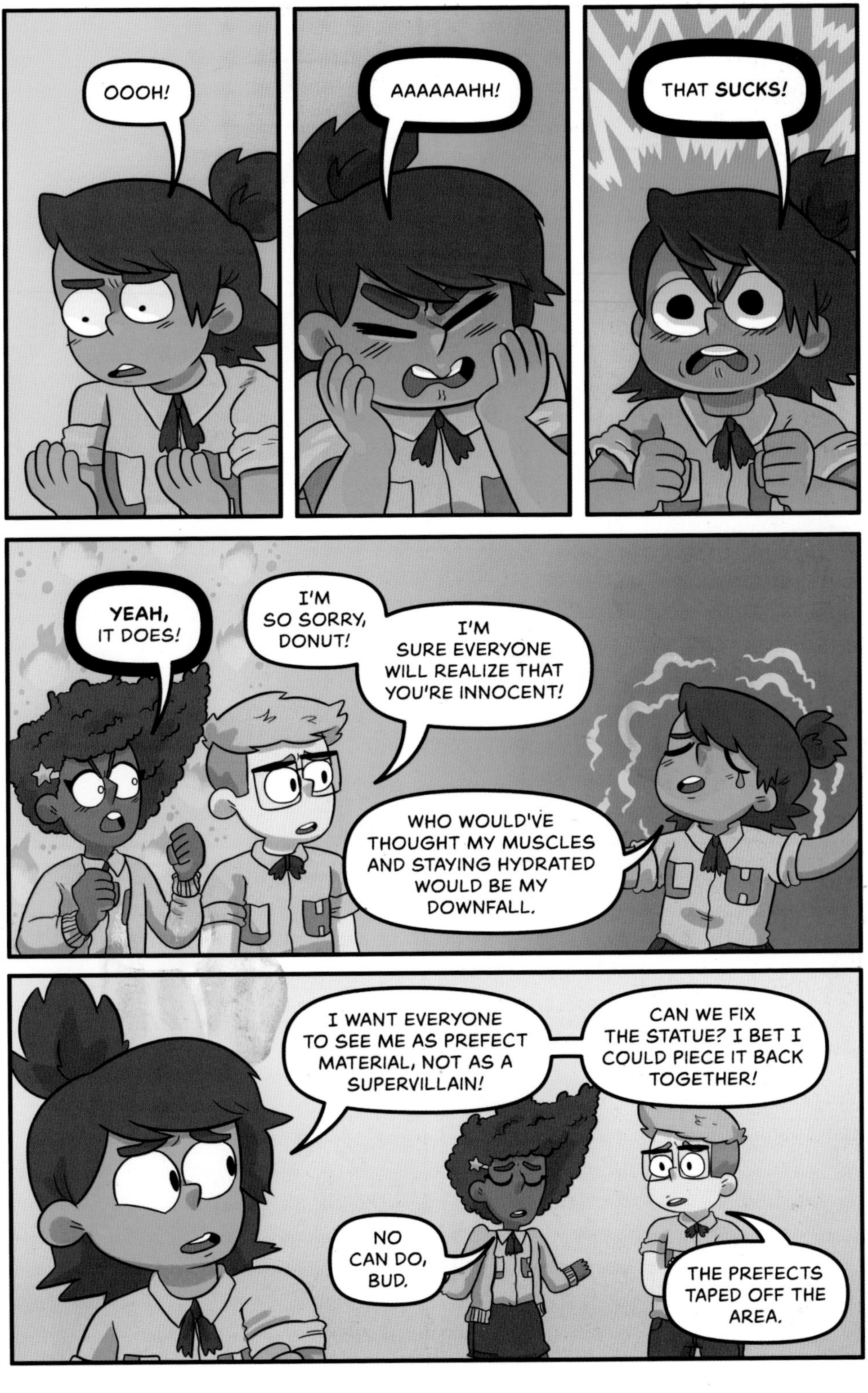
OOOH!
AAAAAAHH!
THAT SUCKS!
YEAH, IT DOES!
I'M SO SORRY, DONUT!
I'M SURE EVERYONE WILL REALIZE THAT YOU'RE INNOCENT!
WHO WOULD'VE THOUGHT MY MUSCLES AND STAYING HYDRATED WOULD BE MY DOWNFALL.
I WANT EVERYONE TO SEE ME AS PREFECT MATERIAL, NOT AS A SUPERVILLAIN!
CAN WE FIX THE STATUE? I BET I COULD PIECE IT BACK TOGETHER!
NO CAN DO, BUD.
THE PREFECTS TAPED OFF THE AREA.

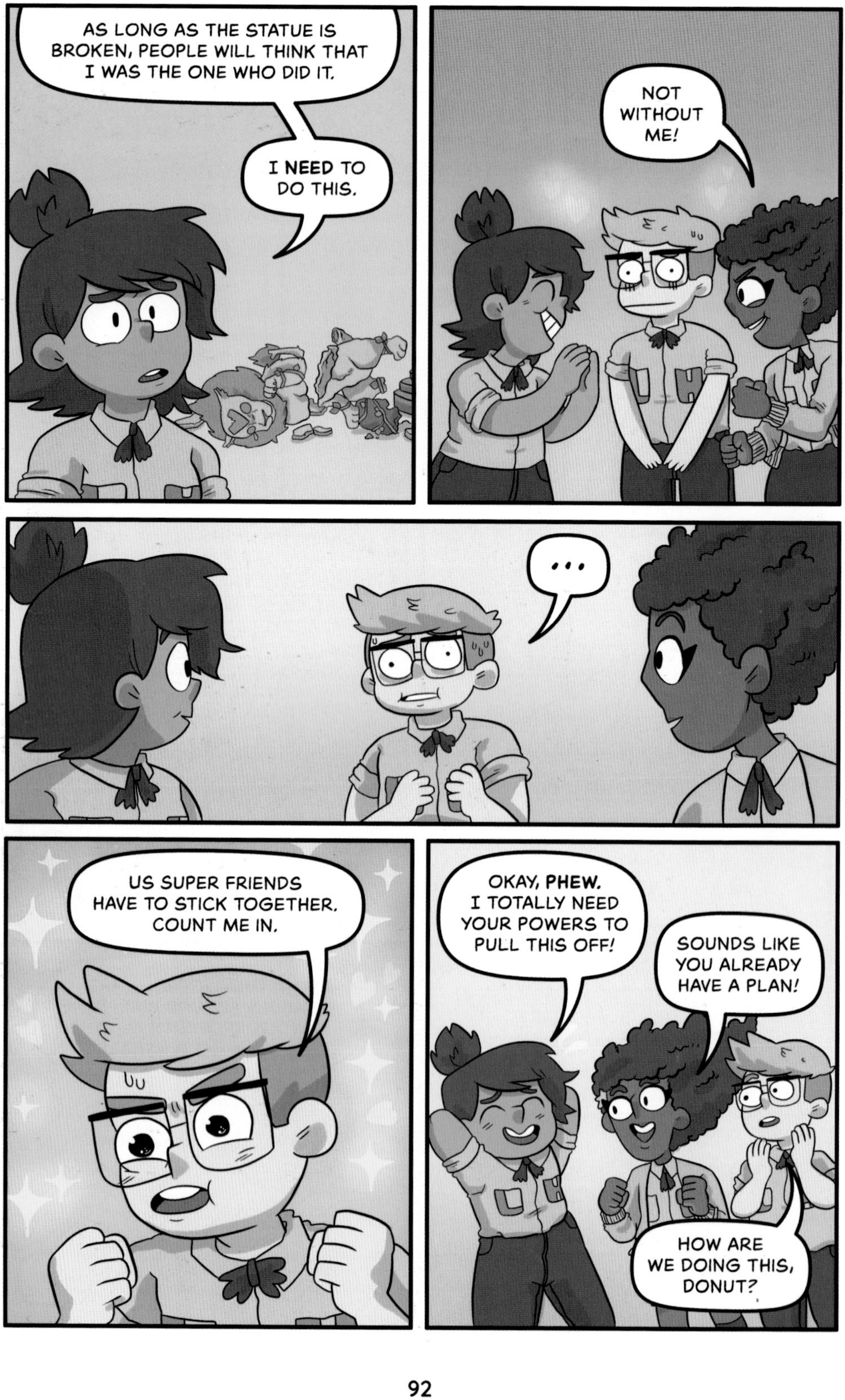
AS LONG AS THE STATUE IS BROKEN, PEOPLE WILL THINK THAT I WAS THE ONE WHO DID IT.
I NEED TO DO THIS.
NOT WITHOUT ME!
...
US SUPER FRIENDS HAVE TO STICK TOGETHER. COUNT ME IN.
OKAY, PHEW. I TOTALLY NEED YOUR POWERS TO PULL THIS OFF!
SOUNDS LIKE YOU ALREADY HAVE A PLAN!
HOW ARE WE DOING THIS, DONUT?

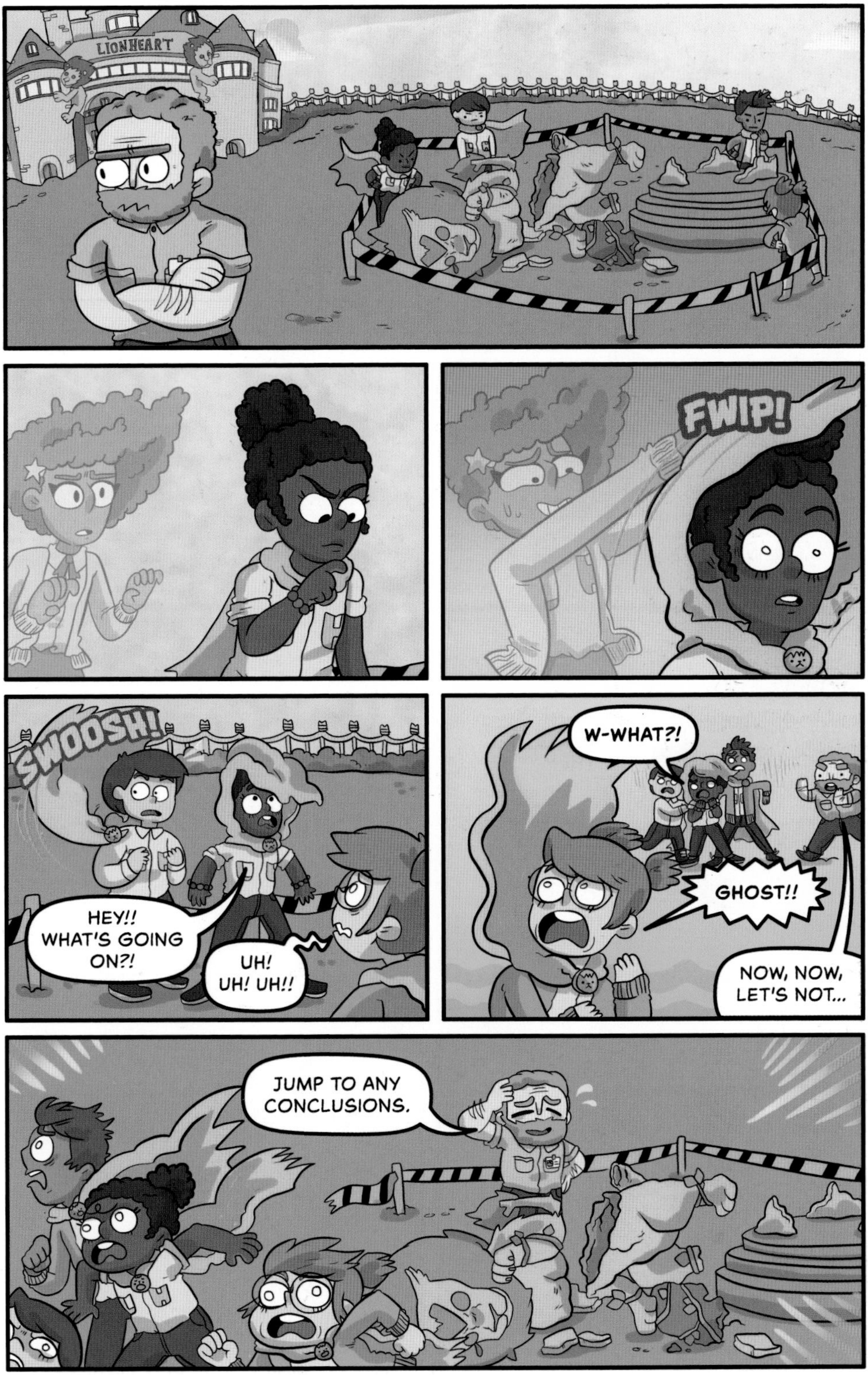
LIONHEART
FWIP!
SWOOSH!
HEY!! WHAT'S GOING ON?!
UH! UH! UH!!
W-WHAT?!
GHOST!!
NOW, NOW, LET'S NOT...
JUMP TO ANY CONCLUSIONS.

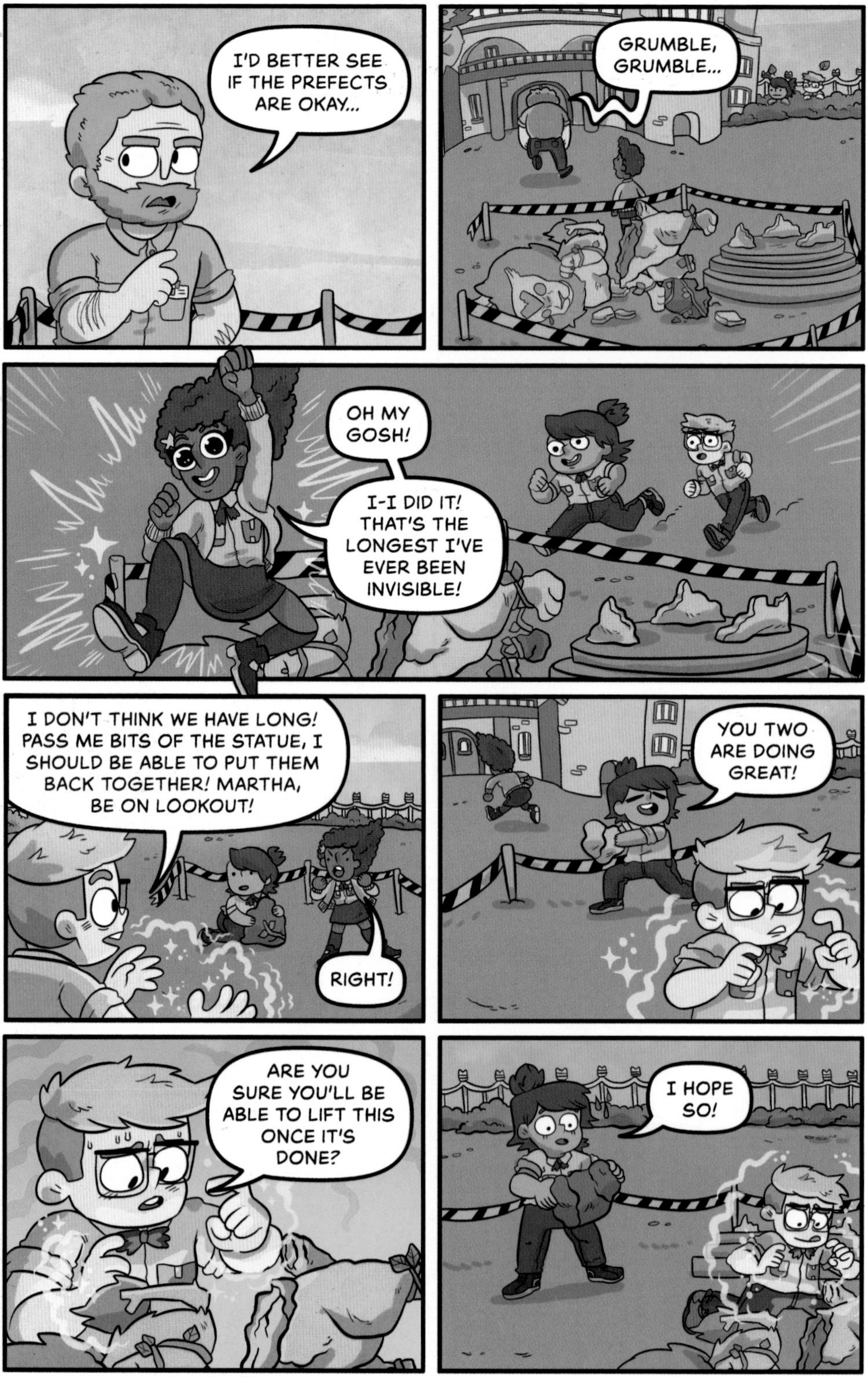
I'D BETTER SEE IF THE PREFECTS ARE OKAY...
GRUMBLE, GRUMBLE...
OH MY GOSH!
I-I DID IT! THAT'S THE LONGEST I'VE EVER BEEN INVISIBLE!
I DON'T THINK WE HAVE LONG! PASS ME BITS OF THE STATUE, I SHOULD BE ABLE TO PUT THEM BACK TOGETHER! MARTHA, BE ON LOOKOUT!
RIGHT!
YOU TWO ARE DOING GREAT!
ARE YOU SURE YOU'LL BE ABLE TO LIFT THIS ONCE IT'S DONE?
I HOPE SO!

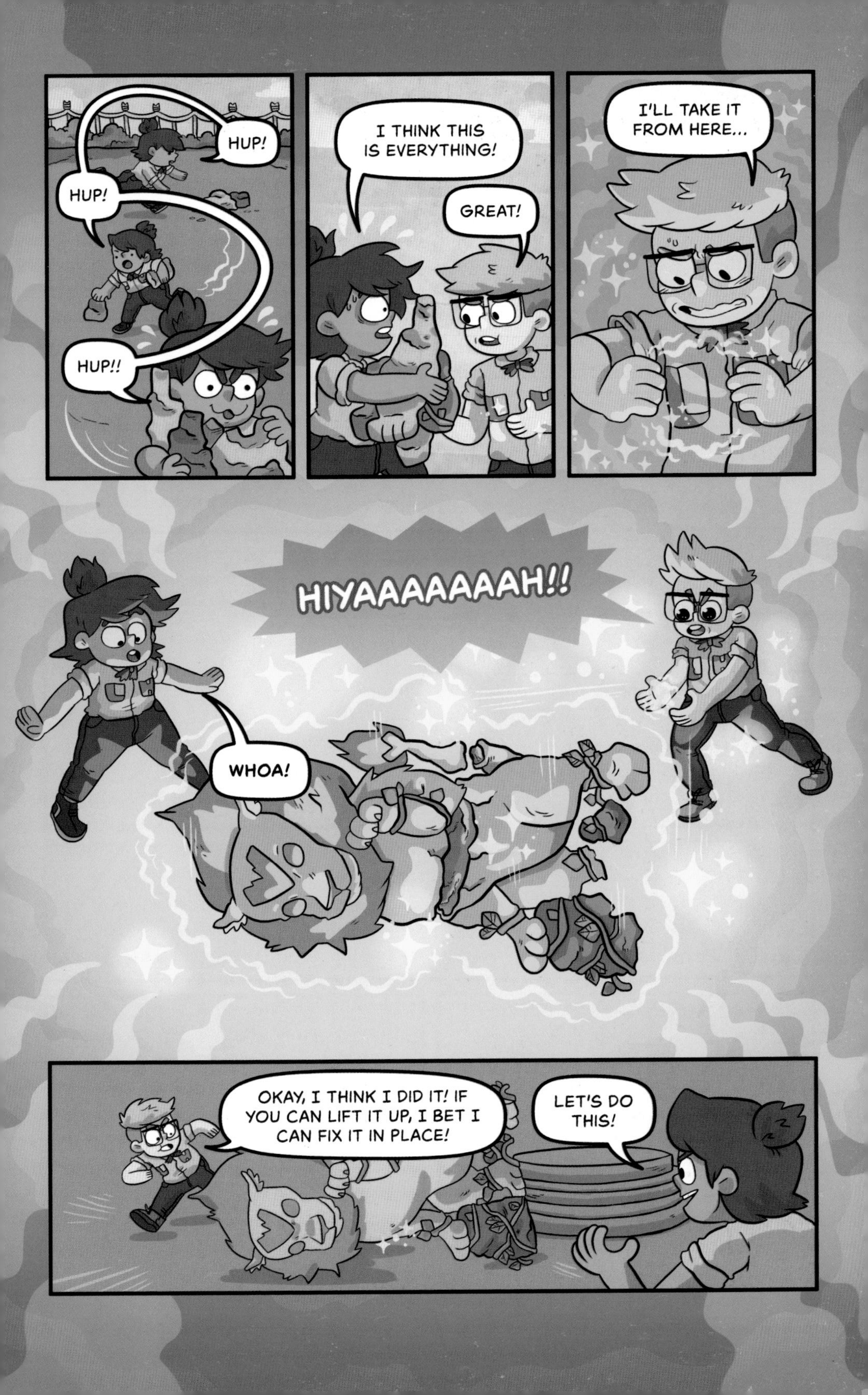
HUP!
HUP!
HUP!!
I THINK THIS IS EVERYTHING!
GREAT!
I'LL TAKE IT FROM HERE...
HIYAAAAAAAH!!
WHOA!
OKAY, I THINK I DID IT! IF YOU CAN LIFT IT UP, I BET I CAN FIX IT IN PLACE!
LET'S DO THIS!

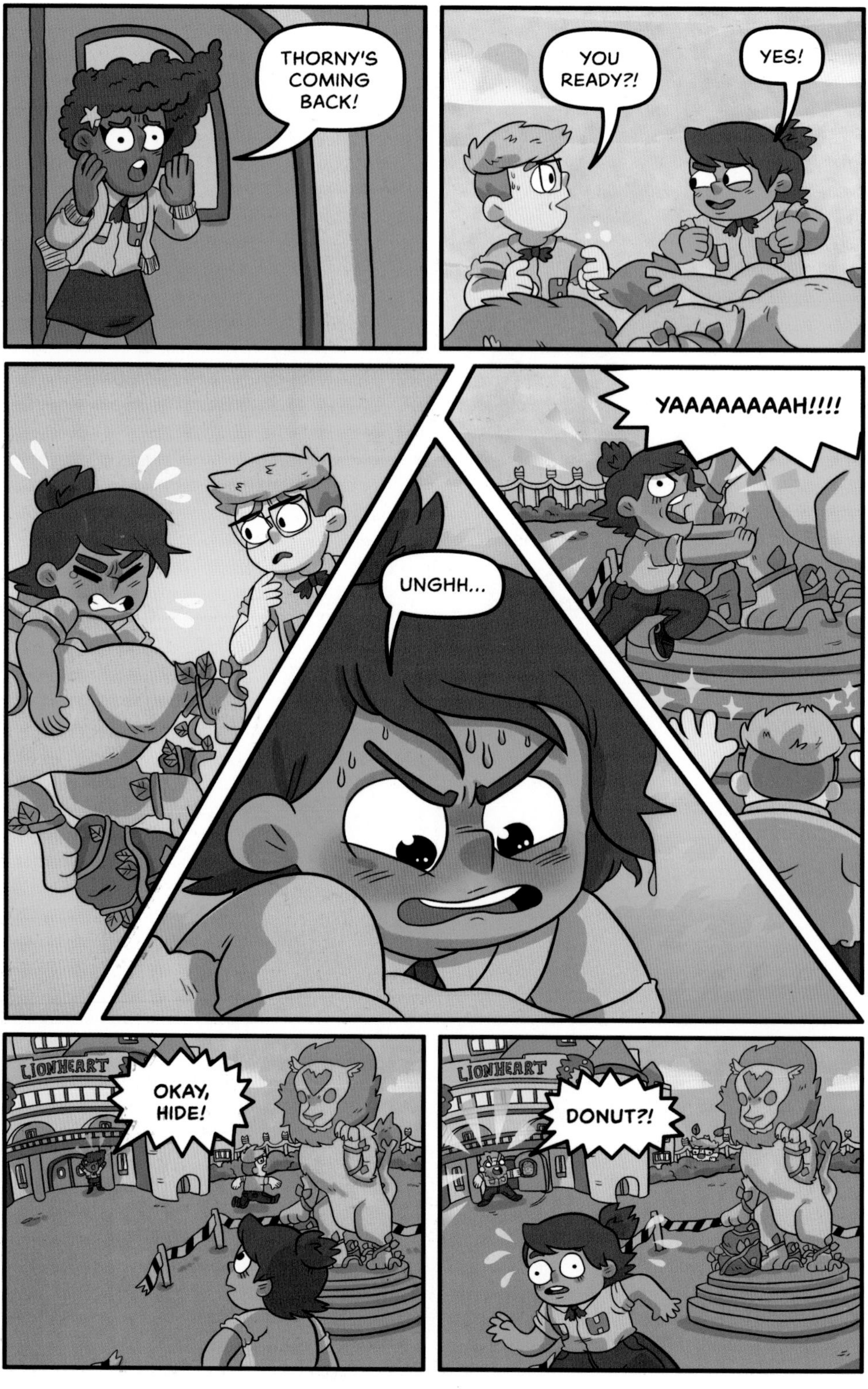
THORNY'S COMING BACK!
YOU READY?!
YES!
UNGHH...
YAAAAAAAAH!!!!
LIONHEART
OKAY, HIDE!
LIONHEART
DONUT?!

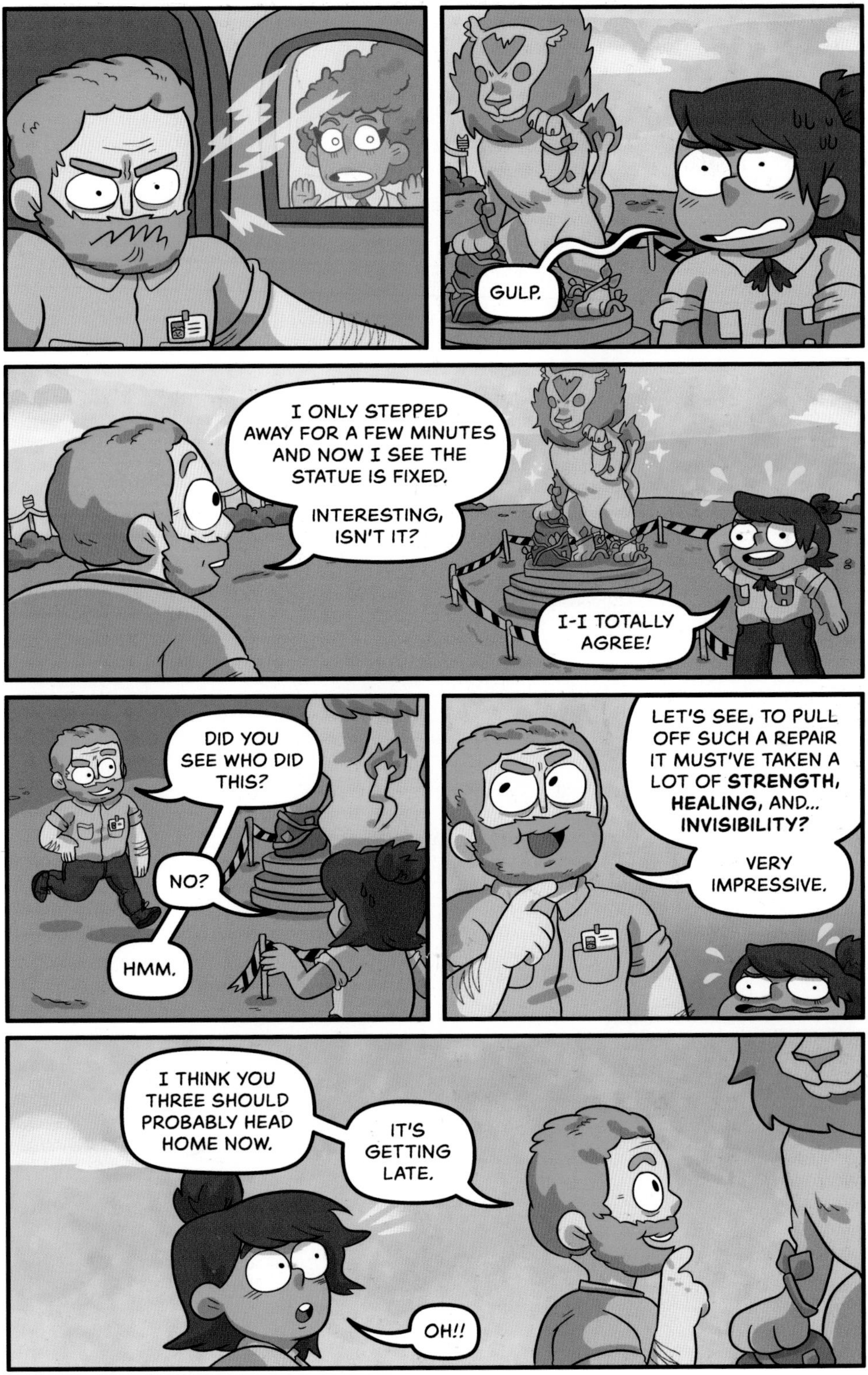
GULP.
I ONLY STEPPED AWAY FOR A FEW MINUTES AND NOW I SEE THE STATUE IS FIXED.
INTERESTING, ISN'T IT?
I-I TOTALLY AGREE!
DID YOU SEE WHO DID THIS?
NO?
HMM.
LET'S SEE, TO PULL OFF SUCH A REPAIR IT MUST'VE TAKEN A LOT OF **STRENGTH, HEALING,** AND... **INVISIBILITY?**
VERY IMPRESSIVE.
I THINK YOU THREE SHOULD PROBABLY HEAD HOME NOW.
IT'S GETTING LATE.
OH!!

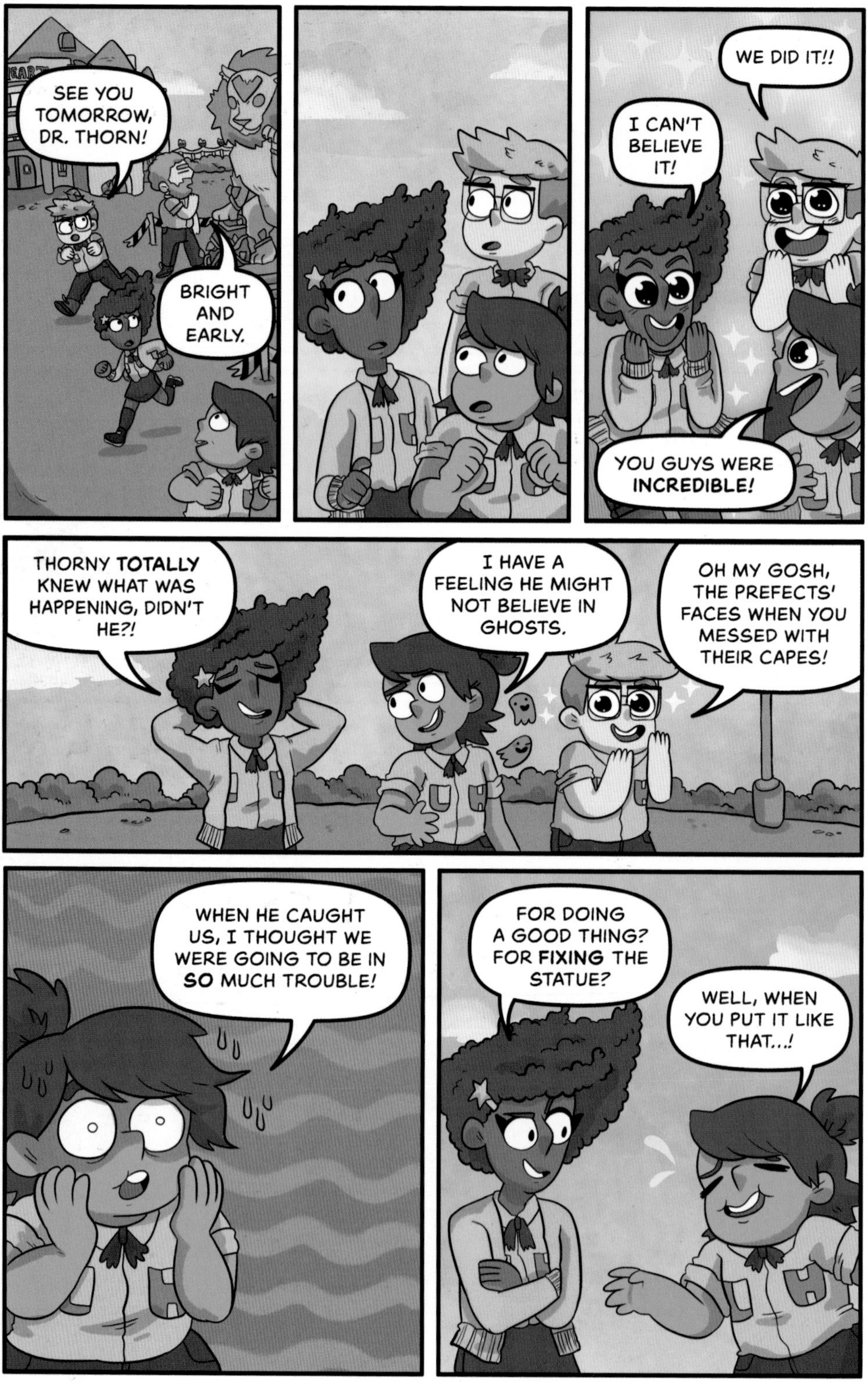
SEE YOU TOMORROW, DR. THORN!
BRIGHT AND EARLY.
WE DID IT!!
I CAN'T BELIEVE IT!
YOU GUYS WERE **INCREDIBLE!**
THORNY **TOTALLY** KNEW WHAT WAS HAPPENING, DIDN'T HE?!
I HAVE A FEELING HE MIGHT NOT BELIEVE IN GHOSTS.
OH MY GOSH, THE PREFECTS' FACES WHEN YOU MESSED WITH THEIR CAPES!
WHEN HE CAUGHT US, I THOUGHT WE WERE GOING TO BE IN **SO** MUCH TROUBLE!
FOR DOING A GOOD THING? FOR **FIXING** THE STATUE?
WELL, WHEN YOU PUT IT LIKE THAT...!

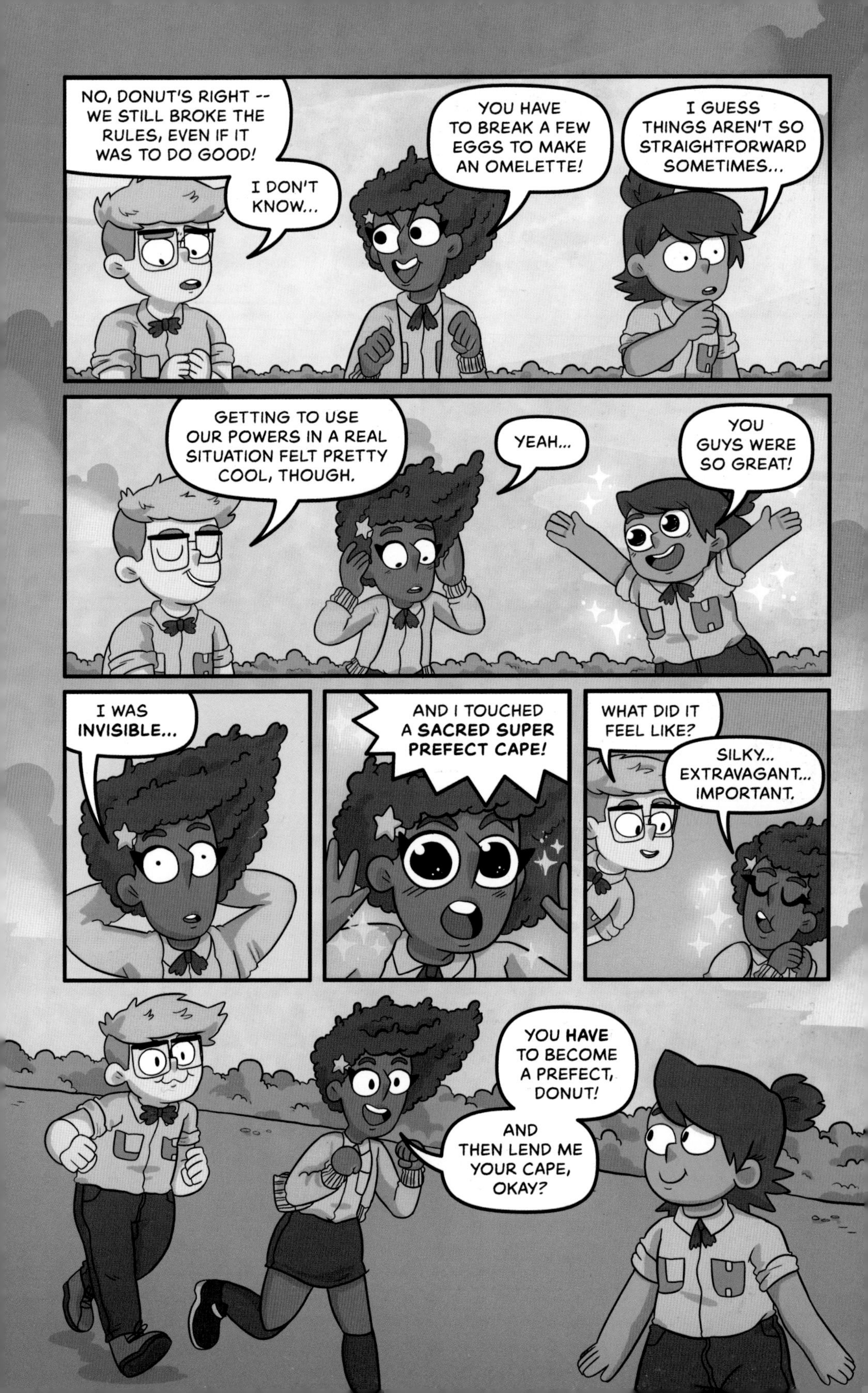
NO, DONUT'S RIGHT -- WE STILL BROKE THE RULES, EVEN IF IT WAS TO DO GOOD!
I DON'T KNOW...
YOU HAVE TO BREAK A FEW EGGS TO MAKE AN OMELETTE!
I GUESS THINGS AREN'T SO STRAIGHTFORWARD SOMETIMES...
GETTING TO USE OUR POWERS IN A REAL SITUATION FELT PRETTY COOL, THOUGH.
YEAH...
YOU GUYS WERE SO GREAT!
I WAS **INVISIBLE**...
AND I TOUCHED A **SACRED SUPER PREFECT CAPE!**
WHAT DID IT FEEL LIKE?
SILKY... EXTRAVAGANT... IMPORTANT.
YOU **HAVE** TO BECOME A PREFECT, DONUT!
AND THEN LEND ME YOUR CAPE, OKAY?

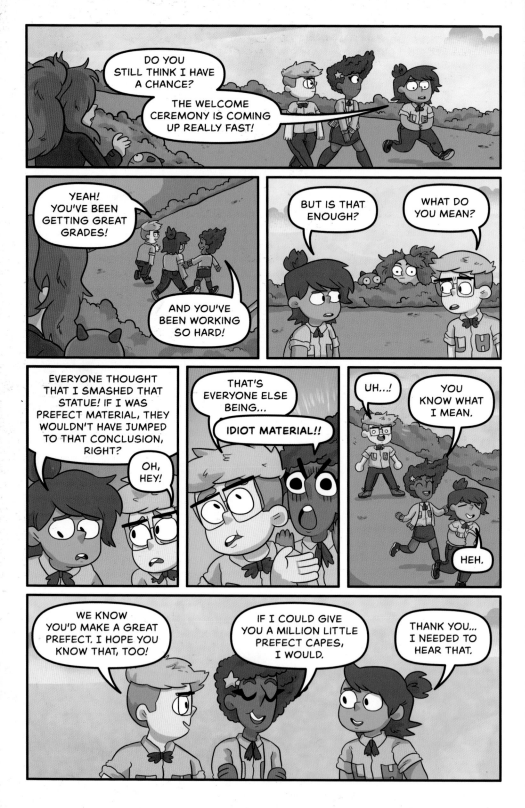

100

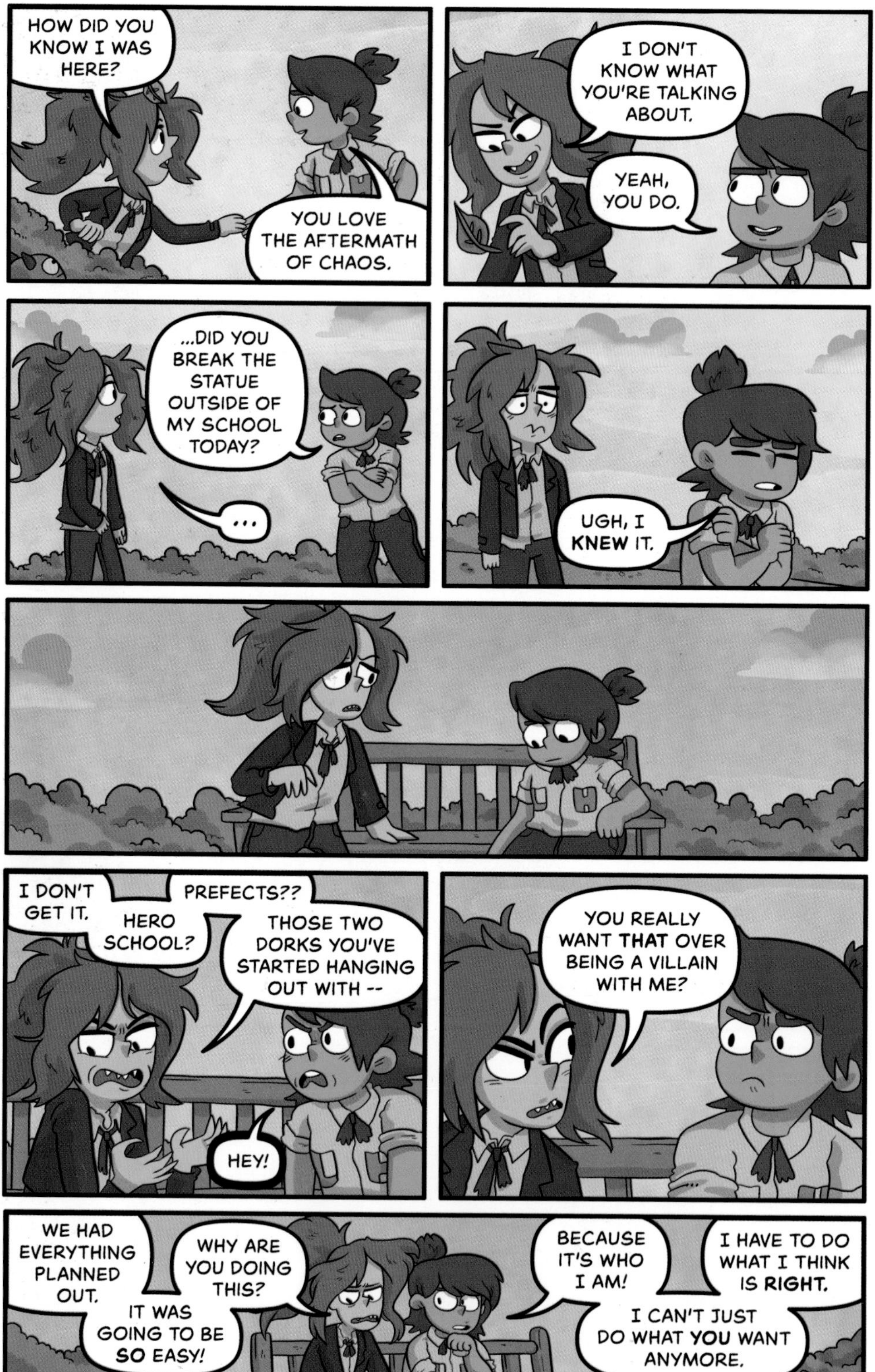
HOW DID YOU KNOW I WAS HERE?
YOU LOVE THE AFTERMATH OF CHAOS.
I DON'T KNOW WHAT YOU'RE TALKING ABOUT.
YEAH, YOU DO.
...DID YOU BREAK THE STATUE OUTSIDE OF MY SCHOOL TODAY?
...
UGH, I **KNEW** IT.
I DON'T GET IT.
HERO SCHOOL?
PREFECTS??
THOSE TWO DORKS YOU'VE STARTED HANGING OUT WITH --
HEY!
YOU REALLY WANT **THAT** OVER BEING A VILLAIN WITH ME?
WE HAD EVERYTHING PLANNED OUT.
IT WAS GOING TO BE **SO** EASY!
WHY ARE YOU DOING THIS?
BECAUSE IT'S WHO I AM!
I HAVE TO DO WHAT I THINK IS **RIGHT.**
I CAN'T JUST DO WHAT **YOU** WANT ANYMORE.

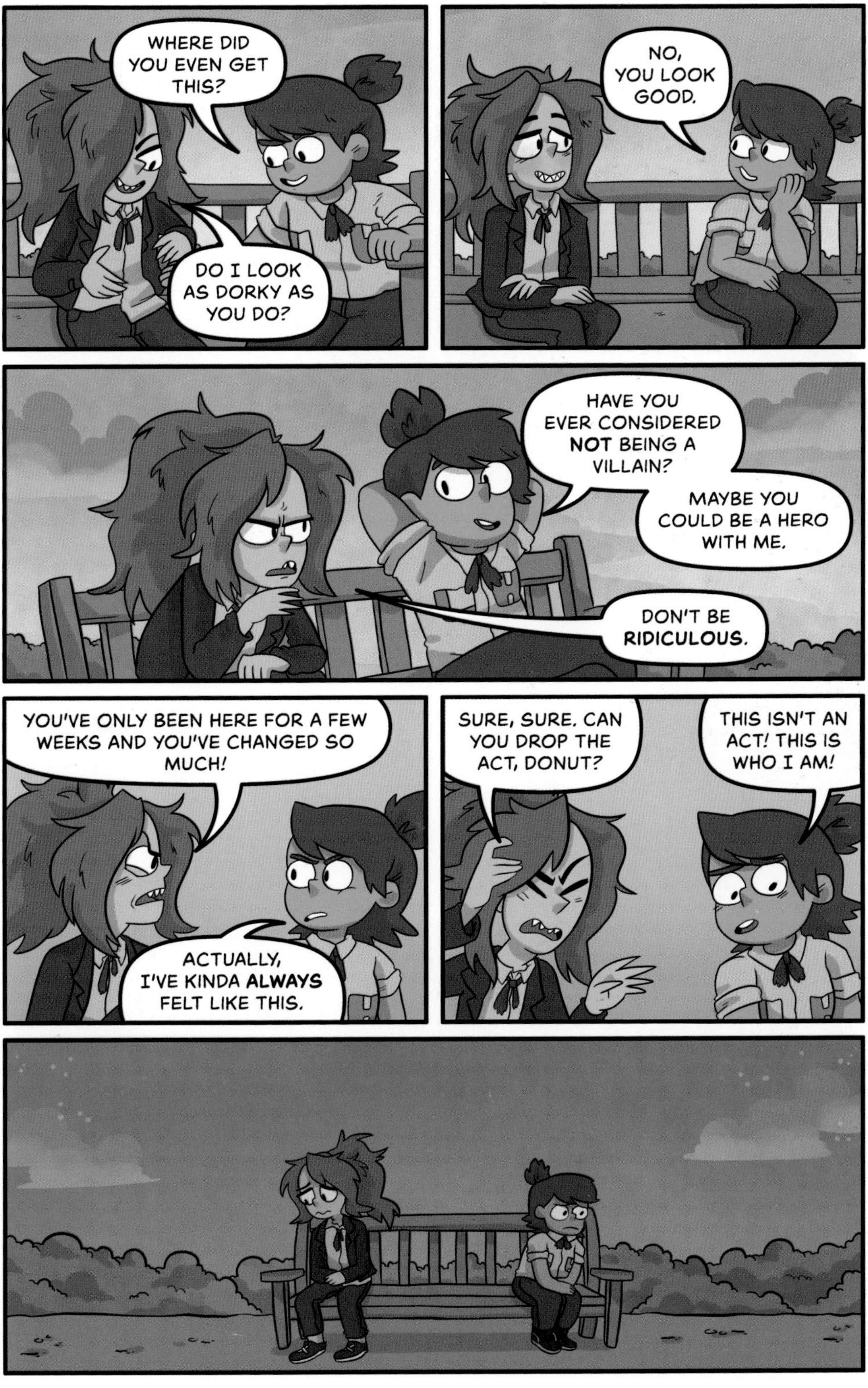
WHERE DID YOU EVEN GET THIS?
DO I LOOK AS DORKY AS YOU DO?
NO, YOU LOOK GOOD.
HAVE YOU EVER CONSIDERED **NOT** BEING A VILLAIN?
MAYBE YOU COULD BE A HERO WITH ME.
DON'T BE **RIDICULOUS.**
YOU'VE ONLY BEEN HERE FOR A FEW WEEKS AND YOU'VE CHANGED SO MUCH!
ACTUALLY, I'VE KINDA **ALWAYS** FELT LIKE THIS.
SURE, SURE. CAN YOU DROP THE ACT, DONUT?
THIS ISN'T AN ACT! THIS IS WHO I AM!

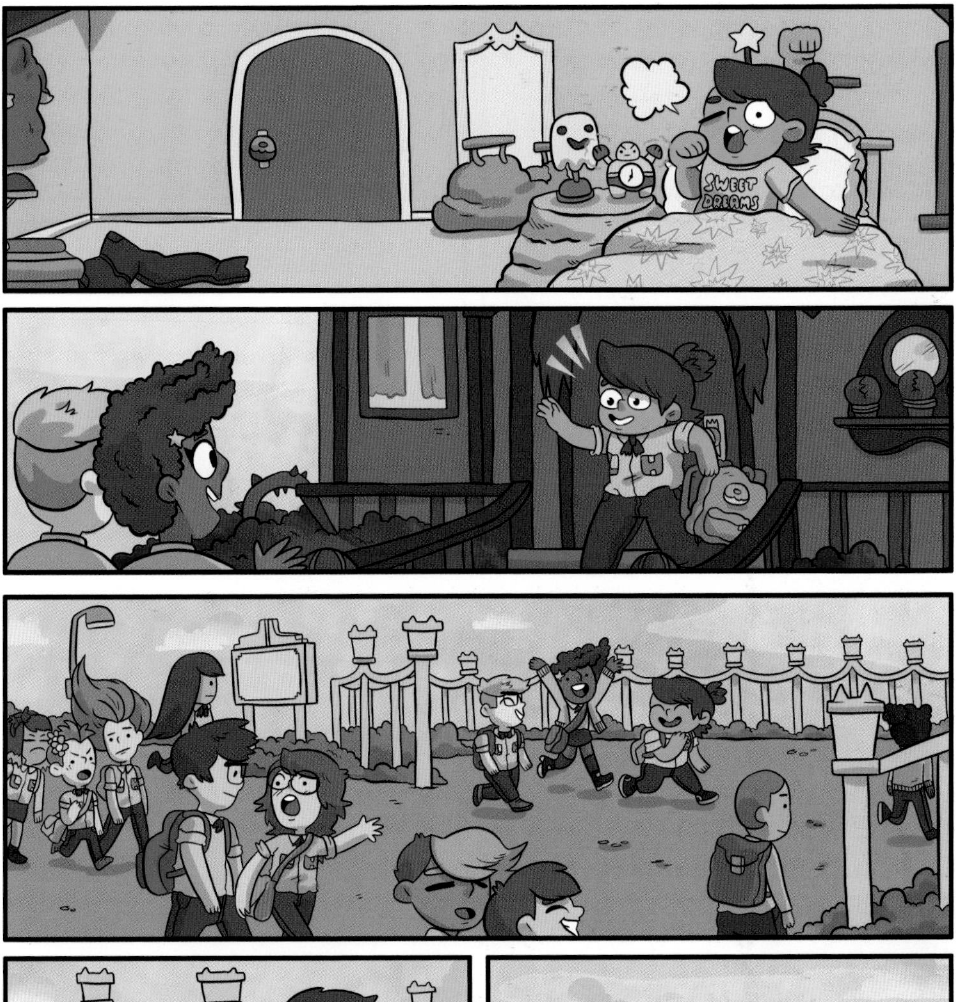
SWEET DREAMS

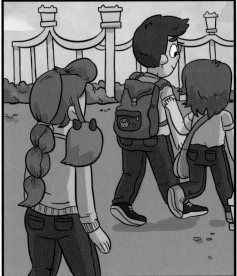

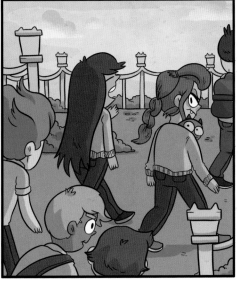

112

116

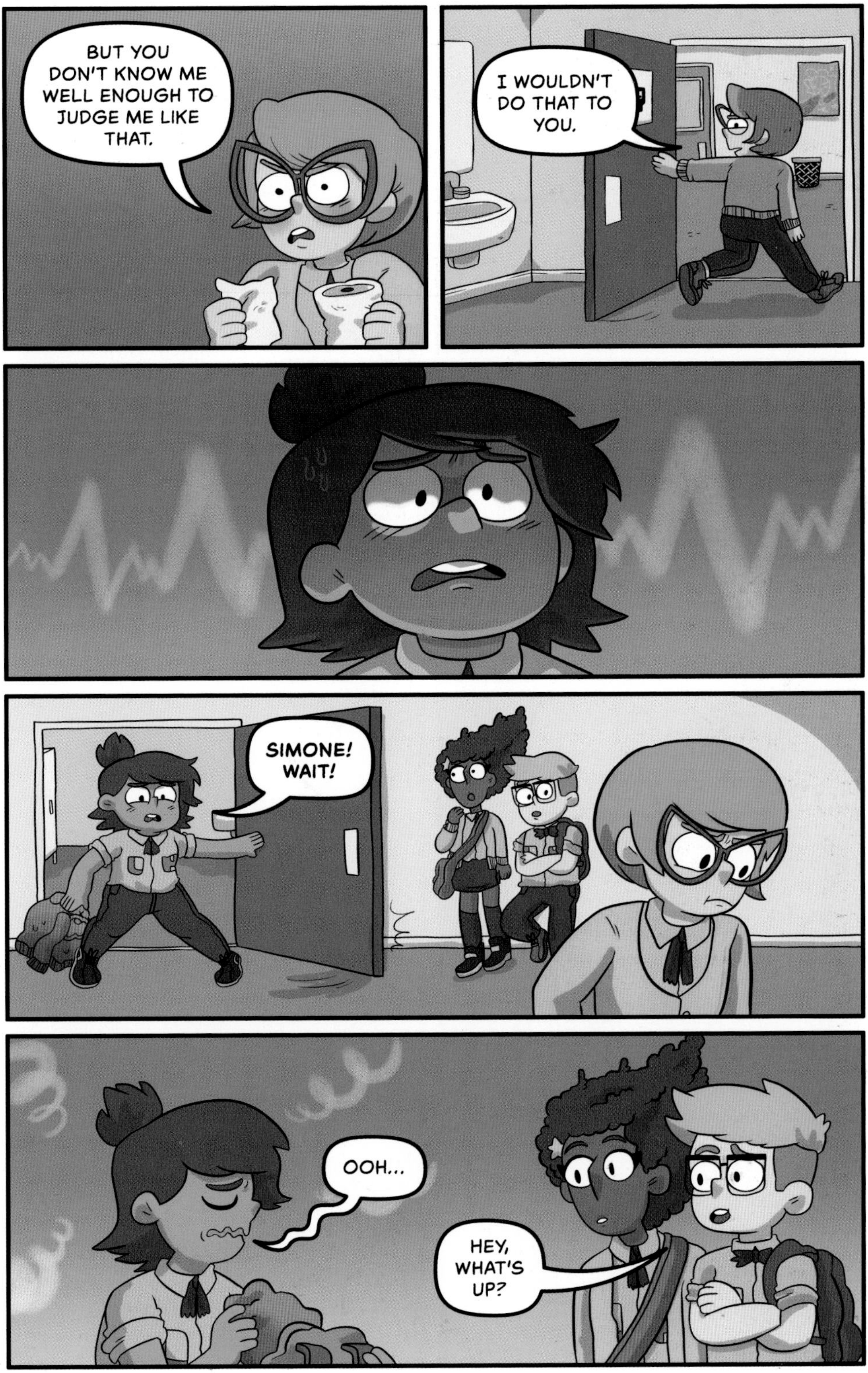
BUT YOU DON'T KNOW ME WELL ENOUGH TO JUDGE ME LIKE THAT.
I WOULDN'T DO THAT TO YOU.
SIMONE! WAIT!
OOH...
HEY, WHAT'S UP?

121

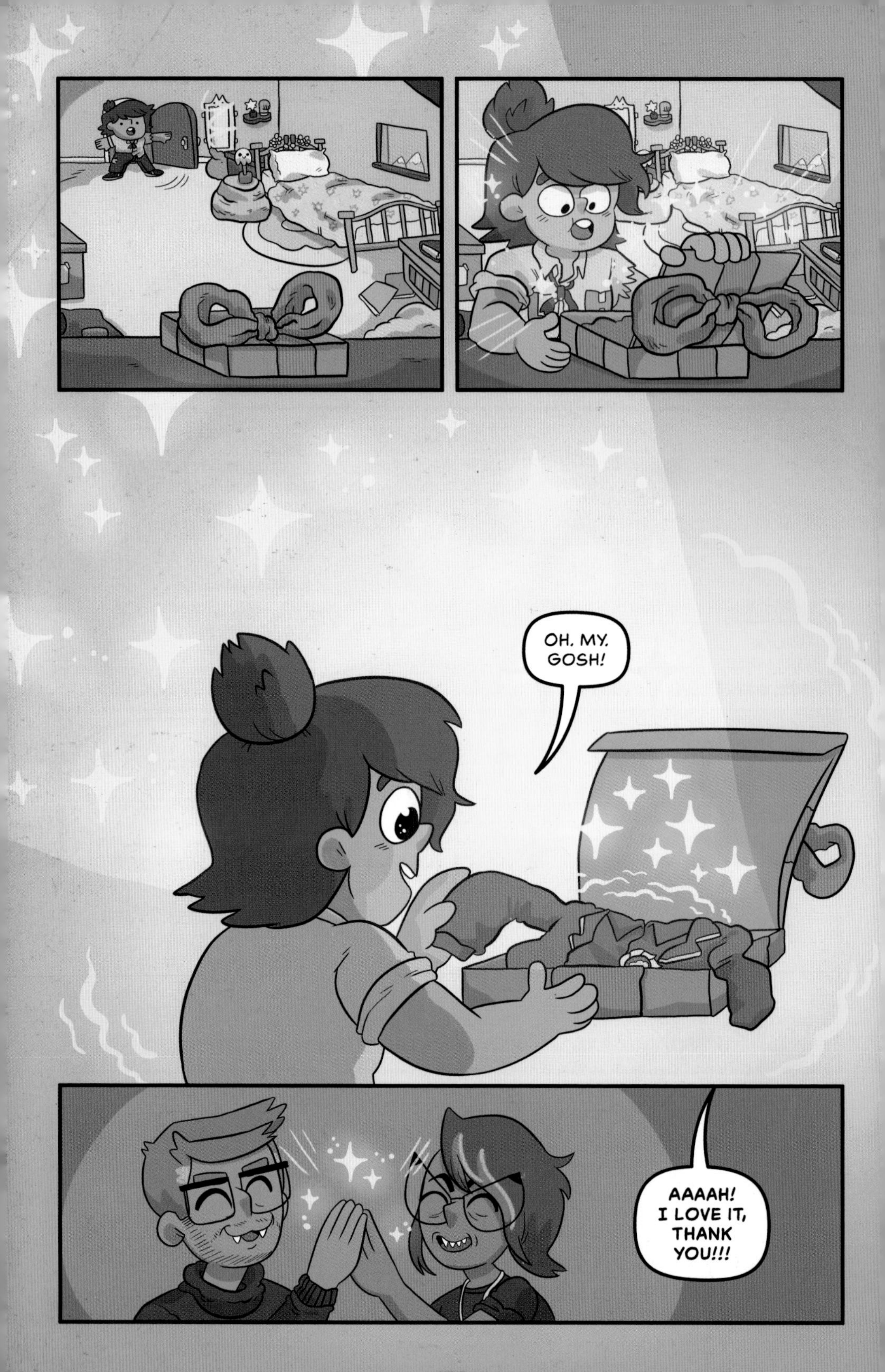
OH, MY, GOSH!
AAAAH! I LOVE IT, THANK YOU!!!

THE NIGHT OF THE WELCOME CEREMONY

135

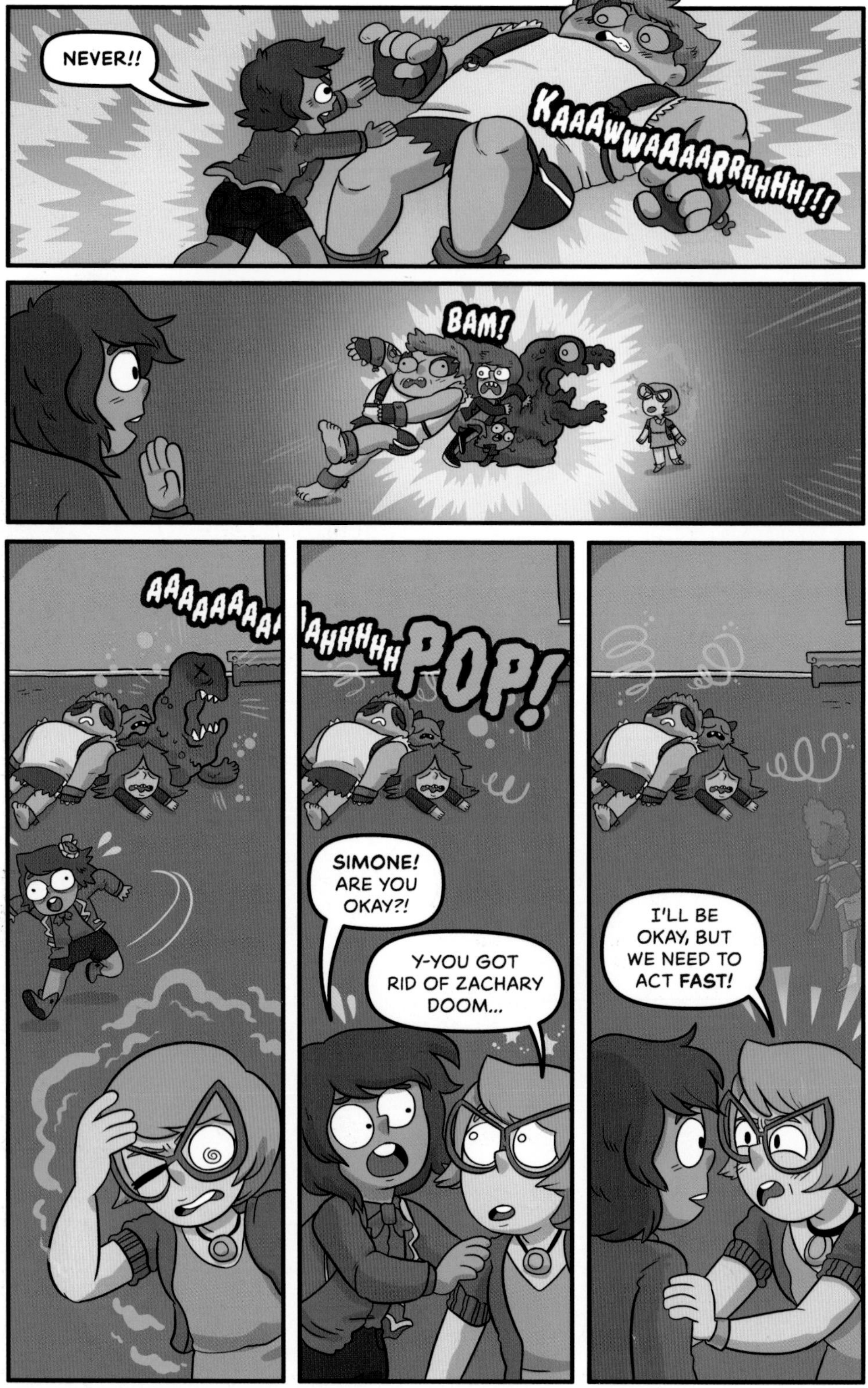
NEVER!!
KAAAWWAAAARRHHHH!!!
BAM!
AAAAAAAAAAHHHHHPOP!
SIMONE! ARE YOU OKAY?!
Y-YOU GOT RID OF ZACHARY DOOM...
I'LL BE OKAY, BUT WE NEED TO ACT FAST!

148

151

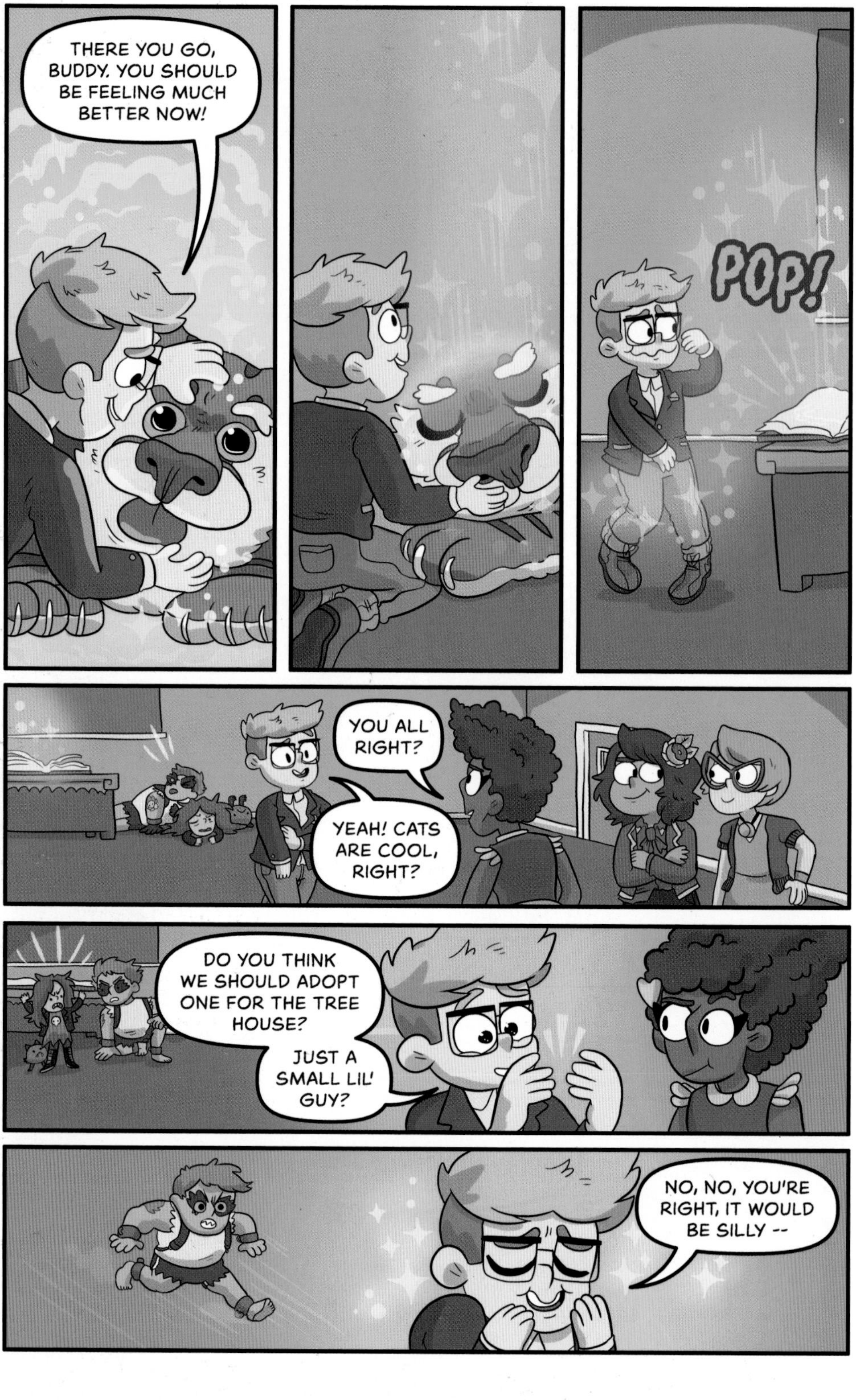
THERE YOU GO, BUDDY. YOU SHOULD BE FEELING MUCH BETTER NOW!
POP!
YOU ALL RIGHT?
YEAH! CATS ARE COOL, RIGHT?
DO YOU THINK WE SHOULD ADOPT ONE FOR THE TREE HOUSE?
JUST A SMALL LIL' GUY?
NO, NO, YOU'RE RIGHT, IT WOULD BE SILLY --

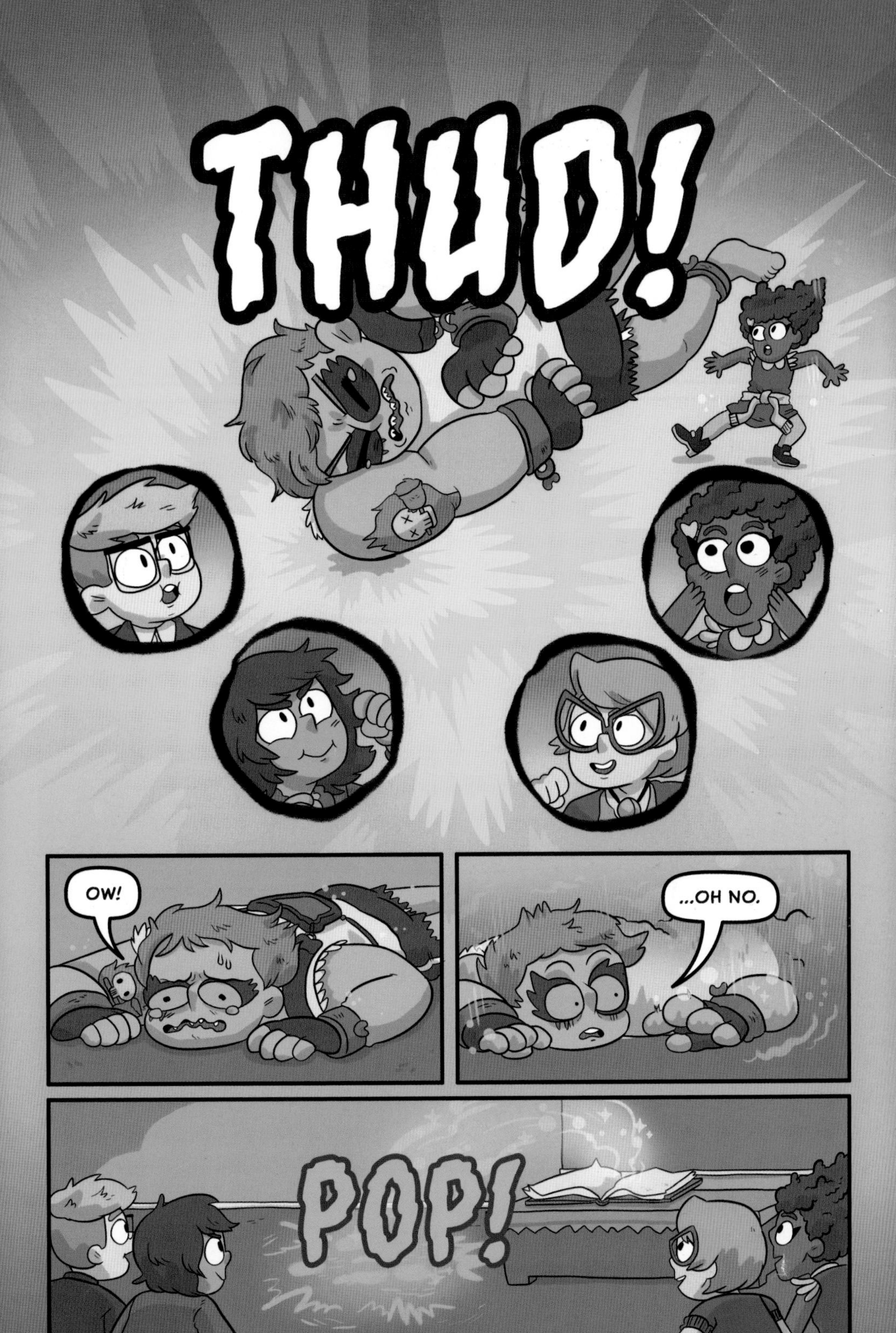
THUD!
OW!
...OH NO.
POP!

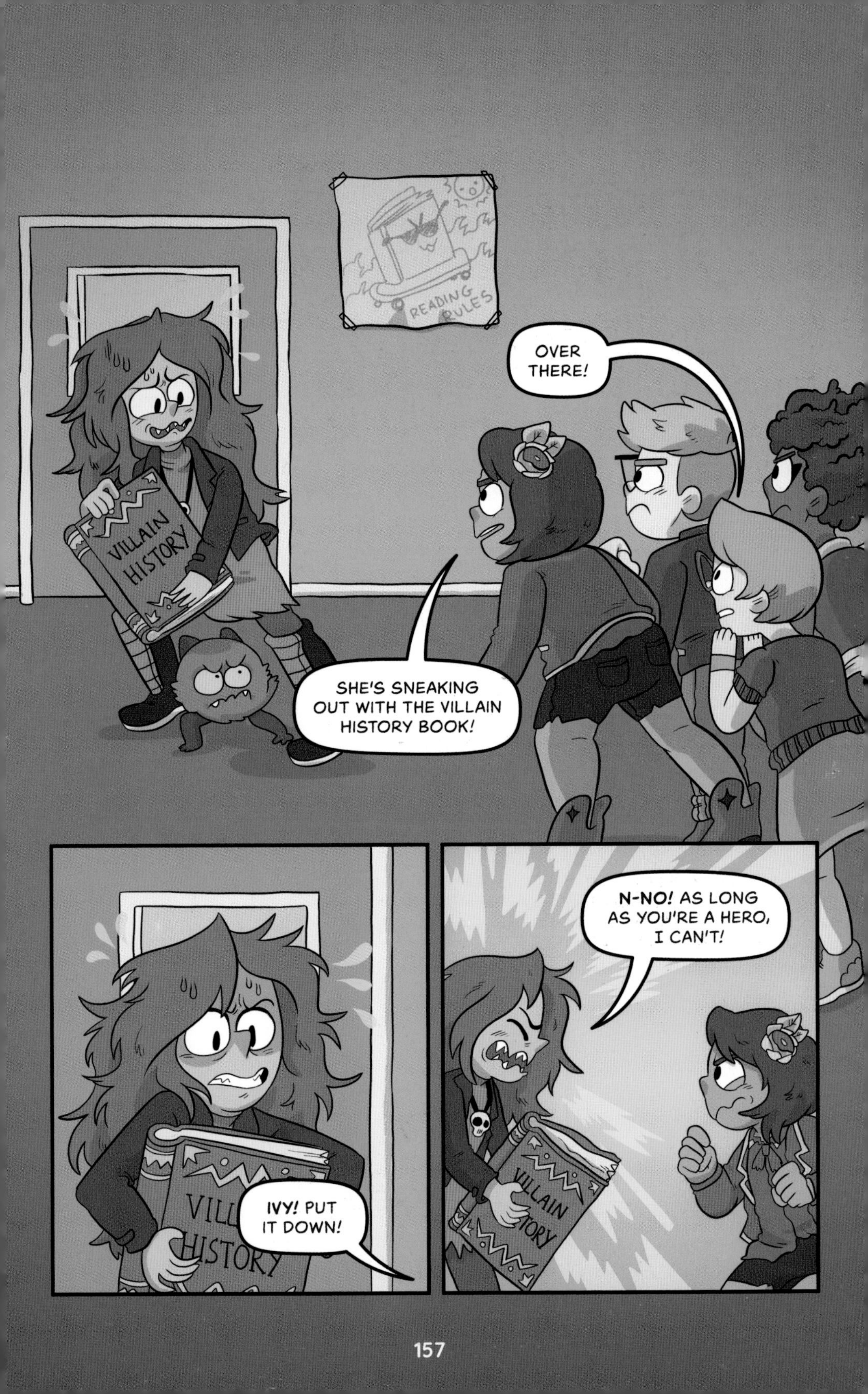
READING RULES
VILLAIN HISTORY
OVER THERE!
SHE'S SNEAKING OUT WITH THE VILLAIN HISTORY BOOK!
IVY! PUT IT DOWN!
N-NO! AS LONG AS YOU'RE A HERO, I CAN'T!

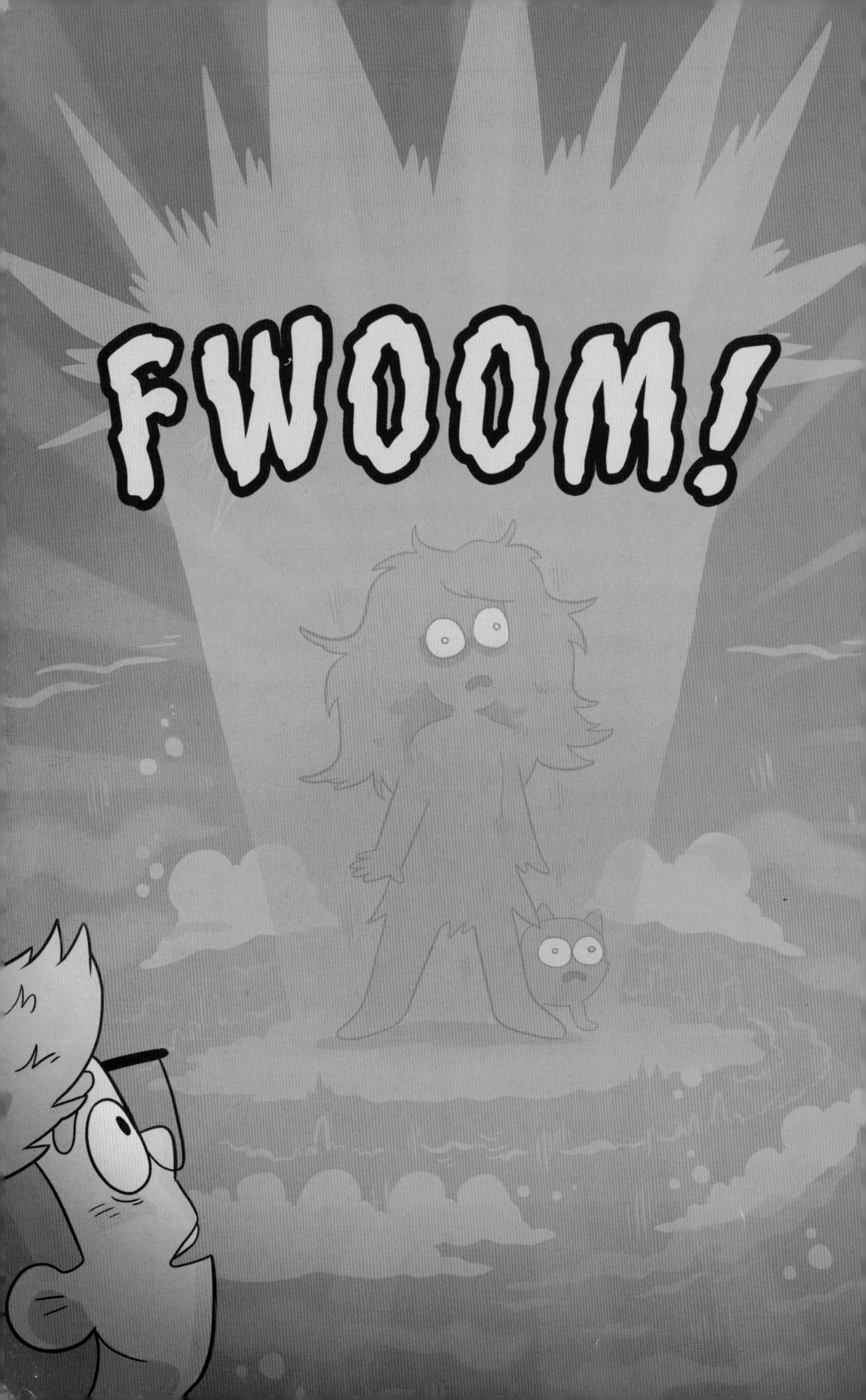
FWOOM!

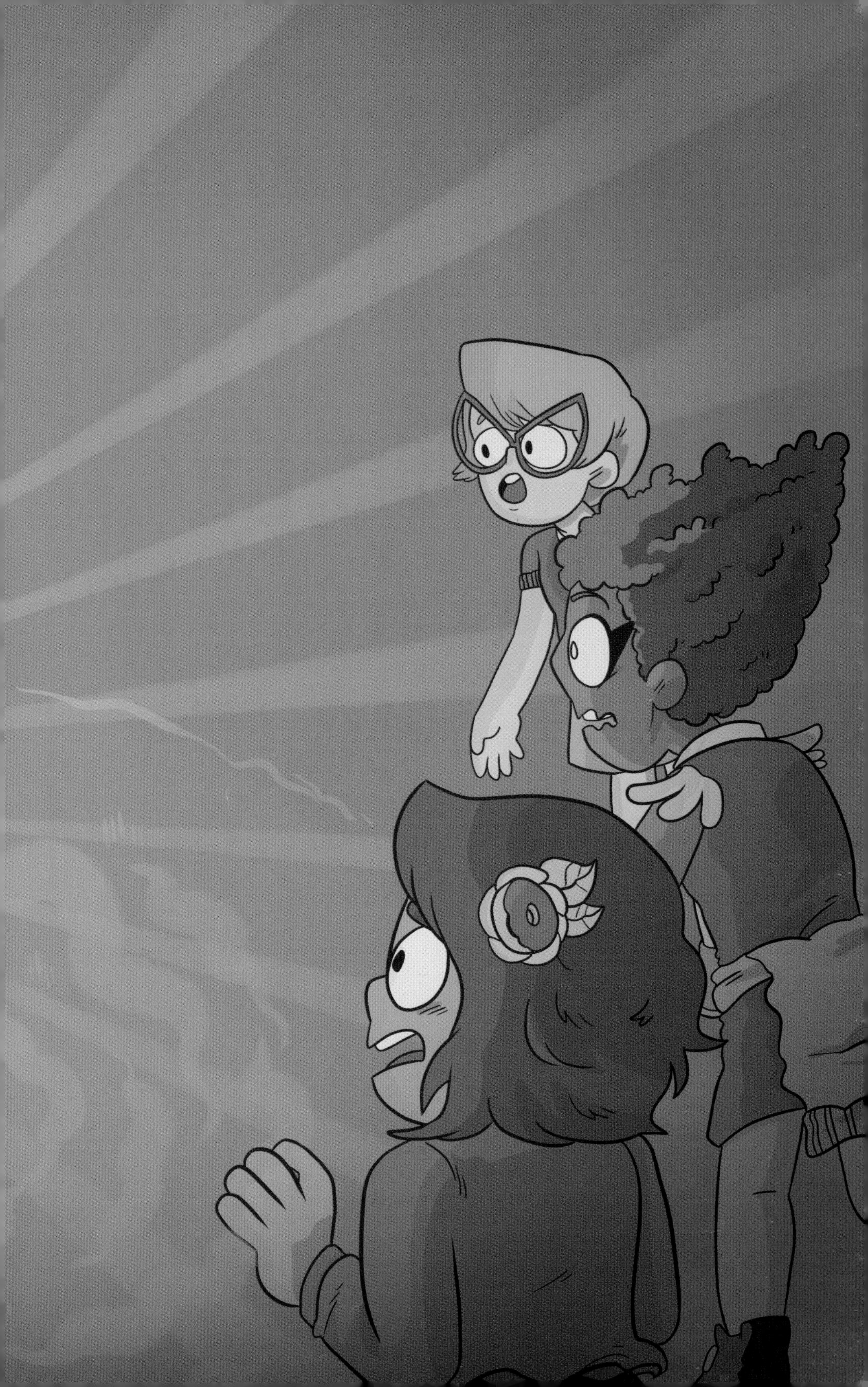

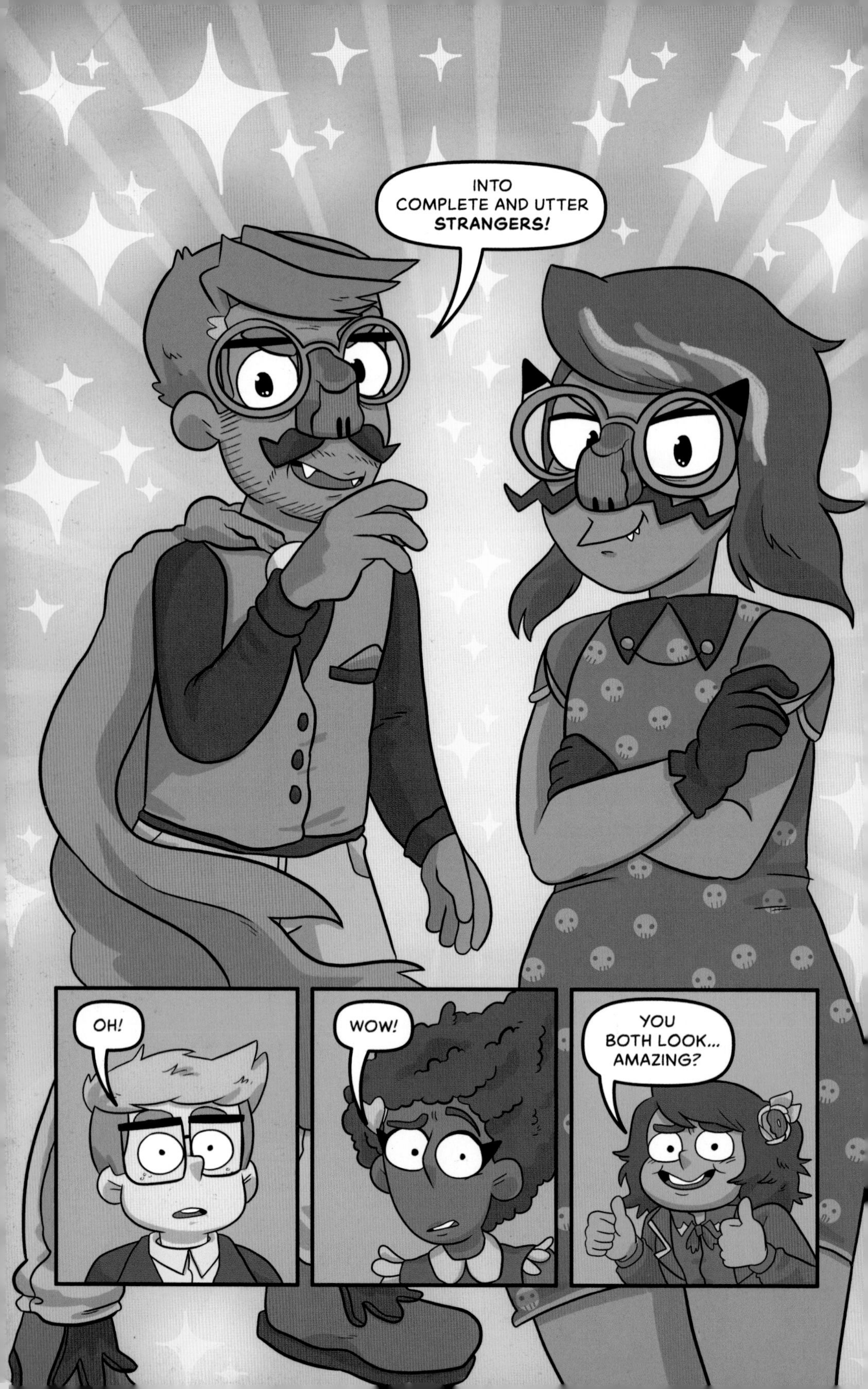
INTO COMPLETE AND UTTER STRANGERS!
OH!
WOW!
YOU BOTH LOOK... AMAZING?

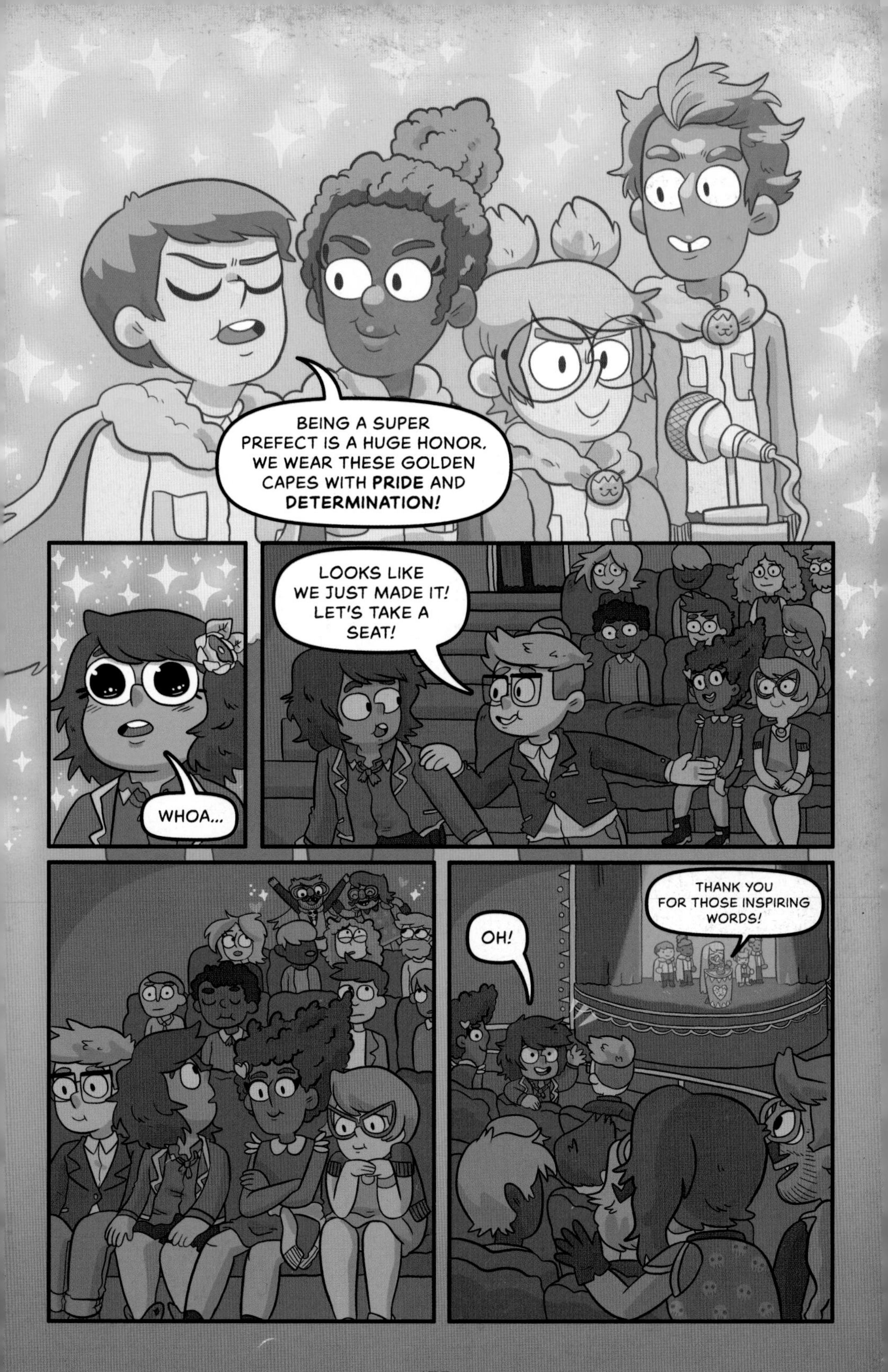
BEING A SUPER PREFECT IS A HUGE HONOR. WE WEAR THESE GOLDEN CAPES WITH PRIDE AND DETERMINATION!
WHOA...
LOOKS LIKE WE JUST MADE IT! LET'S TAKE A SEAT!
OH!
THANK YOU FOR THOSE INSPIRING WORDS!

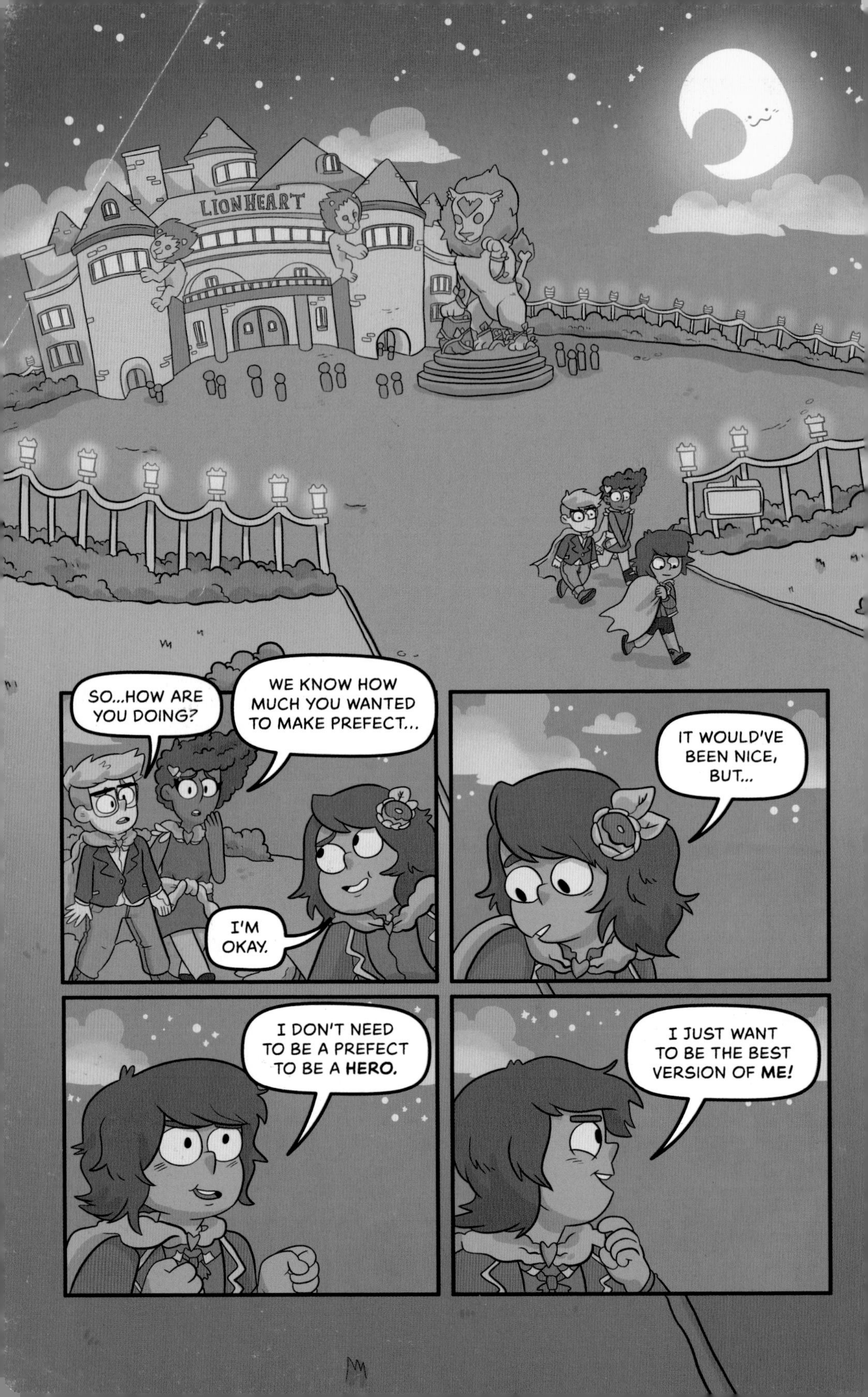
LIONHEART
SO...HOW ARE YOU DOING?
WE KNOW HOW MUCH YOU WANTED TO MAKE PREFECT...
I'M OKAY.
IT WOULD'VE BEEN NICE, BUT...
I DON'T NEED TO BE A PREFECT TO BE A **HERO.**
I JUST WANT TO BE THE BEST VERSION OF **ME!**

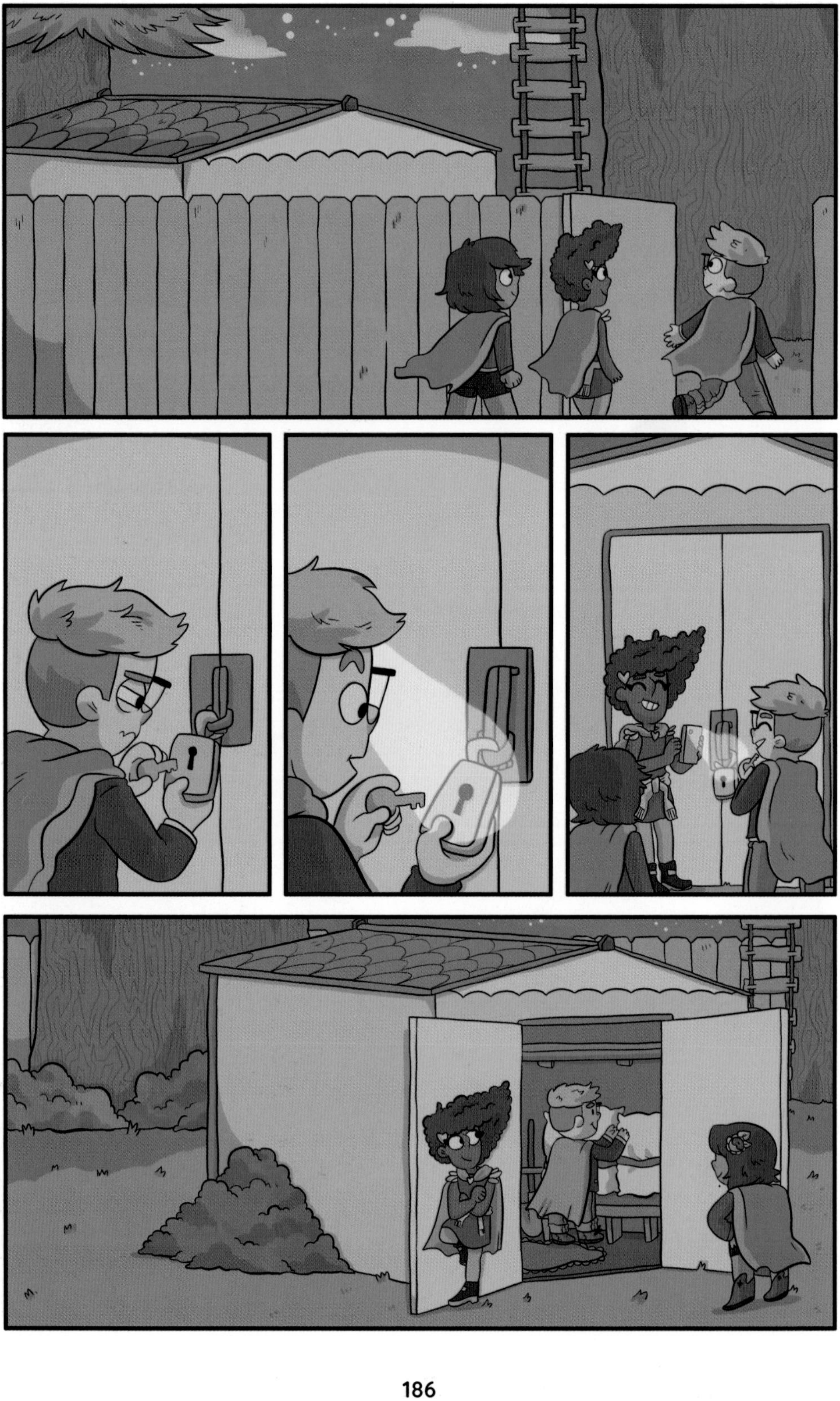

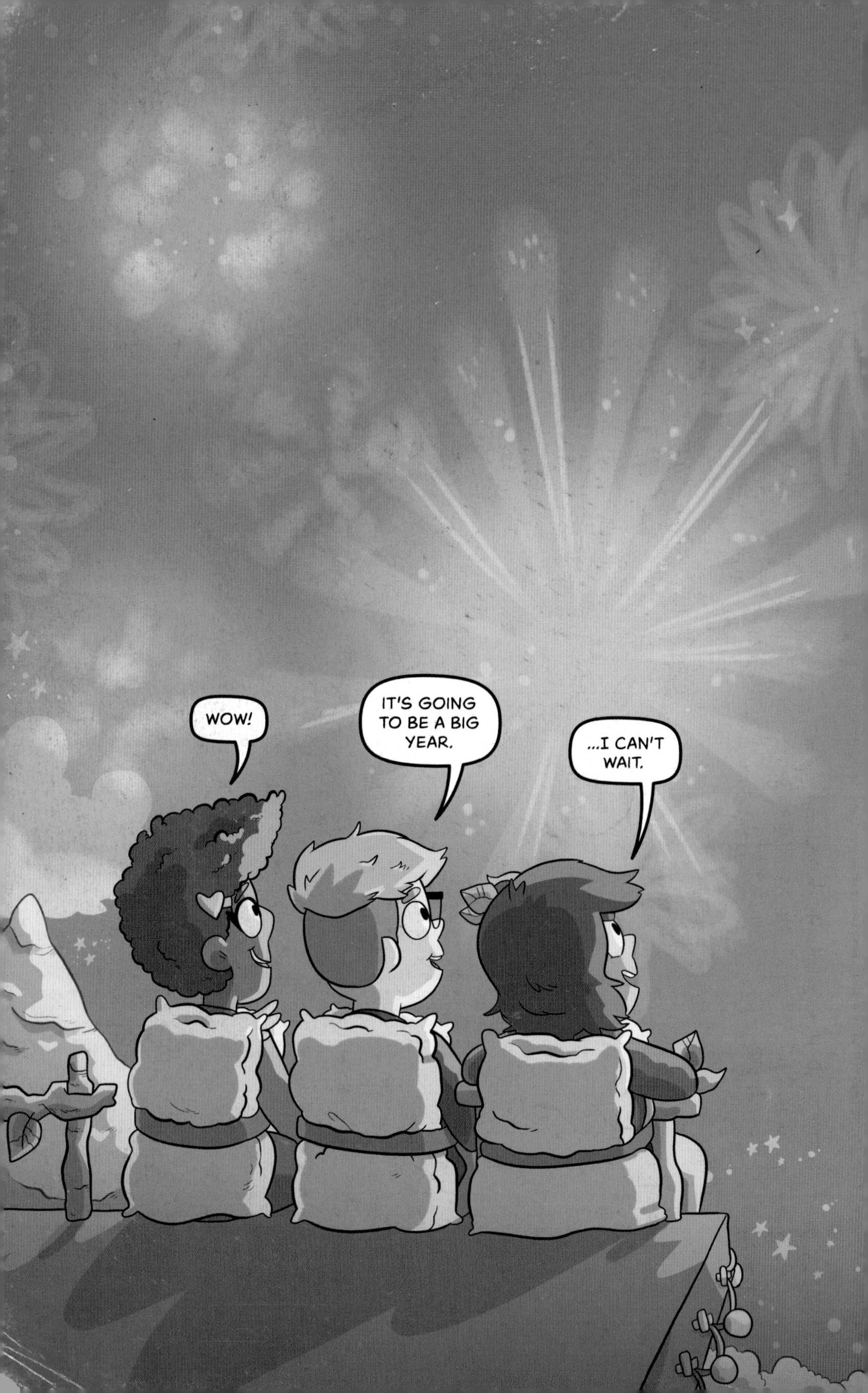
WOW!
IT'S GOING TO BE A BIG YEAR.
...I CAN'T WAIT.